GEPT

全民英檢初級單字100%攻略
左腦式聽力學習×紅膠片高效練習！

User's Guide 使用說明

1 單字全命中！
完整收錄英檢官方指定＆名師特選高分單字

考試和一般學習的差別在於它有「時間壓力」，在有限的準備過程中，走「越少冤枉路」的考生，就能「越快抵達終點」。因此本書收錄的單字皆選自英檢官方指定的範圍，並輔以名師多次應考所特選的單字，避免你浪費時間在艱澀、少考的單字上，只針對出題頻率高、或者容易混淆的重點單字作加強，完全命中真正會考的單字！

Aa Bb Cc Dd Ee Ff Gg Hh Ii Jj

▶ Aa

以下表格是全民英檢官方公告初級「聽、說、讀、寫」所須具備的能力，本書例句皆依此範疇特別設計，只要掃描右方QR code，就能搭配相對應的音軌，實現「眼耳並用」方式，刺激左腦的語言學習功能；同時也可使用本書附贈的紅膠片，將其置於單字上，一面記憶一面自我挑戰，達到雙倍的學習成果！

聽	▶能聽懂與日常生活相關的淺易談話，包含價格、時間及地點等。
說	▶能朗讀簡易文章、簡單地自我介紹，對熟悉的話題能以簡易英語對答，如問候、購物、問路等。
讀	▶可看懂與日常生活相關的淺易英文，並能閱讀路標、交通號誌、招牌、簡單菜單、時刻表及賀卡等。
寫	▶能寫簡單的句子及段落，如寫明信片、便條、賀卡及填表格等。對一般日常生活相關事物，能以簡短的文字敘述或說明。

a [ə] **art.** 一；一（個）　◀ Track 0001
▶She booked a ticket online.
她在網路上訂了一張票。

A.M. = **a.m.** = **AM**　◀ Track 0002
[e-ɛm] **adv.** 午前
▶The baseball game will begin at 10:00 A.M.
棒球賽將在上午十點開始舉行。

ability [əˈbɪlətɪ]　◀ Track 0003
n. 能力；能耐
▶He has the ability to overcome these difficulties.
他有能力克服這些困難。

相關片語 **to the best of one's ability**
就自己能力所及

a·ble [ˈebl]
adj. 有能力的、可以的、會的
▶He won't be able to come tonight because of the typhoon.
因為颱風，他今晚無法回家。

about [əˈbaʊt]
prep. 關於；在……附近；大約
▶The movie is about the Argentina's First Lady, Eva P...
這部電影是在講述關於阿根廷第一夫人‧裴隆的一生。

adv. 到處；在附近；大約
▶Let's look about for someone to help us.
我們看看有沒有人可以幫我們。

相關片語 **up and about**
（病後）可起床走動的

a·ble [ˈebl]
adj. 有能力的、可以...
▶He won't be ...
tonight becau...
因為颱風，他...

above [ə`bʌv]

prep. 在……之上；超過；勝過

► There is a shelf above the desk.
書桌上有一個架子。

adv. 在上面；高於、大於；以上的

► The sun shone above.
太陽在上面閃耀著。

adj. 以上的；前述的

► We hope the above information is helpful to you.
我們希望以上的資訊對你有幫助。

abroad [ə`brɔd]　◀ Track 0007

adv. 在國外；到國外

► He studied abroad after graduating from college.
他大學畢業後就到國外唸書了。

相關片語 **be all abroad** 糊里糊塗

► He was all abroad when two strangers suddenly yelled at him.
當有兩名陌生人突然對他吼叫，他感到莫名其妙。

absence [`æbsns]　◀ Track 0008

n. 不在；缺席

► The absence of his mother's love had a negative impact on his life.
缺乏母愛對他的生命產生很負面的影響。

相關片語 **absence of mind** 心不在焉

► He lost his luggage due to his absence of mind.
他因為心不在焉，而遺失行李。

absent [`æbsnt]　◀ Track 0

adj. 缺席的，不在場的

► She was absent from school o day. 她那天缺課。

► She didn't accept the job offer because of her sudden illness.
她因突然生病，而沒有接受這份工作。

accident [`æksədənt]　◀ Track 0011

n. 意外

► She had brain damage after an accident.
她在意外發生後腦部受傷。

相關片語 **without accident** 安然無恙地；平安無事地

► After being missing for two days, the boy returned home without accident.
男孩失蹤了兩天後，平安無事地回到家。

according [ə`kɔrdɪŋ]　◀ Track 0012

prep. 根據；按照

► According to the recent report, climate change will displace millions of people in the near future.
根據最近的報告，氣候變遷將在不久的未來造成數百萬人流離失所。

補充片語 **according to** 根據，按照

achieve [ə`tʃ

v. 完成、實現　ng missing for t
► She returned home without ac
男孩失蹤了兩天後，平安無事地回到家

according [ə`kɔrdɪŋ]　◀ Track 0012

prep. 根據；按照

► According to the recent report, climate change will displace millions of people in the near future.
根據最近的報告，氣候變遷將在不久的未來造成數百萬人流離失所。

補充片語 **according to** 根據，按照

ieve [ə`tʃiv]

例句最精準！
例句皆按官方公告範圍全新撰寫，絕不魚目混珠

「例句」是單字學習中不可或缺的好幫手，因此合適的例句，對於單字的記憶會有大大加分的效果。本書例句皆依英檢官方公告的初級程度範疇，量身設計撰寫，不會出現「例句單字太難看不懂」或「例句太簡單了學起來沒挑戰性」的狀況，讓你在讀例句的時候，不僅可以複習單字意義，同時也在練習語感，提升聽說讀寫的全面英語力！

**3** **聽力再吸收！**
單字＋例句全錄音，
強化左腦式聽力學習能力

「聽」是人類最原始、最快速、也最直覺的學習管道，即便是不識字的小嬰兒，也能透過聽力來學習語言，所以本書除單字外，特別也為所有的例句全都錄製音檔，讓你能以「視覺＋聽覺」雙重刺激的方式來達到雙倍的記憶效果，只要拿手機一掃書上的QR code，就能立刻聽到完整的例句錄音，且接近真正口語的語速更能訓練你在考場上臨危不亂的能力！

| Aa | **Bb** | Cc | Dd | Ee | | Ff | Gg | Hh | Ii | Jj |

▶ Bb

以下表格是全民英檢官方公告初級「聽、說、讀、寫」所須具備的能力，本書例句皆依此範疇特別設計，只要掃描右方QR code，就能搭配相對應的音軌，實現「眼耳並用」方式，刺激左腦的語言學習功能；同時也可使用本書附贈的紅膠片，將其置於單字上，一面記憶一面自我挑戰，達到雙倍的學習成果！

聽　能聽懂與日常生活相關的淺易談話，包含價格、時間及地點等。

說　能朗讀簡易文章、簡單地自我介紹，對熟悉的話題能以簡易英語對答，如問候、購物、問路等。

讀　可看懂與日常生活相關的淺易英文，並能閱讀路標、交通號誌、招牌、簡單菜單、時刻表及賀卡等。

寫　能寫簡單的句子及段落，如寫明信片、便條、賀卡及填表格等。對一般日常生活相關事物，能以簡短的文字敘述或說明。

baby [`bebɪ] n 嬰兒　◀Track 0145
▶ She helped take care of her sister's baby after school.
她放學後幫忙照顧姐姐的小嬰兒。

相關片語 **sleep like a baby** 睡得很熟

▶ After an exhausting day, he slept like a baby at night.
他忙了一天後，晚上睡得很熟。

babysitter [`bebɪsɪtə] ◀Track 0146
n 臨時保姆
▶ Diana was a babysitter before she married the prince.
黛安娜嫁給王子前是一名保姆。

back [bæk] ◀Track 0147
adv 向後；以前；原處；回覆
▶ She looked back and saw a black dog following her.
她回頭看到一隻黑狗正在跟著她。

n 背部；後面
▶ There is a garden in the back of the house. 屋後有一座庭院。

v 後退；支持
▶ He refused to back her election campaign.
他拒絕支持她的競選活動。

adj 後面的
▶ He sneaked into the classroom through the back door.
他從後門溜進了教室。

backward [`bækwəd] ◀Track 0148
adv 向後；倒回
▶ She looked backward and saw her father.
她向後看，看到了她的爸爸。

adj 向後的；落後的、發展遲緩的
▶ The boy was backward compared with his classmates.
跟同班同學相較之下，這名男童學習遲緩。

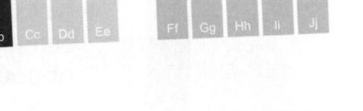
★因各家手機系統不同，若無法直接掃描，仍可以電腦連結https://goo.gl/citFyK 雲端下載收聽

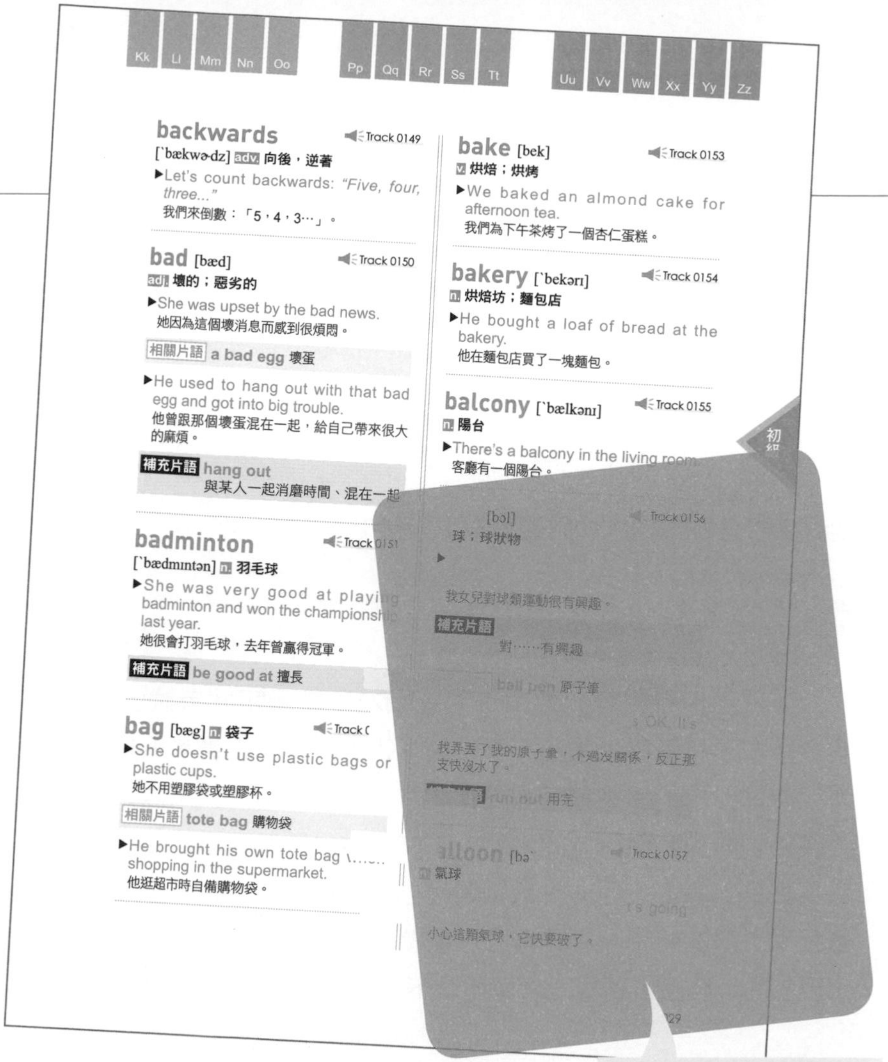

backwards ◀ Track 0149
[`bækwə-dz] adv 向後，逆著
▶Let's count backwards: "Five, four, three..."
我們來倒數：「5，4，3…」。

bad [bæd] ◀ Track 0150
adj 壞的；惡劣的
▶She was upset by the bad news.
她因為這個壞消息而感到很煩惱。

相關片語 a bad egg 壞蛋

▶He used to hang out with that bad egg and got into big trouble.
他曾跟那個壞蛋混在一起，給自己帶來很大的麻煩。

補充片語 hang out
與某人一起消磨時間、混在一起

badminton ◀ Track 0151
[`bædmɪntən] n 羽毛球
▶She was very good at playing badminton and won the championship last year.
她很會打羽毛球，去年曾贏得冠軍。

補充片語 be good at 擅長

bag [bæg] n 袋子 ◀ Track 0
▶She doesn't use plastic bags or plastic cups.
她不用塑膠袋或塑膠杯。

相關片語 tote bag 購物袋

▶He brought his own tote bag when shopping in the supermarket.
他逛超市時自備購物袋。

bake [bek] ◀ Track 0153
v 烘焙；烘烤
▶We baked an almond cake for afternoon tea.
我們為下午茶烤了一個杏仁蛋糕。

bakery [`bekəri] ◀ Track 0154
n 烘焙坊；麵包店
▶He bought a loaf of bread at the bakery.
他在麵包店買了一塊麵包。

balcony [`bælkənɪ] ◀ Track 0155
n 陽台
▶There's a balcony in the living room.
客廳有一個陽台。

[bɔl] ◀ Track 0156
球；球狀物
▶
我女兒對球類運動很有興趣。
補充片語
對……有興趣

ball pen 原子筆

OK. It's
我弄丟了我的原子筆，不過沒關係，反正那支快沒水了。
run out 用完

balloon [bə ◀ Track 0157
n 氣球
's going
小心這顆氣球，它快要破了。

初級

練習高效率！
隨書附贈高效紅膠片，記單字更能同時挑戰自己

身為考生的你一定知道「考試前必須多做練習才行」，但往往在背完一堆單字以後，整個人就筋疲力盡了，哪有心思再做額外的複習？為了避免你虎頭蛇尾，本書附贈的高效紅膠片，幫助你能在記單字的同時就一面做自我挑戰，遮住單字，看看自己到底還記不記得它的意思，如此的練習方式省時又省力，也讓英檢初級考試高分離你更接近！

蓋上後，英文單字和例句消失了！

Preface 作者序

　　全民英檢（GEPT）是台灣最常見、最常考、也最常被學校和企業做為英語能力評估的測驗之一。雖然與托福、雅思這類考試的難度無法比擬，但其仍舊有許多考高分的「眉角」存在。本書就是針對英檢單字部分，以最具經驗的角度，將應考的高分訣竅分享給各位考生為目的而撰寫設計。

全民英檢考生常遇到的難題有以下四種：

1. 經驗值不足

　　即便準備得再多，還是有可能因為不熟悉正式考試的題型與內容，在實際踏上考場時感到緊張，表現失常錯失分數。本書考慮到這點，因此每個單字的例句均依據英檢官方公佈之常見出題範圍（如：聽力的出題範圍多為「價格」、「時間」、「地點」；寫作的出題範圍多為「便條」、「賀卡」「填表格」等），而非一般隨興地自由發揮造句，造一些內容與實際考試完全扯不上邊的句子。相信考生在閱讀本書例句時，同時便可以熟悉考試中出現的內容範圍，正式上考場時就不致驚慌丟分。

2. 字庫量不足

　　單字量不夠，在正式考試時題目看得霧煞煞先不說，口說與寫作測驗時更是腦筋一片空白，遲遲一個字都生不出。事實上，英檢不但考的是你是否認得單字，更考你是否會活用，光是死板地背下每個單字的中文意思是不夠的。幸好，官方公佈了英檢初級、中級所需的所有單字，本書將「英檢初級」所需的單字全數收錄，並加入教育部公佈之國小必備字彙及名師嚴選試題最常出現重點單字作統合，如此完整又精準的內容選擇，相信考生只要熟悉本書中的單字，在考試時的作題能力與臨場的快速反應肯定大幅精進。

3. 練習量不足

　　以為單字已經倒背如流了，但真正上考場時卻一個都記不起來，為什麼呢？因為你沒有做好「複習」與「練習」的動作。本書附贈的紅膠片，就是為了讓考生們能更有效率地複習、練習所因應而生，將紅膠片覆蓋在單字上，就可以快速測試自己是否有真正深刻記憶每個單字，不會讓辛苦記來的單字「左耳進、右耳出」，同時節省下更多時間，有餘裕在腦中補進更多單字。

4. 準備時間不足

　　學生有課業、打工的壓力；上班族有工作的壓力，事實上，並不是每個人都有充裕且完整的時間來準備一次英檢考試，但記憶單字這件事，只用零碎的時間學習，效率往往不高，因此本書才會特別構想，若能透過手機線上聽MP3，就能在通車、睡前等時間裡，好好利用，毫不浪費地準備考試。只要掃描QR code，就能線上聽到MP3音檔，沒有時間與空間的限制，也就沒有考不好的理由了。

　　最後，希望本書的單字選擇、編排設計，線上MP3等等的規劃，可以幫助你用更輕鬆的方式獲得高分，當然也要你自己發揮100%的用心和努力才行，所以一起加油吧！朝著英檢高分的路一步步邁進吧！

張慈庭

全民英檢大解密！

什麼是全民英檢是？

　　全民英檢（GEPT）是「全民英語能力分級檢定測驗（General English Proficiency Test）」的簡稱，為台灣最常見的英文檢定考試之一。此測驗從2000年開始，試題內容分別為「聽、說、讀、寫」四大項目組成，其程度由簡至難共分五等級——1.初級（Elementary）、2.中級（Intermediate）、3.中高級（High- Intermediate）、4.高級（Advanced）、5.優級（Superior），用以評量考生的英語能力，並作為台灣學校、公家機關與民營企業了解考生（受試者）英語程度之參考。

想通過英檢初級，你得具備哪些英語能力？

　　全民英檢初級的檢測對象為一般社會人士及國中以上學生，目的是檢視考生能否理解、使用淺易日常英文用語。其又分為「初試」與「複試」兩次考試，內含聽、讀、寫、說四類測驗，所需具備之能力如下：

聽	能聽懂與日常生活相關的淺易談話，包括價格、時間及地點等。
讀	可看懂與日常生活相關的淺易英文，並能閱讀路標、交通標誌、招牌、簡單菜單、時刻表及賀卡等。
寫	能寫簡單的句子及段落，如寫明信片、便條、賀卡及填表格等。對一般日常生活相關的事物，能以簡短的文字敘述或說明。
說	能朗讀簡易文章、簡單地自我介紹，對熟悉的話題能以簡易英語對答，如問候、購物、問路等。

英檢初級初試的考試內容有什麼？

	初試	
測驗項目	聽力	閱讀
總題數	30題	35題
總作答時間	約20分鐘	35分鐘
滿分分數	120分	120分
測驗內容	看圖辨義 問答 簡短對話 短文聽解	詞彙和結構 段落填空 閱讀理解
總測驗時間（含試前、試後說明）	兩項合計約1.5小時	
通過標準	兩項成績總和達160分，且其中任一項成績不低於72分。	

英檢初級複試的考試內容有什麼？

	複試	
測驗項目	寫作	口說
總題數	16題	18題
總作答時間	40分鐘	約10分鐘
滿分分數	100分	100分
測驗內容	單句寫作 段落寫作	複誦 朗讀句子與短文 回答問題
總測驗時間（含試前、試後說明）	約1小時	約1小時
通過標準	70分	80分

　　全民英檢初級的考試目的旨在檢視考生的基本英語使用能力，因此內容偏向生活化、不艱澀，只要掌握考試要訣並擁有基本的單字概念，想拿到高分並不困難。其他英檢相關資訊（如報名費用、考試時間、採納英檢成績之學校／民營單位／公家機關名單等等），則以英檢官方網站不定期公告的內容為準。

Content 目錄

左腦式聽力學習法，
針對A～Z開頭單字例句錄音QR code線上MP3

在書中，你可能會看到以下代號。原來，它們是這個意思……

n. 名詞	adv. 副詞	aux. 助動詞
v. 動詞	prep. 介系詞	det. 限定詞
adj. 形容詞	pron. 代名詞	interj. 感嘆詞
art. 冠詞	abbr. 縮寫	conj. 連接詞

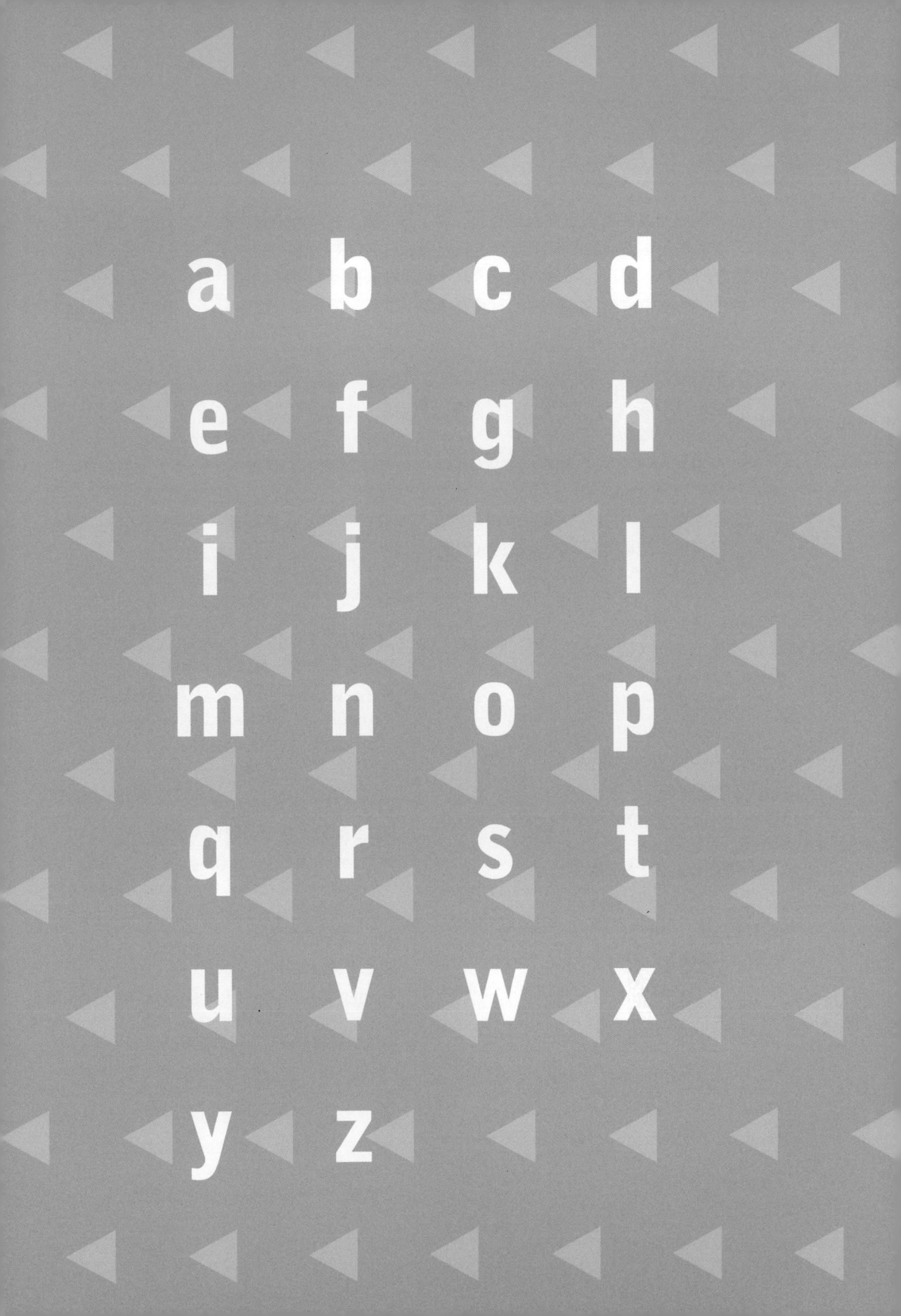

▶ Aa

以下表格是全民英檢官方公告初級「聽、説、讀、寫」所須具備的能力，本書例句皆依此範疇特別設計，只要掃描右方QR code，就能搭配相對應的音軌，實現「眼耳並用」方式，刺激左腦的語言學習功能；同時也可使用本書附贈的紅膠片，將其置於單字上，一面記憶一面自我挑戰，達到雙倍的學習成果！

聽 ▶	能聽懂與日常生活相關的淺易談話，包含價格、時間及地點等。
説 ▶	能朗讀簡易文章、簡單地自我介紹，對熟悉的話題能以簡易英語對答，如問候、購物、問路等。
讀 ▶	可看懂與日常生活相關的淺易英文，並能閱讀路標、交通號誌、招牌、簡單菜單、時刻表及賀卡等。
寫 ▶	能寫簡單的句子及段落，如寫明信片、便條、賀卡及填表格等。對一般日常生活相關事物，能以簡短的文字敘述或説明。

---

a [ə] **art.** 一；一（個）　　◀ Track 0001

▶She booked a ticket online.
她在網路上訂了一張票。

A.M. = a.m.＝AM　　◀ Track 0002

[e-ɛm] **adv.** 午前

▶The baseball game will begin at 10:00 A.M.
棒球賽將在上午十點開始舉行。

---

ability [ə`bɪlətɪ]　　◀ Track 0003

n. 能力；能耐

▶He has the ability to overcome these difficulties.
他有能力克服這些困難。

相關片語 **to the best of one's ability**
就自己能力所及

▶Emma always does her work to the best of her ability.
艾瑪總是盡全力工作。

---

a·ble [`ebl]　　◀ Track 0004

adj. 有能力的、可以的、會的

▶He won't be able to come home tonight because of the typhoon.
因為颱風，他今晚無法回家。

---

about [ə`baʊt]　　◀ Track 0005

prep. 關於；在……附近；大約

▶The movie is about the life of Argentina's First Lady, Eva Perón.
這部電影是在講述關於阿根廷第一夫人伊娃·裴隆的一生。

adv. 到處；在附近；大約

▶Let's look about for someone to help us.
我們看看有沒有人可以幫我們。

相關片語 **up and about**
（病後）可起床走動的

▶She was up and about after the new treatment.
她接受新療法以後，就能起床走動了。

above [ə`bʌv] ◀Track 0006

prep. 在……之上；超過；勝過

▶There is a shelf above the desk.
書桌上有一個架子。

adv. 在上面；高於、大於；以上的

▶The sun shone above.
太陽在上面閃耀著。

adj. 以上的；前述的

▶We hope the above information is helpful to you.
我們希望以上的資訊對你有幫助。

abroad [ə`brɔd] ◀Track 0007

adv. 在國外；到國外

▶He studied abroad after graduating from college.
他大學畢業後就到國外唸書了。

相關片語 **be all abroad** 糊里糊塗

▶He was all abroad when two strangers suddenly yelled at him.
當有兩名陌生人突然對他吼叫，他感到莫名其妙。

absence [`æbsns] ◀Track 0008

n. 不在；缺席

▶The absence of his mother's love had a negative impact on his life.
缺乏母愛對他的生命產生很負面的影響

相關片語 **absence of mind** 心不在焉

▶He lost his luggage due to his absence of mind.
他因為心不在焉，而遺失行李。

absent [`æbsnt] ◀Track 0009

adj. 缺席的，不在場的

▶She was absent from school on that day. 她那天缺課。

accept [ək`sɛpt] **v.** 接受 ◀Track 0010

▶She didn't accept the job offer because of her sudden illness.
她因突然生病，而沒有接受這份工作。

accident [`æksədənt] ◀Track 0011

n. 意外

▶She had brain damage after an accident.
她在意外發生後腦部受傷。

相關片語 **without accident**
安然無恙地；平安無事地

▶After being missing for two days, the boy returned home without accident.
男孩失蹤了兩天後，平安無事地回到家。

according [ə`kɔrdɪŋ] ◀Track 0012

prep. 根據；按照

▶According to the recent report, climate change will displace millions of people in the near future.
根據最近的報告，氣候變遷將在不久的未來造成數百萬人流離失所。

補充片語 **according to** 根據，按照

achieve [ə`tʃiv] ◀Track 0013

v. 完成、實現；達到

▶She finally achieved her dream to be a singer.
她終於實現成為歌手的夢想。

across [ə`krɔs] ◀Track 0014

prep. 橫越、穿過

▶They are building a new skyscraper across the street.
他們正在對街蓋全新的摩天大樓。

初級

adv. 橫過；在對面

▶He glanced across the table and saw his dog sleeping on the carpet.
他朝餐桌瞥了一眼，發現他的小狗睡在地毯上。

相關片語 **come across** 偶然遇見

▶He came across his ex-girlfriend in a banquet.
他在晚宴碰見前女友。

act [ækt] ◀Track 0015
n. 行為、行動；表現

▶The suicide bombing was an act of terrorism.
自殺炸彈是恐怖主義的行為。

v. 行動；做出……舉止；表演

▶She acted on impulse and got herself into big trouble.
她意氣用事，替自己惹來麻煩。

相關片語 **put on an act** 裝腔作勢

▶She put on an act to hide her anxiety.
她裝腔作勢只為掩飾內心的焦慮。

action [`ækʃən] ◀Track 0016
n. 行動，行為

▶Actions speak louder than words.
坐而言不如起而行。

相關片語 **out of action** 不活動；不運轉

▶The elevator went out of action due to mechanical failure.
這部電梯因機械故障而無法運作。

active [`æktɪv] ◀Track 0017
adj. 活躍的；積極的；主動的

▶Although my grandmother is 85, she is still very active.
我的祖母雖已85歲，仍保持身心活躍。

activity [æk`tɪvətɪ] ◀Track 0018
n. 活動

▶She enjoys indoor activities such as reading and watching movies.
她喜歡室內活動，比方閱讀和看電影。

相關片語 **parent-child activity** 親子活動

▶Cycling is a good parent-child activity.
騎腳踏車是很好的親子活動。

actor [`æktɚ] n. 男演員 ◀Track 0019

▶Heath Ledger was a good actor.
希斯‧萊傑是名優秀的男演員。

相關片語 **a bad actor** 做壞事的人；慣犯

▶The boy was a bad actor and constantly bullied his classmates.
這個男童很惡劣，經常欺負同班同學。

actress [`æktrɪs] ◀Track 0020
n. 女演員

▶The girl aspires to be an actress someday.
這個女孩立志有一天要成為一位女演員。

相關片語 **best actress** 最佳女演員

▶Emma Stone won the Best Actress Academy Award for "La La Land."
艾瑪史東因《樂來越愛你》這部片得到奧斯卡最佳女演員獎。

actually [`æktʃʊəlɪ] ◀Track 0021
adv. 實際上、真的

▶He is young, but he's actually quite mature.
他很年輕，但實際上很成熟。

add [æd] v. 加、添加、增加 ◀Track 0022

▶You can add some sea salt and pepper in the salad to add flavors.
你可以在沙拉裡加一點海鹽和胡椒粉來增添風味。

addition [ə`dɪʃən]　◀ Track 0023

n. 加；增加的部分；加法

▶The firstgraders are learning addition and subtraction from their teacher.
這群一年級小學生正在跟老師學加減法。

相關片語 **in addition** 此外

▶Tom is an actor. In addition, he is a movie producer.
湯姆是個演員。此外，他還是電影製作人。

address [ə`drɛs]　◀ Track 0024

n. 地址

▶I lost her email address so I couldn't contact her.
我遺失她的電郵地址，所以無法聯絡她。

相關片語 **address book** 通訊錄

▶I can't find my address book in the iCloud system. What should I do?
我在雲端系統找不到我的通訊錄，我該怎麼做？

admire [əd`maɪr]　◀ Track 0025

v. 欣賞；稱讚

▶I admire her courage to overcome the adversity.
我欣賞她克服逆境的勇氣。

admit [əd`mɪt] **v.** 承認　◀ Track 0026

▶She admitted that she made the wrong decision.
她承認做錯決定了。

adopt [ə`dɑpt]　◀ Track 0027

v. 採取；收養

▶We adopted the kitten after she was abandoned by her mother.
這隻小貓被母貓棄養後，我們就收養了牠。

adult [ə`dʌlt]　◀ Track 0028

n. 成年人

▶You are already 20. You should behave like an adult.
你已經20歲了，應該表現得像個成年人。

相關片語 **adult ticket** 成人票

▶An adult ticket for the amusement park is NT$200.
這家遊樂園的成人票是新台幣200元。

advance [əd`væns]　◀ Track 0029

n. 前進；發展

▶Medical advances have prolonged people's average lifespan.
醫學發展已延長人們的平均壽命。

v. 前進；發展；將……提前

▶The team advanced to the final four in the competition.
這支隊伍在競賽中晉級到前四強。

相關片語 **in advance** 事先；提前

▶If you will drop by, let me know in advance.
如果你要順道來訪，請提前讓我知道。

advantage　◀ Track 0030
[əd`væntɪdʒ]

n. 有利條件；優勢

▶One of the advantages of shopping online is convenience.
網路購物的優勢之一是便利性。

相關片語 **take advantage of**
善用；利用；佔……便宜

▶He took advantage of her kindness and broke her heart.
他利用她的善心佔她的便宜，很傷她的心。

初級

advice [əd`vaɪs]　◀≋Track 0031
n. 勸告，忠告；建議

▶As a financial analyst, she uses spreadsheet and big data to offer advice to her clients.
她是財務分析師，使用試算表和大數據來提供客戶建議。

相關片語 **act on sb.'s advice**
　　　按某人勸告行事

▶He acted on his daughter's advice and quit smoking.
他按女兒的勸告戒菸了。

advise [əd`vaɪz]　◀≋Track 0032
v. 勸告，忠告；建議

▶The doctor advised her to exercise regularly.
醫生勸她要規律運動。

affair [ə`fɛr] **n.** 事情，事件　◀≋Track 0033

▶She is interested in foreign affairs and aspires to be a career diplomat.
她對外交事務很感興趣，並立志要成為職業外交官。

相關片語 **love affair** 戀愛事件，風流韻事

▶I'm not interested in the love affairs of movie stars or singers.
我對電影明星或歌星的戀愛新聞沒興趣。

affect [ə`fɛkt] **v.** 影響　◀≋Track 0034

▶She was affected by the criticism she received and felt frustrated.
她因受到批評而被影響，感到很挫折。

afraid [ə`fred]　◀≋Track 0035
adj. 害怕的；擔心的

▶She is afraid of darkness. 她很怕黑。

after [`æftɚ]　◀≋Track 0036
prep. 在……之後

▶He has a piano lesson after school.
他放學後有鋼琴課。

conj. 在……之後

▶The office was empty after the company went bankrupt.
這家公司破產以後，辦公室變得空蕩蕩的。

相關片語 **after you** 你先請

▶When the elevator door opened, the man said to the lady,"After you."
電梯門打開時，男子對小姐說：「你先請。」

afternoon [`æftɚ`nun]　◀≋Track 0037
n. 下午，午後

▶He usually plays basketball in the afternoon.
他通常在下午打籃球。

again [ə`gɛn] **adv.** 再次地　◀≋Track 0038

▶Come again? I didn't get it.
再說一次好嗎？我剛剛沒聽清楚。

相關片語 **again and again** 再三地

▶He told her again and again that he couldn't live without her.
他一而再再而三地告訴她，他活著不能沒有她。

against [ə`gɛnst]　◀≋Track 0039
prep. 反對；逆著

▶Some people are against death penalty.
有些人反對死刑。

相關片語 **against nature**
　　　違反自然的，不合情理的

▶It is against her nature to take advantage of others.
佔別人的便宜，有違她的本性。

age [edʒ] n. 年紀；年齡　◀ Track 0040
▶He started his own company at the age of only 18.
他十八歲就創業了。

v. 變老
▶She suddenly aged after her husband's death.
她先生過世後，她突然變蒼老了。

ago [ə`go] adv. 在……之前　◀ Track 0041
▶He left the office a few minutes ago.
他幾分鐘之前才離開辦公室。

agree [ə`gri] ◀ Track 0042
v. 贊成，同意
▶I couldn't agree with you more.
我不能同意你更多。（我非常同意你的看法。）

agreement ◀ Track 0043
[ə`grimənt] n. 同意；一致
▶They haven't reached agreement on this issue.
他們在這項議題上仍未達成協議。

ahead [ə`hɛd] ◀ Track 0044
adv. 在前；事前
▶The task was completed ahead of schedule.
這項工作比原先進度提前完成。

相關片語 ahead of time 提前
▶She told him ahead of time that she wouldn't help him again.
她提前告訴他，她不會再幫他了。

aid [ed] n. 幫助；救援　◀ Track 0045
▶He went to the aid of an old lady who fell down on the street.
他去幫助一位在街道上跌倒的老太太。

v. 幫助；救援
▶The charity aided more than 500,000 people across the country last year.
這間慈善機構去年在全國幫助了超過50萬人。

相關片語 first aid 急救；急救護理
▶Every family should have a fist aid kit in case a loved one gets hurt.
家家戶戶都應有急救箱，以防心愛的家人受傷。

AIDS [edz] ◀ Track 0046
n. 愛滋病（後天性免疫不全症候群）
▶The famous singer died of AIDS.
這位知名的歌手死於愛滋病。

aim [em] ◀ Track 0047
v. 針對；瞄準；以……為目標
▶The project aims to help the city's homeless people.
這項計畫以幫助這城市裡無家可歸的人為目標。

n. 瞄準的方向；目的、目標
▶His long-term aim is to establish a hospital for the poor and sick.
他的長期目標是要創辦一家專門幫助貧病人士的醫院。

air [ɛr] n. 空氣　◀ Track 0048
▶He said he needed some fresh air and then excused himself from the table.
他說他需要呼吸一下新鮮的空氣，在離開餐桌席時表示了一下歉意。

相關片語 put on airs 擺架子

初級

▶The Internet celebrity put on airs after becoming famous.
這位網紅成名之後就開始擺架子了。

aircraft [ˈɛrˌkræft] ◀ᴱTrack 0049
n. 飛機

▶The aircraft took off from Heathrow International Airport at 10:00 A.M.
這架飛機在早上10點於倫敦希斯洛機場起飛。

airline [ˈɛrˌlaɪn] ◀ᴱTrack 0050
n. 航線；航空公司

▶The airline has a good safety record.
這家航空公司有良好的飛安記錄。

airplane [ˈɛrˌplen] ◀ᴱTrack 0051
n. =plane 飛機

▶Thanks to the Internet, we can book airplane tickets online.
拜網際網路之賜，我們可以在線上預訂機票。

airport [ˈɛrˌport] n. 機場 ◀ᴱTrack 0052

▶He went to the airport to see his girlfriend off. 他到機場為女友送機。

alarm [əˈlɑrm] ◀ᴱTrack 0053
n. 警報；警報器

▶They left the building soon after the alarm sounded.
他們在警報器響了沒多久後，就離開了這棟建築。

相關片語 **fire alarm** 火警；火警警報器

▶The fire alarm went off when he was in the shower.
火警警報器響時，他正在洗澡。

album [ˈælbəm] ◀ᴱTrack 0054
n. 相簿；集郵簿；唱片

▶He made a photo album for his baby boy. 他幫他的小男娃做了一本相簿。

相關片語 **solo album** 單飛專輯

▶Her latest solo album topped the Billboard 200 chart.
她的最新單飛專輯榮登美國告示牌200強專輯榜冠軍。

alike [əˈlaɪk] ◀ᴱTrack 0055
adv. 一樣地；相似地

▶The mother treated all her children alike.
這位媽媽對她所有的孩子都一視同仁。

adj. 相同的；相像的

▶Tiffany and her sister look alike, but they have very different personalities.
蒂芬妮和她姊姊看起來很像，但是個性截然不同。

相關片語 **young and old alike** 無論老少；老少咸宜

▶The cartoon appeals to young and old alike.
這部卡通是老少咸宜的。

alive [əˈlaɪv] adj. 活著的 ◀ᴱTrack 0056

▶They managed to stay alive in the cave before the rescue effort was properly organized.
在外界救援行動籌備妥當之前，他們在洞穴裡設法保命。

all [ɔl] adj. 全部的；所有的 ◀ᴱTrack 0057

▶The boy ate all the cookies in the cookie jar.
男孩把餅乾罐裡的餅乾全部吃光了。

pron. 全部，一切

▶We ate all of the cakes on the table.
我們吃掉桌子上所有的蛋糕。

adv. 完全地，全然的

▶He has tattoos all over his face.
他的臉上全部都是刺青。

相關片語 **not at all** 一點也不

▶He isn't stupid at all.
他一點也不笨。

allow [ə`laʊ] **v** 允許 🔊 Track 0058

▶She is not allowed to ride the roller coaster because she has a heart disease.
她因為有心臟病，不被允許坐雲霄飛車。

almond [`amənd] 🔊 Track 0059

n. 杏仁；杏樹；杏仁色

▶Almond milk is delicious and nutritious.
杏仁奶既美味又營養。

adj. 杏仁色的；杏仁味的

▶He made an almond tart for dessert.
他做了一個杏仁餡餅當甜點。

almost [`ɔl,most] 🔊 Track 0060

adv. 幾乎，差不多

▶Time flies. My daughter is almost 17.
時光飛逝，我的女兒都快17歲了。

alone [ə`lon] **adv.** 獨自地 🔊 Track 0061

▶He enjoys living alone.
他喜歡獨居。

adj. 單獨的；只有、僅

▶Just go. Leave me alone.
你走開，讓我一個人靜一靜。

along [ə`lɔŋ] 🔊 Track 0062

prep. 沿著……

▶Let's take a walk along the beach.
我們一起沿著沙灘散步吧。

adv. 向前；一起

▶She took her children along with her when she worked.
她工作時也帶著孩子一起去。

aloud [ə`laʊd] 🔊 Track 0063

adv. 大聲地；出聲地

▶He read his poem aloud in the class.
他在課堂大聲地朗讀出他做的詩。

alphabet [`ælfə,bɛt] 🔊 Track 0064

n. 字母系統；全套字母

▶The teacher used teaching aids to help his students learn the alphabet.
老師用教具幫助他的學生學習字母。

already [ɔl`rɛdɪ] 🔊 Track 0065

adv. 已經

▶My dad is already retired.
我爸爸已經退休了。

also [`ɔlso] **adv.** 也，還 🔊 Track 0066

▶She can play the piano, and she can also write computer programs.
她會彈琴，也會寫電腦程式。

although [ɔl`ðo] 🔊 Track 0067

conj. 雖然；儘管

▶Although he's nice, he makes me really nervous.
他雖然人很好，但是他讓我很緊張。

初級

altogether
🔊 Track 0068

[ˌɔltə`gɛðɚ] **adv.** 完全，全然；全部

▶My grandparents have 30 grandchildren altogether.
我的祖父母總共有30個孫子女。

always [`ɔlwez]
🔊 Track 0069

adv. 總是；一直、永遠

▶She always brushes her teeth before she goes to bed.
她睡前總是會刷牙。

am [æm]
🔊 Track 0070

v. 是（用在第一人稱單數現在式）

▶I am a teenager.
我是青少年。

ambulance
🔊 Track 0071

[`æmbjələns] **n.** 救護車

▶She dialed 911 and asked for an ambulance soon after her husband had a heart attack.
她的先生心臟病發作，她立刻就打求救電話請救護車前來。

America [ə`mɛrɪkə]
🔊 Track 0072

n. 美國；美洲

▶She has lived in America for 13 years.
她已在美國住了13年。

相關片語 the United States of America 美利堅合眾國；美國

▶The United States of America is a country located in North America.
美利堅合眾國是位於北美洲的一個國家。

American [ə`mɛrɪkən]
🔊 Track 0073

adj. 美國的；美洲的

▶She speaks English with an American accent.
她說英文帶有美式的口音。

n. 美國人；美洲人

▶Taylor Swift is an American singer.
泰勒絲是美國歌手。

among [ə`mʌŋ]
🔊 Track 0074

prep. 在……之中，在……之間

▶The policy caused a lot of anger among the public.
這項政策在大眾之間引起很大的憤怒。

amount [ə`maʊnt]
🔊 Track 0075

n. 總數，總額；數量

▶He donated a large amount of money to a charity.
他捐了很大一筆錢給一家慈善機構。

an [æn] **art.** 一個、一
🔊 Track 0076

（用於以母音開頭的名詞 之前）

▶That's an excellent idea!
這真是個好主意！

ancient [`enʃənt]
🔊 Track 0077

adj. 古老的；古代的

▶The pyramids were built in ancient Egypt.
這些金字塔是在古埃及時期所建。

and [ænd]
🔊 Track 0078

conj. 和、及；然後

▶Jenny and Betty are my best friends.
珍妮和貝蒂是我最好的朋友。

angel [`endʒl]
🔊 Track 0079

n. 天使；天使般的人

▶She is very sweet and compassionate, just like an angel.
她很討人喜歡又富同心情心，就像個天使。

anger [`æŋgɚ] n. 怒氣
◀ Track 0080

▶He seems to have a lot of anger towards his father.
他似乎對爸爸有很深的怒氣。

angry [`æŋgrɪ]
adj. 生氣的
◀ Track 0081

▶She gets angry easily.
她很容易生氣。

animal [`ænəml] n. 動物
◀ Track 0082

▶An animal lover, he has three dogs and five cats.
他很喜愛動物，養了3隻狗和5隻貓。

相關片語 party animal
熱衷社交聚會的人

▶Wherever there is a party, you'll see Tom here. He's such a party animal.
每當有派對，你一定會在那裡看到湯姆，他很熱衷參加派對。

ankle [`æŋkl] n. 足踝
◀ Track 0083

▶She sprained her ankle when walking down the stairs.
她下樓梯時扭到腳踝了。

another [ə`nʌðɚ]
pron. 另一個；再一個
◀ Track 0084

▶I would like another ice cream, please.
我想要再點一份冰淇淋。

adj. 另一的；另外的

▶I can't wait for another three minutes. My son really needs the doctor's help.
我不能再多等3分鐘了，我的兒子真的很需要醫生的幫忙。

相關片語 one after another 一個接一個

▶One student after another walked onto the stage to receive awards.
學生一個接一個上台去領獎。

answer [`ænsɚ] n. 答案
◀ Track 0085

▶What's the answer to this question?
這道問題的答案是什麼？

v. 回答

▶He hasn't given me an answer whether he will come to the party or not.
他還沒回覆我他會不會來這個派對。

相關片語 answer sb back 頂嘴；辯駁

▶When his dad told him to behave, he answered him back.
他爸爸叫他要注意言行，他頂嘴回去了。

ant [ænt] n. 螞蟻
◀ Track 0086

▶Why are there so many ants in the kitchen?
為什麼廚房有這麼多螞蟻？

相關片語 have ants in one's pants
坐立不安

▶He seemed to have ants in his pants before the presentation.
他在做報告前，看起來很坐立不安。

any [`ɛnɪ]
pron. 任何一人；任何一點
◀ Track 0087

▶Please give me suggestions if you have any.
如果你有建議的話，請提供給我。

初級

adv. 少許；稍微

▶He didn't feel any better after the surgery.
他手術後並沒有感覺比較好。

adj. 任一；絲毫；所有的

▶If you have any questions, please feel free to ask me.
你若有任何問題，請別客氣問我。

anybody [`ɛnɪˌbɑdɪ] ◀Track 0088
pron. 任何人

▶Is there anybody home?
有人在家嗎？

anyhow [`ɛnɪˌhaʊ] ◀Track 0089
adv. 無論如何；總之

▶It may rain this afternoon, but anyhow we will be there on time.
下午可能會下雨，但總之我們會準時抵達。

anyone [`ɛnɪˌwʌn] ◀Track 0090
pron. 任何人

▶Do you know anyone who can speak French?
你有認識任何會說法語的人嗎？

anyplace [`ɛnɪˌples] ◀Track 0091
adv. 任何地方

▶He couldn't find his cell phone anyplace.
他在任何地方都找不到他的手機。

anything [`ɛnɪˌθɪŋ] ◀Track 0092
pron. 任何事

▶Anything is possible.
任何事都可能會發生。

anytime [`ɛnɪˌtaɪm] ◀Track 0093
adv. 任何時候

▶Call me anytime you need someone to talk to.
你想有人陪你說話時，任何時候都可以打電話給我。

anyway [`ɛnɪˌwe] ◀Track 0094
adv. 無論如何，反正

▶Rain or shine, I'll see you next Monday anyway.
無論晴雨，我下週一就是要去看你。

anywhere [`ɛnɪˌhwɛr] ◀Track 0095
adv. 任何地方；無論何處

▶Did you go anywhere during the summer vacation?
你暑假期間，有去任何地方嗎？

apartment ◀Track 0096
[ə`partmənt] **n.** 公寓

▶She lived in an apartment her mother bought as her birthday gift.
她住在母親買來送她作為生日禮物的公寓。

ape [ep] **n.** 猿；大猩猩 ◀Track 0097

▶She adopted an ape and taught him how to use sign language to communicate.
她領養了一隻猩猩，並教他如何用手語來溝通。

相關片語 **go ape**
因興奮或生氣而發狂的、發瘋的

▶He went ape because his ex-girlfriend was going to marry his best friend.
他因為前女友要與他最好的朋友結婚，而氣極敗壞。

apologize
🔊 Track 0098

[ə`pɑləˌdʒaɪz] **v** 道歉；致歉

▶I think you should apologize for your rude behavior.
我認為你應該針對你的無禮行為而道歉。

appear [ə`pɪr]
🔊 Track 0099

v 出現；看來好像

▶She appears to be cold and unfriendly, but she is actually quite nice.
她看起來很冷漠、不友善，但其實她待人很好。

appearance
🔊 Track 0100

[ə`pɪrəns] **n** 出現，顯露；外表，外貌

▶The polar bear cub became a global sensation when he made his first public appearance.
這隻小北極熊首次亮相就造成全球轟動。

appetite [`æpəˌtaɪt]
🔊 Track 0101

n 食慾；胃口

▶The flu may cause loss of appetite.
流感可能導致食慾不振。

apple [`æpl] **n** 蘋果
🔊 Track 0102

▶She baked an apple pie for her boyfriend.
她幫男友烤了一個蘋果派。

相關片語 **the apple of sb.'s eye** 某人的掌上明珠；心愛的人或事物

▶Ivanka is the apple of her father's eyes.
伊凡卡是她父親的掌上明珠。

apply [ə`plaɪ]
🔊 Track 0103

v 塗，敷；申請

▶You can apply some ointment on the wound.
你可以在傷口上敷一點藥膏。

appreciate [ə`priʃɪˌet]
🔊 Track 0104

v 欣賞；感謝

▶We appreciate your comments and will improve our service.
我們感謝你的指教，並將改善我們的服務。

April [`eprəl] **n** 四月
🔊 Track 0105

▶They just got married in April.
他們在四月剛新婚。

相關片語 **April Fool's Day** 愚人節

▶On April 1, he announced on Titter that his company went bankrupt. Later, he said it was a joke on April Fool's Day.
他在四月一日於推特公布他的公司破產了，隨後他說那只是愚人節的玩笑話。

apron [`eprən] **n** 圍裙
🔊 Track 0106

▶She put on her apron and started to prepare for dinner.
她穿上圍裙後，便開始料理晚餐。

are [ɑr]
🔊 Track 0107

v 是（第二人稱或第三人稱複數使用）

▶They are colleagues.
他們是同事。

area [`ɛrɪə] **n** 地區
🔊 Track 0108

▶The famous private school is located in this area.
這間知名的私立學校位在這個地區。

aren't [ɑrnt] **abbr** 不是
🔊 Track 0109

▶They aren't going to the prom.
他們將不參加畢業舞會。

初級

argue [`ɑrgjʊ]
Track 0110

v. 爭執；爭論

▶His children argue with each other all the time.
他的小孩總是在爭吵。

argument
Track 0111

[`ɑrgjəmənt] **n.** 爭執；爭論；爭吵；論點

▶They had an argument with their neighbors last night.
他們昨晚跟鄰居起了爭執。

arm [ɑrm] **n.** 手臂
Track 0112

▶He got a tattoo on his right arm.
他的右手臂有刺青。

armchair [`ɑrm͵tʃɛr]
Track 0113

n. 扶手椅

▶I like to sit in this armchair and read.
我喜歡坐在這個扶手椅上看書。

army [`ɑrmɪ] **n.** 軍隊
Track 0114

▶He had served in the army for five years.
他在軍隊服務了五年。

around [ə`raʊnd]
Track 0115

prep. 在……附近；環繞

▶He looked around to see where his son was.
他看了四周，想知道兒子跑到哪裡了。

adv. 到處、四處；周圍、附近；大約

▶The party will begin around 8:00 P.M.
派對將在晚上八點左右開始。

相關片語 **fool around** 遊手好閒；鬼混

▶If you fool around with drug addicts, you will become one of them sooner or later.
如果你跟吸毒的人在一起鬼混，你早晚也會跟著吸毒。

arrange [ə`rendʒ]
Track 0116

v. 安排；整理

▶He arranged a surprise party for his wife.
他為妻子安排一個驚喜派對。

arrange·ment
Track 0117

[ə`rendʒmənt] **n.** 安排；準備工作；整理

▶He made arrangements for his friend's funeral.
他為他的朋友安排葬禮。

arrest [ə`rɛst]
Track 0118

v. 逮捕；拘留

▶The bank robbers were arrested two days later.
銀行搶劫犯兩天後就被逮捕了。

n. 逮捕；拘留

▶The murderer was finally under arrest.
謀殺犯終於被逮捕了。

相關片語 **house arrest** 軟禁

▶The activist has been put under house arrest.
這個活躍份子已經被軟禁在家了。

arrive [ə`raɪv] **v.** 抵達
Track 0119

▶After hours of traffic jam, we finally arrived home.
塞了幾小時的車後，我們終於到家了。

arrow [`æro] n. 箭　　◀Track 0120

▶He shot an arrow at the hare.
他朝著野兔射了一箭。

art [ɑrt] n. 藝術；美術　　◀Track 0121

▶My favorite subject is art.
我最喜歡的科目是美術。

相關片語 **a work of art** 藝術品

▶The new sculpture in the park is a work of art.
公園裡的新雕像是件藝術品。

article [`ɑrtɪkl] n. 文章　　◀Track 0122

▶Your article is beautifully written.
你的文章寫得真好。

artist [`ɑrtɪst] n. 藝術家　　◀Track 0123

▶Picasso is a famous artist.
畢卡索是知名的藝術家。

相關片語 **street artist** 街頭藝術家

▶She is the only street artist in this city.
她是這個城市裡唯一的街頭藝術家。

as [æz]　　◀Track 0124

conj. 像……一樣；當……時

▶My mother is as busy as a bee.
我媽媽像蜜蜂一樣忙碌。

prep. 像，如同；作為

▶She works in the department store as a makeup advisor.
她在百貨公司當美容顧問。

adv. 一樣地，同樣地

▶She is as beautiful as her mother.
她跟她媽媽一樣美麗。

Asia [`eʃə] n. 亞洲　　◀Track 0125

▶India is one of the countries in Asia.
印度是亞洲的其中一個國家。

Asian [`eʃən]　　◀Track 0126

adj. 亞洲的；亞洲人的

▶She is one of the Asian models invited to attend the New York fashion week.
她是獲邀參加紐約時尚週的亞裔模特兒之一。

n. 亞洲人

▶My father is German and my mother is Asian.
我爸爸是德國人，媽媽是亞洲人。

ask [æsk] v. 問；要求　　◀Track 0127

▶He asked me my name, but I didn't tell him.
他問我的名字，但我沒有告訴他。

asleep [ə`slip]　　◀Track 0128

adj. 睡著的

▶When he came home, his wife was asleep on the sofa.
他到家時，妻子已在沙發上睡著。

相關片語 **fall asleep** 睡著

▶My dog fell asleep soon after she lay down on the carpet.
我的小狗一躺在地毯上，很快就睡著。

補充片語 **lie down** 躺下來

assistant [ə`sɪstənt]　　◀Track 0129

n. 助手

▶She works as an assistant to the editor-in-chief of a fashion magazine.
她擔任一家時尚雜誌總編的助理。

初級

adj. 助理的；有幫助的

▶My father is an assistant professor.
我爸爸是助理教授。

相關片語 **shop assistant** 店員

▶The shop assistant helped me find the clothes I want.
這名店員幫我找到想要的衣服。

assume [ə`sjum] 🔊 Track 0130
v. 以為；假定為；認為

▶She assumed that her husband knew what she wanted for her birthday gift, but he didn't.
她以為她的先生知道她想要什麼生日禮物，但他不知道。

at [æt] **prep.** 在（某地點）； 🔊 Track 0131
在（某時刻）；對著、向

▶I'll meet you at the cafeteria.
我會在自助餐廳和你碰面。

attack [ə`tæk] **n.** 攻擊 🔊 Track 0132

▶There was a terrorist attack that night.
那天晚上發生了恐攻事件。

v. 攻擊

▶He was attacked by a group of gangsters in the parking lot last night.
他昨晚在停車場被一群幫派份子攻擊。

相關片語 **heart attack** 心臟病發作

▶She had an heart attack and was sent to the ER.
她的心臟病發，被送到急診室。

at-tend [ə`tɛnd] 🔊 Track 0133
v. 參加；出席

▶We will attend the music concert tonight.
我們會出席今晚的音樂會。

attention [ə`tɛnʃən] 🔊 Track 0134
n. 注意；注意力

▶The boy pretended that he was kidnapped to get his parents' attention.
男孩假裝被綁架，以獲得他爸媽的關注。

相關片語 **pay attention** 關心；注意

▶Please pay attention to the traffic light when you drive.
開車時請注意交通號誌燈。

audience [`ɔdɪəns] 🔊 Track 0135
n. 觀眾；聽眾；讀者

▶The audience was amused by the comedian.
觀眾被這名喜劇演員逗得很開懷。

August [`ɔgəst] 🔊 Track 0136
n. =Aug. 八月

▶The family always travels abroad in August.
這家人總是會在八月出國旅遊。

aunt [ænt] 🔊 Track 0137
n. =auntie=aunty 阿姨；姑姑；嬸嬸；舅媽

▶My aunt cooks really well.
我姑姑很會料理。

相關片語 **Aunt Flo**
大姨媽（指女子的生理期）

▶I need to take a day-off because Aunt Flo has come to visit.
我今天要請假，因為大姨媽來了。

Australia [ɔ`streljə]   ◀Track 0138
n. 澳洲

▶Chloe was born in Australia.
克蘿伊在澳洲出生。

Australian [ɔ`streljən]   ◀Track 0139
adj. 澳洲的；澳洲人的

▶Nicole Kidman is a great Australian actress.
妮可‧基嫚是一名優秀的澳洲籍女演員。

n. 澳洲人

▶Mr. Yeh married an Australian, and together they have three beautiful children.
葉先生娶了澳洲人，他們有三個漂亮的小孩。

autumn [`ɔtəm] **n.** 秋天   ◀Track 0140
▶We went to Eastern Europe last autumn.
我們去年秋天去了東歐。

相關片語 **Mid-Autumn Festival** 中秋節

▶Chinese people usually eat moon cakes during the Mid-Autumn Festival.
華人常在中秋節吃月餅。

available [ə`veləbl]   ◀Track 0141
adj. 可用的；可取得的；有空的；有效的

▶My boss is not available next Monday. Can you come here next Tuesday?
我的老闆下週一沒空，你方便下週二過來嗎？

avoid [ə`vɔɪd] **v.** 避免   ◀Track 0142
▶I try to avoid going to work during the rush hour.
我出門上班會試著避開交通尖峰時間。

aware [ə`wɛr]   ◀Track 0143
adj. 知道的；察覺的

▶She was not aware that she had a talent for music until now.
她不知道自己有音樂天份，直到現在才發現。

away [ə`we]   ◀Track 0144
adv. 離開；不在；離……多遠；消失

▶She stays away from her friend who has become a drug addict.
她的朋友吸毒成癮，於是她避開她了。

相關片語 **go away** 走開

▶You're such a liar. Go away.
你是個大騙子，你走開。

初級

▶ Bb

以下表格是全民英檢官方公告初級「聽、說、讀、寫」所須具備的能力，本書例句皆依此範疇特別設計，只要掃描右方QR code，就能搭配相對應的音軌，實現「眼耳並用」方式，刺激左腦的語言學習功能；同時也可使用本書附贈的紅膠片，將其置於單字上，一面記憶一面自我挑戰，達到雙倍的學習成果！

聽	▶	能聽懂與日常生活相關的淺易談話，包含價格、時間及地點等。
說	▶	能朗讀簡易文章、簡單地自我介紹，對熟悉的話題能以簡易英語對答，如問候、購物、問路等。
讀	▶	可看懂與日常生活相關的淺易英文，並能閱讀路標、交通號誌、招牌、簡單菜單、時刻表及賀卡等。
寫	▶	能寫簡單的句子及段落，如寫明信片、便條、賀卡及填表格等。對一般日常生活相關事物，能以簡短的文字敘述或說明。

baby [`bebɪ] n. 嬰兒　◀ Track 0145

▶She helped take care of her sister's baby after school.
她放學後幫忙照顧姐姐的小嬰兒。

相關片語 **sleep like a baby** 睡得很熟

▶After an exhausting day, he slept like a baby at night.
他忙了一天後，晚上睡得很熟。

babysitter [`bebɪsɪtɚ] ◀ Track 0146
n. 臨時保姆

▶Diana was a babysitter before she married the prince.
黛安娜嫁給王子前是一名保姆。

back [bæk] ◀ Track 0147
adv. 向後；以前；原處；回覆

▶She looked back and saw a black dog following her.
她回頭看到一隻黑狗正在跟著她。

n. 背部；後面

▶There is a garden in the back of the house. 屋後有一座庭院。

v. 後退；支持

▶He refused to back her election campaign.
他拒絕支持她的競選活動。

adj. 後面的

▶He sneaked into the classroom through the back door.
他從後門溜進了教室。

backward [`bækwɚd] ◀ Track 0148
adv. 向後；倒回

▶She looked backward and saw her father.
她向後看，看到了她的爸爸。

adj. 向後的；落後的、發展遲緩的

▶The boy was backward compared with his classmates.
跟同班同學相較之下，這名男童學習遲緩。

backwards
🔊 Track 0149

[`bækwɚdz] **adv.** 向後，逆著

▶Let's count backwards: *"Five, four, three..."*
我們來倒數：「5，4，3⋯」。

---

bad [bæd]
🔊 Track 0150

adj. 壞的；惡劣的

▶She was upset by the bad news.
她因為這個壞消息而感到很煩悶。

相關片語 **a bad egg** 壞蛋

▶He used to hang out with that bad egg and got into big trouble.
他曾跟那個壞蛋混在一起，給自己帶來很大的麻煩。

補充片語 **hang out**
與某人一起消磨時間、混在一起

---

badminton
🔊 Track 0151

[`bædmɪntən] **n.** 羽毛球

▶She was very good at playing badminton and won the championship last year.
她很會打羽毛球，去年曾贏得冠軍。

補充片語 **be good at** 擅長

---

bag [bæg] **n.** 袋子
🔊 Track 0152

▶She doesn't use plastic bags or plastic cups.
她不用塑膠袋或塑膠杯。

相關片語 **tote bag** 購物袋

▶He brought his own tote bag when shopping in the supermarket.
他逛超市時自備購物袋。

---

bake [bek]
🔊 Track 0153

v. 烘焙；烘烤

▶We baked an almond cake for afternoon tea.
我們為下午茶烤了一個杏仁蛋糕。

---

bakery [`bekərɪ]
🔊 Track 0154

n. 烘焙坊；麵包店

▶He bought a loaf of bread at the bakery.
他在麵包店買了一塊麵包。

---

balcony [`bælkənɪ]
🔊 Track 0155

n. 陽台

▶There's a balcony in the living room.
客廳有一個陽台。

---

ball [bɔl]
🔊 Track 0156

n. 球；球狀物

▶My daughter is interested in ball games.
我女兒對球類運動很有興趣。

補充片語 **be interested in**
對⋯⋯有興趣

相關片語 **ball pen** 原子筆

▶I lost my ball pen, but that's OK. It's running out of ink anyway.
我弄丟了我的原子筆，不過沒關係，反正那支快沒水了。

補充片語 **run out** 用完

---

balloon [bə`lun]
🔊 Track 0157

n. 氣球

▶Watch out for the balloon. It's going to burst.
小心這顆氣球，它快要破了。

初級

補充片語 **watch out** 小心

相關片語 **hot air balloon** 熱氣球

▶How about a hot air balloon ride with me?
要不要和我一起搭熱氣球？

bamboo [bæm`bu] Track 0158
n. 竹；竹子

▶The chair is made of bamboo.
這張椅子是用竹子做成的。

banana [bə`nænə] Track 0159
n. 香蕉

▶She baked a banana cake.
她烤了一個香蕉蛋糕。

band [bænd] Track 0160
n. 帶；細繩；橡皮圈

▶She gave me a beautiful wrist band made by herself.
她送我一條自製的美麗腕帶。

相關片語 **rubber band** 橡皮筋

▶She used a lot of rubber bands to make a jump rope.
她用很多條橡皮筋做成一條跳繩。

bank [bæŋk] Track 0161
n. 銀行

▶He withdrew some money from the bank.
他從銀行提領一些錢。

相關片語 **piggy bank** 存錢撲滿；存錢筒

▶She puts a 5-dollar coin into a piggy bank everyday.
她每天都存一枚5元硬幣在小豬撲滿裡。

banker [`bæŋkə] Track 0162
n. 銀行家

▶His brother is a banker and a financier.
她的弟弟是銀行家和金融家。

bar [bɑr] Track 0163
n. 酒吧；條狀物

▶He runs a hotel bar in California.
他在加州經營飯店酒吧。

相關片語 **monkey bars** （供攀爬的）單槓、握桿

▶The park is equipped with monkey bars and a slide.
這座公園有單槓和溜滑梯。

barbecue =Bar-B-Q [`bɑrbɪkju] Track 0164
n. 烤肉；烤肉餐館

▶My family will have a barbecue tonight.
我們家今晚要烤肉。

v. （在戶外）烤肉

▶We barbecued some vegetables and chicken in the backyard.
我們在後院烤了一些蔬菜和雞肉。

barber [`bɑrbə] Track 0165
n. 理髮師

▶She used to be a barber but now she's a makeup artist.
她以前是理髮師，但現在是化妝師。

相關片語 **barber shop** 理髮店

▶My dad always has his hair cut at this barber shop.
我爸爸總是到這家理髮店理髮。

bark [bɑrk]
◀ Track 0166

v.（狗等）吠叫

▶The dog kept barking at the postman.
那隻狗一直對郵差吠叫。

n. 吠叫聲

▶His dog has a very loud bark.
他的小狗吠叫聲很大。

base [bes]
◀ Track 0167

v. 以……為基礎

▶Based on a true story, the movie is about Argentina's first lady, Eva Perón.
這部電影以真實故事為基礎所拍攝，內容有關阿根廷第一夫人艾薇塔的生平。

n. 基礎；基本部分

▶This moisturizer provides an excellent base for makeup.
這種保濕霜用在化妝前打底效果很好。

baseball [`bes͵bɔl]
◀ Track 0168

n. 棒球

▶He played baseball when he was young.
他小時候打過棒球。

basement [`besmənt]
◀ Track 0169

n. 地下室

▶She put all the old furniture in the basement.
她把所有的舊傢俱都放在地下室。

basic [`besɪk]
◀ Track 0170

adj. 基本的

▶I need some basic knowledge about how to make investments.
我需要一些有關投資的基礎知識

basis [`besɪs]
◀ Track 0171

n. 基礎；根據

▶We made the decision on the basis of big data.
我們根據大數據來做這個決定。

basket [`bæskɪt]
◀ Track 0172

n. 籃子

▶I don't think you should put all your eggs in one basket.
我不認為你應把所有的雞蛋都放在一個籃子裡。（勿孤注一擲）

相關片語 **shopping basket** 購物籃

▶Almost all supermarkets provide shopping baskets for their customers.
幾乎所有超市都提供購客購物籃使用。

basketball
◀ Track 0173

[`bæskɪt͵bɔl] **n.** 籃球

▶He plays basketball after school everyday.
他每天下課都去打籃球。

bat [bæt]
◀ Track 0174

n. 球棒；蝙蝠

▶How can we play baseball without bats?
沒有球棒，我們要怎麼打棒球？

bath [bæθ]
◀ Track 0175

n. 沐浴

▶I gave my dog a bath this afternoon.
我今天下午幫我家小狗洗澡。

相關片語 **swimming bath** 室內游泳池

▶There is a swimming bath next to the house.
這棟房子旁邊有一座室內游泳池。

初級

bathe [beð] ◀Track 0176
v 把……浸入；洗澡；沉浸
▶He bathed his feet in the hot spring.
他在溫泉裡泡腳。

bathroom [`bæθˌrum] ◀Track 0177
n 浴室；洗手間
▶He went to the bathroom during recess.
他下課時去洗手間了。

battle [`bætl̩] ◀Track 0178
n 戰鬥；戰役
▶Many soldiers died at the Battle of Gettysburg.
有很多士兵在蓋茨堡之役身亡。

v 與……作戰；搏鬥
▶She battled against cancer but failed.
她與癌症奮戰，但終究失敗了。

相關片語 **fight a losing battle**
打一場沒有勝算的仗

▶They realized they were fighting a losing battle because their enemies had weapons of mass destruction.
他們知道在打一場沒有勝算的仗，因為他們的敵人有大規模毀滅性武器。

be [bi] ◀Track 0179
v 是；成為；正在（與現在分詞連用）；被（與過去分詞連用）
▶He wanted to be an actor, so he went to Hollywood to give it a try.
他想成為一名演員，所以他到好萊塢去嘗試發展。

beach [bitʃ] ◀Track 0180
n 海邊；海灘
▶It's so hot. Let's go to the beach.
天氣好熱，我們去海邊吧。

相關片語 **beach umbrella** 遮陽傘

▶She didn't want to get a suntan, so she took a rest under the beach umbrella.
她不想被曬黑，所以在遮陽傘下休息。

bead [bid] ◀Track 0181
n 有孔小珠；汗珠；淚珠；水珠
▶She wore a bracelet decorated with colored wooden beads.
她戴著用彩色木珠裝飾的手鏈。

bean [bin] ◀Track 0182
n 豆子
▶The red bean soup tastes so delicious.
這紅豆湯真好喝。

bear [bɛr] **n** 熊 ◀Track 0183
▶The mother bear gave birth to three cubs.
這隻熊生了三隻熊寶寶。

v 忍受；承擔；生（孩子）
▶I can't bear his hot temper anymore.
我再也受不了他的壞脾氣了。

相關片語 **polar bear** 北極熊

▶Polar bears are endangered species due to global warming.
由於氣候暖化，北極熊成了瀕臨絕種的動物。

beard [bɪrd] ◀Track 0184
n 山羊鬍；下巴上的鬍鬚
▶He shaves his beard every morning.
他每天早上都會刮鬍子。

beat [bit] ◀Track 0185
v 打；跳動

▶He was beaten by the bullies and needed to be hospitalized.
他被惡霸痛歐，需要住院住療。

n. 敲打；心跳聲；拍子、節奏

▶My heart skipped a beat when a huge dog started barking at me.
一隻大狗開始對我狂吠，害我嚇了一跳。

補充片語 **one's heart skips a beat**
形容人因為驚嚇、興奮或害怕而心臟差點停止

---

beautiful [ˈbjutəfəl] ◀Track 0186

adj. 美麗的；完美的

▶She has a beautiful heart.
她的心地很善良。

---

beauty [ˈbjutɪ] ◀Track 0187

n. 美貌；美人；美的事物；優點

▶Beauty is in the eye of the beholder.
情人眼裡出西施。

---

because [bɪˈkɔz] ◀Track 0188

conj. 因為

▶She went home because she had a fever.
她因為發燒，所以回家了。

---

become [bɪˈkʌm] ◀Track 0189

v. 成為；變得

▶He grew up and became a great scientist.
他長大後成為一名偉大的科學家。

---

bed [bɛd] **n.** 床 ◀Track 0190

▶I usually go to bed at 10 P.M.
我通常都晚上十點上床睡覺。

---

bedroom [ˈbɛdˌrʊm] ◀Track 0191

n. 臥室

▶She decorated her bedroom with Bob Ross's paintings.
她用鮑伯·羅絲的畫裝飾她的房間。

相關片語 **guest bedroom** 客房

▶When we went to New York, we stayed in the guest bedroom of our uncle's house.
我們去紐約時，我們在叔叔家的客房過夜。

---

bee [bi] **n.** 蜜蜂 ◀Track 0192

▶Her face was stung by a bee and it swelled up horribly.
她的臉被蜜蜂螫到，腫得很可怕。

相關片語 **busy bee** 勤奮的人

▶He works so diligently. There's no doubt that he is a busy bee.
他工作很勤奮，他毫無疑問是個勤奮的人。

---

beef [bif] **n.** 牛肉 ◀Track 0193

▶He order a beef hamburger and a French fries.
他點了一份牛肉漢堡和薯條。

---

beep [bip] ◀Track 0194

v. 吹警笛；發出嗶嗶聲

▶Dr. Weiss was beeped to go to the Emergency Room.
魏斯醫師被呼叫器的嗶嗶聲呼叫去急診室。

n. 嗶聲

▶I left a message after the beep on the answering machine.
我在電話錄音嗶聲後，留了一個口訊。

---

beer [bɪr] **n.** 啤酒 ◀Track 0195

▶I'd like a ginger beer, please.
我要點一杯薑汁啤酒。

初級

相關片語 **beer belly** 啤酒肚

▶He's got a beer belly since he was 40.
他40歲開始有啤酒肚。

beetle [`bitl̩] n. 甲蟲　◀ᴇTrack 0196

▶He kept a beetle as a pet.
他養了一隻甲蟲當寵物。

before [bɪ`for]　◀ᴇTrack 0197
prep. 在……之前

▶I need to go home before 8 P.M.
我得在晚上八點以前回家。

conj. 在……之前

▶He was a brilliant student before his parents divorced.
在他的雙親離婚前，他是很優秀的學生。

adv. 以前

▶She said she had been here before.
她說她曾來過這個地方。

beg [bɛg]　◀ᴇTrack 0198
v. 乞討；懇求

▶I beg your pardon, please?
請再說一遍好嗎？

相關片語 **go begging** 沒人要的

▶If this snowball music box is going begging, I'll buy it.
如果這個雪球音樂盒沒人要，我就會買下它。

begin [bɪ`gɪn]　◀ᴇTrack 0199
v. 開始；著手

▶The forum begins at 10 A.M. in the lecture hall.
這場論壇於上午十點開始在大講堂舉行。

beginner [bɪ`gɪnɚ]　◀ᴇTrack 0200
n. 初學者；新手

▶This yoga class is for beginners.
這個瑜伽課是給初學者上的。

beginning [bɪ`gɪnɪŋ]　◀ᴇTrack 0201
n. 開始；起點

▶In the beginning, she wasn't impressed by him. But years later, she was moved by his sincerity.
她一開始對他的印象不太好，但多年後，她被他的誠意所感動了。

adj. 開始的

▶We are happy to offer you this course which is for beginning level learners.
我們很高興能提供你這堂專給初學者上的課程。

behave [bɪ`hev]　◀ᴇTrack 0202
v. 做出……舉止，表現；行為舉止

▶His parents asked him to behave, but he wouldn't listen.
他的爸媽要求他表現得乖一點，但他不聽話。

behind [bɪ`haɪnd]　◀ᴇTrack 0203
prep. 在……之後

▶The boy was lagging behind the class.
男童的程度在班上落後。

adv. 在背後；(留)在原處、在後；遲

▶She was upset to discover that she had left her laptop behind.
她很氣惱發現居然把筆電留在原地。

相關片語 **leave behind** 忘記帶；未帶

▶The school is committed to making sure that no child is left behind.
這所學校致力於不放棄每個學童。

belief [bɪ`lif]
🔊 Track 0204

n. 信任；相信；信仰

▶I was beyond belief that he would commit such a horrible crime.
他會犯下這麼可怕的案子，簡直讓我難以置信。

補充片語 beyond belief
難以置信的、不可意思的

believble [bɪ`livəbl]
🔊 Track 0205

adj. 可信的

▶He tried to make his story as believable as possible.
他盡可能地讓自己的故事聽來可信。

believe [bɪ`liv]
🔊 Track 0206

v. 相信

▶Don't believe whatever she says. She's a chronic liar.
別盡信她所說的任何事，她是個慣性說謊的人。

bell [bɛl] **n.** 鈴；鐘
🔊 Track 0207

▶Who could possibly ring the door bell this time?
這次到底是誰在按門鈴？

相關片語 ring a bell 使人回想起⋯⋯

▶Wait a minute. Your name rings a bell.
等一下，你的名字聽起來很熟悉。

belong [bə`lɔŋ]
🔊 Track 0208

v. 應被放置某處；屬於；適合

▶The tablet computer belongs to him.
這個平板電腦屬於他的。

below [bə`lo]
🔊 Track 0209

adv. 在下面；以下

▶For more information, please see below.
想了解更多資訊，請見下文。

prep. 在⋯⋯下面；在⋯⋯以下；低於

▶These children are below the age of five.
這些小孩都在五歲以下。

相關片語 hit below the belt
以不正當的手段攻擊

▶She hit below the belt with a lie about you.
她用謊言對你施以不正當的攻擊。

初級

belt [bɛlt]
🔊 Track 0210

n. 帶狀物；腰帶

▶His belt is studded with pieces of metal.
他的皮帶上面鑲有金屬飾品。

bench [bɛntʃ]
🔊 Track 0211

n. 長凳；長椅

▶There are some benches in the park.
公園裡有些長椅。

bend [bɛnd]
🔊 Track 0212

v. 使彎曲、使屈服

▶He bent down to pick up his smart phone.
他彎下腰來撿他的智慧型手機。

n. 彎曲、轉彎處

▶There's a bend in the road on Ontario highway.
安大略高速公路的路段有個轉彎。

beside [bɪˋsaɪd]
◀ Track 0213

prep. 在……旁邊

▶The church is right beside a lake.
教堂就在湖的旁邊。

besides [bɪˋsaɪdz]
◀ Track 0214

prep. 在……之外；除……之外

▶He plays badminton well besides tennis and volleyball.
他除了網球和排球打得很好之外，羽球也打得不錯。

adv. 此外；而且

▶I'm not interested in you at all. Besides, I'm married.
我對你一點興趣都沒有。再說，我已婚了。

best [bɛst]
◀ Track 0215

adv. 最好地；最適當地；最

▶This evening gown suits you best for the banquet.
穿這件晚禮服參加這場晚宴對你最適合。

adj. 最好的；最適當的

▶He is my husband and my best friend.
他是我的先生，也是我最好的朋友。

相關片語 **try one's best** 盡全力

▶The firefighters tried their best to put out the forest fire.
消防人員盡全力撲滅森林大火。

bet [bɛt] **v** 打賭；敢斷言
◀ Track 0216

▶I bet the German team will win the Super Bowl.
我打賭德國隊會贏得世界盃。

n. 打賭；賭注

▶My bet is that she won't win the re-election .
我打賭她不會連任成功。

相關片語 **safe bet**
肯定會發生的事；萬無一失的事

▶It's a safe bet that he will attend his son's wedding.
他一定會參加他兒子的婚禮。

better [ˋbɛtɚ]
◀ Track 0217

adv. 更好地；更適當地；更

▶The team performed better in the second half of the game.
這支隊伍在下半場表現得較好。

adj. 更好的；更適當的

▶Their relationship became better throughout the years.
他們的關係在過去幾年中變得更好了。

相關片語 **better than nothing** 聊勝於無

▶The rice is a bit sticky, but it's better than nothing.
米好像煮得有點太黏了，但有得吃總比沒有好。

between [bɪˋtwin]
◀ Track 0218

prep. 在……之間

▶Her mother doesn't allow her children to eat snacks between meals.
她媽媽不准小孩在三餐之間吃零食。

beyond [bɪˋjɑnd]
◀ Track 0219

prep. 在……另一邊；超出

▶More and more people live beyond the age of 75.
越來越多人活過75歲。

相關片語 **live beyond one's means**
生活入不敷出

▶She has been smart with her money and has never lived beyond her means.
她用錢很謹慎，生活從來不會入不敷出。

bicycle [`baɪsɪkl]
🔊 Track 0220

n. =bike 自行車、單車、腳踏車

▶He rode a bicycle to the grocery store.
他騎腳踏車去雜貨店。

big [bɪg]
🔊 Track 0221

adj. 大的；年齡較長的

▶His dog is big but very gentle.
他的狗體型很大，但很溫和。

相關片語 **have a big mouth**
多話、藏不住秘密

▶She has a big mouth. She talks about people's private lives all the time.
她是個大嘴巴，總是在講別人的私生活。

bill [bɪl] **n.** 帳單
🔊 Track 0222

▶With Internet, you can pay your bill online.
你有網路就可以線上付帳單了。

bind [baɪnd]
🔊 Track 0223

v. 綁；綑；裝訂；黏合

▶The man had been bound in the basement for five days.
男子被綁在地下室長達五天。

biology [baɪ`ɑlədʒɪ]
🔊 Track 0224

n. 生物；生物學

▶My father is a biology professor.
我爸爸是生物學教授。

bird [bɝd] **n.** 鳥
🔊 Track 0225

▶Every year, hundreds of migrant birds gather here for a rest.
這裡每年都有數百隻候鳥聚集在這裡休息。

相關片語 **early bird** 早起的人

▶She is an early bird. She gets up at 5 o'clock and does yoga.
她每天都很早起，她清晨五點起來後就做瑜伽。

birth [bɝθ]
🔊 Track 0226

n. 出生；分娩；出身；家世

▶The cat gave birth to three kittens last week.
這隻貓咪上週生了三隻小貓。

相關片語 **give birth to** 生產；生育

birth·day [`bɝθ,de]
🔊 Track 0227

n. 生日

▶The birthday party will begin at 6:00 P.M.
生日派對將在晚上6點舉行。

相關片語 **birthday boy/ birthday girl**
壽星

▶Jack is the birthday boy today, and there are five candles on his birthday cake.
傑克是今天的壽星，他的生日蛋糕上有5根蠟燭。

bit [bɪt]
🔊 Track 0228

n. 小片；小塊；一點點

▶He smashed the crystal glass into bits.
他把水晶玻璃杯摔成了小碎片。

bite [baɪt] **v.** 咬
🔊 Track 0229

▶She was bitten by a rat.
她被野鼠咬傷。

n. 咬一口；（口）便餐

▶I'm starving. May I have a bite of your hamburger?
我好餓，可以讓我吃一口你的漢堡嗎？

初級

相關片語 **a bite to eat** 吃少量東西

▶I'd like a bite to eat before the state banquet.
參加國宴前，我想先吃點東西。

bitter [ˋbɪtɚ]
🔊 Track 0230

adj. 苦的

▶She feels bitter about the way her mother treats her.
她對於媽媽對待她的方式，心裡感到很苦。

相關片語 **bitter end** 堅忍到底

▶He fought for his ideals to the bitter end.
他為了理想而奮鬥到底。

black [blæk]
🔊 Track 0231

adj. 黑色的；黑人的

▶It's a safe bet to wear black suits in such a formal occasion.
在這麼正式的場合穿黑西裝是絕對不會出錯的。

n. 黑；黑色；（大寫時）指黑人

▶The suspect was in black and ran with a limp.
嫌疑犯穿了一身黑色的衣服，跑起來有一點跛。

相關片語 **black tea** 紅茶

▶Which do you prefer, black tea or coffee?
你想要哪一個，紅茶還是咖啡？

blackboard
🔊 Track 0232

[ˋblæk͵bord] **n.** 黑板

▶The students doodled on the blackboard during recess.
學生在下課時間在黑板上亂畫東西。

blame [blem]
🔊 Track 0233

v. 責怪；責罵

▶She blamed her husband for being inconsiderate.
她責怪先生不體貼。

n. 指責；責備；責任

▶He took the blame even though he didn't do anything wrong.
雖然他沒犯錯，但他把指責都承擔下來了。

blank [blæŋk]
🔊 Track 0234

adj. 空白的；無表情的

▶The TV screen went blank all of a sudden.
電視螢幕突然空白了。

n. 空白；空格處

▶Please write down your complaint in the blank on page 3.
請在第三頁空格處寫下你的申訴事由。

blanket [ˋblæŋkɪt]
🔊 Track 0235

n. 毛毯；毯子

▶She covered the stray dog in a blanket and took him home.
她用毯子把流浪狗裹了起來，並把牠帶回家。

blind [blaɪnd]
🔊 Track 0236

adj. 盲的；視而不見的

▶He became blind when he was 14.
他14歲時變成盲人。

block [blɑk]
🔊 Track 0237

n. 塊狀物；街區

▶The shopping mall is just two blocks away.
購物中心只有兩個街區遠。

v. 阻塞；堵住

▶The pipeline is blocked on both sides.
這條水管兩端都堵住了。

---

blood [blʌd] **n.** 血
Track 0238

▶He was found lying on the floor in a pool of blood.
他被發現躺在血泊中。

相關片語 **blood type** 血型

▶My horoscope is Aquarius and my blood type is O.
我是水瓶座，血型是O。

---

bloody [`blʌdɪ]
Track 0239

adj. 流血的；血淋淋的

▶The boy had a bloody nose and got blood on his shirt.
男孩流鼻血，上衣沾有血跡。

---

blouse [blaʊz]
Track 0240

n.（婦女或孩童的）短上衣

▶I bought a new blouse in the department store.
我在百貨公司買了一件女襯衫。

---

blow [blo] **v.** 吹
Track 0241

▶A gust of wind blew down the fences.
一陣強風把籬笆吹倒了。

n. 吹氣；一擊；（口）強風；精神上的打擊

▶Her husband's death was a serious blow to her.
她先生過世帶給她沉重的打擊。

---

blue [blu]
Track 0242

adj. 藍色的；憂鬱的

▶He bought a pair of blue gloves for his son.
他買了一雙藍手套給兒子。

n. 藍色；沮喪、憂鬱；藍調

▶My favorite color is pastel blue.
我最喜歡的顏色是粉藍色。

相關片語 **feel blue** 感到沮喪、憂鬱

▶She felt blue when she heard that her ex-boyfriend was getting married.
她聽說前男友要結婚了而感到鬱悶。

---

board [bord]
Track 0243

v. 上（船、車或飛機）

▶She boarded a plane to New Zealand early in the morning.
她清晨就登上前往紐西蘭的飛機。

n. 公告欄

▶She left a message on the board.
她把留言寫在公告欄上。

相關片語 **cutting board** 砧板

▶You can use lemon and salt to clean the cutting board.
你可以用檸檬和鹽巴清洗這個砧板。

---

boat [bot] **n.** 小船
Track 0244

▶Dragon Boat Festival is one of the major Chinese holidays.
端午節是華人重要的節日之一。

相關片語 **in the same boat** 相同處境

▶We must work together because we're in the same boat.
我們倆處境相同，所以一定要團結合作。

---

body [`bɑdɪ] **n.** 身體
Track 0245

▶Regular exercise is good for our body.
規律運動對我們的身體有益。

初級

相關片語 **body language** 身體語言

▶His body language shows that he's not a confident man.
他的身體語言顯示他不是一個有自信的男人。

---

boil [bɔɪl]　　　🔊Track 0246

v. （水等）沸騰；烹煮；煮沸

▶I boiled an egg and made a sandwich for my breakfast.
我煮了一顆水煮蛋並做了一份三明治當早餐。

---

bomb [bɑm]　　　🔊Track 0247

n. 炸彈

▶The terrorist who planted a bomb at the station was arrested.
在車站放置炸彈的恐怖份子被逮捕了。

---

bone [bon]　　　🔊Track 0248

n. 骨頭

▶The dog dug out a bone in the park.
那隻狗在公園挖出了一根骨頭。

相關片語 **skin and bone(s)** 瘦得皮包骨

▶The abused child was skin and bones.
這名受虐的小孩瘦成皮包骨了。

---

bony [`bonɪ]　　　🔊Track 0249

adj. 多骨的；骨瘦如柴的

▶According to the doctor, that bony girl is suffering from anorexia.
根據醫師表示，那個骨瘦如柴的女孩有厭食症的困擾。

---

book [bʊk]　　　🔊Track 0250

n. 書；書本

▶Open your book and turn to page five.
打開你的書並翻到第5頁。

v. 預訂；登記

▶He booked a flight ticket to Melbourne.
他訂了一張到墨爾本的機票。

---

bookcase [`bʊk͵kes]　　　🔊Track 0251

n. 書架；書櫥

▶I put literary books on this bookcase.
我把文學類的書都擺在這個書架上。

---

boring [`borɪŋ]　　　🔊Track 0252

adj. 無趣的；乏味的

▶This movie is the most boring one I have ever seen.
這部電影是我看過最無聊的一部。

---

born [bɔrn]　　　🔊Track 0253

adj. 出生的；天生的

▶She was born with congenital diseases.
她出生時就有先天上的缺陷。

---

borrow [`bɑro]　　　🔊Track 0254

v. 借；向……借

▶May I borrow your book?
我可以跟你借書嗎？

---

boss [bɔs] **n.** 老闆；主管　🔊Track 0255

▶My boss is going to retire.
我的老闆快要退休了。

---

both [boθ]　　　🔊Track 0256

adv. 並；又；兩者皆是

▶The boy has two dogs, and he loves them both.
男孩有兩隻狗，他對牠們都一樣喜愛。

adj. 兩個都

▶After the collision, both drivers were taken to the hospital.
兩部車相撞後，兩位駕駛都被送到了醫院。

pron. 兩者；雙方

▶Both of her brothers are entrepreneurs.
她的兩個哥哥都是企業家。

相關片語 **have it both ways** 兩者得兼

▶You need to make up your mind. You can't have it both ways.
你要做個決定，你不能兩邊都選。

bother [`baðɚ]　◀€Track 0257

v. 煩擾；打擾

▶He kept bothering his teachers with strange questions.
他一直問奇怪的問題煩老師。

n. 煩惱；麻煩

▶She is a bother to her family.
她是家族裡的頭痛人物。

bottle [`batl]　◀€Track 0258

n. 瓶子

▶She bought a bottle of perfume for her mother.
她買了一瓶香水送媽媽。

相關片語 **hit the bottle** 大量喝酒

▶After breaking up with his girlfriend, he hit the bottle all night.
他和女友分手後，整晚都在喝酒。

bottom [`batəm]　◀€Track 0259

n. 底部；底層

▶I respect him from the bottom of my heart.
我打從心底尊敬他。

adj. 底部的；最底下的

▶His bottom line was clear—profits.
他最重視的事很清楚，就是利潤。

相關片語 **bell bottoms** 喇叭褲

▶The teenage star was spotted wearing bell bottoms when shopping in Los Angeles.
這位青少女明星被人看見穿著喇叭褲在洛杉磯購物。

bow [bo]　◀€Track 0260

v. 鞠躬

▶They bowed to the king.
他們向國王鞠躬。

n. 鞠躬

▶She took a bow before the curtain fell.
布幕放下來前，她向觀眾鞠躬。

bowl [bol]　◀€Track 0261

n. 碗

▶I eat a bowl of oatmeal every morning.
我每天早上吃一碗燕麥粥。

bowling [`bolɪŋ]　◀€Track 0262

n. 保齡球

▶He used to work in a bowling alley.
他以前在保齡球場上班。

box [baks]　◀€Track 0263

n. 盒子

▶She got a box of chocolates from her boyfriend on Feb. 14.
她在二月十四日情人節收到男友送的一盒巧克力。

相關片語 **lunch box** 便當

初級

▶His mother prepared his lunch box everyday.
他媽媽每天都幫他準備便當。

boy [bɔɪ] ◀Track 0264
n. 男孩；兒子

▶He is a smart boy.
他是很聰明的男孩。

brain [bren] ◀Track 0265
n. 腦；頭腦

▶C'mon, use your brain. You can do it.
快點用腦啊，你可以辦到的。

相關片語 **beat one's brain out**
絞盡腦汁

▶He beat his brain out and finally got the answer to the question.
他絞盡腦汁，終於解出問題的答案。

branch [bræntʃ] ◀Track 0266
n. 支線；分支；分店、分公司

▶The bank has five branches in London.
這間銀行在倫敦有五家分行。

相關片語 **branch office**
分公司；分局；分支機構

▶The company has a branch office in New York.
這家公司在紐約有分公司。

brand [brænd] ◀Track 0267
n. 商標；牌子

▶My wife likes this brand of soy bean sauce.
我太太喜歡這個牌子的醬油。

brave [brev] ◀Track 0268
adj. 勇敢的

▶Before being stationed in a foreign country, he told his little son that he must be brave.
他被派駐到國外前，告訴小兒子一定要勇敢。

bread [brɛd] ◀Track 0269
n. 麵包

▶He spread some butter on his bread.
他在麵包上面塗了一些奶油。

相關片語 **bread and butter**
生計；謀生之道

▶She earned her bread and butter at a restaurant before being scouted as a model.
她被星探發掘成為模特兒之前，在餐廳工作賺錢。

break [brek] ◀Track 0270
v. 打破；破壞

▶She broke her mother's crystal vase.
她把媽媽的水晶花瓶打破了。

n. 休息

▶You really need to take a break after a long exhausting day.
你忙了一整天，真的應該要休息一下。

相關片語 **break up** 結束與某人的婚姻或戀愛關係；分手

▶She broke up with him yesterday.
她昨天跟他分手了。

breakfast [`brɛkfəst] ◀Track 0271
n. 早餐

▶What's for breakfast?
早餐吃什麼？

相關片語 **breakfast television**
晨間電視

▶She watched breakfast television while drinking coffee.
她邊看晨間電視，邊喝咖啡。

brick [brɪk] ◀ Track 0272
n. 磚塊

▶The house was surround by brick walls.
這間房子四周被磚牆包圍住。

相關片語 **like a cat on hot bricks**
如坐針氈；如熱鍋上的螞蟻；形容人非常緊張

▶He was like a cat on hot bricks before the interview.
他在面試前如坐針氈。

bridge [brɪdʒ] **n.** 橋 ◀ Track 0273
▶They built a bridge in the remote area.
他們在一個郊外的地方建了一座橋。

相關片語 **crossover bridge** 天橋

▶They built a crossover bridge between the twin towers.
他們在雙子星塔之間蓋了一座天橋相通。

brief [brif] ◀ Track 0274
adj. 簡短的；短暫的

▶When asked if he had any comments on the issue, he simply gave a brief answer, "No comments."
他被問到對這個議題有什麼看法時，只簡短回應：「不予置評」。

相關片語 **in brief** 簡而言之

▶In brief, he did a wonderful job.
簡而言之，他做得好極了。

bright [braɪt] ◀ Track 0275
adj. 明亮的；晴朗的；聰明的

▶Jack is such a bright boy.
傑克真是個聰明的男孩。

相關片語 **bright and early** 一大早

▶She got up bright and early yesterday morning.
她昨天一大早就起床了。

bring [brɪŋ] **v** 帶來 ◀ Track 0276
▶It might rain today. Don't forget to bring your umbrella.
今天可能會下雨，別忘了帶把傘。

相關片語 **bring up** 養育

▶As a single mother, she brought up three children, who all became very successful.
她是單親媽媽，獨立帶大三個小孩，而且他們後來都很有成就。

Britain [ˈbrɪtən] ◀ Track 0277
n. 英國

▶Have you ever seen the Britain's Got Talent?
你看過《英國達人秀》這個節目嗎？

British [ˈbrɪtɪʃ] ◀ Track 0278
adj. 英國的；英國人的

▶Her British accent sounds very elegant.
她的英式口音聽起來很優雅。

n. 英國人

▶His wife is a British.
他的太太是個英國人。

相關片語 **the best of British luck**
（用作反諷的）祝人好運

初級

▶You want to borrow money from her? The best of British luck to you!
你想跟她借錢？那就祝你好運。

broad [brɔd] ◀Track 0279

adj. 寬闊的；廣泛的；遼闊的

▶She has a broad and radiant smile.
她的笑容很燦爛。

相關片語 **with broad shoulders**
形容人肩膀寬厚，可負重任

▶She is proud of her husband because he is a man with broad shoulders.
她以先生為榮，因為他是個很有肩膀的人。

broadcast ◀Track 0280

[`brɔd͵kæst] **n.** 廣播；廣播節目

▶According to the morning news broadcast, there was a terrorist attack in Boston.
根據晨間新聞廣播節目報導，波士頓發生了恐怖攻擊事件。

v. 播送；廣播

▶The news was broadcast live from the White House.
這則新聞是從白宮現場實況報導的。

brother [`brʌðɚ] ◀Track 0281

n. 兄；弟

▶He doesn't get along with his brothers.
他和兄弟們處得並不好。

相關片語 **half-brother**
同父異母或同母異父的兄弟

▶He was jealous of his half-sister because she got more attention from their father.
他很嫉妒同父異母的妹妹，因為她得到爸爸比較多的關注。

brown [braʊn] ◀Track 0282

adj. 褐色的；棕色的

▶They adopted a brown dog from the animal shelter.
他們從動物庇護所領養了這隻小棕狗。

n. 褐色；棕色

▶Her skin color is dark brown.
她的膚色是深棕色。

相關片語 **as brown as a berry**
皮膚曬得黝黑的

▶He was as brown as a berry when he came back from his holiday.
他渡假回來時，皮膚曬得好黑。

brunch [brʌntʃ] ◀Track 0283

n. 早午餐

▶I woke up at 11 A.M. and had brunch with my friend.
我早上十一點起床，然後跟朋友一起吃早午餐。

brush [brʌʃ] ◀Track 0284

n. 刷子

▶We need a brush to clean the toilet.
我們需要一把刷子來清馬桶。

v. 刷

▶She brushes her teeth thrice a day.
她一天刷三次牙。

bucket [`bʌkɪt] ◀Track 0285

n. =pail 水桶

▶The boy went to the beach with his bucket and spade.
男孩帶著水桶和鏟子去沙灘玩。

相關片語 **bucket list** 人生願望清單

▶Being rich is on the top of his bucket list.
成為有錢人是他人生願望清單的第一項。

buffet [buˋfe]　◀€Track 0286
n. 自助餐；快餐

▶We went to the buffet at a five-star hotel.
我們去五星級飯店吃自助餐

相關片語 **buffet car** 餐車

▶I like the sandwiches sold by that buffet car.
我喜歡吃那家餐車賣的三明治。

bug [bʌg]　◀€Track 0287
n. 蟲子；（口）故障

▶This bug spray can effectively protect you from mosquitoes and other insects.
這瓶防蟲液能有效保護你免受蚊蟲叮咬。

build [bɪld]　◀€Track 0288
v. 興建；建立

▶The city government is going to build a smart library here.
市政府將在這裡蓋一座智慧圖書館。

building [ˋbɪldɪŋ]　◀€Track 0289
n. 建築物

▶This green building is equipped with smart windows that can lower indoor temperatures when it is too hot.
這棟綠建築配備智能窗戶，能在天氣熱時調降室內溫度。

bun [bʌn]　◀€Track 0290
n. 小圓麵包

▶My mother made a few buns and cakes.
我媽媽做了幾個小圓麵包和蛋糕。

bundle [ˋbʌndḷ]　◀€Track 0291
n. 綑；束；大堆、大量

▶She received a bundle of flowers from her boyfriend.
她收到男友送來的一束花。

burger [ˋbɝgɚ]　◀€Track 0292
n. 漢堡；漢堡牛肉餅

▶I'd like a burger and an egg tart, please.
麻煩你，我要點一個漢堡和蛋塔。

burn [bɝn]　◀€Track 0293
v. 燃燒；著火；燒傷；燒死

▶She got burned in the fire and had scars on her arm.
她在火災中被燒傷，手臂上有疤。

相關片語 **burn oneself out** 讓自己累垮

▶Don't burn yourself out trying to finish your dissertation within one week.
別急著在一個禮拜內寫完論文，把自己累垮了。

burst [bɝst]　◀€Track 0294
v. 爆炸；突然發生

▶She burst out crying when hearing the bad news.
她聽到壞消息，突然哭出來了。

bus [bʌs] **n.** 公車　◀€Track 0295

▶I took a bus to the train station.
我搭公車到火車站。

相關片語 **school bus** 校車

初級

▶He takes the school bus to and from school everyday.
他每天都搭校車上學。

business [ˈbɪznɪs]
🔊 Track 0296

n. 職業；商業；生意；公司

▶His major was business administration when he was in college.
他大學時主修企業管理。

相關片語 **monkey business**
胡鬧；惡作劇

▶Stop your monkey business in the class, or I'll give you more homework.
停止上課胡鬧，不然我就出更多作業給你們。

businessman
🔊 Track 0297

[ˈbɪznɪsmən] **n.** 生意人；實業家

▶He is a great businessman and investor.
他是傑出的實業家和投資家。

busy [ˈbɪzɪ]
🔊 Track 0298

adj. 忙碌的；繁忙的

▶My dad has been too busy to come home for dinner lately.
我爸爸最近太忙，無法回家吃晚餐。

but [bʌt]
🔊 Track 0299

conj. 但是；卻

▶She is smart, but she has a dark side, too.
她很聰明，但她也有暗黑的一面。

prep. 除……以外

▶She is anything but stupid.
她一點都不笨。

butter [ˈbʌtɚ]
🔊 Track 0300

n. 奶油

▶She spread some butter on the pancake.
她在鬆餅上面塗了一些奶油。

相關片語 **butter sb. up**
討好某人、巴結某人

▶You don't need to butter people up to please everyone.
你不用為了取悅別人而到處巴結人。

butterfly [ˈbʌtɚˌflaɪ]
🔊 Track 0301

n. 蝴蝶

▶My dog is chasing butterflies in the park.
我的小狗在花園裡追著蝴蝶跑。

相關片語 **have butterflies in one's stomach** 緊張

▶He had butterflies in his stomach when he went to see his girlfriend's parents.
他去見女友父母時感到很緊張。

button [ˈbʌtn]
🔊 Track 0302

n. 鈕扣；按鈕

▶Simply push the button on the remote and you can turn on the TV.
只要按下搖控器的按鈕，你就能打開電視了。

v. 扣上；扣住

▶It's very cold outside. Button up your coat before you go out.
外面天氣很冷，出門前先把大衣扣上。

相關片語 **belly button** 肚臍

▶She still wears a belly button ring although she is pregnant.
她雖然懷孕了，仍戴著肚臍環。

buy [baɪ]

◀ Track 0303

v. 買、購買

▶He just bought a house in this neighborhood.
他剛在這個鄰近的地區買了一間房子。

---

by [baɪ]

◀ Track 0304

prep. 在……旁；在……（時間）之前；透過；被

▶The audience was amazed by her singing talent.
觀眾被她的歌唱天賦震撼，而感到驚歎不已。

adv. 經過；在旁邊

▶He walked by without saying anything.
他什麼都沒説就走過去了。

初級

▶ Cc

以下表格是全民英檢官方公告初級「聽、說、讀、寫」所須具備的能力，本書例句皆依此範疇特別設計，只要掃描右方QR code，就能搭配相對應的音軌，實現「眼耳並用」方式，刺激左腦的語言學習功能；同時也可使用本書附贈的紅膠片，將其置於單字上，一面記憶一面自我挑戰，達到雙倍的學習成果！

聽	▶ 能聽懂與日常生活相關的淺易談話，包含價格、時間及地點等。
說	▶ 能朗讀簡易文章、簡單地自我介紹，對熟悉的話題能以簡易英語對答，如問候、購物、問路等。
讀	▶ 可看懂與日常生活相關的淺易英文，並能閱讀路標、交通號誌、招牌、簡單菜單、時刻表及賀卡等。
寫	▶ 能寫簡單的句子及段落，如寫明信片、便條、賀卡及填表格等。對一般日常生活相關事物，能以簡短的文字敘述或說明。

cabbage [`kæbɪdʒ] ◀ Track 0305
n. 甘藍菜；捲心菜

▶ Tear up the cabbage into bite-sized bits so you can eat them with a spoon.
把甘藍菜撕成可以入口的小片，以便用湯匙吃。

相關片語 **Chinese cabbage** 大白菜

▶ I made Chinese cabbage stew with carrots. 我用胡蘿蔔一起滷了大白菜。

cabinet [`kæbənɪt] ◀ Track 0306
n. 內閣

▶ The president has reshuffled his cabinet.
總統已將內閣改組。

相關片語 **kitchen cabinet** 餐具櫃

▶ There are three crystal glasses in the kitchen cabinet.
餐具櫃裡有三個水晶玻璃杯。

cable [`kebl] n. 電纜 ◀ Track 0307

▶ They towed away the car with a cable.
他們用電纜把車子拖走。

café [kə`fe] ◀ Track 0308
n. 咖啡廳；小餐館

▶ We grabbed a bite at the café in the food court .
我們在美食街的小餐館吃了點心。

相關片語 **Internet café** 網路咖啡店

▶ Have you ever been to an Internet café.
你去過網咖嗎？

cafeteria [ˌkæfə`tɪrɪə] ◀ Track 0309
n. 自助餐廳

▶ I'm starving. Let's go to the school cafeteria.
我好餓，我們去學校餐廳吧。

cage [kedʒ]
🔊 Track 0310

n. 鳥籠；獸籠

▶ The mokey was locked in a cage.
猴子被鎖在籠子裡。

cake [kek] **n.** 蛋糕
🔊 Track 0311

▶ My mother made a birthday cake for me.
我媽媽為我做了一個生日蛋糕。

相關片語 **a piece of cake**
輕而易舉的事

▶ The exam was a piece of cake for him.
這次考試對他來說太簡單了。

calendar [`kæləndə]
🔊 Track 0312

n. 月曆；行事曆

▶ I kept my boss's schedules on my calendar.
我把老闆的行程記在行事曆上。

相關片語 **Chinese calendar**
陰曆；農曆

▶ Many Chinese communities use Chinese calendar for traditional purposes.
許多華人社區為了傳統習俗而使用農曆。

call [kɔl]
🔊 Track 0313

v. 喊叫；稱呼；打電話

▶ His name is Robert, but everyone calls him Bob.
他的名字叫羅伯特，但大家都叫他鮑伯。

n. 打電話

▶ Make a call if you need any support.
若你需要任何支援，隨時打電話過來。

calm [kɑm]
🔊 Track 0314

adj. 冷靜的；鎮定的

▶ When the accident happened, he remained cool, calm, and collected.
意外發生時，他保持地非常鎮定。

v. 使冷靜；使鎮定

▶ Stop fidgeting. You need to calm down.
不要坐立不安的，你要冷靜下來。

camel [`kæml]
🔊 Track 0315

n. 駱駝

▶ That's the last straw on a camel's back.
那是壓跨駱駝的最後一根稻草。

camera [`kæmərə]
🔊 Track 0316

n. 相機

▶ She brings a camera wherever she goes.
她無論到哪裡都帶著一台相機。

camp [kæmp]
🔊 Track 0317

n. 露營活動

▶ These children will attend a summer camp in July.
這些孩子將在七月參加一個夏令營。

v. 露營

▶ My family went camping last weekend.
我們家上週末去露營。

campus [`kæmpəs]
🔊 Track 0318

n. 校園

▶ Students at this private school are required to wear uniforms on campus.
這所私立學校要求學生在校內要穿制服。

補充片語 **on campus** 校內

初級

can [kæn]　◀️ Track 0319
aux. 表示「可以；能夠；可能」的助動詞
▶Can you give me your phone number?
你可以給我電話號碼嗎？

Canada [`kænədə]　◀️ Track 0320
n. 加拿大
▶She has been living in Canada for 10 years.
她在加拿大住了十年。

Canadian [kə`nedɪən]　◀️ Track 0321
adj. 加拿大的；加拿大人的
▶He has Canadian and US citizenships.
他擁有加拿大和美國公民身分。

n. 加拿大人
▶Her husband is a Canadian.
她的先生是加拿大人。

cancel [`kænsl̩]　◀️ Track 0322
v. 取消
▶We cancelled the party due to the typhoon.
因為颱風的關係，我們取消了派對。

cancer [`kænsɚ]　◀️ Track 0323
n. 癌
▶He was diagnosed with pancreatic cancer three months ago.
他三個月前被診斷出罹患胰臟癌。

candle [`kændl̩]　◀️ Track 0324
n. 蠟燭
▶The wind blew out the candles.
風吹熄了蠟燭。

補充片語 **blow out** 吹熄

candy [`kændɪ]　◀️ Track 0325
=sweet（英式英文）**n.** 糖果
▶Remember to brush your teeth after eating candy.
吃完糖果記得要刷牙。

相關片語 **eye candy** 養眼的人或事
▶Look at him. What an eye candy.
看看他，長相真養眼。

cannot [`kænat]　◀️ Track 0326
abbr. 不能、不會
▶We cannot make a decision without your consent.
沒有你的同意，我們無法做決定。

can't [kænt]　◀️ Track 0327
abbr. 不能、不會
▶He can't speak French.
他不會說法文。

cap [kæp]　◀️ Track 0328
n. 無邊便帽；制服帽
▶He always wears a baseball cap to uncover his disheveled hair.
他總是戴著棒球帽子，以掩蓋他的一頭亂髮。

captain [`kæptɪn]　◀️ Track 0329
n. 船長；機長；隊長；領隊
▶Jeremy was the captain of this baseball team.
傑瑞米是這支棒球隊的隊長。

car [kɑr] **n.** 汽車　◀️ Track 0330
▶He crashed his new car the first time he drove it.
他第一次開新車，就把它撞爛了。

相關片語 **booster car seat**
（汽車內）兒童座椅

▶He strapped his child into a booster car seat.
他把小孩繫在兒童安全座椅裡。

card [kɑrd]　◀Track 0331
n. 卡片

▶She received a greeting card from her best friend.
她收到最好的朋友送來的問候卡。

care [kɛr]　◀Track 0332
n. 看護；照料；所關心之事；用心

▶The patient was sent to the intensive care unit.
這病人被送到加護中心。

v. 關心；在意；喜歡

▶She doesn't care about what people say and stays true to herself.
她不在意別人怎麼說，就是忠於做自己。

career [kə`rɪr]　◀Track 0333
n. 事業；（終身）職業

▶He is a career diplomat.
他是職業外交官。

careful [`kɛrfəl]　◀Track 0334
adj. 小心的；注意的

▶Be careful when you cross the street.
過馬路要小心。

care·less [`kɛrlɪs]　◀Track 0335
adj. 粗心的

▶He is careless about his appearance.
他不太在意自己的外表。

carpet [`kɑrpɪt]　◀Track 0336
n. 地毯

▶His dog is sleeping on the carpet.
他的小狗正在地毯上睡覺。

carrot [`kærət]　◀Track 0337
n. 紅蘿蔔

▶She made beef stew with carrots and potatoes.
她用紅蘿蔔和馬鈴薯一起燉牛肉。

carry [`kærɪ]　◀Track 0338
v. 扛、抱、拿、背、提、搬等

▶Whether it's rainy or not, Jimmy always carries an umbrella with him.
無論有沒有下雨，吉米身上總是帶著一把雨傘。

cart [kɑrt]　◀Track 0339
n. 手推車

▶Don't put your cart before the horse.
不要把馬車放在馬的前面（不要本末倒置）。

相關片語 **shopping cart** 購物推車

▶Most shopping malls provide shopping carts for their customers.
大部分的賣場都有提供購物推車給消費者使用。

cartoon [kɑr`tun]　◀Track 0340
n. 卡通

▶She enjoys watching cartoons even though she is not young.
她雖然不年輕了，還是喜歡看卡通。

case [kes]　◀Track 0341
n. 箱子、盒子；事件、案例

初級

▶The confidential files are put in this case.
機密檔案文件都放在這個箱子裡。

相關片語 in case 假如、萬一

▶We'd better make a backup of this document just in case.
我們最好把這份文件做一個備份，以防萬一。

cash [kæʃ]
🔊 Track 0342

n. 現金

▶Many people prefer to use a debit card instead of cash.
許多人比較喜歡用簽帳金融卡而不是現金。

v. 兌現

▶Please read these terms before you cash this check.
兌現這張支票之前，請先閱讀這些條款。

相關片語 cash desk 付款處

▶The cash desk is at the entrance on the ground floor.
付款處在一樓入口處。

cassette [kə`sɛt]
🔊 Track 0343

n. 卡式錄音帶或錄影帶

▶Nowadays, it is almost impossible to find video cassettes.
現在幾乎已經找不到卡式錄影帶了。

castle [`kæsl]
🔊 Track 0344

n. 城堡

▶This castle is one of the most famous tourist destinations in Europe.
這座城堡是歐洲最著名的觀光景點之一。

cat [kæt]
🔊 Track 0345

n. 貓

▶She is an animal lover. She has two dogs and three cats.
她很喜歡動物，有二隻狗和三隻貓。

catch [kætʃ]
🔊 Track 0346

v. 抓、接；趕上

▶If you want to catch the bus, you'd better go now.
如果你要搭到公車，現在最好就出發。

n. 抓、接

▶The fisherman was very happy with his catch today.
漁夫很滿意今天的收獲。

cause [kɔz]
🔊 Track 0347

v. 引起、導致

▶He caused a lot of trouble to his family.
他給家裡添了很多麻煩。

n. 原因、起因；理由

▶The police is investigating the cause of the accident.
警方正在調查意外發生的原因。

cave [kev]
🔊 Track 0348

n. 洞穴；洞窟

▶They found a cave in a deep forest.
他們在濃密的森林裡發現了一個洞窟。

v. 塌陷；屈服

▶After the customer's complaint, the company caved and gave him a refund.
顧客抱怨後，公司妥協並給他全額退費。

CD [si-di]
🔊 Track 0349
=compact disk

n. 光碟

▶People don't use video cassettes now; even CDs are hard to come by.
人們現在已不使用卡式錄音帶了，即使CD也很少見了。

ceiling [ˋsilɪŋ]　◀ Track 0350
n. 天花板

▶The ceiling light is very classy.
這個天花板燈很有品味。

相關片語 **hit the ceiling** 勃然大怒

▶She hit the ceiling when she found she was betrayed by her best friend.
她發現被好友背叛時，勃然大怒。

celebrate [ˋsɛləˌbret]　◀ Track 0351
v. 慶祝

▶My parents are going to celebrate their wedding anniversary.
我爸媽要慶祝他們的結婚週年紀念日。

cell [sɛl]　◀ Track 0352
n. 細胞

▶The new treatment targets on cancer cells only.
新療法只鎖定對付癌細胞。

相關片語 **cell phone** 手機

▶She bought a new cell phone.
她買了一支新手機。

cent [sɛnt]　◀ Track 0353
n. 一分（美元）

▶The candy costs only ten cents.
這個糖果只要花十分錢。

相關片語 **five-and-ten-cent store** 廉價商店

▶The drawing bought from a five-and-ten-cent store turned out to be Picasso's hand-drawn sketches.
這幅在廉價商店裡買到的圖畫結果被發現是畢卡索的手繪素描。

center [ˋsɛntɚ]　◀ Track 0354
=centre （英式英文）
n. 中心點；中央

▶There is a beautiful tower in the center of Paris.
巴黎市中心有一座美麗的高塔。

v. 以……為中心；使集中

▶Conversations with him are always centered on sports or computer games.
和他聊天的話題老是以運動或電腦遊戲為中心。

centimetre [ˋsɛntəˌmitɚ]　◀ Track 0355
=centimetre （英式英文）
n. 公分

▶The basketball player is 210 centimeters tall.
這名籃球員有二百一十公分高了。

central [ˋsɛntrəl]　◀ Track 0356
adj. 中心的；中央的

▶New York's Central Park is a famous tourist destination.
紐約的中央公園是知名的觀光景點。

century [ˋsɛntʃʊrɪ]　◀ Track 0357
n. 世紀

▶His political career spanned over half a century.
他的政治生涯長達逾半世紀。

初級

cereal [`sɪrɪəl]
Track 0358

n. 麥片；穀類加工食品

▶He had cereals and a pancake for breakfast.
他早餐吃麥片和一個鬆餅。

certain [`sɝtən]
Track 0359

adj. 確信的；某……；某種程度的

▶Are you certain that he will attend the ceremony?
你確定他會參加慶典嗎？

certainly [`sɝtənlɪ]
Track 0360

adv. 無疑地；當然

▶She will certainly pass the exam.
她無疑地會通過考試。

chair [tʃɛr]
Track 0361

n. 椅子

▶My grandfather likes to sit in the rocking chair.
我祖父喜歡坐在這張搖椅。

chairman [`tʃɛrmən]
Track 0362

n. 主席；議長；（大學）系主任

▶The chairman of the committee will resign due to the scandal.
委員會主席因為醜聞案即將請辭。

chalk [tʃɔk]
Track 0363

n. 粉筆

▶He used a piece of chalk and drew a circle on the blackboard.
他用粉筆在黑板上畫了一個圓圈。

相關片語 **as different as chalk and cheese** 天差地遠

▶Tom and Jack are as different as chalk and cheese, but they get along fine.
湯姆和傑克迥然不同，但他們處得還不錯。

chance [tʃæns]
Track 0364

n. 機會

▶This is a chance of a lifetime. You should cherish it.
這是畢生難逢的機會，你要珍惜啊。

change [tʃendʒ]
Track 0365

n. 改變；變化

▶The manager made fundamental changes in the company's marketing strategy.
經理把公司的行銷策略做了很徹底的變革。

v. 改變；變動

▶He changed his diet and lost some weight.
他改變飲食並減了一些體重。

channel [`tʃænḷ]
Track 0366

n. 水道；航道；頻道

▶I like watching National Geographic and Discovery Channel.
我喜歡看國家地理和探索頻道。

chapter [`tʃæptɚ]
Track 0367

n. （書籍的）章；回

▶Let's review Chapter 7 of the textbook.
我們來複習教科書第七章內容吧。

charac·ter [`kærɪktɚ]
Track 0368

n. （人的）性格；（事物的）特質；（戲劇或小說的）人物角色

▶He's quite a character.
他是很有個性的人。

charge [tʃɑrdʒ] ◀€Track 0369

n. 費用；掌管

▶My mother is in charge of our family's business.
我媽媽負責主導家族事業。

補充片語 in charge of sth.
負責某事；掌管某物

v. 索費；指控

▶The private school charged US$ 10,000 for one semester.
這所私立學校一學期要收一萬美元。

chart [tʃɑrt] ◀€Track 0370

n. 圖表

▶He used a pie chart to show how the company's debts have increased over the years.
他用一張圓形圖表顯示公司債務在過去幾年來所增加的情形。

相關片語 eye chart 視力檢查表

▶The eye doctor asked me to read an eye chart to determine whether my vision is 20/20.
眼科醫師要我看視力檢查表來測試我的視力是不是二點零。

chase [tʃes] ◀€Track 0371

v. 追逐；追求

▶The policemen are chasing after a thief.
警察正在追一個小偷。

相關片語 chase rainbows
妄想；不切實際

▶He kept chasing rainbows without taking any action.
他老在妄想，而不採取任何行動。

cheap [tʃip] ◀€Track 0372

adj. 便宜的；廉價的

▶The restaurant provides good food with cheap prices.
這家餐廳提供物美價廉的食物。

cheat [tʃit] ◀€Track 0373

v. 欺騙；行騙；作弊

▶The student was found cheating on the exam.
學生被發現考試作弊。

n. 騙子；欺詐；作弊

▶His financial transaction was found to be a great cheat.
他的金融交易被發現是個大騙局。

check [tʃɛk] ◀€Track 0374

n. 檢查；帳單；支票

▶May I cash the check, please?
我想對兌這張支票，麻煩了。

v. 檢查

▶She double-checked the essay and found several typos.
她仔細檢查這篇論文，發現有幾個字打錯了。

補充片語 double check
仔細檢查；再次確認

cheer [tʃɪr] ◀€Track 0375

v. 歡呼；使振奮、高興

▶He tried to cheer his sister up by playing magic.
他為了讓姊姊開心，表演起魔術。

n. 歡呼；喝彩；鼓勵

▶His campaign speech was received with cheers and applause.
他的競選演説受到熱烈歡呼和鼓掌。

初級

相關片語 **cheer up**
高興起來；振作起來

▶Cheer up. Everything will be alright.
振作起來！事情會好轉的。

cheese [tʃiz] ◀Track 0376
n. 乳酪；乾酪

▶She added some cheese and pepper in her salad.
她在沙拉加了一些乳酪和胡椒調味。

chemical [`kɛmɪkl̩] ◀Track 0377
n. 化學製品；化學藥品

▶The bug spray does not contain any chemicals. It's 100% natural.
這罐驅蟲劑不包含任何化學物質，百分之百純天然。

adj. 化學的；化學上的

▶The country acknowledged that it possesses chemical weapons.
這個國家承認擁有化學武器。

chess [tʃɛs] ◀Track 0378
n. 西洋棋

▶Alpha Zero masters chess in only four hours.
Alpha Zero在四小時內即精通西洋棋。

相關片語 **Chinese chess** 中國象棋

▶I played Chinese chess with my grandfather yesterday evening.
我昨晚和祖父在下象棋。

chick [tʃɪk] ◀Track 0379
n. 小雞；少女；小妞

▶The hen hatched the eggs and raised the chicks.
母雞孵蛋並養小雞。

chicken [`tʃɪkɪn] ◀Track 0380
n. 小雞；雞肉

▶She made chicken soup and tomato rice stew for dinner.
她做雞湯和蕃茄燉食當晚餐。

相關片語 **get up with the chickens**
早起

▶He got up with the chickens in order to catch the early flight.
他為了搭一早的班機而早起。

chief [tʃif] ◀Track 0381
adj. 主要的；等級最高的

▶The meeting's chief concern is about how to reduce carbon emission.
會議主要關切的議題是如何減少碳排放。

n. 首長；長官

▶My husband is the chief fire officer.
我的先生是消防局局長。

child [tʃaɪld] ◀Track 0382
n. 孩子；孩童

▶As a child, he showed a talent for music.
他從小就展現音樂天賦。

相關片語 **only child** 獨生子（女）

▶She is the only child in the family.
她是家中的獨生女。

childhood ◀Track 0383
[`tʃaɪld‚hʊd] **n.** 童年

▶As the only child in the family, he was very lonely in his childhood.
身為家中的獨子，他的童年過得很孤獨。

childish [`tʃaɪldɪʃ] ◀Track 0384
adj. 孩子般的；幼稚的

▶Stop being so childish. You're already 30 years old.
別幼稚了，你已經三十歲了。

childlike [`tʃaɪld,laɪk] ◀€Track 0385
adj. 孩子般的；天真的；單純的

▶She has a childlike face.
她有一張如同孩子般的臉蛋。

chin [tʃɪn] **n.** 下巴 ◀€Track 0386

▶After burning the midnight oils for a week, she got some pimples on her chin.
她熬夜了一個星期，下巴冒出了一些痘子。

| 相關片語 **keep one's chin up**
不灰心；不氣餒

▶Keep your chin up. You can do it.
不要灰心，你做得到的。

Chinese [`tʃaɪ`niz] ◀€Track 0387
adj. 中國的；中國人的

▶The chef makes delicious Chinese food.
這位大廚能做出很美味的中國料理。

n. 中國人

▶He is a German and his wife is a Chinese.
他是德國人，太太是中國人。

cho·co·late [`tʃakəlɪt] ◀€Track 0388
n. 巧克力；巧克力糖；巧克力飲料

▶She received a box of chocolate from her boyfriend.
她收到男友送的一盒巧克力。

choice [tʃɔɪs] ◀€Track 0389
n. 選擇

▶He had no choice but to cancel his business trip.
他別無選擇，只能取消出差。

| 補充片語 **have no choice but...**
別無選擇，只得……；不得不

choose [tʃuz] ◀€Track 0390
v. 選擇

▶The family chose to move to London.
這家人選擇搬到倫敦。

| 相關片語 **pick and choose** 挑挑揀揀

▶We'd better take our time to pick and choose the right time to invest in emerging markets.
我們最好不要急，挑選合適的時機投資新興市場。

| 補充片語 **take one's time**
從容進行；不著急

chopstick [`tʃap,stɪk] ◀€Track 0391
n. 筷子

▶He's right-handed, but he can also use chopsticks with his left hand.
他是右撇子，但也能用左手使用筷子。

Christmas [`krɪsməs] ◀€Track 0392
=Xmas **n.** 聖誕節

▶We are decorating our Christmas tree.
我們在裝飾聖誕樹。

chubby [`tʃʌbɪ] ◀€Track 0393
adj. 豐腴的；圓胖的

▶The little boy is chubby and funny.
小男孩圓圓胖胖的，而且很逗趣。

初級

church [tʃɝtʃ]

n. 教堂

▶The church is situated at the foot of a hill.

教堂位在小山丘腳下。

相關片語 **church mouse**
　　　　一貧如洗的人；窮到極點的人

▶Once a billionaire, he's now as poor as a church mouse.

他曾經是億萬富翁，如今一貧如洗了。

circle [`sɝkl]

n. 圓圈

▶The boy drew a circle on the blackboard.

男孩在黑板上畫一個圓圈。

citizen [`sɪtəzn]

n. 市民；居民；公民

▶She applied to become a Danish citizen.

她申請成為丹麥公民。

相關片語 **senior citizen**
　　　　老年人；退休老人

▶Senior citizens enjoy a fare discount when taking public transportation.

老年人搭乘大眾運輸可以享有票價折扣的優惠。

city [`sɪtɪ] **n.** 城市

▶She is tired of city life.

她已厭倦了城市生活。

claim [klem]

v. 要求；主張；聲稱

▶The terrorist group claimed that it was responsible for the attack.

恐怖組織宣稱他們發動了這次的攻擊。

n. 要求；主張；斷言

▶He gave concrete evidence to support his claim.

他給出具體的證據支持他的說法。

clap [klæp]

v. 拍（手）；鼓（掌）

▶The audience clapped until the pianist played an encore.

觀眾拍手直到鋼琴家加演一首曲目。

n. 拍手鼓掌；喝彩

▶We gave a big clap for the winning team.

我們給優勝的隊伍熱烈的鼓掌。

class [klæs]

n. 班級；課；（社會）階級、等級

▶She attends a yoga class to stay in shape.

她參加瑜伽課程來維持好體態。

相關片語 **first class** 頭等；第一流

▶Elon always travels first class.

伊隆旅行總是坐頭等艙。

classic [`klæsɪk]

adj. 典型的；經典的

▶The design of the jewelry is classic and timeless.

這件珠寶的設計很經典，而且不會過時。

n. 典型事物；著名事件；經典名著

▶Adventures of Huckleberry Finn by Mark Twain is a classic of American literature.

馬克吐溫的《頑童歷險記》是美國經典文學。

classical [`klæsɪkl]

adj. 經典的，古典的

▶I learned classical music when I was a child, and I still love it.
我小時候學古典音樂，現在還是很熱愛它。

classmate
Track 0403
[`klæsˌmet] **n.** 同班同學
▶We were classmates when we studied in junior high school.
我們讀國中時是同班同學。

claw
[klɔ] Track 0404
n. 爪子；手
▶Tigers have sharp claws.
老虎的爪子很銳利。

v. 用爪子抓、撕、挖；費力奪回
▶Oh no! My cat clawed my teddy bear!
毀了，我的貓咪用爪子撕了我的泰迪熊！

clay
[kle] Track 0405
n. 黏土；泥土
▶The roof tiles were made from clay.
屋頂的磚瓦是用泥土製成的。

cleaner
[`klinɚ] Track 0406
n. 清潔工；乾洗店；清潔劑
▶She is a road cleaner.
她是道路清潔工。

clear
[klɪr] Track 0407
adj. 清楚的；清澈的
▶Her explanation is very clear.
她的解釋很清楚。

v. 清除；收拾；使乾淨；使清楚
▶The department store is holding sales to clear its winter stock.
百貨公司正在舉辦特惠促銷來清理冬季庫存。

clerk
[klɝk] Track 0408
n. 店員；辦事員
▶She is a bank clerk.
她是銀行櫃員。

clever
[`klɛvɚ] Track 0409
adj. 聰明的；靈巧的
▶Bobo is a clever dog. He knows how to open a door.
波波是隻聰明的小狗，牠知道怎麼開門。

climate
[`klaɪmɪt] Track 0410
n. 氣候
▶The climate is very humid in this country.
這個國家氣候很潮濕。

climb
[klaɪm] Track 0411
v. 爬；攀爬
▶He climbed up Jade Mountain and took a lot of selfies.
他爬上玉山並拍了很多自拍照。

clock
[klɑk] Track 0412
n. 時鐘
▶I was late for school because my alarm clock didn't go off this morning.
我今天上課遲到，因為早上鬧鐘沒響。

close
[klos] Track 0413
v. 關起；關閉；結束
▶The convenient store doesn't close even during typhoon days.
超商即使在颱風天也不打烊。

n. 結束；末尾
▶He finally drew the meeting to a close.
他總算把會議做個總結。

初級

adj. （距離）近的；（關係）親近的

▶My dog is very close with my family.
我的小狗和我的家人都很親。

adv. 接近地；緊密地

▶We should stay close together for warmth.
我們應該待在一起取暖。

相關片語 **close call** 千鈞一髮；險遭意外

▶The woman came very close to being hit by a car, but that was a close call.
女子差一點就被車子撞到，真是千鈞一髮。

closet [`klɑzɪt] ◀Track 0414

n. 衣櫃

▶She has four closets of clothes.
她有四個衣櫃的衣服。

相關片語 **water closet (WC)** 沖水馬桶

▶It's important to provide more facilities in this office building, such as water closets.
這棟辦公大樓應提供更多設施，比如沖水馬桶。

cloth [klɔθ] ◀Track 0415

n. 布；織物；衣料

▶She used a cleaning cloth to mop the floor.
她用一塊清潔用的抹布來拖地。

clothe [kloð] ◀Track 0416

n. 為⋯⋯穿衣；為⋯⋯提供衣服

▶He clothed himself in tuxedo for the formal occasion.
他為了正式場合而穿上燕尾服。

clothes [kloz] ◀Track 0417

n. 衣服

▶You look gorgeous in these clothes.
你穿這些衣服真漂亮。

clothing [`kloðɪŋ] ◀Track 0418

n. 衣服；衣著

▶He works in a clothing factory.
他在製衣廠上班。

cloudy [`klaʊdɪ] ◀Track 0419

adj. 多雲的；陰天的

▶The weather is dark and cloudy. Don't forget to bring an umbrella just in case.
天氣很陰暗又多雲。別忘了帶把傘，以備不時之需。

clown [klaʊn] ◀Track 0420

n. 小丑

▶When he was a child, he was a family clown. His parents laughed their heads off when he impersonated a politician.
他小時候是家裡的小丑，當他扮演某政客時，爸媽笑到不行。

補充片語 **laugh one's head off**
使某人笑死

club [klʌb] ◀Track 0421

n. （運動、娛樂等的）俱樂部；會所

▶We joined an English conversation club to practice our English.
我們參加英語會話俱樂部來練習英文。

相關片語 **club sandwich** 總匯三明治

▶She ordered a club sandwich for brunch.
她點了一份總匯三明治當早午餐。

coach [kotʃ] ◀Track 0422
n. （運動隊的）教練；巴士；長途公車
▶He is a basketball coach.
他是籃球教練。

coal [kol] ◀Track 0423
n. 煤；煤塊；木炭
▶Some people think coal-fired power plants are not environmentally friendly.
有人認為火力發電並不環保。

coast [kost] ◀Track 0424
n. 海岸
▶Taroko Gorge is located on the east coast of Taiwan.
太魯閣位在台灣的東海岸。

coat [kot] ◀Track 0425
n. 外套；（動物的）皮毛
▶Button up your coat. It's cold outside.
把外套扣子扣好，外面很冷。

相關片語 **down coat** 羽絨外套
▶The online shopping mall is holding sales on down coats.
這家線上購物城正在舉辦羽絨外套特惠活動。

cock [kak] **n.** 公雞 ◀Track 0426
▶He was woken early in the morning by a cock crowning repeatedly.
他大清早就被一陣陣的公雞啼聲叫醒。

相關片語 **cock of the walk** 自命不凡的男子
▶He thought he was the cock of the walk.
他自以為很了不起。

cockroach [`kak͵rotʃ] ◀Track 0427
=**roach** **n.** 蟑螂
▶She hates cockroaches.
她痛恨蟑螂。

cocoa [`koko] ◀Track 0428
n. 可可粉
▶She sprinkled some cocoa powder on top of the cake.
她在蛋糕最上層撒了一些可可粉。

coffee [`kɔfɪ] ◀Track 0429
n. 咖啡
▶He always needs a cup of coffee to start the morning.
他早上總得來一杯咖啡。

coin [kɔɪn] ◀Track 0430
n. 錢幣
▶They flipped a coin to decide which team would start with the ball.
他們丟擲一枚錢幣來決定哪一隊先開球。

相關片語 **the other side of the coin** 事情的另一面
▶She likes the white dress, but the other side of the coin is that it gets dirty easily.
她喜歡白色的洋裝，但從另一面來看，它比較容易變髒。

Coke [kok] ◀Track 0431
n. 可樂
▶He drinks a bottle of Coke everyday.
他每天都喝一瓶可樂。

cold [kold] ◀Track 0432
adj. 冷的

▶When you have a flu, try to drink some warm water instead of cold beverages.
你有流感時，喝點溫開水，不要喝冷飲。

n. 寒冷；感冒

▶He had a cold and took a day-off.
他感冒了，所以請假一天。

相關片語 **catch a cold** 感冒

▶She caught a cold from her sister and went to see a doctor.
她被妹妹傳染感冒，去看醫生了。

---

collect [kə`lɛkt]　◀ Track 0433
v. 收集；領取

▶He enjoys collecting stamps.
他喜歡收集郵票。

---

collection [kə`lɛkʃən]　◀ Track 0434
n. 收集；收藏品

▶The fashion house just launched a beautiful winter collection.
這間時尚公司剛推出了美麗的冬裝商品。

相關片語 **collection box** 募捐箱

▶They put some money in the collection box to help the homeless.
他們放了些錢到募捐箱裡來幫助無家可歸的人。

---

college [`kɑlɪdʒ]　◀ Track 0435
n. 大學

▶The twin went to the same college.
這對雙胞胎上同一所大學。

---

color [`kʌlə]　◀ Track 0436
=colour （英式英文）**n.** 顏色；色彩

▶Orange is my favorite color.
橘色是我最愛的顏色。

v. 著色；塗上顏色

▶She drew a sun and colored it yellow.
她畫了一個太陽並把它塗成黃色。

相關片語 **a horse of a different color**
完全另外一回事

▶You thought the guy that was with Jenny was her boyfriend, but that's a horse of a different color. That's her cousin.
你以為跟珍妮在一起的男生是她的男友，但完全是另外一 回事，他是她的表哥。

---

colourful [`kʌləfəl]　◀ Track 0437
=colourful （英式英文）
adj. 色彩豐富的；多彩多姿的

▶She lives a very colorful life.
她的生活很多彩多姿。

---

comb [kom]　◀ Track 0438
n. 梳子；梳理

▶He always carries a comb in his briefcase.
他的公事包裡總帶著一把梳子。

v. 梳頭

▶Comb your hair when you wake up each morning.
早上起來要梳一下頭髮。

---

come [kʌm] **v.** 來　◀ Track 0439
▶Come visit us when you drop by Seattle.
你到西雅圖時可以到我們這裡會個面。

---

comfortable　◀ Track 0440
[`kʌmfətəbl] **adj.** 舒適的；自在的

▶She felt comfortable when living in the countryside.
她住在鄉間感到很舒服。

comic [`kɑmɪk]　◀ Track 0441

adj. 喜劇般的；連環漫畫的

▶She enjoys reading comic books.
她喜歡看漫畫書。

補充片語 comic book 漫畫書

n. 連環漫畫；連環漫畫書

▶I used to read the comics as a kid and got a lot of fun from it.
我小時候會看連環漫畫，並從中得到很多樂趣。

command [kə`mænd]　◀ Track 0442

v. 命令，指揮

▶The general commanded the soldiers to withdraw immediately.
將軍指揮士兵立即撤退。

comment [`kɑmɛnt]　◀ Track 0443

n. 批評；議論

▶Thank you for your forthright comments.
謝謝你坦率的評論。

v. 發表意見；評論

▶She refused to comment on the controversial issue.
她拒絕對這個很有爭議的議題發表意見。

common [`kɑmən]　◀ Track 0444

adj. 一般的；共同的

▶They shared common goals in life.
他們有共同的生活目標。

相關片語 common sense 常識

▶When you have a cold, you need to avoid drinking iced water. It's common sense.
感冒時要避免喝冰水，這是常識。

company [`kʌmpənɪ]　◀ Track 0445

n. 公司

▶The company is situated in the city center.
公司位在市中心。

compare [kəm`pɛr]　◀ Track 0446

v. 比較；對照

▶We compared the house prices before making a decision.
我們做決定前，先比較了房價。

相關片語 beyond compare
無可比擬；無以倫比

▶His intelligence is beyond compare.
他的智力無人能比。

complain [kəm`plen]　◀ Track 0447

v. 抱怨

▶He's pain in the neck. He complains about everything.
他很討人厭，什麼事都要抱怨。

complete [kəm`plit]　◀ Track 0448

v. 完成；使完整

▶She completed her college education at the age of 14.
她十四歲就完成大學的學業。

adj. 完整的；結束的

▶You make my life complete.
你讓我的生命更完整。

completion　◀ Track 0449
[kəm`pliʃən] **n.** 完整

▶The construction of the building is nearing completion.
這棟建築快要完工了。

初級

computer [kəm`pjutɚ] ◀Track 0450
n. 電腦

▶You can't find a job if you don't have computer skills.
你若沒有電腦技能，就找不到工作。

concern [kən`sɜn] ◀Track 0451
n. 關心的事；掛念

▶We thank you for your concern about this matter.
我們謝謝你對這件事的關心。

v. 關於；關係到；使關心、使擔心、使不安

▶He is very concerned about his daughter's safety.
他很擔心女兒的安全。

confident [`kɑnfədənt] ◀Track 0452
adj. 自信的；有信心的

▶I am confident that you can ace the exam.
我很有信心你能考得很好。

confirm [kən`fɜm] ◀Track 0453
v. 確定；確認

▶The White House confirmed that the president would visit Russia.
白宮證實總統將訪問俄羅斯。

conflict [kən`flɪkt] ◀Track 0454
n. 衝突

▶There was a lot of conflicts between her and her mother.
她們母女之間存在很多衝突。

Confucius [kən`fjuʃəs] ◀Track 0455
n. 孔子

▶Confucius's teachings are practical.
孔子的學說很實用。

confuse [kən`fjuz] ◀Track 0456
v. 使困惑；搞亂

▶He confused me with my twin brother.
他把我當成是我的雙胞胎弟弟。

congratulation ◀Track 0457
[kən͵grætʃə`leʃən] **n.** 恭喜

▶Let me extend my heartfelt congratulations on your re-election.
我由衷恭喜你競選連任成功。

consider [kən`sɪdɚ] ◀Track 0458
v. 考慮；認為

▶I consider her my best friend.
我認為她是我最好的朋友。

contact [`kɑntækt] ◀Track 0459
n. 接觸；聯繫

▶He lost contact with his parents.
他與父母失聯了。

v. 與……接觸；與……聯繫

▶You can contact us via email.
你可以透過電郵與我們聯繫。

相關片語 **eye contact** 眼神接觸

▶Children are not used to making eye contact with strangers.
孩子不習慣與陌生人做眼神的接觸。

contain [kən`ten] ◀Track 0460
v. 包含

▶Natural food contains rich nutrients that are good for our body.
天然食物含有豐富的營養素，對人體有益。

continue [kən`ten] ◀Track 0461
v. 繼續

▶He couldn't continue his education because of the high tuition.
因為學費太高，他無法繼續就學了。

contract [kən`trækt]
🔊 Track 0462

n. 合約

▶The two companies signed a contract yesterday.
這兩間公司昨天簽了合約。

v. 訂契約

▶The company was contracted to develop auto-pilot cars.
這間公司剛簽合約，要開發無人駕駛汽車。

control [kən`trol]
🔊 Track 0463

n. 控制

▶It is beyond my control.
這件事超出我的控制之中。

v. 控制

▶He doesn't know how to control his dog.
他不知道該怎麼控制他的小狗。

相關片語 **out of control** 失控

▶The situation is getting horribly out of control.
情況已經失控得一塌糊塗了。

controller [kən`trolɚ]
🔊 Track 0464

n. 管理人；控制器；主計員

▶Her father used to be an air-traffic controller.
她爸爸曾是航空交通指揮員。

convenient
🔊 Track 0465

[kən`vinjənt] **adj.** 方便的；便利的

▶It's very convenient to shop online.
線上購物很方便。

conversation
🔊 Track 0466

[ˌkɑnvɚ`seʃən] **n.** 對話；對談

▶She is my English conversation teacher.
她是我的英語會話老師。

cook [kʊk]
🔊 Track 0467

v. 烹煮；做菜

▶He's a chef at a five-star hotel. He can cook really delicious food.
他是五星級飯店的大廚，能做很美味的料理。

n. 廚師

▶My mother is a good cook.
我媽媽是個出色的廚師。

相關片語 **cook the books**
做假帳；偽造帳目

▶It's a shame that the chief financial officer was found cooking the books.
財務長被抓包做假帳，真是令人遺憾。

cooker [`kʊkɚ]
🔊 Track 0468

n. 炊具；爐灶；烹調器具

▶She doesn't have any cookers or cooking utensils in her dorm.
她的宿舍沒有任何的電鍋或炊具。

補充片語 **cooking utensil** 炊具

cookie [`kʊkɪ]
🔊 Track 0469

=cooky **n.** 甜餅乾

▶The dog ate all the cookies on the table.
小狗把餐桌上的餅乾吃光了。

cool [kul]
🔊 Track 0470

adj. 涼爽的；冷靜的；冷淡的；
（口）極好的

初級

▶It was a cool afternoon.
那是個涼爽的下午。

v. 使涼快；使冷卻；使（情緒）平息

▶She placed the pie on the table to cool it down.
她把派擺在餐桌上放涼。

相關片語 **play it cool** 泰然處之

▶She managed to play it cool when her child threw a tantrum.
她的小孩在亂發脾氣時，她維持泰然處之的態度。

copy [kul]
🔊 Track 0471

n. 抄本；複製品

▶He gave me a copy of his new book.
他送我一本他的新書。

v. 抄寫；抄襲；模仿

▶She copied a dissertation and was flunked by her teacher.
她抄襲一篇論文，被老師當掉了。

corn [kɔrn]
🔊 Track 0472

n. 小麥、穀物；玉米

▶I like corn chowder.
我喜歡玉米濃湯。

corner [ˋkɔrnə]
🔊 Track 0473

n. 角、角落

▶The restaurant is just around the corner.
餐廳就在轉角處。

補充片語 **around the corner** 很近

相關片語 **turn the corner**
度過難關、好轉

▶The company turned the corner and started to make profits.
公司狀況好轉，開始獲利了。

correct [kəˋrɛkt]
🔊 Track 0474

adj. 正確的

▶He gave the correct answer to the question.
他給出問題的正確答案。

v. 糾正、訂正

▶The teacher corrected the student's English pronunciation.
老師糾正學生的英文發音。

cost [kɔst]
🔊 Track 0475

n. 費用；成本；代價

▶The company is trying to reduce its personnel costs.
公司正在嘗試減少人事成本。

v. 花費（時間、金錢、勞力等）

▶How much does this chandelier cost?
這個吊飾燈要花多少錢？

costly [ˋkɔstlɪ]
🔊 Track 0476

n. 貴重的；昂貴的；代價高的

▶The new system is too costly.
新系統太貴了。

cotton [ˋkɑtn]
🔊 Track 0477

n. 棉；棉花

▶The hat is made of pure cotton.
這帽子是用純棉製成的。

相關片語 **cotton candy** 棉花糖

▶He makes a living by selling cotton candy.
他以賣棉花糖為生。

couch [kaʊtʃ]
🔊 Track 0478

n. 長沙發

▶His dog is lying on the couch.
他的小狗正躺在長沙發上。

相關片語 **couch potato**
成天躺在沙發上看電視的人；懶惰的人

▶He is a couch potato. He always watches TV after work.
他下班後總是看電視，是個電視迷。

cough [kɔf]　　◀ Track 0479

v. 咳嗽

▶She coughed terribly last night.
她昨晚咳得很厲害。

n. 咳嗽；咳嗽聲

▶The patient had a hacking cough.
病人劇烈咳嗽。

could [kʊd]　　◀ Track 0480

aux. 助動詞can的過去式；表示假設語氣的「可以、但願」

▶He wishes he could colonize Mars.
他但願能殖民火星。

couldn't [`kʊdnt]　　◀ Track 0481

abbr. 不能（could not的縮寫）

▶He couldn't believe that his son was a murderer.
他無法置信兒子是個謀殺犯。

count [kaʊnt]　　◀ Track 0482

v. 數；算；將……計算在內；有意義；依賴

▶Let's count from one to ten.
我們從一數到十吧。

n. 計算；總數

▶His white cell blood count is too low.
他的白血球數量過少。

country [`kʌntrɪ]　　◀ Track 0483

n. 國家；鄉下、郊外

▶Germany is a country in Europe.
德國是位在歐洲的一國。

countryside　　◀ Track 0484

[`kʌntrɪˌsaɪd] **n. 鄉村；農間**

▶We went to the countryside and saw a waterfall.
我們去鄉下看到了瀑布。

county [`kaʊntɪ]　　◀ Track 0485

n. 縣；郡

▶He lives in Harris County, Houston.
他住在休士頓的哈里斯郡。

couple [`kʌpl]　　◀ Track 0486

n. 夫妻；一對

▶The newly-wed couple just had a baby.
這對新婚夫妻剛迎接了小寶寶的誕生。

courage [ˌkɝ·ɪdʒ]　　◀ Track 0487

n. 勇氣

▶He showed great courage in the crisis.
他在危機中展現了巨大的勇氣。

course [kors]　　◀ Track 0488

n. 課程；習慣的程序；一道菜

▶I'm going to take a writing course next semester.
我下學期想修寫作課。

相關片語 **of course** 當然

▶Of course. I'll attend your wedding.
當然，我會參加你的婚禮。

court [kort]　　◀ Track 0489

n. 法庭；場地

初級

▶If you don't make the payment, I'm afraid we'll have to appeal to the court.
如果你不付帳款，我們恐怕必須訴諸法院了。

cousin [ˋkʌzn]　◀Track 0490
n. 表或堂兄弟姐妹

▶My cousin who lives in the United States is going to visit us this summer.
我們住在美國的表妹這個暑假要來拜訪我們。

cover [ˋkʌvɚ]　◀Track 0491
v. 覆蓋

▶She covered her dog with a blanket and took him to the animal hospital.
她用毯子裹住她的小狗，帶牠到動物醫院。

n. 遮蓋物；書皮（封面或封底）

▶She used to be the cover girl of the fashion magazine.
她曾是這本時尚雜誌的封面女郎。

相關片語 **from cover to cover**
（書）從頭到尾

▶The novel was incredibly funny and witty that I read it from cover to cover within a day.
這本小說真是太有趣、詼諧了，我一天內就把它從頭到尾讀完了。

cow [kaʊ]　◀Track 0492
n. 母牛；奶牛

▶They raise cows and horses in their farm.
他們在農場養了幾頭母牛和馬。

相關片語 **cash cow**
搖錢樹；巨大財源

▶Unfortunately, the child star became a cash cow for the family.
很遺憾的是，這名童星變成全家人的搖錢樹。

cowboy [ˋkaʊbɔɪ]　◀Track 0493
n. 牛仔；牧牛人

▶Heath Ledger played a cowboy in the movie Brokeback Mountain.
希斯‧萊傑在電影《斷背山》中飾演一名牛仔。

crab [kræb]　◀Track 0494
n. 螃蟹；蟹肉

▶Most crabs live in the sea.
大部份的螃蟹住在海邊。

crane [kren]　◀Track 0495
n. 鶴；起重機

▶He is a crane operator.
他是起重機操作員。

v. 用起重機搬運；伸長脖子看

▶The crowd craned forward to see Prince William.
群眾伸長脖子看威廉王子。

crayon [ˋkreən]　◀Track 0496
n. 蠟筆

▶The boy used crayons to draw a flower.
男孩用蠟筆畫一朵花。

crazy [ˋkrezɪ]　◀Track 0497
adj. 瘋狂的；失常的

▶His rudeness drives me crazy.
他的無禮把我逼得快發瘋了。

cream [krim]
◀ Track 0498

n. 奶油；乳脂食品；乳膏狀物

▶ She put some cream on the blueberry muffin.
她放了一些奶油在藍莓鬆餅上。

相關片語 **hand cream** 護手霜

▶ This hand cream moisturizes very well.
這條護手霜滋潤效果很好。

create [krɪ`et]
◀ Track 0499

v. 創造；創作

▶ Blake Edwards and Peter Sellers created the animated character Pink Panther.
布萊克·艾德華和彼德·瑟勒創造了頑皮豹這個動畫角色。

crime [kraɪm]
◀ Track 0500

n. 罪行；罪過

▶ He committed several crimes, including theft.
他犯了很多的罪，包括竊盜。

crisis [`kraɪsɪs]
◀ Track 0501

n. 危機；危險期

▶ She lost a lot of money during the financial crisis.
她在金融危險中損失很多錢。

crop [krɑp]
◀ Track 0502

n. 作物；莊稼；收成

▶ Rice is a staple crop for many Asian people.
米是許多亞洲人的主食。

cross [krɔs]
◀ Track 0503

v. 穿越；橫過

▶ Cross the street when the green light is on.
綠燈亮了再過馬路。

n. 十字形；十字架

▶ He wears a silver cross.
他戴著一條銀製的十字架。

crow [kro]
◀ Track 0504

v. （雞）報曉；啼

▶ The cock crowed a second time.
公雞啼叫了第二聲。

n. （公雞）啼叫聲

▶ I woke up before the cock's crow.
我是被公雞的啼叫聲給叫醒的。

crowd [kraʊd]
◀ Track 0505

n. 人群

▶ The arrival of the superstar attracted a huge crowd waiting at the airport.
巨星的到來吸引大匹群眾在機場等候。

crowded [`kraʊdɪd]
◀ Track 0506

adj. 擁擠的

▶ The bus was so crowded this morning.
今早公車真是擁擠。

cru·el [`kruəl]
◀ Track 0507

adj. 殘忍的；痛苦傷人的

▶ The dictator was cruel and merciless.
獨裁者既殘忍又無情。

cry [kraɪ]
◀ Track 0508

v. 哭；哭泣；喊叫

▶ Upon hearing the bad news, he broke down and cried.
他一聽到壞消息，就崩潰痛哭了。

初級

n. 叫喊聲；哭

▶Many people heard her cries for help when she was robbed.
許多人在她被搶劫時聽見她的呼救聲。

相關片語 **cry wolf**
喊狼來了；發假情報；騙人

▶Pay no attention. He is crying wolf again.
別在意，他又在騙人了。

culture [ˋkʌltʃɚ]　🔊Track 0509
n. 文化

▶The tribe has very unique cultures.
這個部落擁有很獨特的文化。

cup [kʌp]　🔊Track 0510
n. 杯子；（一）杯

▶The government put a ban on plastic cups.
政府實施塑膠杯的禁令。

相關片語 **one's cup of tea**
某人喜歡的事或物

▶He's not my cup of tea.
他不是我喜歡類型的男生。

cure [kjʊr]　🔊Track 0511
n. 治療；痊癒；療法

▶Researchers are developing a new cure for the disease.
研究人員正在開發治療這個疾病的新療法。

v. 治癒；消除（弊病等）

▶The new drug Gleevec can cure leukemia.
基利克這個新藥可以治療白血病。

相關片語 **kill or cure**
不成功便成仁；孤注一擲的

▶Chemotherapy can be kill or cure treatment.
化療可能是成敗在此一舉的療法。

curious [ˋkjʊrɪəs]　🔊Track 0512
adj. 好奇的；渴望知道的

▶The students are very curious about their new teacher.
學生們對於他們的新老師感到很好奇。

current [ˋkɝənt]　🔊Track 0513
adj. 現在的；當前的

▶If the current trend continues, there will be more plastic wastes than fish in the oceans.
若照現在的趨勢持續下去，海洋裡的塑膠垃圾會比魚兒多。

n. 流動；氣流；潮流

▶Ocean currents carry plastic wastes into five major ocean gyres.
洋流把塑膠垃圾帶往全球五大海洋環流圈。

curtain [ˋkɝtn]　🔊Track 0514
n. 窗簾；門簾；（舞台上的）幕

▶The curtain is beautifully designed.
窗簾的設計很美觀。

curve [kɝv]　🔊Track 0515
n. 曲線；弧線

▶She exercises regularly to enhance her curves.
她定期運動以提升身材曲線。

v. 彎曲

▶With closer observations, we can see the arrow curves slightly in the air.
如果我們仔細觀察，我們可以看見這枝箭在空氣中輕微地彎曲。

custom [`kʌstəm] ◀Track 0516
n. 習俗；習慣

▶It is the custom of the Chinese community to celebrate the Dragon Boat Festival.
慶祝端午節在華人世界是項習俗。

cus·tom·er ◀Track 0517
[`kʌstəmə˙] **n.** 顧客

▶The customer requested a refund.
顧客要求退款。

> 相關片語 **ugly customer**
> 奧客；粗暴、可怕的人

▶The ugly customer was very demanding and overbearing.
那個奧客要求很多又霸道。

cut [kʌt] ◀Track 0518
v 剪；切

▶The chef cut the cucumber beautifully.
主廚把小黃瓜切得很漂亮。

n. 剪、切的傷口，割痕

▶The cut went so deep and through the skin that the doctor put in two layer of stitches.
傷口如此之深達到肌肉層，以致於醫師縫了兩層線。

cute [kjut] ◀Track 0519
adj. 可愛的；漂亮的

▶The puppy is so cute.
小狗狗好可愛。

初級

Dd

以下表格是全民英檢官方公告初級「聽、說、讀、寫」所須具備的能力，本書例句皆依此範疇特別設計，只要掃描右方QR code，就能搭配相對應的音軌，實現「眼耳並用」方式，刺激左腦的語言學習功能；同時也可使用本書附贈的紅膠片，將其置於單字上，一面記憶一面自我挑戰，達到雙倍的學習成果！

聽 ▶	能聽懂與日常生活相關的淺易談話，包含價格、時間及地點等。
說 ▶	能朗讀簡易文章、簡單地自我介紹，對熟悉的話題能以簡易英語對答，如問候、購物、問路等。
讀 ▶	可看懂與日常生活相關的淺易英文，並能閱讀路標、交通號誌、招牌、簡單菜單、時刻表及賀卡等。
寫 ▶	能寫簡單的句子及段落，如寫明信片、便條、賀卡及填表格等。對一般日常生活相關事物，能以簡短的文字敘述或說明。

dad [dæd] =daddy=papa=pa=pop
◀ Track 0520

n. 爸爸

▶His dad is a baker.
他爸爸是烘焙師。

daily [`delɪ]
◀ Track 0521

adj. 每天的

▶She practices ballet on a daily basis.
她每天都練習芭蕾。

adv. 每天

▶He goes jogging daily.
他每天慢跑。

相關片語 **daily bread** 生計

▶Sher works at the night club to earn her daily bread.
她在夜總會上班維持生計。

damage [`dæmɪdʒ]
◀ Track 0522

n. 損害；損失

▶The hurricane caused serious damage to the city.
颶風造成這座城市嚴重的損失。

v. 損害；毀壞

▶The castle was badly damaged in the fire.
城堡在火災中遭到嚴重的毀損。

dance [dæns]
◀ Track 0523

v. 跳舞

▶She danced to the music.
她隨著音樂跳舞。

n. 跳舞

▶They performed folk dance at the event.
他們在慶典上表演民族舞蹈。

dancer [ˋdænsɚ]
◀Track 0524

n. 舞者；舞蹈家

▶She is an outstanding dancer.
她是個傑出的舞者。

danger [ˋdendʒɚ]
◀Track 0525

n. 危險

▶The patient was out of danger after the operation.
病人手術後已脫離危險。

dangerous
◀Track 0526

[ˋdendʒərəs] **adj.** 危險的

▶The criminal is extremely dangerous.
這名罪犯相當危險。

dark [dɑrk]
◀Track 0527

adj. 暗的；黑的

▶It's so dark here. Turn on the light.
這裡好黑，把電燈打開。

n. 黑暗

▶She cried silently in the dark.
她在黑暗中啜泣。

darken [ˋdɑrkn]
◀Track 0528

v. 使變暗

▶The road darkened as night fell.
夜幕降臨，路面暗了起來。

data [ˋdetə]
◀Track 0529

n. 資料；數據

▶She is a data scientist.
她是資料科學家。

date [det]
◀Track 0530

n. 日期；約會；約會對象

▶She had a date with Tom yesterday.
她昨天跟湯姆約會。

v. 確定年代；註明日期；和⋯⋯約會

▶The time capsule can be dated back to 200 years ago.
這個時空膠囊可以追溯到兩百年前。

daughter [ˋdɔtɚ]
◀Track 0531

n. 女兒

▶Her daughter is studying in Paris.
她的女兒在巴黎讀書。

dawn [dɔn]
◀Track 0532

n. 黎明；破曉

▶They arrived in Frankfurt at the break of dawn.
他們在破曉以前抵達法蘭克福。

v. 破曉；天亮

▶She came home as the day was dawning.
天將破曉時她才回到家。

day [de]
◀Track 0533

n. 一天；日；白晝

▶How was your day?
你今天過得好嗎？

dead [dɛd]
◀Track 0534

adj. 死的；無效的；已廢的

▶The volcano is dead.
這是座死火山。

相關片語 **dead letter**
無法投遞的郵件

▶It cost $30,000 for the post office to handle these dead letters last year.
郵局去年花費三萬元處理這些無法投遞的郵件。

初級

deaf [dɛf] ◀Track 0535
adj. 聾的

▶He became deaf after the age of four.
他四歲後就聽不見了。

deal [dil] ◀Track 0536
v. 處理；對付

▶What's the hardest thing you have ever dealt with?
你曾處理過最困難的事情是什麼？

n. 交易

▶She made a business deal with Mark Zuckerberg.
她和祖克伯達成商業交易。

相關片語 **big deal**
重要的事；了不起的事

▶He cancelled the party. No big deal.
他取消了派對，沒什麼大不了的。

dear [dɪr] ◀Track 0537
adj. 親愛的

▶Dear Amy, I miss you so much.
親愛的艾咪，我好想妳。

int. （感歎詞）哎呀

▶Oh, dear! I totally forgot to lock the door.
哎呀，我完全忘記要鎖門！

n. 親愛的（人）

▶She is such a dear. She took care of me when I was sick.
她是個大好人，我生病時她照顧我。

相關片語 **Dear John letter**
（女友寫的）分手信

▶He was devastated when he got a Dear John letter from his girlfriend.
他收到女友寫的分手信時感到痛徹心扉。

death [dɛθ] ◀Track 0538
n. 死；死亡

▶The cause of her death is still unclear.
她的死因仍然不明。

相關片語 **at death's door** 性命垂危

▶He still remains at death's door. Let's pray for him.
他現在仍性命垂危，讓我們為他祈福。

debate [dɪ`bet] ◀Track 0539
n. 辯論；辯論會

▶A group of prisoners beat Harvard students in a debate in 2015.
在二〇一五年，一群囚犯在辯論會擊敗了哈佛的高材生。

v. 辯論；爭論

▶They are debating whether they should purchase a new computerized production system.
他們在辯論是否應添購一套全新的電腦化生產系統。

debt [dɛt] **n.** 債；負債 ◀Track 0540

▶She paid off her debt in five years.
她花了五年時間還清債務。

December
=Dec. [dɪ`sɛmbɚ] **n.** 十二月 ◀Track 0541

▶His date of birth is December 5, 2006.
他的生日是二〇〇六年十二月五日。

decide [dɪ`saɪd] ◀Track 0542
v. 決定

▶He decided to break up with his sassy girlfriend.
他決定與野蠻女友分手了。

decision [dɪˋsɪʒən]
◀≋Track 0543

n. 決定

▶They finally made the decision to move to Arizona.
他們終於決定要搬到亞利桑那州。

decorate [ˋdɛkəˌret]
◀≋Track 0544

v. 裝飾；佈置

▶We decorated the Christmas tree with pink and silver ornaments.
我們用粉紅色和銀色飾品裝飾聖誕樹。

decrease [ˋdikris]
◀≋Track 0545

v. 減少；降低

▶Unemployment rate has decreased over the year.
過去一年來失業率已降低。

n. 減少；降低

▶The decrease in the number of visitors has little impact on this area.
遊客數量的減少對這個區域的影響很小。

deep [dip]
◀≋Track 0546

adj. 深的

▶Be careful. The well is deep.
要小心，這口井很深。

adv. 深地

▶The ship sank deep under the ocean.
船隻沉在海底很深的地方。

deer [dɪr]
◀≋Track 0547

n. 鹿

▶We saw a deer when walking in the forest.
我們在森林漫步時看見一隻鹿。

degree [dɪˋgri]
◀≋Track 0548

n. 程度；度數；學位

▶She holds a doctorate degree in psychology.
她有心理學博士的學位。

delay [dɪˋle]
◀≋Track 0549

n. 延遲；耽擱

▶You're one hour late. What caused the delay?
你遲到了一小時，什麼事耽擱了？

v. 耽擱；延期

▶Our plane was delayed due to the typhoon.
我們的班機因為颱風而被延誤。

delicious [dɪˋlɪʃəs]
◀≋Track 0550

adj. 美味的

▶This apple pie is so delicious.
這道蘋果派真美味。

deliver [dɪˋlɪvə]
◀≋Track 0551

v. 運送；投遞

▶The online store just delivered the goods I ordered.
網路商店剛把我訂的貨物寄過來了。

democracy
◀≋Track 0552

[dɪˋmɑkrəsɪ]

n. 民主；民主政體；民主國家

▶Sometimes democracy can be abused.
有時民主會被濫用。

democratic
◀≋Track 0553

[ˌdɛməˋkrætɪk]

adj. 民主的；民主政體的

▶The United States is a democratic country.
美國是一個民主國家。

初級

dentist [ˋdɛntɪst] 🔊 Track 0554
n. 牙醫

▶He is a pediatric dentist.
他是兒科牙醫。

deny [dɪˋnaɪ] 🔊 Track 0555
v. 否認

▶The politican denied the accusation that he had an affair with his assistant.
政客否認他與助理有緋聞的指控。

department 🔊 Track 0556
[dɪˋpɑrtmənt] **n.** 部門

▶He works at the advertising department.
他在廣告部門工作。

相關片語 **department store**
百貨公司

▶He made a lot of purchases when the department store was having a sale.
百貨公司舉行特賣時,他買了很多東西。

補充片語 **have a sale** 舉行特賣

depend [dɪˋpɛnd] 🔊 Track 0557
v. 依賴;信賴;視……而定

▶You can't depend on him. He doesn't practice what he preaches.
你不能信賴他,他說一套做一套。

depth [dɛpθ] 🔊 Track 0558
n. 深度;厚度

▶The depth of the pond is 12 inches.
這個池塘有十二吋深。

相關片語 **out of one's depth** 非某人所
能理解;非某人能力所及

▶He was hopelessly out of his depth in the advanced chemistry classes.
他對化學進階班的課程內容完全無法理解。

describe [dɪˋskraɪb] 🔊 Track 0559
v. 形容;描述

▶He described what the robber looked like.
他描述了搶劫犯的長相。

desert [ˋdɛzɚt] 🔊 Track 0560
n. 沙漠

▶They didn't bring enough water when crossing the desert.
他們穿越沙漠時,沒帶足夠的水。

v. 逃跑;拋棄;遺棄 [dɪˋzɚt]

▶He deserted his wife when she was diagnosed with cancer.
他在妻子被診斷罹患癌症時遺棄了她。

design [dɪˋzaɪn] 🔊 Track 0561
n. 設計

▶The design of the jewelry is exquisite.
這件珠寶的設計很精緻。

v. 設計

▶The computer course is designed for beginners.
這堂電腦課是設計給初級者的。

desire [dɪˋzaɪr] 🔊 Track 0562
n. 渴望

▶Many people have no desire to have children because their wages are too low.
很多人因為工資太低,沒有想要孩子願望。

v 渴望

▶He desired to live peacefully in the countryside.
他渴望在鄉間平靜過生活。

---

desk [dɛsk] **n.** 書桌
◀€Track 0563

▶There are magainzes and newspapers on the desk.
書桌上有雜誌和報紙。

相關片語 **desk potato** 桌邊馬鈴薯（做任何事都窩在辦公桌前的人）

▶He is a desk potato. He rarely leaves his seat until 5 P.M.
他很習慣窩在辦公桌前，直到下午五點才會離開他的座位。

---

dessert [dɪ`zɝt]
◀€Track 0564

n. 甜點；餐後點心

▶I made a banana cake for dessert.
我做了個香蕉蛋糕當甜點。

---

detect [dɪ`tɛkt]
◀€Track 0565

v. 發覺；察覺；看穿

▶The fire alarm went off as soon as the smoke was detected.
火警警報器一偵測到冒煙就響了。

---

determine [dɪ`tɝmɪn]
◀€Track 0566

v. 決心；決定

▶She is determined to achieve her dream as an actress.
她決心要實現成為女演員的夢想。

---

develop [dɪ`vɛləp]
◀€Track 0567

v. 建立；發展

▶Parents should help their children develop reading habits.
家長應該協助孩子培養閱讀的習慣。

---

development
◀€Track 0568

[dɪ`vɛləpmənt]

n. 發展；發育；進展；開發

▶The development of the new drug is too costly.
這個新藥的發展成本太高了。

---

dew [dju]
◀€Track 0569

n. 露水；露

▶The morning dew on the flowers looks lovely.
花朵上的震露看起來很可愛。

---

dial [`daɪəl]
◀€Track 0570

v. 撥打

▶Dial 911 when an emergency occurs.
有緊急事件時，撥打911專線。

n. 表盤；鐘盤

▶There is a picture of Hello Kitty on the dial of the clock.
時鐘上的錶盤有一個凱蒂貓的圖案。

---

diamond [`daɪəmənd]
◀€Track 0571

n. 鑽石

▶Janet was showing off her 14-carat diamond given by her boyfriend.
珍妮在炫耀她男友送她的十四克拉鑽戒。

補充片語 **show off** 炫耀；愛現

---

diary [`daɪərɪ]
◀€Track 0572

n. 日記

▶He kept a diary when he was young.
他年輕時有寫日記的習慣。

---

dictionary
◀€Track 0573

[`dɪkʃən͵ɛrɪ] **n.** 字典

初級

▶She is a diligent student. Whenever she comes across a new word, she always look it up in the dictionary.
她是用功的學生，每當遇到不認識的字，她總會查字典。

補充片語 **come across** 遇到；**look up** 查閱

相關片語 **walking dictionary/living dictionary** 活字典

▶If you don't know a word, ask Elon. He is a walking dictionary.
如果你有不懂的單字，可以問伊隆，他是一部活字典。

didn't [`dɪdnt]
🔊 Track 0574

abbr. 未、沒有做（**did not**的縮寫）

▶We didn't hear from him since then.
我們從那時起就沒有聽到他的消息了。

die [daɪ] **v** 死；死去
🔊 Track 0575

▶The man died of heart attack.
男子死於心臟病發。

相關片語 **die laughing** 笑死

▶The host of the talk show was hilarious. We nearly died laughing.
脫口秀的主持人很爆笑，我們差點被他笑死。

diet [`daɪət]
🔊 Track 0576

n. 飲食；特種飲食

▶The man keeps a healthy diet and exercises regularly.
男子維持健康飲食和規律運動。

v 節食；只吃規定的飲食

▶She lost some weight by carefully deiting.
她透過小心控制飲食而減了一些體重。

adj. 減重的；節食的

▶He drinks diet cola several times a day.
他每天都喝幾次健怡可樂。

相關片語 **on a diet** 控制飲食

▶The model was on a diet to prepare for the fashion week.
模特兒為了準備時尚週登台而進行飲食控制。

difference [`dɪfərəns]
🔊 Track 0577

n. 不同；差異

▶The invention of the world wide web has made a huge difference to our lives.
全球網際網路的發明已徹底改變了人們的生活方式。

different [`dɪfərənt]
🔊 Track 0578

adj. 不同的

▶They are good friend, but they have very different personalities.
他們是好友，但個性迥然不同。

difficult [`dɪfəˌkəlt]
🔊 Track 0579

adj. 困難的；難處理的；難對付的

▶He is very difficult to work with.
他很難跟人共事。

difficulty [`dɪfəˌkʌltɪ]
🔊 Track 0580

n. 困難；難處

▶She overcame a lot of difficulties to bring up her children.
她克服很多困難才把孩子撫養長大。

dig [dɪg] **v** 挖；掘
🔊 Track 0581

▶He dug a hole and buried a time capsule.
他挖了個洞，把一個時空膠囊埋進去。

相關片語 **dig in** 開始吃

▶Dinner is ready. Let's dig in.
晚餐準備好了，我們開動吧。

diligent [`dɪlədʒənt]　◀ Track 0582

adj. 勤勞的

▶She is a diligent teacher.
她是很勤勞的老師。

dinner [`dɪnɚ]　◀ Track 0583

n. 晚餐

▶They had a candlelit dinner last night.
他們昨晚共進燭光晚餐。

dinosaur [`daɪnəˌsɔr]　◀ Track 0584

n. 恐龍

▶Jurassic Park is a movie about dinosaurs.
《侏羅紀公園》是有關恐龍的一部電影。

diplomat [`dɪpləˌmæt]　◀ Track 0585

n. 外交官

▶Before being the Secretary of State, he was an excellent diplomat.
他擔任美國國務卿之前，是位傑出的外交官。

direct [daɪ`rɛkt]　◀ Track 0586

adj. 直接的

▶He is very direct. He doesn't beat around the bush.
他很直接，不會拐彎抹角的。

v. 指揮；指導；指路

▶Many police officers were directing the traffic during New Year's Eve.
除夕有很多警察在指揮交通。

direction [daɪ`rɛkʃən]　◀ Track 0587

n. 方向

▶He just moved here and doesn't have a good sense of direction in the neighborhood.
他剛搬來，對於這附近還沒有很強的方向感。

補充片語 **a sense of direction**
方向感

director [daɪ`rɛktɚ]　◀ Track 0588

n. 主管；指揮；導演

▶Peter Hedges is the director of Ben Is Back.
彼得·海吉斯是《班恩回家》的導演。

dirty [`dɝtɪ]　◀ Track 0589

adj. 髒的

▶Clean your room. It's too dirty.
打掃你的房間，實在太髒了。

v. 弄髒

▶The kid dirtied the wall with his boots.
小孩用靴子把牆壁弄髒了。

相關片語 **dirty look** 厭惡的表情

▶He gave Mary a dirty look when she walked by.
瑪莉經過時，他對她露出厭惡的表情。

disagree [ˌdɪsə`gri]　◀ Track 0590

v. 意見不和；爭論；不一致

▶He disagreed with his wife on how to bring up their children.
他和太太對於如何教養小孩意見不一致。

disagreement　◀ Track 0591

[ˌdɪsə`grimənt]

n. 意見不一；爭論；不符

初級

▶They had a disagreement over the safety of the treatment.
他們對於這個療法的安全性意見不一致。

disappear [ˌdɪsə`pɪr] ◀Track 0592
v. 消失；不見

▶My tabby cat disappeared a month ago.
我的斑貓一個月前不見了。

discover [dɪs`kʌvɚ] ◀Track 0593
v. 發現

▶The scientist discovered tyrosine kinases by accident.
科學家意外發現了酪氨酸激酶。

discuss [dɪ`skʌs] ◀Track 0594
v. 討論

▶They discussed the project at the meeting.
他們在會議討論這項計畫。

discussion ◀Track 0595
[dɪ`skʌʃən] **n.** 討論

▶The chairman had a pleasant discussion with the guests.
主席和貴賓相談甚歡。

相關片語 under discussion
正在討論中

▶The proposal is still under discussion and needs to be assessed.
這項提案還在討論階段，而且尚待評估。

dish [dɪʃ] ◀Track 0596
n. 盤；碟；菜餚

▶Slice some cucumber and arrange it around the edge of the dish.
把小黃瓜切片並擺設在菜餚的周圍。

相關片語 side dish 小菜；配菜

▶The roasted potatoes make a perfect side dish for any dinner party.
烤馬鈴薯在任何晚宴派對中，都是絕佳的配菜。

dishonest [dɪs`ɑnɪst] ◀Track 0597
adj. 不誠實的

▶The politican was dishonest about his medical condition.
政客並未誠實公布他的病情。

display [dɪ`sple] ◀Track 0598
v. 陳列；展出；顯示

▶Monet's paintings were displayed at the Palace of Fine Arts last year.
莫內的畫作去年在藝術宮展出。

n. 展覽；陳列；陳列品

▶The fireworks display was absolutely stunning.
煙花表演實在精彩極了。

distance [`dɪstəns] ◀Track 0599
n. 距離

▶She looks like Gemma Ward from a distance.
她從遠處看有點像潔瑪·沃德。

相關片語 keep one's distance from
與某人保持距離

▶Sadly, he became a drug dealer, so I had to keep my distance from him.
可惜他成為毒梟，所以我必須與他保持距離。

distant [`dɪstənt] ◀Track 0600
adj. 遠的；遠離的；遠親的；
冷淡的、疏遠的

▶ Norway is a distant country from here.
挪威對我們來說是遙遠的國家。

divide [dəˈvaɪd]
◀ Track 0601

v. 分；劃分

▶ The teacher divided the class into four groups.
老師把班上學生分成四組。

division [dəˈvɪʒən]
◀ Track 0602

n. 部門

▶ She works at the sales division.
她在銷售部門工作。

dizzy [ˈdɪzɪ]
◀ Track 0603

adj. 暈的

▶ She felt so dizzy that she had to lie down.
她頭暈到必須要躺下休息。

do [du]
◀ Track 0604

v. 做

▶ Can you do me a favor?
你可以幫我一個忙嗎？

aux. 構成疑問句、否定句、強調句或倒裝句的助動詞

▶ He does enjoy learning English.
他的確很喜歡學英文。

doctor [ˈdɑktɚ]
◀ Track 0605

=doc.=physician
=Dr （英式中文）**n.** 醫生

▶ The doctor was very attentive to his patients.
這名醫生很關心他的病人。

document
◀ Track 0606

[ˈdɑkjəmənt] **n.** 文件

▶ Please sign your name on this document.
請在這份文件上簽你的名字。

doesn't [ˈdʌznt]
◀ Track 0607

abbr. 不（**does not** 的縮寫）

▶ She doesn't like you.
她不喜歡你。

dog [dɔg]
◀ Track 0608

n. 狗

▶ Her dog is her best friend.
她的小狗是她最好的朋友。

相關片語 **dog's chance**
極微小的機會

▶ The candidate doesn't have a dog's chance of winning the election.
這名候選人根本沒有機會贏得選舉。

doll [dɑl]
◀ Track 0609

n. 洋娃娃

▶ The supermodel has a doll face with beautiful green eyes.
這位超模有洋娃娃的臉蛋和美麗的綠色眼珠。

dollar [ˈdɑlɚ]
◀ Track 0610

=buck **n.** 元；美元、加幣

▶ It cost me $3,000 to fix the car.
修車花了我三千元。

相關片語 **feel like a million dollars**
覺得身體很好、非常健康

▶ She feels like a million dollars after improving her diet.
她改善飲食習慣後，覺得身體很健康。

初級

dolphin [ˋdɑlfɪn]
🔊 Track 0611

n. 海豚

▶We saw a school of dolphins when we went into the whale hot spot .
我們去賞鯨熱門景點時看到一群海豚。

donkey [ˋdɑŋkɪ]
🔊 Track 0612

n. 驢子；傻瓜

▶The donkey collapsed due to overwork.
驢子因為工作過勞而倒下了。

相關片語 **donkey's years**
很長的時間

▶She's been working as a waitress for donkey's years.
她擔任服務生很長一段時間了。

don't [dont]
🔊 Track 0613

abbr. 不（do not的縮寫）

▶We don't have any pets.
我們沒有養任何的寵物。

door [dor]
🔊 Track 0614

n. 門

▶Lock the door before you go to school.
上學前記得要鎖門。

dot [dɑt]
🔊 Track 0615

n. 點；小圓點

▶Her dress was white with polka dots.
她的洋裝是白色帶有圓點的。

相關片語 **on the dot** 準時地

▶We arrived at the meeting on the dot.
我們準時抵達會議。

double [ˋdʌb!]
🔊 Track 0616

adj. 兩倍的；成雙的；雙人的

▶He ordered a double cheeseburger.
他點了一份雙層起士漢堡。

v. 使加倍；增加一倍

▶The company's profits doubled after the introduction of new technology.
引進新技術後，公司利潤增加了一倍。

adv. 兩倍數量地

▶He paid double for the coat.
他花兩倍的價格買了這件大衣。

doubt [daʊt]
🔊 Track 0617

n. 懷疑；疑慮

▶She is one of the most talented singers of our time, without a doubt.
她無疑地是我們這個年代最有才華的歌手。

補充片語 **without a doubt** 無疑地

v. 懷疑；不相信

▶I never doubted his integrity.
我從未懷疑過他的正直。

相關片語 **in doubt**
不確定的；不肯定的

▶When in doubt, don't make a decision.
如果心裡存有疑慮，就不要做決定。

doughnut [ˋdoˏnʌt]
🔊 Track 0618

=donut **n.** 油炸圈餅；炸麵圈

▶Doughnuts are my comfort food.
甜圈圈是讓我有幸福感的食物。

dove [dʌv]
🔊 Track 0619

n. 鴿；溫和派人士

▶She opened the cage and set the doves free.
她打開籠子讓鴿子自由飛走。

down [daʊn]
◀ Track 0620

adv. 向下地；（程度、數量）減緩、減少地

▶The elevator is going down.
電梯向下開。

prep. 在……下方；沿著

▶We sailed our ship down the river.
我們沿著這條河把船往下開。

n. 下降；失敗；蕭條

▶He's been through ups and downs in life.
他經歷了人生的起落。

adj. 向下的；（情緒）低落的

▶He was a bit down because he flunked the exam.
他因為考試考不好，情緒有點低落。

相關片語 **break down** 故障；失靈

▶His scooter broke down so he was late for work.
他的機車拋錨，所以上班遲到了。

downstairs
◀ Track 0621

[ˌdaʊnˈstɛrz]

adv. 在樓下；往樓下

▶They went downstairs to the meeting room.
他們下樓到會議室。

adj. 樓下的

▶He checked the downstairs bathroom to see if anything needed to be repaired.
他檢查樓下的浴室，看看是否有任何需要修繕的地方。

downtown
◀ Track 0622

[ˌdaʊnˈtaʊn]

adv. 往城市商業區

▶We went downtown to see our children.
我們進城去探視子女。

adj. 城市商業區的

▶My office is in downtown San Francisco.
我的辦公室位在舊金山市中心。

n. 城市商業區；鬧區

▶They live in the downtown.
他們住在鬧區。

dozen [ˈdʌzn]
◀ Track 0623

n. 一打；許多

▶He bought a dozen of eggs in the supermarket.
他在超市買了一打的蛋。

相關片語 **talk nineteen to the dozen**
喋喋不休地說著

▶They talked nineteen to the dozen until midnight.
他們喋喋不休地聊個沒完，直到深夜才停止。

Dr. [ˈdɑktɚ]
=doctor
◀ Track 0624

n. 博士；醫生；大夫；學者；教師

▶Dr. Lee is a forensic expert.
李博士是法醫專家。

drag [dræg]
◀ Track 0625

v. 拉；拖；拖曳；慢吞吞地進行

▶He dragged the chair behind him.
他拉著椅子。

相關片語 **drag one's feet**
拖拖拉拉

初級

▶They dragged their feet over the decision.
他們做決定拖拖拉拉的。

dragon [`drægən]
◀≷Track 0626

n. 龍

▶Dragons are considered auspicious in Chinese culture.
華人的文化認為龍是吉祥的。

相關片語 **dragon fruit** 火龍果

▶Dragon fruit is popular among people who are health-conscious.
火龍果在有健康意識的人群中很受歡迎。

Dragon Boat Festival [`drægən-bot-`fɛstəv!]
◀≷Track 0627

n. 端午節

▶Dragon Boat Festival is an annual holiday in the Chinese community.
端午節在華人世界是重要的年度節慶。

dragonfly
◀≷Track 0628

[`drægən͵flaɪ] **n.** 蜻蜓

▶There are butterflies and dragonflies in the garden.
庭院有蝴蝶和蜻蜓。

drama [`dramə]
◀≷Track 0629

n. 戲劇；戲劇性

▶He starred in many TV dramas.
他演過許多電視劇。

相關片語 **drama queen**
　　　　喜歡小題大作的人

▶You're a drama queen. Stop making a song and dance about everything.
你很常大驚小怪的，別再每件事情都小題大作。

補充片語 **make a song and dance about** 小題大作

drape [drep]
◀≷Track 0630

n. 簾；幔

▶She drew the drapes and then locked the door.
她拉上窗簾，接著鎖門。

v. 覆蓋；垂掛

▶Her coffin were draped with a British national flag.
她的棺木被英國國旗覆蓋著。

draw [drɔ]
◀≷Track 0631

v. 畫

▶He drew a house and a rainbow with crayon.
他用蠟筆畫了房子和彩虹。

drawer [`drɔɚ]
◀≷Track 0632

n. 抽屜

▶She hid her pocket money in the drawer.
她把私房錢藏在抽屜裡。

drawing [`drɔɪŋ]
◀≷Track 0633

n. 描繪；圖畫

▶I learned oil painting and drawing when I was a child.
我小時候學油畫和素描。

dream [drim]
◀≷Track 0634

n. 夢；夢想

▶Her dream is to become a chef.
她的夢想是成為一名大廚。

v. 做夢；夢到

▶He dreamed that he could fly.
他夢到自己能飛。

相關片語 **like a dream**
完美地；十分順利地

▶The machine worked like a dream.
機器運作很順暢。

---

dress [drɛs]
🔊 Track 0635

v. 給……穿衣；使穿著；穿衣；打扮

▶She dressed like a duchess.
她穿著像公爵夫人。

n. 衣服；女裝；連身裙

▶The dress is incredibly beautiful.
這件洋裝美極了。

相關片語 **be dressed up to the nines**
穿著講究

▶He was dressed up to the nines for the state banquet.
他穿著講究前來參加國宴。

---

dresser [`drɛsɚ]
🔊 Track 0636

n. 附有鏡子的衣櫥；附有抽屜的梳妝台

▶There's a dresser in the guest room.
客房裡有座梳妝台。

---

drink [drɪŋk]
🔊 Track 0637

v. 喝

▶She only drinks water and juice.
她只喝開水和果汁

n. 飲料

▶I had no drink this entire morning.
我整個早上都沒喝東西。

相關片語 **soft drink** 汽水

▶He prefers soft drink to water.
比起白開水，他更喜歡喝汽水。

---

drinking [`drɪŋkɪŋ]
🔊 Track 0638

n. 喝，喝酒

▶Binge drinking is not good for your health.
大量飲酒對健康沒有益處。

---

drive [draɪv]
🔊 Track 0639

v. 開車，駕駛

▶He drives to work everyday.
他每天開車上班。

n. 開車兜風；駕車旅行

▶It's a long drive from the east to the west coast.
從東海岸到西海岸的車程很遠。

---

driver [`draɪvɚ]
🔊 Track 0640

n. 駕駛人；司機

▶The school bus driver was kind and patient.
校車司機很慈祥有耐心。

---

drop [drɑp]
🔊 Track 0641

v. 滴下；丟下；下（車）

▶He dropped me off at the main entrance of the school.
他載我到校門口下車。

n. 滴；落下；降落

▶There were little drops of paint on the floor of the living room.
客廳地板有幾滴油漆。

相關片語 **drop off to sleep**
打瞌睡

▶He dropped off to sleep on the couch.
他在沙發上打瞌睡。

---

drug [drʌg]
🔊 Track 0642

n. 藥；毒品

▶His son died of drug abuse.
他的兒子因吸毒過量而死。

drugstore [`drʌg͵stor] ◀Track 0643
n. 藥局

▶Please help me get some cough syrup when you go to the drugstore.
你去藥局時，請順便幫我買一些咳嗽糖漿。

drum [drʌm] ◀Track 0644
n. 鼓

▶He plays the drum in the band.
他在樂團負責打鼓。

dry [draɪ] ◀Track 0645
adj. 乾的

▶My hands are dry. I need a hand cream.
我的手好乾，我需要擦護手霜。

v. 弄乾；使乾燥

▶She dried her hair with a hair dryer.
她用吹風機把頭髮吹乾。

相關片語 **high and dry** 孤立無援；處於困境

▶His wife took all the money and left him high and dry.
他太太拿走所有的錢，讓他陷入了困境。

dry·er [`draɪɚ] ◀Track 0646
n. 乾燥器；吹風機；烘乾機

▶She put the damp clothes in the dryer.
她把濕衣服放進烘乾機

相關片語 **hair dryer** 吹風機

▶The hair dryer doesn't leave your hair frizzy.
這支吹風機不會把你的頭髮吹得很毛燥。

duck [dʌk] ◀Track 0647
n. 鴨子；鴨肉

▶We used to have some ducks in the farm.
我們的農場以前有養一些鴨子。

相關片語 **duck face** 鴨嘴臉（指自拍時做出的嘟嘴臉）

▶She likes to make a duck face when taking pictures.
她拍照時喜歡嘟嘴。

dull [dʌl] ◀Track 0648
adj. 晦暗的；模糊的；陰沈的；乏味的、單調的

▶Oh man. The lecture is so dull.
老天爺，這堂課好乏味。

dumb [dʌm] ◀Track 0649
adj. 啞的；不能說話的；沉默寡言的；愚笨的

▶She's usually quiet, but she's not dumb.
她平常很安靜，但她並不笨。

相關片語 **deaf and dumb** 聾啞的

▶Although he is deaf and dumb, he can paint really well.
他雖然聾啞，但很會畫畫。

dumpling [`dʌmplɪŋ] ◀Track 0650
n. 餃子；水煎包等

▶The dumplings in the restaurant are delicious.
這家餐廳的餃子很好吃。

during [`djʊrɪŋ]

◀≡ Track 0651

prep. 在……期間

▶They went to Italy during winter vacation.
他們寒假去義大利玩。

duty [`djutɪ]

◀≡ Track 0652

n. 職責；任務

▶It is everyone's duty to protect children.
保護小孩是每個人的責任。

相關片語 **on duty** 當值；上班

▶He was on duty when the accident happened.
意外發生時，他正在值班。

初
級

Ee

　　以下表格是全民英檢官方公告初級「聽、說、讀、寫」所須具備的能力，本書例句皆依此範疇特別設計，只要掃描右方QR code，就能搭配相對應的音軌，實現「眼耳並用」方式，刺激左腦的語言學習功能；同時也可使用本書附贈的紅膠片，將其置於單字上，一面記憶一面自我挑戰，達到雙倍的學習成果！

聽	▶ 能聽懂與日常生活相關的淺易談話，包含價格、時間及地點等。
說	▶ 能朗讀簡易文章、簡單地自我介紹，對熟悉的話題能以簡易英語對答，如問候、購物、問路等。
讀	▶ 可看懂與日常生活相關的淺易英文，並能閱讀路標、交通號誌、招牌、簡單菜單、時刻表及賀卡等。
寫	▶ 能寫簡單的句子及段落，如寫明信片、便條、賀卡及填表格等。對一般日常生活相關事物，能以簡短的文字敘述或說明。

each [itʃ]
◀ Track 0653

pron. 每一個

▶ The teacher prepared gifts for each of her students.
老師為每個學生準備了一份禮物。

adj. 每一的；各自的

▶ Each child got a slice of cake in the party.
每個孩子在派對上得到一片蛋糕。

adv. 每一

▶ The cheese cake is $80 each.
起士蛋糕每塊八十元。

相關片語 **each other** 彼此；互相

▶ They didn't know each other until they met in the pub.
他們在酒吧見面之前，從不認識彼此。

eagle [`igḷ]
◀ Track 0654

n. 老鷹

▶ The eagle soared higher and higher into the sky.
老鷹在空中越飛越高。

相關片語 **eagle eye** 目光銳利的人；銳利的目光

▶ She has an eagle eye for fashion.
她很有時尚的眼光。

ear [ɪr] **n.** 耳；聽力
◀ Track 0655

▶ She turned a deaf ear to her father's warning.
她對父親的警告充耳不聞。

補充片語 **turn a deaf ear to** 對……充耳不聞

相關片語 **be all ears** 洗耳恭聽；全神貫注地聽

▶ I'm all ears, and I'll protect your privacy.
我洗耳恭聽，而且會保護你的隱私。

early [ˋɝlɪ]
🔊 Track 0656

adj. 早的

▶She is an early bird.
她是早起的鳥兒。

adv. 早地

▶He went to bed early because he had an important meeting the next morning. 他很早就去睡覺，因為隔天一早有重要會議。

補充片語 go to bed 去睡覺

earn [ɝn]
🔊 Track 0657

v. 賺得；贏得

▶She earned $1 million a year.
她年薪百萬。

相關片語 earn a living 謀生

▶He earned money by being a street artist.
他靠當街頭藝人賺錢。

earth [ɝθ]
🔊 Track 0658

n. 地球，泥土

▶We should protect our earth from further pollution.
我們應保護地球讓它不再被進一步地污染了。

earthquake
🔊 Track 0659

[ˋɝθ͵kwek] **n.** 地震

▶I slept so well that I didn't know there was a big earthquake last night.
我昨晚睡得很熟，不知道有大地震。

ease [iz]
🔊 Track 0660

v. 減輕；緩和；使安心

▶The painkiller can ease the pain.
止痛藥能減輕疼痛。

n. 舒適；悠閒；容易；放鬆；自在

▶The team won the competition with ease. 這支隊伍輕鬆奪得冠軍。

east [ist]
🔊 Track 0661

n. 東方

▶There will be a snowstorm in the east. 東部將有暴風雪。

adv. 東邊地，往東邊地

▶They drove east for a few miles and then turn left.
他們向東開了幾英哩，接著往左轉。

adj. 東邊的

▶The building is on the east coast of New York.
這棟建築在紐約的東岸。

Easter [ˋistɚ]
🔊 Track 0662

n. 復活節

▶How was your Easter?
你的復活節過得如何？

east·ern [ˋistɚn]
🔊 Track 0663

adj. 東邊的

▶Some people think that eastern countries are a bit mysterious.
有些人認為東方國家帶有一些神秘色彩。

easy [ˋizɪ]
🔊 Track 0664

adj. 容易的；輕鬆的

▶Learning physics is easy for him.
對他來說，學習物理很簡單。

相關片語 easy money
橫財；得來容易的錢

▶She made some easy money by getting lucky on the stock market.
她靠著在股市的好運氣輕鬆賺錢。

初級

eat [it]
🔊 Track 0665

v. 吃

▶He doesn't have any cooking utensils, so he always eats out.
他沒有炊具，所以總是外食。

補充片語 **eat out**
外食；在外面吃飯

edge [ɛdʒ]
🔊 Track 0666

n. 邊；邊緣

▶Slice some carrot and arrange it around the edge of the dish.
把胡蘿蔔切片，並擺飾在菜餚的周圍。

相關片語 **on a knife-edge**
處境困難；對未來發生的事感到焦慮

▶Investors were living on a knife-edge during the financial crisis.
金融危機期間，投資客都感到焦慮不安。

education
🔊 Track 0667

[ˌɛdʒʊˋkeʃən] **n.** 教育

▶He went to Germany to further his education.
他去德國深造。

effect [ɪˋfɛkt]
🔊 Track 0668

n. 影響；作用

▶The medicine has some side effects.
這個藥有些副作用。

v. 造成；達到（目的）；產生

▶The politician tried to effect a change in the country's health care system.
這名政治人物試圖改善國家的醫療體系。

相關片語 **of no effect**
無效的；無濟於事的；完全沒用的

▶His warning about climate change was of no effect.
他發出氣候變遷的警告，卻無人理會。

effec·tive [ɪˋfɛktɪv]
🔊 Track 0669

adj. 有效的

▶The medicine contains effective painkilling ingredients.
這個藥具有效止痛的成份。

effort [ɛˋfət]
🔊 Track 0670

n. 努力

▶The chef put a lof of effort in each dish.
主廚在每道佳餚都花了很多功夫。

相關片語 **with no effort**
毫不費力地

▶He boasted that he could finish the task with no effort.
他吹牛自己可以不費吹灰之力就完成這項工作。

egg [ɛg]
🔊 Track 0671

n. 蛋

▶I boiled an egg and made a pancake for my breakfast.
我煮了一顆水煮蛋又做了一個薄煎餅當早餐。

eight [et]
🔊 Track 0672

pron. 八個

▶He sold twenty egg tarts, and I sold eight of them.
他賣出二十個蛋塔，而我賣出其中八個。

n. 八；八個

▶He learned how to cook at the age of eight.

他八歲就學烹飪了。

adj. 八的；八個的
▶I have eight ball pens.
我有八支原子筆。

eighteen [`e`tin]　◀≣Track 0673
pron. 十八（個）
▶Most students at the school were fine, but eighteen of them were still not out of the woods.
大部份的學生都沒事，但是有十八位尚未脫離險境。

n. 十八；十八個
▶He started his own business at the age of eighteen.
他十八歲就創業了。

adj. 十八的；十八個的
▶She has eighteen pairs of shoes.
她有十八雙鞋。

eighty [`etɪ]　◀≣Track 0674
pron. 八十（個）
▶The farmer harvested one hundred apples, but eighty of them are damaged due to the heavy rain.
這名農夫收成了一百顆蘋果，但是其中八十顆因大雨受到損傷。

n. 八十；八十個
▶He married again at the age of eighty.
他八十歲梅開二度。

adj. 八十的；八十個的
▶Eighty students attended the seminar.
八十位學生參加了研討會。

either [`iðɚ]　◀≣Track 0675
adv. 也（用於否定句）
▶He doesn't eat nuts and his brother doesn't either.
他不吃堅果，弟弟也不吃堅果。

pron. （兩者中）任一
▶"Do you prefer chicken or steak?" "I don't like either."
「你喜歡吃雞肉還是牛排？」「任何一樣我都不喜歡。」

adj. （兩者中）任一的
▶"Do you want the shipment ready for Monday or Tuesday?" "Either day is fine for me."
「你希望貨運星期一或星期二準備就緒嗎？」「任一天都可以。」

conj. 或者
▶We will go mountain climbing either today or tomorrow.
我們今天或明天要去登山。

elder [`ɛldɚ]　◀≣Track 0676
n. 長者；前輩
▶We need to take care of our elders.
我們必須照顧長者。

adj. 年紀較大的
▶His elder brother is a banker.
他哥哥是銀行家。

補充片語 elder brother 哥哥

elect [ɪ`lɛkt]　◀≣Track 0677
v. 選舉；推選；選擇
▶He was elected governor of California.
他被選為加州州長。

election [ɪ`lɛkʃən]　◀≣Track 0678
n. 選舉；當選
▶The doctor ran for mayoral election.
這名醫師競選市長。

初級

相關片語 **general election** 大選

▶He lost in the general election.
他在大選落敗。

electric [ɪˋlɛktrɪk] ◀ Track 0679
adj. 電的；導電的；電動的

▶The company produces electric vehicles.
這家公司生產電動車。

element [ˋɛləmənt] ◀ Track 0680
n. （化）元素；成分；要素

▶The TV series have all the elements of a good sci-fi story.
這部電視影集具備一個精彩科幻故事應有的一切元素。

相關片語 **in one's element**
如魚得水；得心應手；樂得其所

▶She was in her element when swimming.
她游泳時感到如魚得水。

elephant [ˋɛləfənt] ◀ Track 0681
n. 大象

▶We went to the zoo and saw animals such as elephants and giraffes.
我們去動物園看到大象和長頸鹿等動物。

eleven [ɪˋlɛvn] ◀ Track 0682
pron. 十一（個）

▶They have thirty gem stones, and eleven of them are rubies.
他們有三十顆寶石，其中十一個是紅寶石。

n. 十一；十一個

▶She's turning eleven next month.
她下個月就十一歲了。

adj. 十一的；十一個的

▶Mr. Smith has eleven grandchildren.
史密斯先生有十一個孫子女。

else [ɛls] ◀ Track 0683
adv. 其他；另外

▶Who else knows what happened?
還有誰知道當時發生什麼事了？

adj. 其他的；另外的

▶The gift is not what he desires. He wants something else.
這個禮物不是他想要的，他要的是其他的東西。

e-mail [ˋiˋmel] ◀ Track 0684
n. 電子郵件

▶I wrote an e-mail to him, but he didn't reply.
我寫了一封電郵給他，但他沒回覆。

v. 用電子郵件發送；寄電子郵件給……

▶You can e-mail us and tell us your request.
你可發電郵告訴我們你的需求。

embarrass ◀ Track 0685
[ɪmˋbærəs] **v.** 使困窘

▶She embarrassed her son by telling people the ridiculous things he did.
她告訴大家兒子所做的可笑事情，讓他很困窘。

emotion [ɪˋmoʃən] ◀ Track 0686
n. 情緒；情感

▶She couldn't control her emtion and burst into tears.
她無法控制情緒，淚如雨下。

emphasize
◀ Track 0687

[`ɛmfə͵saɪz]

=emphasise （英式）

v. 強調

▶He used a highlighter to emphasize the important paragraphs in the article.
他用螢光筆註記強調文章重要的段落。

employ [ɪm`plɔɪ]
◀ Track 0688

v. 聘雇；雇用

▶She employed a nurse to take care of her sick child.
她雇用一名護士照顧生病的孩子。

相關片語 **employ oneself in** 忙於

▶He employed himself in teaching math.
他忙於教數學。

empty [`ɛmptɪ]
◀ Track 0689

adj. 空的；未占用的

▶The barn is empty.
穀倉是空的。

v. 使成為空的

▶He quickly emptied the dorm and moved back home.
他很快就清空宿舍，搬回家住了。

相關片語 **on an empty stomach** 空著肚子

▶She went to the office on an empty stomach.
她空著肚子去上班。

encourage [ɪn`kɝɪdʒ]
◀ Track 0690

v. 鼓勵

▶The teacher encouraged his students to read books.
這名老師鼓勵他的學生閱讀。

encouragement
◀ Track 0691

[ɪn`kɝɪdʒmənt]

n. 鼓勵；獎勵

▶She was grateful for her teacher's encouragement.
她對老師對她的鼓勵充滿感激。

end [ɛnd]
◀ Track 0692

n. 結局；終點；盡頭；結束

▶The end of the the movie is unexpected.
電影的結局出乎我的意料之外。

v. 結束；了結；作為……的結尾

▶The story ended with happy reconciliation.
故事是以愉快的和解收尾。

相關片語 **meet one's end** 死亡

▶His dog met his death when he got hit by a car.
他的小狗被車禍撞到而死亡。

ending [`ɛndɪŋ]
◀ Track 0693

n. 結局；結尾

▶The movie has a confusing ending.
這部電影的結局令人困惑。

enemy [`ɛnəmɪ]
◀ Track 0694

n. 敵人

▶Why do you have so many enemies?
為什麼你的敵人這麼多？

en·er·gy [`ɛnɚdʒɪ]
◀ Track 0695

n. 精力；活力；能量

初級

▶She was too sick to have the energy to go to work.
她生病太嚴重，沒有精力去上班。

相關片語 **energy crisis** 能源危機

▶Researchers are trying to find solutions to our current energy crisis.
研究人員正在尋找解決能源危機的方法。

engine [`ɛndʒən]
◀Track 0696

n. 引擎；發動機

▶The engine is making a strange noise.
引擎正發出奇怪的聲音。

engineer [͵ɛndʒə`nɪr]
◀Track 0697

n. 工程師

▶He is a senior engineer in the company.
他是公司裡的資深工程師。

England [`ɪŋglənd]
◀Track 0698

n. 英國；英格蘭

▶We went to England for sightseeing last month.
我們上個月去英國觀光。

English [`ɪŋglɪʃ]
◀Track 0699

adj. 英文的；英國的；英國人的

▶She enjoys reading English literature.
她喜歡讀英國文學。

n. 英語；英國人

▶He speaks excellent English.
他的英文說得很棒。

Englishman
◀Track 0700

[`ɪŋglɪʃmən] **n.** 英國人

▶Her husband is an Englishman.
她先生是英國人。

enjoy [ɪn`dʒɔɪ]
◀Track 0701

v. 喜愛；享受

▶We enjoyed singing at the karaoke.
我們喜歡去卡拉OK唱歌。

enjoyment
◀Track 0702

[ɪn`dʒɔɪmənt]

n. 樂趣；享受；令人愉快的事

▶The pianist expressed great enjoyment in his performance.
鋼琴師在演出中傳達了喜悅之情。

enough [ə`nʌf]
◀Track 0703

adv. 足夠地

▶I've had enough. Leave me alone.
我受夠了，讓我靜一靜。

adj. 足夠的

▶They don't have enough money to buy a house.
他們沒有足夠的錢買房子。

pron. 足夠的東西

▶My dog can never have enough of potato chips.
我的小狗愛吃薯片，怎麼吃也吃不夠。

相關片語 **enough is enough**
適可而止

▶Enough is enough. You're 30. Be mature!
夠了！你已經三十歲了，成熟點。

enter [`ɛntə]
◀Track 0704

v. 進入

▶He entered the classroom during the lesson.
他在上課中進入教室。

entire [ɪn`taɪr]
Track 0705

adj. 整個的;全部的

▶I ate the entire pizza.
我吃掉一整個比薩。

entrance [`ɛntrəns]
Track 0706

n. 入口;進入;入學

▶My mother dropped me off at the entrance of the school.
我媽媽在學校入口放我下車。

相關片語 **entrance fee**
入場費

▶The entrance fee for the amusement park is $200.
這間遊樂園入場費是兩佰元。

envelope [`ɛnvə‚lop]
Track 0707

n. 信封

▶He put some money in an envelope and gave it to his friend who was broke.
他在信封放了點錢,把它拿給了破產的朋友。

相關片語 **red envelope** 紅包

▶Children receive red envelopes during the Chinese New Year.
孩子在過年能拿到紅包。

environment
Track 0708

[ɪn`vaɪrənmənt] **n.** 環境

▶We still have a lot to do to protect our environment.
我們還有很多要努力的地方,來保護我們的環境。

envy [`ɛnvɪ]
Track 0709

n. 羨慕;妒忌

▶He was green with envy when hearing his colleague's promotion.
他聽到同事升遷,心裡充滿了羨慕。

v. 羨慕;妒忌

▶The married man envied his friend's single lifestyle.
已婚男很羨慕他單身朋友的生活。

equal [`ikwəl]
Track 0710

adj. 平等的;相等的

▶One kilometer is equal to one thousand meters.
一公里等於一千公尺。

v. 等於;比得上

▶Four times three equals twelve.
四乘三等於十二。

n. (地位或能力)相同的人;相等的事物

▶Her boss treats them all as equals.
她的老闆對他們一視同仁。

eraser [ɪ`resɚ]
Track 0711

n. 橡皮擦;板擦

▶I lost my eraser. I need to buy a new one.
我的橡皮擦掉了,我需要買個新的橡皮擦。

error [`ɛrɚ]
Track 0712

n. 錯誤;失誤

▶He found the solution to the problem after several trial and errors.
經過很多的嘗試和失敗,他找到解決問題的方法了。

especially [ə`spɛʃəlɪ]
Track 0713

adv. 尤其;特別是

▶She is especially interested in classical music.
她對古典樂特別感興趣。

初級

Europe [`jʊrəp] ◀Track 0714

n. 歐洲

▶She is on business in Europe. Do you want to leave a message?
她人在歐洲出差,你要留話給她嗎?

補充片語 on business 出差

European [ˌjʊrə`piən] ◀Track 0715

adj. 歐洲的;歐洲人的

▶They went to several European countries for their honeymoon.
他們度蜜月造訪了幾個歐洲國家。

n. 歐洲人

▶Her husband is a European.
她的先生是歐洲人。

---

eve [iv] ◀Track 0716

n. (節日的)前夕;
(大事發生的)前 一刻

▶The prime minister had a press conference on the eve of his visit to France.
首相出訪法國前夕舉辦了記者說明會。

相關片語 Christmas Eve 平安夜

▶We are going to have a big dinner on Christmas Eve.
我們平安夜要吃大餐。

---

evening [`ivnɪŋ] ◀Track 0717

n. 夜晚;晚上

▶This is BBC news. Good evening.
這是英國廣播公司,大家晚安。

---

event [ɪ`vɛnt] ◀Track 0718

n. 事件;項目

▶We wish the event a great success.
我們敬祝大會圓滿成功。

相關片語 at all events 無論如何

▶At all events, we will make our country great again.
無論如何,我們將讓國家再次偉大。

---

ever [`ɛvɚ] ◀Track 0719

adv. 從來;任何時候;究竟

▶Have you ever been to Berlin?
你去過柏林嗎?

相關片語 forever and ever 永遠

▶I will miss you forever and ever.
我會永遠地想著你。

---

every [`ɛvrɪ] ◀Track 0720

adj. 每一個;一切的

▶He watches cartoons every evening.
他每天晚上都看卡通。

---

everybody

[`ɛvrɪˌbɑdɪ] ◀Track 0721

pron. 每個人;人人;各人

▶You can't please everybody.
你無法取悅每個人。

---

everything [`ɛvrɪˌθɪŋ] ◀Track 0722

pron. 每件事;事事

▶Don't worry. Everything will be fine.
別擔心,事情會好轉的。

---

everywhere ◀Track 0723

[`ɛvrɪˌhwɛr]

adv. 到處;處處;每個地方

▶They looked for the child everywhere, but in vain.
他們到處尋找這名小孩,但徒勞無功。

相關片語 here, there and everywhere 到處

▶He has a lot of money and lives a care-free life. He's been spotted here, there and everywhere enjoying life.
他很有錢，過著無憂無慮的生活，到處都可見到他享受人生的蹤跡。

evil [`ivl]
◀Track 0724
n. 邪惡；禍害

▶The movie is about a battle between good and evil.
這部電影是關於善與惡的較量。

adj. 邪惡的；惡毒的

▶The evil king killed a lot of innocent people.
邪惡的國王殺害了很多無辜的老百姓。

相關片語 for good or evil 不論好歹

▶For good or evil, they are my students.
不論好歹，他們都是我的學生。

exact [ɛg`zækt]
◀Track 0725
adj. 精確的；確切的

▶We still don't know the exact number of casualties.
我們還不知道確切的傷亡人數。

exam [ɛg`zæm]
◀Track 0726
n. 考試；測驗

▶He aced his physics exam.
他的物理考試考得很好。

examine [ɛg`zæmɪn]
◀Track 0727
v. 檢查

▶Forensic scientists carefully examined the body.
法醫科學家小心地檢查屍體。

example [ɛg`zæmpl]
◀Track 0728
n. 例子；榜樣

▶The cathedral is a perfect example of medieval architecture.
這所教堂是中古世紀建築的完美典範。

excellent [`ɛkslənt]
◀Track 0729
adj. 出色的；優秀的

▶He is an excellent painter.
他是傑出的畫家。

except [ɛk`sɛpt]
◀Track 0730
conj. 除了；要不是

▶They did nothing except talk.
他們除了聊天，什麼都沒做。

prep. 除……之外

▶We all left the party that night except Sarah.
除了莎拉以外，我們那晚都離開派對了。

excite [ɛk`saɪt]
◀Track 0731
v. 刺激；使激動

▶The successful launch of Falcon 9 rocket has excited the whole world.
獵鷹九號火箭成功發射，振奮了全世界。

excited [ɛk`saɪtɪd]
◀Track 0732
adj. 感到興奮的

▶She was very excited to be an exchange student.
她成為交換學生感到很興奮。

exciting [ɛk`saɪtɪŋ]
◀Track 0733
adj. 刺激的；令人激動的

▶The movie was so exciting, and I highly recommend it.
這部電影好刺激，我很推薦它。

初級

excuse [ɛk`skjuz] ◀≣Track 0734

n. 理由；藉口

▶What a lame excuse. Your dog ate the document?
真是糟透的藉口，你的狗吃掉了文件？

v. 原諒；辯解

▶Excuse me. Could you tell me how to get to the Eiffel Tower?
不好意思，可以請你告訴我怎麼到艾菲爾鐵塔嗎？

exercise [`ɛksɚˌsaɪz] ◀≣Track 0735

n. 運動；練習；習題

▶This exercise can help develop your muscles.
這個運動能幫你鍛鍊肌肉。

v. 做運動

▶She exercises on a daily basis.
她每天都運動。

exist [ɛg`zɪst] ◀≣Track 0736

v. 存在

▶Slavery still exists in this country.
這個國家仍存在奴隸制度。

exit [`ɛksɪt] ◀≣Track 0737

n. 出口

▶Where is the nearest exit to the building?
這棟大樓最近的出口在哪裡？

v. 出去；離去

▶He exited by the side door.
他從側門離開了。

expect [ɛk`spɛkt] ◀≣Track 0738

v. 期待；預期

▶She didn't expect to see her ex-boyfriend there.
她沒料到會在那裡見到前男友。

expensive ◀≣Track 0739

[ɛk`spɛnsɪv]

adj. 昂貴的；高價的

▶The house is too expensive.
這棟房子太貴了。

experience ◀≣Track 0740

[ɛk`spɪrɪəns]

n. 經驗；經歷

▶He has the experience for this kind of job.
他有這類工作的經歷。

v. 經歷；體驗

▶He experienced a lot of pain after his wife passed away.
他的妻子過世後，他經歷了很大的痛苦。

expert [`ɛkspɚt] ◀≣Track 0741

n. 專家；能手

▶He is an expert in psychiatry.
他是精神病學的專家。

explain [ɛk`splen] ◀≣Track 0742

v. 解釋；說明

▶The librarian explained clearly about how to use the smart library.
館員清楚地解釋如何使用這間智慧圖書館。

export ◀≣Track 0743

[`ɛksport] [ɛks`port]

n. 出口，出口產品

▶The company plans to increase their exports over the next three years.
公司計畫在接下的三年增加商品的出口。

v. 出口

▶ Korean pop music has been successfully exported all over the world.
韓國流行樂已成功輸出到全世界。

express [ɪk`sprɛs]

◀€ Track 0744

v. 表達

▶ Let me express my heartfelt congratulations to you for winning the election.
我由衷地恭喜你贏得這次的選舉。

n. 特快車

▶ We took the express to get here.
我們搭特快車來到這裡。

adj. 特快的

▶ The bank sent me the check by express delivery.
銀行用快遞寄給我這張支票。

extra [`ɛkstrə]

◀€ Track 0745

adj. 額外的

▶ She works as a babysitter to earn some extra money.
她兼差當保姆賺取額外的收入。

eye [aɪ] n. 眼睛

◀€ Track 0746

▶ His eyes are mesmerizing.
他的眼睛很迷人。

相關片語 **catch one's eye**
吸引某人

▶ The fluffy polar bear cub caught my eye, and I fell in love with her immediately.
這隻毛茸茸的小北極熊吸引了我的注意，我立刻就愛上她了。

初級

▶ Ff

以下表格是全民英檢官方公告初級「聽、說、讀、寫」所須具備的能力，本書例句皆依此範疇特別設計，只要掃描右方QR code，就能搭配相對應的音軌，實現「眼耳並用」方式，刺激左腦的語言學習功能；同時也可使用本書附贈的紅膠片，將其置於單字上，一面記憶一面自我挑戰，達到雙倍的學習成果！

聽 ▶	能聽懂與日常生活相關的淺易談話，包含價格、時間及地點等。
說 ▶	能朗讀簡易文章、簡單地自我介紹，對熟悉的話題能以簡易英語對答，如問候、購物、問路等。
讀 ▶	可看懂與日常生活相關的淺易英文，並能閱讀路標、交通號誌、招牌、簡單菜單、時刻表及賀卡等。
寫 ▶	能寫簡單的句子及段落，如寫明信片、便條、賀卡及填表格等。對一般日常生活相關事物，能以簡短的文字敘述或說明。

face [fes]　◀ Track 0747

n. 臉；面子

▶ I could see from her face that she was genuinely happy.
我可以從她的臉上看出她發自內心地快樂。

v. 面對

▶ Let's face the fact and be practical.
我們要面對問題，實際一點。

相關片語 pull a long face
愁眉苦臉

▶ The child pulled a long face because his mother didn't allow him to play the cell phone.
小孩愁眉苦臉的，因為媽媽不讓他玩手機。

fact [fækt]　◀ Track 0748

n. 事實，實情

▶ They will have to accept the fact sooner or later.
他們遲早要接受事實的。

補充片語 sooner or later
遲早

相關片語 in fact
事實上

▶ In fact, she doesn't love you.
事實上，她不愛你。

factory [ˈfæktərɪ]　◀ Track 0749

n. 工廠

▶ The company is going to shut down one of its five factories.
公司計畫要關閉五間廠房的其中一間。

fail [fel]　◀ Track 0750

v. 失敗；不及格

▶ He failed the bar exam and became an actor.
他沒有通過律師考試，反倒成為演員了。

failure [ˋfeljɚ]
◀€ Track 0751

n. 失敗

▶The experiment was a total failure.
這個實驗徹底失敗。

相關片語 **heart failure**
心臟衰竭

▶He was diagnosed with heart failure five years ago.
他五年前被診斷出有心臟衰竭的毛病。

fair [fɛr]
◀€ Track 0752

adj. 公平的；公正的

▶Life is not fair.
生命本來就不公平。

n. 集市；露天的娛樂集會；廟會

▶There will be a book fair in the Taipei World Trade Center next week.
台北世貿中心下週將舉辦書展。

補充片語 **book fair** 書展

相關片語 **fair and square**
光明正大，公正公平

▶He won the election fair and square.
他光明正大贏了選舉。

fall [fɔl]
=autumn
◀€ Track 0753

n. 秋天

▶Fall is coming, and the temperature eventually drops.
秋天來了，氣溫終於下降了。

v. 落下；跌倒；下降

▶She fell down the stairs and strained her ankle.
她跌下樓梯，扭傷了腳踝。

相關片語 **fall in love**
愛上；戀上

▶I think I fall in love with the guy I met in the cafeteria.
我想我愛上了在自助餐廳遇見的那位男士。

false [fɔls]
◀€ Track 0754

adj. 假的，不正確的

▶She wore false eyelashes to finish her look.
她戴上假睫毛，完成她的妝容。

family [ˋfæməlɪ]
◀€ Track 0755

n. 家庭；家人

▶This firm is a family business.
這家公司是家族企業。

相關片語 **start a family**
開始生兒育女

▶He got married and started his own family.
他結婚並生兒育女了。

famous [ˋfeməs]
◀€ Track 0756

adj. 有名的

▶The singer is famous for her angelic voice.
這名歌手因有天籟的聲音而聞名。

fan [fæn]
◀€ Track 0757

n. 風扇；狂熱愛好者；粉絲

▶The movie star has a lot of fans all over the world.
這名影星在世界各地擁有很多粉絲。

相關片語 **fan club**
追星族俱樂部

▶She is a member of Amanda Seyfried's fan club.
她是亞曼達‧塞佛瑞影迷俱樂部的一員。

初級

fanatic [fə`nætɪk]

Track 0758

n. 狂熱者；極端分子

▶He is a fitness fanatic.
他是個健身迷。

adj. 入迷的；狂熱的

▶He is fanatic about sports cars and his son is fanatic about rockets.
他對超跑很狂熱，他的兒子對火箭很著迷。

fancy [`fænsɪ]

Track 0759

adj. 別緻的；花俏的；特級的

▶She opened a fancy restaurant in Shanghai last month.
她上個月在上海開了一家高檔的餐廳。

相關片語 **fancy fair**
義賣會

▶They organized a fancy fair to raise funds for the nursing home.
他們籌辦一場義賣會來為安養院募款。

fantastic [fæn`tæstɪk]

Track 0760

adj. 極好的；了不起的

▶You look fantastic in the suit.
你穿西裝真好看。

far [fɑr]

Track 0761

adv. 遠地

▶She felt out of place and far from home.
她覺得格格不入，又離家鄉很遠。

adj. 遠的

▶The theater isn't far from here.
電影院離這裡並不遠。

相關片語 **so far** 到目前為止

▶We've made $1 million so far.
到目前為止，我們賺了一百萬。

farm [fɑrm]

Track 0762

n. 農場

▶He owns a dairy farm in Scotland.
他在蘇格蘭擁有一座乳牛場。

相關片語 **truck farm**
蔬菜農場

▶The villagers buy organic vegetables from the truck farm.
村民向蔬菜農場買有機蔬菜。

farmer [`fɑrmɚ]

Track 0763

n. 農夫

▶He is a farmer who grows organic vegetables.
他是種植有機蔬菜的農夫。

fashionable [`fæʃənəb!]

Track 0764

adj. 流行的；時尚的；趕時髦的

▶Bell bottoms used to be fashionable in the 1970s.
喇叭褲在一九七○年代曾經很時髦。

fast [fæst]

Track 0765

adj. 快的；迅速的

▶He is a fast runner.
他跑步很快。

adv. 快地

▶Tina's heart beats fast when she sees Tom.
蒂娜一看到湯姆就心跳加速。

相關片語 **fast food** 速食

▶She is very health-conscious. But she eats fast food once in a while.
她很有健康意識，不過偶爾也吃速食。

補充片語 **once in a while**
偶爾；有時

fat [fæt] ◀Track 0766

adj. 肥的；胖的；高脂的

▶Many women think they are too fat.
很多女人都覺得自己太胖。

n. 脂肪；油脂

▶The product contains vegetable fats.
這個商品含有植物油。

相關片語 **low fat** 低脂

▶Our company sells organic low fat milk.
本公司販賣有機低脂牛奶。

father [`faðɚ] ◀Track 0767

n. 父親

▶His father is a financial analyst.
他爸爸是金融分析師。

相關片語 **father-in-law**
公公；岳父

▶My father-in-law doesn't live far from here.
我公公的住處離這裡不遠。

faucet [`fɔsɪt] ◀Track 0768

n. 水龍頭

▶Turn off the faucet when you don't use water.
不用水時要關掉水龍頭。

fault [fɔlt] ◀Track 0769

n. 缺點；錯誤

▶He admitted that it was all his fault.
他承認一切都是他的錯。

相關片語 **find fault**
挑毛病；找碴

▶She seems to enjoy finding fault with people around her.
她似乎很喜歡找身邊所有人的碴。

favor [`fevɚ] ◀Track 0770
=favour （英式英文）

v. 贊同；偏愛、偏袒

▶I favor taking a walk in the evening.
我喜歡在夜裡散步。

n. 贊成；偏愛；恩惠；幫忙

▶He just emailed me asking for a favor.
他剛傳電郵請我幫他一個忙。

favorite [`fevərɪt] ◀Track 0771
=favourite （英式英文）

adj. 最喜歡的

▶Chopin is my favorite musician.
蕭邦是我最愛的音樂家。

n. 最喜歡的人或事物

▶Donald loves all his children, but Ivanka is his favorite.
唐納愛他所有的小孩，但是伊凡卡是他最寵愛的孩子。

fear [fɪr] ◀Track 0772

n. 恐懼

▶The passengers were trembling with fear when the airplane was going to crash.
飛機要墜機時，乘客嚇得發抖。

v. 害怕；恐懼

▶Investigators feared that no one survived in the crash.
調查人員擔心空難中沒有人生還。

初級

fearful [ˈfɪrfəl]
◀ Track 0773

adj. 可怕的；擔心的、害怕的

▶She is fearful that her husband will abandon her for another woman.
她擔心先生將為了別的女人而棄她而去。

February =Feb.
◀ Track 0774
[ˈfɛbrʊˌɛrɪ]

n. 二月

▶His birthday is on February 28.
二月二十八日是他的生日。

fee [fi]
◀ Track 0775

n. 費用

▶He couldn't afford university fees so he dropped out.
他無法負擔大學學費，所以輟學了。

feed [fid]
◀ Track 0776

v. 餵食

▶The zookeeper is feeding the polar bear cub.
動物管理員正在餵食小北極熊。

feel [fil]
◀ Track 0777

v. 感覺；覺得

▶He felt weak after the surgery.
他在手術後覺得很虛弱。

feeling [ˈfilɪŋ]
◀ Track 0778

n. 感覺；看法；預感

▶He has the feeling that he will be heartbroken if his girlfriend decides to break up with him.
他有感覺如果他的女朋友決定和他分手，他會心碎。

補充片語 break up 分手

feelings [ˈfilɪŋz]
◀ Track 0779

n. 感情；感性

▶Undoubtedly, animals have feelings, too.
無疑地，動物也是有感情的。

fellow [ˈfɛlo]
◀ Track 0780

n. 男人；傢伙；同事；伙伴

▶He is a decent fellow.
他是個正派的人。

adj. 同伴的；同事的

▶The former CIA agent betrayed his fellow countrymen and women.
前美國中情局探員背叛了國家的同胞。

female [ˈfimel]
◀ Track 0781

adj. 女的；雌的

▶Female deer do not have antlers.
母鹿沒有鹿角。

n. 女性；雌性動物

▶This koala is a female.
這隻無尾熊是母的。

fence [fɛns]
◀ Track 0782

n. 柵欄；籬笆

▶They built a fence around the farm.
他們在農場四周築了一道柵欄。

相關片語 on the fence
保持中立

▶I'm on the fence about euthanasia.
我對於安樂死這個議題保持中立態度。

festival [ˈfɛstəv!]
◀ Track 0783

n. 節慶；節日

▶Christmas is an important festival of the year.
聖誕節是一年之中重要的節日。

fever [ˈfivɚ]
Track 0784

n. 發燒；發熱

▶She had a fever and a headache.
她發燒又頭痛。

few [fju]
Track 0785

pron. 幾個；很少數

▶"How many guavas do you want?"
"Just a few, thanks."
「你要幾顆芭樂？」「幾個就夠了，謝謝。」

adj. 幾個的；幾乎沒有的；少數的

▶Few people attended the seminar.
只有少數人參加這場研討會。

> 相關片語 **quite a few**
> 相當多

▶He's been to Japan quite a few times.
他去日本很多次了。

field [fild]
Track 0786

n. 原野；運動場；領域

▶The field is planted with cherry trees.
這塊地種了很多櫻桃樹。

> 相關片語 **field day**
> 戶外活動日

▶The students are anticipating the annual field day.
學生們很期待年度的戶外活動日。

fifteen [ˈfɪfˈtin]
Track 0787

pron. 十五（個）

▶Fifteen of the best restaurants in California are located in this city.
加州最好的十五家餐廳都位在這個城市。

n. 十五；十五歲

▶The two-year-old child can count from one to fifteen.
這個二歲的孩子可以從一數到十五。

adj. 十五的；十五個的

▶My sister is fifteen years old.
我妹妹十五歲。

fifty [ˈfɪftɪ]
Track 0788

pron. 五十（個）

▶We made one hundred blueberry pies, and donated fifty of them to a nursing home.
我們做了一百個藍莓派，並把其中五十個捐給安養院。

n. 五十

▶The singer is already fifty.
這名歌手已經五十歲了。

adj. 五十的；五十個的

▶The documentary was made fifty years ago.
紀錄片是五十年前製作的。

> 相關片語 **fifty-fifty**
> 機會各半的；平分的

▶They had a fifty-fifty share in the business.
他們在這筆生意中獲利平分。

fight [faɪt]
Track 0789

v. 打架；搏鬥；爭吵

▶A group of gangsters were fighting in the night club.
有一群幫派份子在夜總會打架。

n. 打架；爭吵

▶She had a fight with her husband last night.
她昨晚跟先生吵架。

fighter [ˈfaɪtɚ]
Track 0790

n. 戰士；鬥士

▶The little boy with cancer is a fighter.
罹癌的男童是個生命鬥士。

相關片語 **firefighter** 救火隊員

▶Firefighters risk their lives to save others.
消防員冒著生命危險救人。

figure [ˋfɪgjɚ]　◀€Track 0791
n. 外形；體形；數字；人物

▶She earned a seven-figure annual income.
她的年薪有七位數。

v. 計算；認為；料到

▶I figured that they would offer her the job.
我認為他們會給她這份工作。

fill [fɪl]　◀€Track 0792
v. 裝滿；充滿

▶He filled the flask with hot water.
他在保溫瓶裡裝滿熱開水。

film [fɪlm]　◀€Track 0793
n. 影片；電影；底片

▶Her favorite film is Breakfast at Tiffany's.
她最喜歡的電影是《第凡內早餐》。

final [ˋfaɪnḷ]　◀€Track 0794
adj. 最後的；確定的

▶It's up to the CEO to make the final decision.
執行長要做最後的決定。

n. 決賽；期末考

▶The team made it to the final.
這支隊伍進入了決賽。

finally [ˋfaɪnḷɪ]　◀€Track 0795
adv. 最後地；終於

▶She finally landed her dream job.
她終於獲得夢寐以求的工作。

find [faɪnd]　◀€Track 0796
v. 發現；找到

▶Can you help me find my dog?
你可以幫我找我的小狗嗎？

fine [faɪn]　◀€Track 0797
adj. 美好的；很好的

▶She was sick yesterday, but she's fine now.
她昨天生病，不過今天好多了。

v. 處以罰金

▶The driver was fined heavily for driving under the influence.
這名駕駛因酒駕被處以巨額罰款。

n. 罰金

▶The maximum penalty for animal cruelty is $300,000 fine.
虐待動物最高可判罰三十萬元。

finger [ˋfɪŋgɚ]　◀€Track 0798
n. 手指

▶She cut her finger when slicing cucumber.
她在切小黃瓜時切到手指。

相關片語 **finger food**
手指食物（不需餐具，直接拿著吃的小餐點）

▶My favorite finger food is French fries.
我最喜愛的手指食物是薯條。

finish [ˋfɪnɪʃ]　◀€Track 0799
v. 結束；完成

▶Have you finished reading the novel?
你把那本小說讀完了嗎？

n. 結束；終結；最後階段

▶The athlete won in a close finish.
這名運動員在比分接近的比賽中獲勝。

相關片語 **from start to finish**
自始至終

▶The famous painter showed us how to paint from start to finish in thirty minutes.
這名畫家向我們展示如何在三十分鐘內從頭完成一張畫。

fire [faɪr]　◀ミTrack 0800
n. 火

▶Firefighters put out the fire in no time.
消防員很快就把火撲滅了。

補充片語 **put out** 撲滅；
in no time 很快地

v. 開火射擊；解僱；起火燃燒

▶Trump fired a high-ranking official again.
川普又開除了高階官員。

相關片語 **on fire**
著火；火力全開

▶He was not home when his house was on fire.
他家著火時，他不在家。

fireman [`faɪrmən]　◀ミTrack 0801
n. 消防隊員；救火隊員

▶Many firemen lost their lives during the 911 terrorist attacks.
許多消防員在九一一恐攻事件喪失了生命。

firewoman　◀ミTrack 0802
[`faɪrwʊmən]
n. 女消防員

▶My sister is a firewoman, and I am proud of her.
我妹妹是女消防員，我以她為榮。

firm [fɝm]　◀ミTrack 0803
n. 商行；公司

▶Erin works in a law firm.
艾琳在律師事務所工作。

adj. 牢固的；堅定的

▶The company remained firm on its long-term investment strategy.
公司堅定維持其長期投資策略 。

first [fɝst]　◀ミTrack 0804
adj. 第一的；最前面的

▶Their first baby is due in April.
他們的第一個寶寶在四月將誕生。

adv. 最先；首先

▶He came first in the marathon race.
他在馬拉松比賽獲得第一名。

pron. 第一；第一個

▶The robot is the first of its kind in the world with the capability to carry out multiple tasks at the same time.
這是世界上第一個能同時執行數項工作的機器人。

fish [fɪʃ]　◀ミTrack 0805
n. 魚

▶When he went diving, he saw more plastic bags than fish.
他去潛水時，看到的塑膠袋比魚還多。

v. 釣魚

▶We went fishing last Saturday.
我們上週六去釣魚。

相關片語 **a fish out of water**
格格不入；尷尬不自在

初級

▶He felt like a fish out of water in the big city.
他在大城市裡感到格格不入。

fisherman [ˋfɪʃɚmən] ◀€ Track 0806
n. 漁夫

▶The fisherman accidentally discovered a scary sea creature.
漁夫意外發現一種很嚇人的海洋生物。

fit [fɪt] ◀€ Track 0807
v. 適合；相稱

▶These boots fit you nicely.
你穿這雙靴子很合腳。

five [faɪv] ◀€ Track 0808
pron. 五（個）

▶I bought ten apples in the market, five for me and five for you.
我在市場買了十顆蘋果，五個我自己留著吃，五個給你。

n. 五；五歲

▶Tim is at the age of five.
提姆五歲了。

adj. 五的；五個的

▶The library has five floors.
圖書館有五層樓。

fix [fɪks] ◀€ Track 0809
v. 修理；處理；安排

▶He helped me fix the computer.
他幫我修理電腦。

flag [flæg] ◀€ Track 0810
n. 旗子

▶Our national flags are flapping in the breeze.
我們的國旗在微風中飄揚。

補充片語 national flag
國旗

flashlight [ˋflæʃ͵laɪt] =flash ◀€ Track 0811
n. 手電筒；閃光燈

▶There's a power outage. Do you have a flashlight?
停電了，你有手電筒嗎？

flat [flæt] ◀€ Track 0812
n. =apartment 一層樓；一層公寓

▶She bought a flat in Munich.
她在慕尼黑買了一層公寓。

adj. 平坦的；單調無聊的

▶His performance was a bit flat.
他的表演有一點平淡。

flight [flaɪt] ◀€ Track 0813
n. 班機；飛航

▶She missed her flight.
她錯過班機了。

相關片語 take flight
逃跑

▶The trespassing dog took flight and jumped over the small fence.
闖入的小狗逃跑了並跳越過小籬笆。

floor [flor] ◀€ Track 0814
n. 地板；樓層

▶The meeting room is on the third floor.
會議室在三樓。

flour [flaʊr] ◀€ Track 0815
n. 麵粉；（穀類磨成的）粉

▶She mixed the flour with butter and raisins in a bowl.
她在碗裡把麵粉和奶油、葡萄乾混合拌在一起。

flow [flo] ◀Track 0816

n. 流動；流暢

▶The flow of traffic is moving much faster than the speed limit.
車流量移動的速度比速限還高。

v. 流動；湧（進或出）

▶The video shows how the blood flows through the heart.
影片顯示血液如何流過心臟。

相關片語 **go with the flow**
順其自然

▶Take it easy and go with the flow.
放輕鬆，順其自然吧。

flower [`flaʊɚ] ◀Track 0817

n. 花

▶The teacher got a bouquet of flowers from her students.
老師得到學生送她的一束花。

相關片語 **flower girl** （女）花童

▶Zoe was the flower girl in our wedding.
柔伊是我們婚禮的花童。

flu [flu] ◀Track 0818

n. 流行性感冒

▶She had a flu and a stomach virus.
她得流感和腸胃型病毒。

相關片語 **bird flu** 禽流感

▶When the bird flu was detected, the government took measures to prevent the virus from spreading.

禽流感被發現後，政府即採取措施以避免病毒傳染。

flute [flut] ◀Track 0819

n. 長笛；橫笛

▶She has not played the flute for two weeks.
她兩個星期沒練長笛了。

相關片語 **teach a pig to play on a flute**
做不可能做到的事

▶Don't force me. It's like teaching a pig to play on a flute.
別逼我。這是我不可能做到的事。

fly [flaɪ] ◀Track 0820

v. 飛；駕駛飛機；搭飛機旅行

▶She flew to Tokyo this morning.
她今早乘飛機到東京。

n. 蒼蠅

▶A fly just landed on your sandwich.
剛剛有一隻蒼蠅停在你的三明治。

focus [`fokəs] ◀Track 0821

v. 使集中；使聚焦

▶The program focused on the impact of high housing prices on society.
這個節目聚焦在高房價對社會的影響。

n. 焦點；重點

▶The focus of this report is about microplastic and our environment.
這篇報告的重點是有關塑膠微粒和我們的環境

fog [fɑg] ◀Track 0822

n. 霧

▶The fog is expected to clear away in

初級

two hours.
這層霧預計兩小時後會散去。

foggy [`fɑgɪ]
◀ Track 0823

adj. 有霧的；多霧的；朦朧的

▶It was very foggy this morning.
今早的霧很濃。

follow [`fɑlo]
◀ Track 0824

v. 跟隨；跟著；接著

▶My little sister followed me whenever I went.
我的小妹不論我到哪都跟著我走。

following [`fɑləwɪŋ]
◀ Track 0825

adj. 接著的；其次的；下述的

▶The stock market recovered in the following days.
股市在接下來的幾天有些起色。

prep. 在……以後

▶The weeks following the coup d'état were extremely chaotic.
政變之後的幾個星期情勢極度混亂。

pron. 下列人員或事物

▶The following is the abstract of my dissertation.
以下是我的論文摘要。

n. 追隨者

▶The followers of the cult were forced to commit suicide by their leader.
邪教的跟隨者被他們的領袖逼迫自殺。

food [fud]
◀ Track 0826

n. 食物

▶I love Thai food.
我喜歡泰式食物。

相關片語 **junk food**
垃圾食物

▶Her mom does not allow her to eat junk food.
她媽媽不准她吃垃圾食物。

fool [ful]
◀ Track 0827

n. 笨蛋；傻瓜

▶She is a chronic liar. You are a fool if you believe in her.
她是慣性撒謊者，如果你相信她的話，你就是笨蛋。

v. 愚弄；鬼混

▶He was fooled by her appearance.
他被她的外表給騙了。

相關片語 **fool around**
遊手好閒；鬼混

▶Don't fool around with the flamethrower.
不要亂弄噴火器。

foolish [`fulɪʃ]
◀ Track 0828

adj. 愚蠢的；荒謬可笑的

▶It was so foolish of you to buy that stuff. 你買這個東西很愚蠢。

foot [fʊt]
◀ Track 0829

n. 腳；英尺

▶My office isn't far from where I live, so I go to work on foot.
我的辦公室離住處不遠，所以我走路上班。

補充片語 **on foot**
以步行方式；走路

相關片語 **foot the bill** 付帳

▶When we went to the fancy restaurant, my boyfriend footed the bill.

我們去那家高檔餐廳用餐，我的男友付帳。

football [ˋfʊtˌbɔl]
◀┋Track 0830
n. 足球

▶That was the most exciting football game I had ever seen.
那是我看過最刺激的足球賽。

for [fɔr]
◀┋Track 0831
prep. 為了

▶He bought the diamond ring for his fiancée.
他買了一只鑽戒給未婚妻。

conj. 因為；由於

▶We are all happy for her, for she finally found someone who truly loves her。
我們都很替她高興，因為她終於找到真心愛她的人。

force [fors]
◀┋Track 0832
n. 力量；武力；勢力

▶The police used force to quell the protestors.
警方使用武力驅散抗議者。

v. 強迫；迫使；強行攻佔

▶She had to force herself to be nice to him.
她必須強迫自己對他和顏悅色。

foreign [ˋfɔrɪn]
◀┋Track 0833
adj. 外國的；外來的

▶He works at the Ministry of Foreign Affairs.
他在外交部工作。

foreigner [ˋfɔrɪnɚ]
◀┋Track 0834
n. 外國人

▶Generally speaking, Chinese society is friendly to foreigners.
大致上來說，華人社會對外國人很友善。

forest [ˋfɔrɪst]
◀┋Track 0835
n. 森林

▶We nearly got lost in the forest.
我們差一點就在森林裡迷路了。

相關片語 **forest bath**
森林浴

▶Taking a forest bath can help release pressure.
森林浴有助釋放壓力。

forget [fɚˋgɛt]
◀┋Track 0836
v. 忘記

▶Oops, I forgot to bring my purse.
糟了，我忘了帶錢包。

forgive [fɚˋgɪv]
◀┋Track 0837
v. 原諒

▶Sometimes it's very hard to forgive.
有時饒恕是很困難的。

fork [fɔrk]
◀┋Track 0838
n. 叉子

▶He used a fork to eat pizza.
他用叉子吃比薩。

form [fɔrm]
◀┋Track 0839
n. 外形；類型；表格

▶He filled in the online application form and e-mailed it to the company.
他填好線上表格並用電郵寄給公司。

初級

v. 形成；塑造；養成

▶The students quickly formed into lines.
學生們很快就排好隊了

formal [`fɔrml]　◀ Track 0840
adj. 正式的

▶He was invited to attend a formal function.
他受邀參加一場正式的活動。

former [`fɔrmɚ]　◀ Track 0841
pron. 前者

▶Of the two computer systems, he preferred the former.
這兩套電腦系統中，他比較喜歡前者。

adj. 從前的；前者的；前任的

▶Willy Brandt was the former chancellor of Germany.
威利‧布蘭特是德國前總理。

forty [`fɔrtɪ]　◀ Track 0842
pron. 四十（個）

▶She has fifty books, and he borrows forty of them.
她有五十本書，而他借了其中四十本。

n. 四十

▶He became a world-renowned doctor by the time he was forty.
他四十歲時成為世界知名的醫師。

adj. 四十的；四十個的

▶There are forty employees in the company.
公司有四十名員工。

forward [`fɔrwɚd]　◀ Track 0843
adv. 向前；提前；今後

▶He leaned forward to give his daughter a kiss.
他向前傾，親他的女兒一下。

adj. 前面的；早的；早熟的

▶He is forward-thinking, ambitious, and committed.
他很有前瞻性、具上進心，並且很熱誠。

相關片語 **look forward to**
期待

▶We look forward to visiting you in Taipei.
我們期待去台北拜訪你們。

forwards [`fɔrwɚdz]　◀ Track 0844
adv. 往前的

▶Please move forwards.
請往前進。

four [for]　◀ Track 0845
pron. 四個

▶I ordered five hamburgers, and he ate four of them.
我點了五個漢堡，他吃了其中四個。

n. 四；四個

▶My son is nearly four.
我的兒子快要四歲了。

adj. 四的；四個的

▶The village has four temples.
這個村莊有四間廟宇。

fourteen [`for`tin]　◀ Track 0846
pron. 十四（個）

▶He has fifteen dollars, and I borrow fourteen of them.
他有十五元，而我借了其中十四元。

n. 十四

▶Seven times two equals fourteen.
七加二等於十四。

adj. 十四個

▶The handbag cost fourteen pounds.
這個手提包要價十四英鎊。

---

fox [fɑks]　◀ Track 0847

n. 狐狸；狡猾的人

▶The politician is sly like a fox.
這名政客像狐狸一樣狡猾。

補充片語 sly like a fox
非常狡猾

France [fræns]　◀ Track 0848

n. 法國

▶I bought this fragrance in France.
我在法國時買了這瓶香水。

---

frank [fræŋk]　◀ Track 0849

adj. 老實的；坦白的

▶To be frank, she is very nasty.
坦白說，她為人很卑鄙。

---

free [fri]　◀ Track 0850

adj. 自由的；免費的；不受限制的

▶I have some free tickets for Céline Dion's concert.
我有一些席琳．迪翁演唱會的免費門票。

v. 釋放；使自由

▶The hostages were freed after a two-day siege.
人質經過兩天的圍困後獲釋。

相關片語 free time
空閒時間

▶She enjoys reading and listening to music in her free time.
她有空的時候喜歡看書、聽音樂。

---

freedom [`fridəm]　◀ Track 0851

n. 自由

▶People enjoy much more freedom these days.
現在人們的自由多了。

---

freezer [`frizɚ]　◀ Track 0852

n. 冰箱；冷藏箱；冷凍櫃

▶She bought a frost-free freezer from a local supply store.
她在當地供應商店買了一個無霜冷凍櫃。

初級

French [frɛntʃ]　◀ Track 0853

adj. 法國的；法國人的；法語的

▶We spent our summer vacation in a small French town.
我們暑假在一個法國小鎮度假。

n. 法國人；法語

▶Can you speak French?
你會說法文嗎？

相關片語 French toast
法式吐司

▶I had French toast with cinnamon for brunch.
我的早午餐是法式肉桂吐司。

---

fresh [frɛʃ]　◀ Track 0854

adj. 新鮮的

▶He is fresh out of college and very diligent.
他剛剛大學畢業，為人很勤奮。

相關片語 fresh blood
新血；新成員

▶They need some fresh blood to lighten up the school.
他們需要新成員，讓學校比較有活力。

Friday [`fraɪ͵de] =Fri. n. 星期五
◀╒Track 0855

▶Thank God it's Friday. Let's go to the movie after work.
感謝老天終於星期五了，我們下班去看電影吧。

fridge [frɪdʒ]
n. 冰箱
◀╒Track 0856

▶Fruit and vegetables stay fresh much longer in a fridge.
蔬果在冰箱可以保存比較久。

friend [frɛnd]
n. 朋友
◀╒Track 0857

▶Amy is my bosom friend.
艾咪是我的閨密。

相關片語 **make friends**
交朋友

▶He made many foreign friends when he was an exchange student in Korea.
他在韓國當交換學生時，結交了很多外國友人。

friendly [`frɛndlɪ]
adj. 友善的；友好的
◀╒Track 0858

▶I met many friendly Germans when travelling there.
我在德國旅行時，遇到很多友善的德國人。

friendship [`frɛndʃɪp]
n. 友誼
◀╒Track 0859

▶Christy and John's friendship blossomed into love.
克莉斯蒂和約翰的友誼升級成戀人關係。

fright [fraɪt]
n. 驚嚇；恐怖
◀╒Track 0860

▶The cat ran off in fright.
貓咪受到驚嚇跑走了。

frighten [`fraɪtn]
v. 使驚嚇；使害怕
◀╒Track 0861

▶The children were frightened by the violent behavior of their mother.
孩子們被母親的暴力行為嚇到了。

frisbee [`frɪzbi]
n. 飛盤
◀╒Track 0862

▶They are playing frisbee in the yard.
他們在院子裡玩飛盤。

frog [frɑg]
n. 青蛙
◀╒Track 0863

▶I refused to dissect a frog in our biology class.
我拒絕在我們的生物課解剖青蛙。

from [frɑm]
prep. 從
◀╒Track 0864

▶She came from London to visit us.
她從倫敦來看我們。

front [frʌnt]
n. 前方
◀╒Track 0865

▶The front of the Sun Yat-sen Memorial Hall is magnificent.
國父紀念館的正面很壯觀。

adj. 前面的

▶Two of her front teeth are missing.
她的前兩顆門牙掉了。

fruit [frut]　◀Track 0866
n. 水果

▶What's your favorite fruit?
你最喜歡吃哪一種水果？

相關片語 **fruit farm** 果園

▶He bought a fruit farm in France.
他在法國買了一個果園。

fry [fraɪ]　◀Track 0867
v. 炸；煎；炒

▶I fried an egg and made a hamburger for the homeless young man.
我煎了一顆蛋並做了一個漢堡給那位無家可歸的年輕男子。

n. 油炸物；薯條

▶French fries are tasty, but they contain too many calories.
薯條很美味，但卡路里太高。

相關片語 **have other fish to fry**
另有要事

▶My boyfriend is not going to the soccer match. He has other fish to fry.
我男友不會去看足球賽，他有別的事要忙。

full [fʊl]　◀Track 0868
adj. 滿的；吃飽的

▶The metro was full of people during the New Year's Eve.
新年前夕期間，捷運裡滿滿地都是人。

相關片語 **in full** 全部地；無省略地

▶He published a medical report in full.
他以全文發表了一份醫學報告。

fun [fʌn]　◀Track 0869
n. 樂趣

▶They had a lot of fun in the prom.
他們在畢業舞會玩得很開心。

補充片語 **have fun** 玩得開心

adj. 有趣的；開心的

▶We had a fun shopping last night.
我們昨晚購物很開心 。

function [ˋfʌŋkʃən]　◀Track 0870
n. 功能

▶The new cell phone features functions that match its rival brands but comes at a lower price.
這款新手機配備與競爭品牌同樣的功能，但價格較低廉。

v. 作用；運作

▶The laptop functioned normally until yesterday.
筆電在昨天之前都還運作正常。

funny [ˋfʌnɪ]　◀Track 0871
adj. 有趣的；可笑的；古怪的

▶His reaction was so funny that I couldn't contain myself from laughing.
他的反應太好笑了，以致於我無法控制大笑。

furniture [ˋfɝnɪtʃɚ]　◀Track 0872
n. 傢俱

▶They just bought the furniture for their new house.
他們剛為新家添購這些傢俱。

further [ˋfɝðɚ]　◀Track 0873
adv. 進一步地；更遠地

初級

▶We've got to do something. We can't just sit there and see her sink further and further into depression.
我們要做點事情，不能坐視她一天天消沉下去。

adj. 更遠的；更深層的；進一步的

▶Was that you at the further end of the hall?
當時走廊另一頭那個人是你嗎？

---

future [ˈfjutʃɚ]

◀ Track 0874

n. 未來

▶He plans to study in Denmark in the future.
他計畫未來要去丹麥求學。

adj. 未來的

▶We studied future tense in our grammar class.
我們在文法課學習將來式。

▶ Gg

以下表格是全民英檢官方公告初級「聽、説、讀、寫」所須具備的能力，本書例句皆依此範疇特別設計，只要掃描右方QR code，就能搭配相對應的音軌，實現「眼耳並用」方式，刺激左腦的語言學習功能；同時也可使用本書附贈的紅膠片，將其置於單字上，一面記憶一面自我挑戰，達到雙倍的學習成果！

聽	▶	能聽懂與日常生活相關的淺易談話，包含價格、時間及地點等。
說	▶	能朗讀簡易文章、簡單地自我介紹，對熟悉的話題能以簡易英語對答，如問候、購物、問路等。
讀	▶	可看懂與日常生活相關的淺易英文，並能閱讀路標、交通號誌、招牌、簡單菜單、時刻表及賀卡等。
寫	▶	能寫簡單的句子及段落，如寫明信片、便條、賀卡及填表格等。對一般日常生活相關事物，能以簡短的文字敘述或説明。

初級

gain [gen] ◀ Track 0875

v. 贏得；得到

▶The candidate gained a lot of support from young people.
候選人得到很多年輕人的支持。

n. 獲得；獲利；收益

▶The director abused power for his personal gain.
主任濫用權利謀取私利。

相關片語 **gain weight**
增加體重

▶She gained a lot of weight during pregnancy.
她懷孕期間增加很多體重。

game [gem] ◀ Track 0876

n. 遊戲；比賽

▶The basketball game will start at 10:00 A.M. tomorrow.
籃球賽明早十點開始。

garage [gə`rɑʒ] ◀ Track 0877

n. 車庫

▶He backed his car into the garage.
他把車子倒入車庫。

相關片語 **garage sale**
車庫拍賣會

▶I bought this lamp at a garage sale.
我在車庫特賣會買了這盞檯燈。

garbage [`gɑrbɪdʒ] ◀ Track 0878

n. 垃圾

▶There was some garbage at the beach.
海灘上有些垃圾。

相關片語 **garbage truck**
垃圾車

▶The cyclist was hit and injured by a private garbage truck in Manhattan.
一位騎腳踏車的人士在曼哈頓被私人垃圾車撞倒受傷。

garden [`gɑrdn] ◀⋶Track 0879
n. 花園

▶She planted roses and petunias in the garden.
她在花園種了玫瑰和牽牛花。

gardener [`gɑrdənɚ] ◀⋶Track 0880
n. 園丁

▶Both she and her sisters are professional gardeners.
她和妹妹都是專業的園丁。

gas [gæs] ◀⋶Track 0881
n. 氣體；瓦斯

▶The police used tear gas to disperse the rioters.
警方使用催淚瓦斯驅散暴民。

gasoline [`gæsəˌlin] ◀⋶Track 0882
=gas=petrol
n. 汽油

▶The truck driver filled the tank with gasoline.
卡車司機在油槽加滿汽油。

gate [get] ◀⋶Track 0883
n. 大門；登機門

▶We went to gate 24 for boarding.
我們到24號登機口登機。

相關片語 gate money
入場費

▶The gate money from ticket sales in the first match will be donated to a charity.
第一場賽事的門票入場費將捐到一家慈善機構。

gather [`gæðɚ] ◀⋶Track 0884
v. 聚集；收集；召集

▶They gathered their things together and left the library.
他們收拾好自己的東西後就離開圖書館了。

general [`dʒɛnərəl] ◀⋶Track 0885
adj. 一般的；普通的；大體的；全體的；大眾性的

▶He left a vague and genera impression on her.
她對他的印象很模糊、普通。

n. 一般；一般情況

▶In general, he is a nice guy.
大致上來說，他為人不錯。

generation [ˌdʒɛnəˈreʃən] ◀⋶Track 0886
n. 世代

▶The disease is passed down from one generation to the next.
這個疾病是世代遺傳的。

generous [`dʒɛnərəs] ◀⋶Track 0887
adj. 慷慨的；大方的

▶She is a generous and kind lady.
她是慷慨、仁慈的女士。

genius [`dʒinjəs] ◀⋶Track 0888
n. 天才；天賦才能

▶He showed signs of genius from the age of two.
他從兩歲開始就表現出天賦。

gentle [`dʒɛnt!] ◀⋶Track 0889
adj. 溫和的；輕柔的；有教養的；文靜的

▶My grandmother is very gentle with all his grandchildren.
我的祖母對所有的孫子女都很溫和。

gentleman
🔊 Track 0890
[`dʒɛnt!mən]

n. 紳士；男士

▶This gentleman whom I'm with is Mr. Calvin Moore.
和我同行的這位紳士是凱爾文・摩爾先生。

geography
🔊 Track 0891
[`dʒɪ`agrəfɪ]

n. 地理學；地勢；地形

▶My favorite subjects are literature and geography.
我最喜歡的科目是文學和地理。

German [`dʒɜˑmən]
🔊 Track 0892

adj. 德國的；德語的；德國人的

▶This Germany documentary was produced by German broadcaster ARD.
這部德國紀錄片是由德國公共廣播聯盟所製作。

n. 德語；德國人

▶My husband is a German.
我的先生是德國人。

Germany [`dʒɜˑmənɪ]
🔊 Track 0893

n. 德國

▶The German Institute Taipei is a representative office of Germany in Taiwan.
德國在台協會是德國駐台的代表處。

gesture [`dʒɛstʃə]
🔊 Track 0894

n. 姿勢；手勢

▶He made a rude gesture at his teacher.
他對老師做了粗魯的手勢。

v. 用手勢表示

▶I gestured to my dog to come forward.
我跟我家小狗比了手勢要他過來。

get [gɛt]
🔊 Track 0895

v. 得到；理解；到達；有機會

▶Pardon me, I didn't get it.
不好意思，我剛沒聽懂。

相關片語 **get along**
相處和睦

▶He didn't get along with his family.
他跟家人處不來。

ghost [gost]
🔊 Track 0896

n. 鬼

▶The girl said she can see ghosts.
女孩說她看得見鬼。

相關片語 **ghost story**
鬼故事

▶I'm not interested in ghost stories.
我對鬼故事沒興趣。

giant [`dʒaɪənt]
🔊 Track 0897

adj. 巨大的

▶The dog looks giant, but he is actually very timid.
這隻狗外表很大隻，但實際上牠很膽小。

n. 巨人；偉人

▶He is one of the intellectual giants of our time.
他是我們這個年代知識界的巨擘之一。

相關片語 **giant panda**
大熊貓

初級

▶The giant pandas in the zoo attracted many visitors to see them each year.
動物園的大熊貓每年都吸引很多遊客去看牠們。

gift [gɪft]　　🔊 Track 0898
n. 禮物；天賦

▶Her father bought her a horse as a birthday gift.
她父親買了一匹馬送她當生日禮物。

gi·raffe [dʒəˋræf]　　🔊 Track 0899
n. 長頸鹿

▶She drew a giraffe and a giant panda on a sheet of paper.
她在紙上畫了一隻長頸鹿和大貓熊。

girl [gɝl]　　🔊 Track 0900
n. 女孩；女兒

▶The girl standing there is my sister.
站在那裡的女孩是我的姊姊。

相關片語 **office girl**
（辦公室的）小妹

▶She was an office girl, who took acting jobs part-time.
她是辦公室小妹，兼差當演員。

give [gɪv]　　🔊 Track 0901
v. 給予；舉辦

▶I gave her a crystal vase as a wedding gift.
我送她的結婚禮物是一個水晶花瓶。

相關片語 **give up** 放棄

▶I have no clues. I give up.
我一點頭緒也沒有，我放棄。

glad [glæd]　　🔊 Track 0902
adj. 高興的

▶I'm so glad to see you again. How have you been these years?
我好高興再見到你，你這些年過得好嗎？

glass [glæs]　　🔊 Track 0903
n. 玻璃；玻璃杯

▶Please give me a glass of water.
請給我一杯水。

相關片語 **looking glass**
全身鏡

▶She has a looking glass hanging on the wall in her room.
她的房間牆上掛有一面全身鏡。

glasses [ˋglæsɪz]　　🔊 Track 0904
n. 眼鏡

▶My grandfather wears reading glasses when he reads books or newspapers.
我祖父看書報都會戴老花眼鏡。

補充片語 **reading glasses**
老花眼鏡

相關片語 **field glasses**
望遠鏡

▶I used a pair of field glasses to watch the marsh birds.
我用望遠鏡觀察沼澤的鳥類。

glove [glʌv]　　🔊 Track 0905
n. 手套

▶The hand-knitted glove looks nice and warm.
這雙手織的手套看起來很漂亮、暖和。

glue [glu]
🔊 Track 0906

n. 膠水；黏著劑

▶ You can stick the envelope with a bit of glue.
你可以用膠水來黏信封。

v. 黏牢；緊附；如用黏著劑固定

▶ He's a couch potato. He glues his eyes to TV after work.
他是電視迷，下班後眼睛都盯著電視。

go [go]
🔊 Track 0907

v. 去；離去；行走；從事（活動）

▶ We plan to go hiking next Sunday.
我們計畫下週日去健行。

n. 輪到的機會；嘗試；進行

▶ Have a go. It's easier than you think.
試試看，比你想像的簡單。

goal [gol]
🔊 Track 0908

n. 目標

▶ The company has set a series of goals to achieve by the end of the year.
公司已設定年底要達成的一系列目標。

goat [got]
🔊 Track 0909

n. 山羊

▶ Goat cheese contains lower lactose.
羊乳酪含有較少的乳糖。

相關片語 **get one's goat**
激怒、惹惱某人

▶ She tried to get my goat by teasing me.
她嘲弄我，試圖激怒我。

god [gad]
🔊 Track 0910

n. 上帝；造物主；神祇

▶ May God keep you safe when you are in danger.
願上帝保佑你在危難中能夠平安無事。

goddess ['gadɪs]
🔊 Track 0911

n. 女神；受尊崇或仰慕的女子

▶ Miranda is his goddess. He adores her so much.
米蘭達是他的女神，他非常寵愛她。

gold [gold]
🔊 Track 0912

n. 金；金色；金幣；金牌

▶ He ran fast and took the gold.
他跑得很快，奪得金牌。

相關片語 **as good as gold**
表現很好

▶ The kids were as good as gold all afternoon.
孩子們整個下午都表現得很好。

golden ['goldn]
🔊 Track 0913

adj. 金的；金色的；黃金般的；絕好的；珍貴的

▶ She wore a golden necklace around her neck.
她的頸部戴了金項練。

相關片語 **golden opportunity**
良機

▶ It is a golden opportunity for you to forget about your work and relax.
這對你是個忘掉工作、好好放鬆的良機啊。

golf [galf]
🔊 Track 0914

n. 高爾夫球運動

▶ Ivanka and her father often play a round of golf at the weekend.
伊凡卡和她爸爸常在週末打一場高爾夫球。

初級

good [gʊd]
◀ Track 0915

adj. 好的；愉快的；令人滿意的；擅長的

▶They had a good time at the party.
他們在派對度過了愉快的時光。

補充片語 have a good time
玩得愉快

n. 利益；好處；善事

▶It won't do you good to jump to a conclusion.
倉促下結論對你沒有任何好處。

相關片語 for good 永久

▶He quit drugs for good.
他已永久戒掉毒癮了。

good-bye [gʊd`baɪ]
◀ Track 0916

n. 再見；道別

▶They exchanged e-mails and then said good-bye to their host family.
他們和寄宿家庭彼此留下電郵後互道再見。

goose [gus]
◀ Track 0917

n. 鵝；鵝肉

▶I saw a flock of goose in the lake.
我看見一群鵝在湖裡。

govern [`gʌvən]
◀ Track 0918

v. 統治；管理；控制

▶The country is governed by a dictator.
這個國家被獨裁者統治。

government
◀ Track 0919

[`gʌvənmənt]

n. 政府

▶The government has done little to control the high housing prices.
政府對於高房價沒有什麼作為。

grade [gred]
◀ Track 0920

n. 分數；年級；等級

▶My son is in fifth grade.
我兒子讀五年級。

相關片語 get good grades
取得好成績

▶He always gets good grades in every subject.
他在任何的科目總能取得好成績。

gram [græm]
◀ Track 0921

n. 克

▶The glass weighs 740 grams.
這個玻璃杯重七百四十公克。

grand [grænd]
◀ Track 0922

adj. 雄偉的；偉大的；重要的

▶Her job has a grand title, but in fact she is just a clerk.
她的職稱很好聽，但事實上她只是個職員。

grandchild
◀ Track 0923

[`grænd͵tʃaɪld]

n. 孫子（女）；外孫（女）

▶His grandchildren are well-educated.
他的孫子女都受到很好的教育。

granddaughter
◀ Track 0924

[`græn͵dɔtə]

n. 孫女；外孫女

▶Never had he expected that his granddaughter would become a princess.
他從沒料到孫女會成為王妃。

grandfather
◀ Track 0925

[`grænd͵faðə]

n. 祖父；外祖父

▶His grandfather is turning ninety next month.
他的祖父下個月就九十歲了。

grandmother
◀Track 0926

[`grænd͵mʌðɚ]

n. 祖母；外祖母

▶He was brought up by his grandmother after his parents separated.
他的父母分居後，他就由祖母帶大。

補充片語 bring up 養育

grandson
◀Track 0927

[`grænd͵sʌn]

n. 孫子；外孫

▶She has three lovely grandsons.
她有三個可愛的孫子。

grape
[grep]
◀Track 0928

n. 葡萄

▶I like grape and watermelon.
我喜歡葡萄和西瓜。

grass
[græs]
◀Track 0929

n. 草；草地

▶He sat on the grass and read books.
他坐在草地上看書。

相關片語 a snake in the grass
口蜜腹劍的人；表面和善卻陰險的人

▶Alice looked friendly, but she turned out to be a snake in the grass.
艾莉絲看起來很友善，結果她是個面善卻陰險的人。

補充片語 turn out 結果是

grassy
[`græsɪ]
◀Track 0930

adj. 長滿草的；草綠色的；有草味的

▶He took a picture of the grassy hillside.
他把長滿草的山坡景觀照了下來。

gray
[gre]
◀Track 0931

adj. 灰色的；灰的；蒼白的；頭髮灰白的

▶His face was gray and gaunt.
他的臉色灰暗又消瘦。

n. 灰色；灰色衣服

▶Dressed in gray, he looked depressed.
他穿著灰色衣服，看起來心情不太好。

相關片語 gray hair 灰白頭髮

▶She started to have gray hair in her mid-thirties.
她在三十五歲左右頭髮就變灰白了。

great
[gret]
◀Track 0932

adj. 棒的；極好的；偉大的

▶Céline Dion is one of the greatest singers of all time.
席琳·狄翁是最偉大的歌手之一。

補充片語 of all time
永遠的，無論何時的

greedy
[`gridɪ]
◀Track 0933

adj. 貪婪的；貪吃的

▶She is greedy and stingy.
她很貪心又吝嗇。

green
[grin]
◀Track 0934

adj. 綠色的；（臉色）發青的

▶She looked good in the green dress.
她穿綠色的洋裝很好看。

初級

n. 綠色

▶I like the curtain in pastel green.
我喜歡這個粉綠色的窗簾。

相關片語 **green tea** 綠茶

▶He always has a glass of green tea after lunch.
他午餐後總要喝一杯綠茶。

greet [grit]　◀Track 0935
v. 迎接；問候；打招呼

▶My dog greeted me at the door.
我的狗在門口迎接我。

ground [graʊnd]　◀Track 0936
n. 地面

▶He sat down on the ground and ate his sandwich.
他坐在地上吃起三明治。

group [grup]　◀Track 0937
n.（一）群；群；類；組

▶A group of students visited the museum this morning.
今早有一群學生參觀博物館。

grow [gro]　◀Track 0938
v. 生長；成長；種植

▶The plant grows best in the sun.
這種植物曬太陽長得最好。

growth [groθ]　◀Track 0939
n. 成長；發育；生長物；種植

▶The country has a large population grow.
這個國家有很高的人口增長。

guard [gard]　◀Track 0940
n. 警衛；看守員；護衛隊

▶The security guard was shot and seriously injured by the gunman.
保安被持槍的男子擊中而身受重傷。

v. 保衛；防衛

▶Three prison officers guarded the felon.
三名獄警看守這個重刑犯。

相關片語 **guard dog** 看門狗；警衛狗

▶The guard dog was trained to protect livestock in the farm.
看門狗被訓練看守農場的家畜。

guava [`gwavə]　◀Track 0941
n. 芭樂

▶He ate a lot of guavas when he came back to Taiwan.
他回台灣時，吃了很多的芭樂。

guess [gɛs]　◀Track 0942
v. 猜；猜想

▶Guess what? I won the lottery.
你猜發生什麼事？我贏了大樂透。

n. 猜

▶My guess is that she will never be back.
我猜她永遠都不會回來了。

guest [gɛst]　◀Track 0943
n. 客人；賓客

▶We invited more than two hundred guests to attend the celebration.
我們邀請超過兩百位賓客參加這場慶典。

相關片語 **guest room** 客房

▶I stayed in the guest room of my cousin's house when I was in Helsinki.
我在赫爾辛基時，住在表弟房子裡的客房。

guide [gaɪd]   ◀⁞Track 0944
n. 導遊；嚮導；指導者

▶This travel guide is very informative.
這本旅遊手冊資訊很豐富。

v. 領路；帶領；引導

▶The curator guided us through the museum.
館長帶領我們參觀博物館。

相關片語 **guide dog** 導盲犬

▶When a guide dog is on duty, it is not the time to play or socialize.
導盲犬工作時，不能玩耍或與他人交流。

guitar [gɪˋtɑr]   ◀⁞Track 0945
n. 吉他

▶He sat on the bed, strumming his guitar.
他坐在床上彈奏吉他。

gun [gʌn]   ◀⁞Track 0946
n. 槍

▶Hundreds of thousands of people urge gun control across the United States.
數以萬計的美國人民呼籲進行槍枝管控。

相關片語 **go great guns**
成功；順利

▶The economy is going great guns, and some businesses begin to expand their presence in other countries.
景氣很好，有些企業開始擴展國外的據點。

guy [gaɪ]   ◀⁞Track 0947
n. 傢伙；朋友；人

▶She married the guy she met at the party.
她嫁給在派對遇到的男子。

相關片語 **bad guy** 壞人

▶Stay away from that bad guy. He is violent.
遠離那個壞人，他很暴力。

gym [dʒɪm]   ◀⁞Track 0948
n. 體育館；健身房

▶She works out in the local gym everyday.
她每天都到當地的健身房健身。

補充片語 **work out**
做大量體能鍛鍊

初級

▶ Hh

　　以下表格是全民英檢官方公告初級「聽、說、讀、寫」所須具備的能力，本書例句皆依此範疇特別設計，只要掃描右方**QR code**，就能搭配相對應的音軌，實現「眼耳並用」方式，刺激左腦的語言學習功能；同時也可使用本書附贈的紅膠片，將其置於單字上，一面記憶一面自我挑戰，達到雙倍的學習成果！

聽 ▶	能聽懂與日常生活相關的淺易談話，包含價格、時間及地點等。
說 ▶	能朗讀簡易文章、簡單地自我介紹，對熟悉的話題能以簡易英語對答，如問候、購物、問路等。
讀 ▶	可看懂與日常生活相關的淺易英文，並能閱讀路標、交通號誌、招牌、簡單菜單、時刻表及賀卡等。
寫 ▶	能寫簡單的句子及段落，如寫明信片、便條、賀卡及填表格等。對一般日常生活相關事物，能以簡短的文字敘述或說明。

habit [`hæbɪt]
◀ Track 0949

n. 習慣

▶The teacher helped her students develop reading habits.
老師幫助她的學生培養閱讀習慣。

hadn't [`hædnt]
◀ Track 0950

abbr. 未曾、還沒（**had not**的縮寫）

▶She was disappointed that Kevin hadn't called her.
她很失望凱文還沒打電話給她。

hair [hɛr]
◀ Track 0951

n. 頭髮

▶She has beautiful blond hair.
她有一頭美麗的棕髮。

相關片語	**not turn a hair**
	面不改色

▶The actor has high EQ. He hasn't turned a hair at anything that has been thrown at him.
這名演員的情商很高，他對任何不利他的傳聞都面不改色。

haircut [`hɛr͵kʌt]
◀ Track 0952

n. 剪髮

▶He had a really awful haircut.
他的髮型真難看。

half [hæf]
◀ Track 0953

pron. 半；一半；二分之一

▶I have a dozen of eggs, and he breaks half of them.
我有一打的蛋，他打碎了其中一半。

adj. 一半的；二分之一的

▶The team struggled in the second half of the game.
這支隊伍在下半場的表現有些吃力。

n. 半；二分之一

▶He was born in the latter half of the 19th century.
他出生於十九世紀後半葉。

adv. 一半地；相當地

▶The boy was half deaf when he was born.
男童出生時就半聾了。

hall [hɔl]
◀Track 0954

n. 會堂；大廳

▶She lost her luggage in the hall.
她在大廳遺失了行李。

相關片語 **music hall** 音樂廳

▶The famous pianist will perform at the music hall tonight.
這名有名的鋼琴家今晚要在音樂廳表演。

Halloween [ˌhælo`in]
◀Track 0955

n. 萬聖節

▶He wore a Spiderman costume at the Halloween party.
他在萬聖節派對穿著蜘蛛人衣服。

ham [hæm]
◀Track 0956

n. 火腿

▶He had a ham sandwich and pumpkin pie for dinner.
他晚餐吃了一個火腿三明治和南瓜派。

hamburger
[`hæmbɚgɚ]

=burger
◀Track 0957

n. 漢堡

▶I'd like a king-size hamburger, please.
我要一份特大漢堡，麻煩了。

hammer [`hæmɚ]
◀Track 0958

n. 榔頭；鎚子

▶He used a hammer to nail the picture frame into the wall.
他用鎚子把畫框釘在牆上。

hand [hænd]
◀Track 0959

n. 手

▶He held her hand when crossing the road.
他牽起她的手過馬路。

v. 遞交；傳遞

▶He read the document and handed it to his co-workers.
他讀完文件並交給同事傳閱。

相關片語 **helping hand** 幫助；援手

▶His neighbors gave him a helping hand when he was in destitute.
他在貧困潦倒時，鄰居伸出援手幫助他。

handkerchief
[`hæŋkɚˌtʃif]
◀Track 0960

n. 手帕

▶She used a handkerchief to dry her tears when she heard the bad news.
她聽到壞消息時，用手帕擦乾眼淚。

handle [`hænd!]
◀Track 0961

v. 處理；對待；操作

▶We need to handle this issue carefully.
我們要小心地處理這個議題。

n. 把手；柄狀物；落人口實的把柄

▶The door handle was made of gold and porcelain.
這個門把是用金子和陶瓷做的。

初級

相關片語 **love handles** 腰間贅肉

▶She felt that her love handles looked like a swimming tube.
她覺得她的腰間贅肉看起來像一個泳圈。

handsome [`hænsəm] ◀Track 0962
adj. 英俊的;可觀的

▶Jim is such a handsome guy.
吉姆是個美男子。

hang [hæŋ] ◀Track 0963
v. 懸掛;吊起

▶He hung his coat on the rack at the entrance of the house.
他把外套吊在房子入口的架子上。

相關片語 **hang on** 等待不掛斷(電話)

▶Please hang on. I'll transfer your call.
請不要掛斷,我將為你轉接電話。

hanger [`hæŋɚ] ◀Track 0964
n. 衣架;掛鉤

▶I bought extra hangers and donated them to a nursing home.
我多買了一些衣架並把它們捐到一家安養院。

happen [`hæpən] ◀Track 0965
v. 發生

▶What happened to you? You look so sad.
你發生什麼事了? 你看起來很難過。

相關片語 **happen to** 恰好;碰巧

▶We happened to see Justin Bieber on the street.
我們在街上碰巧遇到小賈斯汀。

happy [`hæpɪ] ◀Track 0966
adj. 高興的;樂意的;滿意的

▶Luke seems a lot happier since he met Ella.
路克自從認識艾拉之後就快樂多了。

相關片語 **happy medium** 折衷辦法

▶The designer of the clothes found a happy medium between luxury and affordability.
服裝設計師找到介於奢華和可負擔範圍的折衷辦法。

hard [hɑrd] ◀Track 0967
adj. 堅硬的;困難的;努力的

▶It's so hard to forgive his evil behavior.
要饒恕他的邪惡行為很困難。

adv. 努力地;困難地;猛烈地

▶He studied very hard for the final exams.
他很努力地準備期末考。

相關片語 **hard up** 缺錢

▶He has been a bit hard up for cash lately.
他最近手頭有點緊。

hardly [`hɑrdlɪ] ◀Track 0968
adv. 幾乎不;簡直不

▶She hardly ate anything in the cocktail party.
她在雞尾酒會幾乎什麼都沒吃。

hasn't [`hæznt] ◀Track 0969
abbr. 還沒、未曾(**has not**的縮寫)

▶She hasn't finished her homework.
她還沒寫完功課。

hat [hæt]　Track 0970
n. 帽子

▶She wore a straw hat at the beach.
她在海灘戴了一頂草帽。

hate [het]　Track 0971
v. 厭惡；討厭

▶Molly hates her boss.
莫莉討厭她的上司。

n. 仇恨；厭惡；反感

▶He admitted that he could not overcome his feelings of hate for Emily.
他承認他無法克服對艾蜜莉的反感。

hateful [`hetfəl]　Track 0972
adj. 可憎的；討厭的

▶She is indeed a hateful person. Nobody wants to make friends with her.
她的確是個令人討厭的人，沒有人想和她做朋友。

補充片語 make friends with sb.
和某人做朋友

have [hæv]　Track 0973
v. 有；吃；使做……

▶How many sisters do you have?
你有幾個姊妹？

aux. 已經（完成式的助動詞）

▶I have never heard of him before. Who's he?
我從沒聽過他，他是誰？

haven't [`hævnt]　Track 0974
abbr. 還沒、未曾（have not的縮寫）

▶We haven't been to Seoul before.
我們還沒去過首爾。

he [hi]　Track 0975
pron. 他

▶He is a wise man.
他是個有智慧的男人。

head [hɛd]　Track 0976
n. 頭

▶She fell and banged her head on the bus.
她在公車裡跌倒撞到頭。

v. 前往

▶They headed back before it became dark.
他們在天黑前趕回家。

相關片語 turn one's head
使某人得意忘形

▶Jason didn't allow success to turn his head.
傑森不容許自己讓成功沖昏了頭。

headache [`hɛdˌek]　Track 0977
n. 頭痛；令人頭痛的事

▶She has a terrible headache. We need to take her to the hospital.
她頭痛得很厲害，我們必須帶她去醫院。

health [hɛlθ]　Track 0978
n. 健康

▶He quit because of poor health.
他因健康不佳而辭掉工作。

相關片語 in the pink of health
極健康的

▶After taking a break for a year, she's back in the pink of health.
她休息了一年，現在容光煥發地回來了。

healthy [`hɛlθɪ]
🔊 Track 0979

adj. 健康的

▶The baby is healthy and happy.
寶寶很健康、快樂。

hear [hɪr]
🔊 Track 0980

v. 聽到；聽見

▶We heard a noise on the roof.
我們聽到天花板有吵嘈聲。

heart [hɑrt]
🔊 Track 0981

n. 心；心臟

▶Elizabeth has a beautiful heart.
伊麗莎白是心地善良的人。

相關片語 **have a heart**
【口】發發慈悲；做好事

▶I wish that our boss would have a heart and give us a raise.
但願我們老闆發發慈悲，給我們調薪。

heat [hit]
🔊 Track 0982

n. 熱；熱氣；高溫

▶The heat of summer is crazy here.
這裡的夏天炎熱得不得了。

v. 加熱；使變熱

▶He heated up some food for us with the microwave.
他用微波爐加熱了一些食物給我們。

heater [`hitɚ]
🔊 Track 0983

n. 暖氣機；加熱器

▶The room didn't have a heater and it was super cold at night.
房間沒有暖氣，晚上超級冷的。

heavy [`hɛvɪ]
🔊 Track 0984

adj. 沉重的；大的；繁忙的

▶Her luggage was heavy.
她的行李很重。

相關片語 **heavy heart**
沉重的心情

▶The governor wrote letters with a heavy heart to the victims' families.
州長懷著沉重的心情寫信給罹難者家屬。

he'd [hid]
🔊 Track 0985

abbr. 他會（he would、he had的縮寫）

▶He'd already arrived in Manchester two months ago.
他兩個月前就抵達曼徹斯特了。

height [haɪt]
🔊 Track 0986

n. 高；高度

▶The suspect is about average height.
嫌犯大約中等個子。

helicopter [`hɛlɪkaptɚ]
🔊 Track 0987

n. 直升機

▶My uncle is a helicopter pilot.
我叔叔是直升機駕駛員。

相關片語 **helicopter parent**
直升機家長

▶You need to stop being a helicopter parent and allow your kids to learn from mistakes.
你別當直升機家長了，要容忍孩子從錯誤中學習。

he'll [hil]
🔊 Track 0988

abbr. 他會（he will的縮寫）

▶The president said he will make America great again.
總統說他會讓美國再次偉大。

hello [hə`lo]

n. 表示問候的招呼；哈囉

▶He just dropped by and said hello to us.
他剛順道拜訪問候我們。

interj. 喂；你好；哈囉

▶Hello, I'd like to book a flight ticket to Paris.
你好，我想訂飛往巴黎的機票。

help [hɛlp]

v. 幫助

▶My dad helped me pay my college tuition.
我爸爸幫我付大學的學費。

n. 幫助

▶Do you need any help?
你需要幫忙嗎？

helpful [`hɛlpfəl]

adj. 有幫助的

▶This reference book is very helpful.
這本參考書很有用。

hen [hɛn]

n. 母雞

▶She got four hens and they followed her all around.
她養了四隻母雞，牠們每天到處跟著她。

相關片語 hen house 雞舍

▶She built a hen house and raised some chickens.
她造了一間雞舍，在裡面養了一些雞。

her [hɜ˞]

pron. 她

▶He gave her a beautiful necklace.
他送她一條美麗的項鍊。

here [hɪr]

adv. 這裡

▶Something went terribly wrong here.
這裡出了很大的差錯。

補充片語 go wrong 出錯

相關片語 here and now
此時此刻

▶I'm not in the mood to think about my retirement. I'm busy focusing on the here and now.
我沒心情想退休生活，我忙著專注過好現在的日子。

hero [`hɪro]

n. 英雄；受崇拜的人

▶Nikola Tesla is my hero.
尼古拉·特斯拉是我的英雄。

her·o·ine [`hɛro͵ɪn]

n. 女英雄；女傑；受崇拜的女子

▶Neerja Bhanot died a heroine after saving 359 passengers on board Pan Am Flight 73.
妮嘉·巴洛特犧牲生命，救了泛美航空第73號班機上的三百五十九名乘客，而成為女英雄。

hers [hɜ˞z]

pron. 她的

▶I have dark hair, but hers is darker than mine.
我有深色頭髮，但她的髮色比我的更深。

初級

herself [hɚˋsɛlf]
🔊 Track 0998

pron. 她自己

▶She kept telling herself she could do it.
她不斷告訴自己她可以做到。

he's [hiz]
🔊 Track 0999

abbr. 他是、他已（**he is**、**he has**的縮寫）

▶He's a great basketball player.
他是很傑出的籃球員。

hey [he]
🔊 Track 1000

interj. 嘿

▶Hey, how's it going?
嘿，近來如何？

hi [haɪ]
🔊 Track 1001

interj. 嗨（招呼語）

▶Hi, may I speak to Jerry?
嗨，我可以跟傑瑞講電話嗎？

hide [haɪd]
🔊 Track 1002

v. 藏；躲藏

▶He hid her picture in the drawer.
他把她的照片藏在抽屜裡。

相關片語 **hide-and-seek**
捉迷藏

▶When we were young, we loved playing hide-and-seek.
我們小時候喜歡玩捉迷藏。

high [haɪ]
🔊 Track 1003

adj. 高的；（價值）高的；高速的

▶He has high blood pressure.
他有高血壓。

adv. 高地

▶He hit the ball quite high over the net with lots of spin.
他把球打得很高，球越過網子並旋轉了好幾圈。

highway [ˋhaɪ͵we]
🔊 Track 1004

n. 公路；道路

▶The highway connects Manhattan and New York City.
這條公路連接曼哈頓和紐約市。

hike [haɪk]
🔊 Track 1005

n. 徒步旅行

▶The trail has been dubbed the world's best hike.
這條步道被全世界封為最佳健走景點。

v. 徒步旅行

▶They went hiking in the forest.
他們到森林裡徒步旅行。

hill [hɪl]
🔊 Track 1006

n. 小山；丘陵

▶We have a cabin on the top of the hill.
我們在山丘頂上有一間小木屋。

相關片語 **over the hill**
已經過了巔峰時刻的

▶Although the singer is over the hill, he is still well-respected.
這名歌手雖然已經過氣了，仍然很受到敬重。

him [hɪm]
🔊 Track 1007

pron. 他

▶If you see Ben, tell him that I miss him.
如果你有看見班恩，告訴他我很想他。

himself [hɪm`sɛlf]
◀ Track 1008

pron. 他自己

▶ Have you seen Fred? He hasn't been quite himself lately.
你有看到佛列德嗎？ 他最近看起來不太對勁。

補充片語 **not oneself**
不太對勁

hip [hɪp]
◀ Track 1009

n. 臀部；屁股

▶ She practices yoga to trim her hips and thighs.
她練瑜伽讓臀部和大腿變得苗條。

hippopotamus
◀ Track 1010

[ˌhɪpə`pɑtəməs]

=hippo

n. 河馬

▶ Hippopotamus can be found in the wild.
野外可以看到河馬的蹤跡。

hire [haɪr]
◀ Track 1011

v. 雇用；租用

▶ He couldn't afford to hire a lawyer.
他無法負擔雇用律師的費用。

n. 租用；雇用

▶ The camping shop has tents for hire.
這家露營用品店有帳篷供人租用。

his [hɪz]
◀ Track 1012

det. 他的；他的東西

▶ His favorite color is indigo.
他最喜愛的顏色是靛藍色。

history [`hɪstərɪ]
◀ Track 1013

n. 歷史；由來；過去的經歷；故事

▶ She studied ancient Chinese history at college.
她在大學裡學的是中國古代歷史。

hit [hɪt]
◀ Track 1014

v. 打；打擊；碰撞

▶ She was hit in the arm by a stray bullet.
她被流彈擊中手臂。

n. 打擊；碰撞；成功而風行一時的事物

▶ The boy band had several number-one hits in the 1990s。
這個男孩樂團在一九九〇年代推出了好幾首冠軍歌曲。

相關片語 **hit-and-run**
肇事逃逸的

▶ He was suspected of being the driver in the fatal hit-and-run accident.
他被懷疑是這場致命肇事逃逸的駕駛。

hobby [`hɑbɪ]
◀ Track 1015

n. 嗜好

▶ Vera's main hobby is photography.
薇拉的主要嗜好是攝影。

hold [hold]
◀ Track 1016

v. 握住；抓住；舉行

▶ The little boy held his father's hand.
小男孩握著爸爸的手。

n. 抓住；支撐

▶ He lost hold of the reigns and the horse bolted forward.
他沒抓住韁繩，馬兒仍往前直奔。

相關片語 **hold on** 不掛電話

初級

▶Hold on a few seconds. I'll transfer your call.
請稍等不要掛斷，我將為你轉接電話。

holder [`holdɚ] ◀Track 1017
n. 持有者；保有者；支托物

▶He is a British passport holder.
他持有英國護照。

hole [hol] **n.** 洞 ◀Track 1018

▶He dug a hole and planted the seedling.
他挖了一個洞，種下一株小樹苗。

holiday [`halə‚de] ◀Track 1019
n. 假日；節日；休假日

▶I don't like to go out on holidays because there are people everywhere.
我不喜歡在假日時出門，因為到處都是人。

home [hom] ◀Track 1020
n. 家

▶Will you come home for dinner tonight?
你今晚會回家吃晚飯嗎？

adv. 在家；回家；到家

▶She is on her way home now.
她現在正在回家的路上。

adj. 家庭的；本國的；總部的

▶The company provides home care for elder people.
這公司提供針對老年人的居家照護。

相關片語 **home bird**
　　　　喜歡待在家裡的人

▶My brother likes to go out with friends, but I am a home bird.
我哥哥喜歡跟朋友出去，但我喜歡窩在家裡。

homesick [`hom‚sɪk] ◀Track 1021
adj. 想家的

▶I got homesick a lot when I was studying in America.
我在美國讀書的時候常常很想家。

homework ◀Track 1022
[`hom‚wɝk]
n. 回家作業

▶The teacher gave us a lot of homework today.
老師今天給我們很多的回家作業。

honest [`anɪst] ◀Track 1023
adj. 誠實的；用正當手段取得的；坦白的

▶Be honest with me and tell me everything.
對我誠實地說出一切吧。

honesty [`anɪstɪ] ◀Track 1024
n. 誠實

▶Honesty is the best policy.
誠實為上策。

honey [`hʌnɪ] ◀Track 1025
n. 蜂蜜

▶He likes to eat French toast with honey on it.
他喜歡吃上面有淋上蜂蜜的法國吐司。

Hong Kong [hɔŋ-kɔŋ] ◀Track 1026
n. 香港

▶Chris Patten is the former governor of Hong Kong.
彭定康是前香港總督。

hop [hɑp] ◀Track 1027
v. （人）單足跳；（動物）齊足跳；跳舞

▶The kangaroo hopped across the grass.
袋鼠蹦跳穿越草地。

n. 跳躍

▶Frankfurt to Munich is just a short hop by plane.
法蘭克福到慕尼黑只是很短的一段飛行旅程。

相關片語 **job-hop** 跳槽

▶He job-hopped a lot until he finally found what he was passionate about.
他找到熱衷的事業前經常跳槽。

hope [hop] ◀€Track 1028
v. 希望

▶He hopes that he will see Alicia again.
他希望能再見到艾莉西亞。

n. 希望

▶They haven't given up hope that their child will be found.
他們還沒放棄小孩能被找到的希望。

horrible [`hɔrəb!] ◀€Track 1029
adj. 可怕的；糟透的

▶Why do some people do horrible things to their children?
為什麼有些父母對小孩做出可怕的事情？

horse [hɔrs] ◀€Track 1030
n. 馬

▶I learned how to ride a horse when I was a kid.
我小時候學會騎馬。

相關片語 **eat like a horse**
食量很大

▶Peter has a huge appetite. He eats like a horse.
彼得的食慾很好，他的食量驚人。

hospital [`hɑspɪt!] ◀€Track 1031
n. 醫院

▶My husband is a doctor in a general hospital.
我先生是綜合醫院的醫生。

host [host] ◀€Track 1032
n. 主人；東道主；主持人

▶The host of the banquet was very welcoming and nice to everybody.
晚宴的主持人對每位來賓都表達誠摯歡迎並態度和善。

v. 主持；主辦；以主人身份招待

▶Japan will be hosting the next Olympic Games.
日本將主辦下屆奧運會。

相關片語 **host city** 主辦城市

▶Taipei was the host city of the 2017 World Universiade.
台北是2017年世界大學運動會的主辦城市。

hot [hɑt] adj. ◀€Track 1033
熱的；辣的

▶It's too hot. Let's turn on the air-conditioner.
天氣太熱了，我們打開冷氣吧。

相關片語 **hot potato**
燙手山芋；棘手問題

▶The issue of racial discrimination is a hot potato.
種族歧視是棘手的議題。

hotel [ho`tɛl] ◀€Track 1034
n. 飯店

初級

▶We stayed at a four-star hotel in New York.
我們在紐約一家四星級飯店過夜。

hour [aʊr] ◀ Track 1035

n. 小時

▶I sleep eight hours a day.
我花了睡八個小時。

相關片語 **school hours**
上課時間

▶The average school hours here are thirty-five hours per week.
這裡每週上課時數是三十五個小時。

house [haʊs] ◀ Track 1036

n. 屋子；房子

▶He lives in a big house alone.
他獨自住在一間大房子裡。

v. 給……房子住；將……收藏在屋內

▶It is difficult to house all the homeless people.
要收容所有的遊民是很困難的事。

how [haʊ] ◀ Track 1037

adv. 怎樣；多麼；為何

▶How could he possibly know how much I earned?
他怎麼會知道我賺多少錢？

conj. 如何；怎麼

▶She wondered how George found her.
她想知道喬治是如何找到她的。

相關片語 **how come** 為何如此

▶How come I never heard of you since last time we met?
為什麼上次跟你見面後，就沒聽到你的消息了？

however [haʊˋɛvɚ] ◀ Track 1038

adv. 無論如何；不管用什麼方法

▶However hungry she is, she always follows table manners.
她無論有多餓，都保持良好的餐桌禮儀。

conj. 然而

▶I tried to explain. However, he wouldn't listen to me.
我盡可能地解釋了，然而他不願意聽我說。

how's [haʊz] ◀ Track 1039

abbr. 如何（ **how is** 的縮寫）

▶How's Johnny?
強尼還好嗎？

Hualian [ˋhwɑˋliɛn] ◀ Track 1040

n. 花蓮

▶Taroko National Park is located in Hualian.
太魯閣國家公園位於花蓮。

huge [hjudʒ] ◀ Track 1041

adj. 巨大的；龐大的

▶Polar bears are huge and powerful animals.
北極熊是體型龐大又強而有力的動物。

hum [hʌm] ◀ Track 1042

v. 發嗡嗡聲；發哼聲；哼曲子

▶He hummed to himself as he walked back home.
她在回家的路上邊走邊哼著曲子。

n. 哼聲；哼曲子的聲音；嗡嗡聲

▶There is an annoying hum when the amplifier is switched on.
擴音器一打開，就傳來惱人的嗡嗡聲。

human [`hjumən]　◀ Track 1043

adj. 人的；人類的；有人性的

▶ We are not perfect. After all, we are only human.
我們都不完美，畢竟我們只是凡人。

n. 人；人類

▶ Foxes are actually very shy animals. They don't attack humans.
狐狸事實上是很害羞的動物，牠們不會襲擊人類。

相關片語 **human nature**
人性；人類的天性

▶ It's human nature to be curious about others.
對別人感到好奇是人類的天性。

humble [`hʌmb!]　◀ Track 1044

adj. 謙遜的；卑微的；簡陋的

▶ An intellectual giant, he remains very humble.
他是知識界巨擘，但他仍然十分謙遜。

humid [`hjumɪd]　◀ Track 1045

adj. 潮濕的

▶ The room is humid and stuffy.
這個房間又濕又悶。

humor [`hjumɚ]　◀ Track 1046

n. 幽默

▶ My father has a very good sense of humor.
我爸爸很有幽默感。

humorous　◀ Track 1047

[`hjumərəs] **adj.** 幽默的；詼諧的

▶ His articles are very humorous.
他的文章很幽默。

hundred [`hʌndrəd]　◀ Track 1048

n. 一百

▶ The handbag costs me hundreds of dollars.
這個手提包花了我數百元。

pron. 一百個；一百

▶ The terrorist attack killed ten people, and injured hundreds.
這場恐攻造成十人死亡，數百人受傷。

adj. 一百的；一百個的

▶ There are one hundred students in this school.
學校裡有一百個學生。

相關片語 **a hundred and one**
許多

▶ I have a hundred and one things to do today.
我今天有許多事情要做。

hunger [`hʌŋgɚ]　◀ Track 1049

n. 饑餓；渴望

▶ I started to feel hunger around ten o'clock.
我十點的時候開始感到很餓。

hungry [`hʌŋgrɪ]　◀ Track 1050

adj. 餓的；饑餓的；渴望的

▶ He was so hungry that he could eat a horse.
他餓扁了，餓到可以把一匹馬吃下去。

hunt [hʌnt]　◀ Track 1051

v. 追獵；獵取；尋找；追求

▶ Nocturnal animals hunt at night.
夜行動物在夜間獵食。

初級

n. 打獵；搜索

▶The FBI agents are on the hunt for the serial killer.
美國聯邦調查局探員正在搜捕那個連續殺人犯。

hunter [`hʌntɚ]   ◀ Track 1052

n. 獵人；追求者；搜尋者

▶This polar bear is a good hunter.
這隻北極熊很擅長獵取食物。

相關片語 **job hunter**
求職者；找工作的人

▶She is a serious job hunter.
她很認真在找工作。

hurry [`hɝɪ]   ◀ Track 1053

v. 使趕快；催促；趕緊；匆忙

▶They hurried to the police station to pick up their three-year-old son.
他們急忙趕到警察局去接三歲的兒子。

n. 急忙；倉促

▶She left in such a hurry that she forgot to bring her lunch.
她太倉促離開，忘了帶午餐。

相關片語 **in a hurry** 迅速地

▶The police were in a hurry to hunt the criminal.
警察正急著搜捕罪犯。

hurt [hɝt]   ◀ Track 1054

v. 傷害；使疼痛；疼痛

▶My back hurts.
我的背很痛。

相關片語 **get hurt** 受傷

▶He had a traffic accident yesterday, and he got hurt.
他昨天發生交通事故而受傷。

husband [`hʌzbənd]   ◀ Track 1055

n. 丈夫；老公

▶My husband is a professor.
我的先生是教授。

▶ Ii

　　以下表格是全民英檢官方公告初級「聽、說、讀、寫」所須具備的能力，本書例句皆依此範疇特別設計，只要掃描右方QR code，就能搭配相對應的音軌，實現「眼耳並用」方式，刺激左腦的語言學習功能；同時也可使用本書附贈的紅膠片，將其置於單字上，一面記憶一面自我挑戰，達到雙倍的學習成果！

聽 ▶	能聽懂與日常生活相關的淺易談話，包含價格、時間及地點等。
說 ▶	能朗讀簡易文章、簡單地自我介紹，對熟悉的話題能以簡易英語對答，如問候、購物、問路等。
讀 ▶	可看懂與日常生活相關的淺易英文，並能閱讀路標、交通號誌、招牌、簡單菜單、時刻表及賀卡等。
寫 ▶	能寫簡單的句子及段落，如寫明信片、便條、賀卡及填表格等。對一般日常生活相關事物，能以簡短的文字敘述或說明。

初級

I [aɪ]　　　　　🔊 Track 1056
pron. 我

▶ I am Sam.
　我是山姆。

---

ice [aɪs]　　　　🔊 Track 1057
n. 冰

▶ The lake was frozen into ice.
　湖水結成了冰。

相關片語 **ice cream**
　　　　冰淇淋

▶ I like vanilla ice cream.
　我喜歡香草冰淇淋。

I'd [aɪd]　　　　🔊 Track 1058
abbr. 我會、我已（I would或I had 的 縮寫）

▶ I'd like a cheese cake and a cup of coffee, please.
　我要一個起士蛋糕和一杯咖啡，麻煩了。

---

idea [aɪˋdɪə]　　🔊 Track 1059
n. 想法；主意；計劃；打算；概念

▶ Your idea is fantastic.
　你的主意好極了。

相關片語 **have no idea**
　　　　不知道

▶ They have no idea how to talk to her.
　他們不知道要如何跟她溝通。

---

if [[ɪf]　　　　🔊 Track 1060
conj. 如果；是否

▶ If it's not rainy, we'll go hiking tomorrow.
　如果明天不下雨，我們就要去健走。

ignore [ɪg`nor]
◀Track 1061

v 不顧；忽視

▶The child was totally ignored by his parents.
孩子被他的雙親完全忽視。

I'll [aɪl]
◀Track 1062

abbr 我會（I will的縮寫）

▶I'll go to the prom with you.
我會跟你去畢業舞會。

ill [ɪl]
◀Track 1063

adj 病的；不健康的；壞的；邪惡的

▶She's been ill with cirrhosis.
她因肝硬化病了好一陣子。

I'm [aɪm]
◀Track 1064

abbr 我是（I am的縮寫）

▶I'm a bank clerk.
我是銀行行員。

image [`ɪmɪdʒ]
◀Track 1065

n 肖像；形象；印象；概念

▶The company's image was bad due to its tainted oil.
這家公司因為劣質油而形象很差。

imagine [ɪ`mædʒɪn]
◀Track 1066

v 想像

▶Can you imagine how it feels to be deaf?
你能想像失聰的感覺嗎？

impolite [ˌɪmpə`laɪt]
◀Track 1067

adj 無禮的

▶It was impolite of you to swear at her.
你講髒話罵她，這樣很無禮。

import
◀Track 1068

[`ɪmport] [ɪm`port]

n 進口；輸入；進口商品

▶The country imposed restrictions on some foreign imports.
這個國家對部分外國進口商品設有限制。

v 進口；輸入；引進

▶We import high quality cars from Germany.
我們從德國進口高品質的汽車。

importance
◀Track 1069

[ɪm`portns]

n 重要性

▶The case highlights the importance of equality and respect.
這個案子突顯平等與尊重的重要性。

important [ɪm`portnt]
◀Track 1070

adj 重要的

▶My son's birthday is the most important day of the year.
我兒子的生日是一年中最重要的日子。

impossible
◀Track 1071

[ɪm`pɑsəb!]

adj 不可能的

▶It was impossible to work in such a noisy environment.
要在這麼吵雜的環境工作幾乎是不可能的。

improve [ɪm`pruv]
◀Track 1072

v 進步；改進；改善

▶He attended the English class to improve his English.
他上英文班，以改善他的英文。

improvement

◀≣ Track 1073

[ɪm`pruvmənt]

n. 改進；改善

▶We try to serve our customers with the highest quality. However, there is still room for improvement.
我們盡力給予顧客最高品質的服務，然而還有改善的空間。

in [ɪn]

◀≣ Track 1074

prep. 在……裡；在……方面；穿著

▶Are you still in bed?
你還在睡覺嗎？

adv. 進；在裡頭

▶Can you take the boxes in for me?
你可以幫我把這些盒子拿進來嗎？

adj. 在裡面的；流行的

▶Neon lipsticks are in this season.
雙色漸變唇膏這季很當紅。

inch [ɪntʃ]

◀≣ Track 1075

n. 英吋

▶She had a cut an inch long below her lower lip.
她的下唇有一道一英寸長的傷口。

相關片語 **by inches**
差一點；險些

▶The car missed her by inches.
她險些被車子撞到。

include [ɪn`klud]

◀≣ Track 1076

v. 包含；包括

▶The bill includes your food and service charge.
帳單包括餐點和服務費。

including [ɪn`kludɪŋ]

◀≣ Track 1077

prep. 包含

▶Many singers will attend the Christmas concert, including Mariah Carey.
許多歌手都會參加聖誕音樂會，包括瑪麗亞‧凱莉。

income [ɪn`kʌm]

◀≣ Track 1078

n. 收入

▶She spent a large proportion of her income on clothes.
她大部分的收入都花在置裝。

increase [ɪn`kris]

◀≣ Track 1079

v. 增加；增長

▶The company's productivity increased by five percent each year.
公司成長率每年增加了百分之五。 。

n. 增加；增強；增長

▶The increase in production cost will lower the profit margin.
成本上升會降低毛利率。

independence

◀≣ Track 1080

[͵ɪndɪ`pɛndəns]

n. 獨立；自立

▶The United States declared independence from Great Britain in 1776.
美國在一七七六年宣布脫離大英國協，成為獨立的國家。

independent

◀≣ Track 1081

[͵ɪndɪ`pɛndənt]

adj. 獨立的

初級

143

▶She has been financially independent since she was sixteen.
她從十六歲起在經濟上就自食其力。

indicate [ˋɪndəˌket] ◀Track 1082
v. 指示；指出；表明

▶Her reply indicated that she didn't consider it a problem.
她的回應表示她並不認為這是個問題。

individual ◀Track 1083
[ˌɪndəˋvɪdʒʊəl]
adj. 個人的；個體的；特有的

▶The volunteer teachers try to help students on an individual basis.
一群志工老師試著以個案處理的方式幫助每個學生。

n. 個人；個體

▶Every individual should protect our environment by minimizing waste.
我們每個人都應減少廢棄物量，來保護我們的環境。

industry [ˋɪndəstrɪ] ◀Track 1084
n. 工業；企業；行業

▶The country's tourism industry has suffered considerably since the terrorist attacks.
這個國家的觀光業因為恐攻事件受到重創。

補充片語 **tourism industry**
觀光業

influence [ˋɪnflʊəns] ◀Track 1085
n. 影響；作用；影響力

▶He is a bad influence on his brothers.
他對弟弟們有很不好的影響。

v. 影響

▶The politician is good at influencing the public.
這名政治人物擅長對大眾施加影響。

相關片語 **have an influence on**
對……有影響

▶The advance in technology has a huge influence on our daily life.
科技的日新月益對我們的日常生活有重大的影響。

information ◀Track 1086
[ˌɪnfɚˋmeʃən]
n. 資料；資訊；消息

▶For further information, please visit our official website.
欲知詳情，請上我們的官方網站。

injury [ˋɪndʒərɪ] ◀Track 1087
n. 傷害；損害

▶She suffered awful injuries in the accident.
她在意外受到重傷。

ink [ˋɪnk] ◀Track 1088
n. 墨水

▶The felt-tip pen is running out of ink.
簽字筆快沒墨水了。

補充片語 **felt-tip pen**
簽字筆

insect [ˋɪnsɛkt] ◀Track 1089
n. 昆蟲

▶Mosquitoes, dragonflies, and butterflies are all insects.
蚊子、蜻蜓和蝴蝶都是昆蟲。

inside [`ɪn`saɪd] ◀≣Track 1090

prep. 在……裡面

▶Inside the box is a teddy bear.
箱子裡有一隻泰迪熊。

adv. 在裡面；往裡面

▶It was difficult for him to cope with the frustrations he felt inside.
對他來說，要處理內心的挫折感很困難。

n. 裡面；內部；內側

▶She cleaned the inside of the car.
她把車子內部清理乾淨。

相關片語 inside out
裡朝外地

▶He wore his shirt inside out.
他把襯衫穿反了。

insist [ɪn`sɪst] ◀≣Track 1091

v 堅持

▶He insisted on doing everything on his own.
他堅持親自做所有的事。

inspire [ɪn`spaɪr] ◀≣Track 1092

v 鼓舞；激勵

▶After her pleasant trip to Germany, she felt inspired to learn German.
她在德國愉快的旅遊經驗促使她學習德文。

instance [`ɪnstəns] ◀≣Track 1093

n. 例子；實例

▶He has many health problems, for instance, diabetes.
他有很多健康問題，例如糖尿病。

補充片語 for instance
舉例來說，例如

instant [`ɪnstənt] ◀≣Track 1094

adj. 立即的；緊迫的；速食的

▶Instant noodles are popular convenience food all over the world.
速食麵在全球是很受歡迎的方便食品。

補充片語 instant noodles
速食麵；泡麵

n. 剎那；頃刻

▶The facial cleanser leathers up in an instant.
洗面乳立即就能起泡。

補充片語 in an instant
傾刻間；剎那間

instrument ◀≣Track 1095
[`ɪnstrəmənt]

n. 儀器；器具；樂器

▶Piano is a kind of musical instrument.
鋼琴是樂器的一種。

intelligent ◀≣Track 1096
[ɪn`tɛlədʒənt]

adj. 有才智的；聰明的；有理性的

▶Mark is a highly intelligent young man.
馬克是很聰明的年輕人。

相關片語 AI robot
人工智慧機器人

▶The AI robot can assist doctors in diagnosing diseases based on a patient's symptoms.
這個人工智慧型機器人能協助醫師根據病人症狀診斷疾病。

補充說明 artificial intelligence (AI)
人工智慧

初級

interest [`ɪntərɪst] ◀≡ Track 1097

n. 興趣；愛好

▶She showed great interest in music.
她對音樂很感興趣。

v. 使感興趣；使發生興趣

▶Calculus has never really interested me.
我從沒有對微積分真正感興趣過。

interested ◀≡ Track 1098

[`ɪntərɪstɪd]

adj. 感興趣的

▶I'm interested in geometry.
我對幾何學很感興趣。

international ◀≡ Track 1099

[ˌɪntɚˋnæʃən!]

adj. 國際的

▶He is the CEO of an international company.
他是一家國際公司的執行長。

Internet [`ɪntɚˌnɛt] ◀≡ Track 1100

n. 網路

▶I learned about the bad news from the Internet.
我從網路得知這個壞消息。

interrupt [ˌɪntɚˋrʌpt] ◀≡ Track 1101

v. 打斷

▶She was very impatient and kept interrupting our conversation.
她很沒耐心，一直打斷我們的對話。

interview [`ɪntɚˌvju] ◀≡ Track 1102

n. 訪談；面談；接見

▶He had an interview for a job with a semi-conductor company.
他參加了一個半導體公司的求職面試。

v. 會見；訪談；採訪

▶The journalist is going to interview Rachel Weisz.
這名記者將要採訪瑞秋・懷茲。

into [`ɪntu] ◀≡ Track 1103

prep. 到……裡；進入到；成為

▶He got into bed after taking a shower.
他洗完澡後就上床睡覺了。

introduce ◀≡ Track 1104

[ˌɪntrəˋdjus]

v. 介紹

▶Let me introduce my friend Linda to you.
容我向你介紹我的朋友琳達。

invent [ɪnˋvɛnt] ◀≡ Track 1105

v. 發明

▶Sir Tim Berners-Lee invented the world wide web.
提姆・柏納・李爵士發明了網際網路。

investigate ◀≡ Track 1106

[ɪnˋvɛstəˌget]

v. 調查

▶The central government was investigating the problem of inner city violence.
中央政府在調查城市內的暴力問題。

invitation ◀≡ Track 1107

[ˌɪnvəˋteʃən]

n. 邀請；邀請函；請帖

▶ I received an invitation to a wedding feast scheduled next Monday.
我收到邀請參加下週一的婚宴。

invite [ɪn`vaɪt] ◀ Track 1108
v 邀請

▶ We invited her to a dinner party.
我們邀請她參加晚宴派對。

iron [`aɪən] ◀ Track 1109
n 鐵；鐵質；熨斗

▶ Red meat is a particularly rich source of iron.
紅肉含有特別豐富的鐵質。

v 用熨斗燙平

▶ It took me ten minutes to iron the dress.
燙這件洋裝花了我十分鐘。

相關片語 **have many irons in the fire**
同時有幾件事要辦

▶ I can't talk to you now. I have many irons in the fire.
我現在不能跟你聊天，我同時有好幾件事情要做。

is [ɪz] ◀ Track 1110
v 是（用於第三人稱單數現在式）

▶ He is a kind man.
他是個仁慈的男人。

island [`aɪlənd] ◀ Track 1111
n 島；島嶼

▶ The billionaire bought an island and built a castle on it.
億萬富翁買了一座島嶼並在上面蓋了一座城堡。

相關片語 **traffic island**
安全島

▶ The motorist hit the traffic island and got seriously injured.
機車騎士撞到安全島並受到重傷。

isn't [`ɪznt] ◀ Track 1112
abbr 不是（is not的縮寫）

▶ She isn't a secretary. She is a teacher.
她不是秘書，她是老師。

it [ɪt] ◀ Track 1113
pron 它；牠

▶ It's a very beautiful sweater.
這是件很漂亮的毛衣。

item [`aɪtəm] ◀ Track 1114
n 項目；品項

▶ There are five items on the agenda.
議事日程上有五個項目。

it'll [`ɪt!] ◀ Track 1115
abbr 它會（it will的縮寫）

▶ It'll be difficult to find another translator as good as Jane.
要找到像珍這麼能幹的譯者會很困難。

its [ɪts] ◀ Track 1116
pron 它的；牠的

▶ The cat hurt its claw.
貓咪弄傷了牠的爪子。

it's [ɪts] ◀ Track 1117
abbr 它是（it is的縮寫）

▶ It's my turn to do the presentation.
輪到我做報告了。

itself [ɪt`sɛlf] ◀ Track 1118
pron 它自己；牠自己

初級

▶The cat is grooming itself.
貓咪正在清理自己的毛。

I've [aɪv] ◀Track 1119

abbr. 我已、我有（**I have**的縮寫）

▶I've been to the United States ten years ago.
我十年前就去過美國了。

▶ Jj

以下表格是全民英檢官方公告初級「聽、說、讀、寫」所須具備的能力，本書例句皆依此範疇特別設計，只要掃描右方QR code，就能搭配相對應的音軌，實現「眼耳並用」方式，刺激左腦的語言學習功能；同時也可使用本書附贈的紅膠片，將其置於單字上，一面記憶一面自我挑戰，達到雙倍的學習成果！

聽 ▶	能聽懂與日常生活相關的淺易談話，包含價格、時間及地點等。
說 ▶	能朗讀簡易文章、簡單地自我介紹，對熟悉的話題能以簡易英語對答，如問候、購物、問路等。
讀 ▶	可看懂與日常生活相關的淺易英文，並能閱讀路標、交通號誌、招牌、簡單菜單、時刻表及賀卡等。
寫 ▶	能寫簡單的句子及段落，如寫明信片、便條、賀卡及填表格等。對一般日常生活相關事物，能以簡短的文字敘述或說明。

初級

jacket [`dʒækɪt]
Track 1120
n. 夾克；上衣

▶I put my keys in my jacket pocket.
我把鑰匙放在我的夾克口袋裡。

jam [dʒæm]
Track 1121
n. 果醬；堵塞

▶They were stuck in the traffic jam for three hours.
他們塞車塞了三小時。

相關片語 money for jam
能容易賺錢的工作

▶Selling ice cream is money for jam for him.
賣冰淇淋對他來說是能輕鬆賺錢的工作。

January [`dʒænjʊˌɛrɪ] =Jan.
Track 1122
n. 一月

▶We went to Canada last January.
我們去年一月去加拿大。

Japan [dʒə`pæn]
Track 1123
n. 日本

▶He is on a business trip in Japan.
他目前在日本出差。

Japanese [ˌdʒæpə`niz]
Track 1124
n. 日語；日本人

▶Can you speak Japanese?
你會說日語嗎？

adj. 日本的；日本人的；日語的

▶This Japanese drama was very popular in Asia.
這齣日劇在亞洲很受歡迎。

jazz [dʒæz]
Track 1125
n. 爵士樂；爵士舞

▶ She listened to the jazz on the radio.
她聽著廣播裡播放的爵士音樂。

jealous [`dʒɛləs]
🔊 Track 1126

adj. 妒忌的；吃醋的

▶ He is very jealous of his little sister.
他很妒忌他的妹妹。

jeans [dʒinz]
🔊 Track 1127

n. 牛仔褲

▶ She never wears jeans to work.
她從不穿牛仔褲上班。

jeep [dʒip]
🔊 Track 1128

n. 吉普車

▶ He crashed his jeep and luckily, he escaped the vehicle fire.
他撞毀了他的吉普車，不過幸好他逃出了著火的車子。

job [dʒɑb]
🔊 Track 1129

n. 工作；分內事情；成果

▶ He applied for a job as a computer programmer.
他應徵了一份電腦程式設計師的工作。

相關片語 **out of a job** 失業

▶ How long has he been out of the job?
他多久沒工作了？

jog [dʒɑg]
🔊 Track 1130

v. 慢跑

▶ She goes jogging every morning to keep fit.
她每早去慢跑，以保持健康。

join [dʒɔɪn]
🔊 Track 1131

v. 加入；參加

▶ He joined the army when he was twenty-four.
他二十四歲時加入陸軍。

joint [dʒɔɪnt]
🔊 Track 1132

adj. 聯合的；連接的；合辦的

▶ She holds joint citizenship in Canada and the United States.
她有加拿大和美國的雙重國籍身分。

n. 接合點；關節

▶ Her ankle joint is incredibly fragile.
她的腳踝關節非常地脆弱。

joke [dʒok]
🔊 Track 1133

n. 笑話；玩笑

▶ He cracked jokes to cheer her up.
他說笑話逗她開心。

v. 開玩笑

▶ He wasn't joking when he said he wanted a divorce.
他說要離婚，不是開玩笑的。

相關片語 **be no joke**
不是開玩笑的；不是鬧著玩

▶ Marriage is no joke. It is serious business.
結婚可不是鬧著玩的，是很正經的事。

journalist [`dʒɝ-nəlɪst]
🔊 Track 1134

n. 新聞工作者；新聞記者

▶ The journalist risked his life to bring the viewers the latest news in the war zone.
這名記者冒著生命危險，在戰區為觀眾報導最新消息。

joy [dʒɔɪ]
🔊 Track 1135

n. 歡樂；樂趣

▶She cried tears of joy when her boyfriend proposed to her.
她的男友向她求婚時，她喜極而泣。

judge [dʒʌdʒ]　🔊 Track 1136
n. 法官；裁判

▶The judge overruled her objection.
法官駁回她的異議。

v. 判決；判斷；評斷

▶You can't judge a book by its cover.
不要以貌取人。

judgement [ˋdʒʌdʒmənt]　🔊 Track 1137
n. 審判；判斷；判斷力；看法

▶Just listen and don't make judgement until you see the whole picture.
先傾聽，在了解事情全貌前先別論斷。

juice [dʒus]　🔊 Track 1138
n. 果汁

▶I had a glass of grape juice.
我喝了一杯葡萄汁。

juicy [ˋdʒusɪ]　🔊 Track 1139
adj. 多汁的

▶The organic orange is so sweet and juicy.
這顆有機柳丁真香甜多汁。

July [dʒuˋlaɪ]　🔊 Track 1140
n. 七月

▶The children are going to a summer camp in July.
孩子們七月要參加夏令營。

jump [dʒʌmp]　🔊 Track 1141
v. 跳

▶Stop jumping on the couch. You'll ruin the springs.
不要在沙發一直跳，你會把彈簧跳壞。

n. 跳躍；跳一步的距離

▶He woke up with a jump when he felt a cool hand on his forehead.
他在睡夢中感覺有隻冰冷的手摸著他的額頭而猛然跳起，驚醒了。

相關片語 **jump the couch**
行為突然失控

▶He jumped the couch and destroyed my smart phone.
他突然失控，把我的智慧型手機給毀了。

June [dʒun]　🔊 Track 1142
n. 六月

▶They are going to get married in June.
他們六月要結婚。

just [dʒʌst]　🔊 Track 1143
adv. 僅；只是；正好

▶I just finished my homework. Now I'm going to play basketball.
我剛寫完功課，現在要去打籃球。

相關片語 **just now** 剛才

▶She was talking to her friend on the phone just now.
她剛剛在跟朋友講電話。

初級

▶ Kk

　　以下表格是全民英檢官方公告初級「聽、說、讀、寫」所須具備的能力，本書例句皆依此範疇特別設計，只要掃描右方QR code，就能搭配相對應的音軌，實現「眼耳並用」方式，刺激左腦的語言學習功能；同時也可使用本書附贈的紅膠片，將其置於單字上，一面記憶一面自我挑戰，達到雙倍的學習成果！

聽 ▶	能聽懂與日常生活相關的淺易談話，包含價格、時間及地點等。
說 ▶	能朗讀簡易文章、簡單地自我介紹，對熟悉的話題能以簡易英語對答，如問候、購物、問路等。
讀 ▶	可看懂與日常生活相關的淺易英文，並能閱讀路標、交通號誌、招牌、簡單菜單、時刻表及賀卡等。
寫 ▶	能寫簡單的句子及段落，如寫明信片、便條、賀卡及填表格等。對一般日常生活相關事物，能以簡短的文字敘述或說明。

kangaroo [ˌkæŋgəˈru] ◀Track 1144
n. 袋鼠

▶Three people were injured after a driver swerved his car to avoid hitting a kangaroo on the road.
小轎車駕駛為了閃避撞到袋鼠，造成三人受傷。

Kaohsiung [ˈkɑʊˈʃɔŋ] ◀Track 1145
n. 高雄

▶My wife came from Kaohsiung.
我的妻子是高雄人。

keep [kip] ◀Track 1146
v. 保持；持有；繼續不斷

▶He kept silent until his lawyer came.
他在律師抵達前都不發一語。

相關片語	**keep sb. company**
	陪伴某人

My sister was lonely so I stayed and kept her company.
我妹妹覺得很孤單，所以我留下來陪她。

keeper [ˈkipɚ] ◀Track 1147
n. 飼養人；保管者；看守人

▶The keeper brought up the orphaned polar bear cub.
動物飼養員把小北極熊孤兒養大。

ketchup [ˈkɛtʃəp] ◀Track 1148
n. 番茄醬

▶Do you want ketchup with your French fries?
你的薯條要加番茄醬嗎？

key [ki] ◀Track 1149
n. 鑰匙；關鍵

▶Oops, I left my door keys in the office.
糟了，我把家門的鑰匙留在辦公室。

adj. 主要的；關鍵的

▶The SEAL captured a key figure of ISIS from Afghanistan.
美國海豹突擊隊在阿富汗捕獲極端組織伊斯蘭國的關鍵人物。

kick [kɪk]　◀Track 1150

v. 踢

▶He kicked the ball so powerfully that it flew over the wall.
他踢球力道之猛，以致於球飛到牆外。

n. 踢；一時的愛好或狂熱

▶He's on a science fiction kick at the moment.
他現在愛看科幻小說。

kid [kɪd]　◀Track 1151

n. 小孩；年輕人

▶She is the youngest of the three kids.
她是三個孩子中年紀最小的。

kill [kɪl]　◀Track 1152

v. 殺死；引起死亡

▶His brother was killed in the campus shooting spree.
他的哥哥在校園槍擊案中身亡。

相關片語 **kill time**
打發時間

▶He played his cell phone to kill time.
他玩手機來打發時間。

kilogram [`kɪlə‚græm]　◀Track 1153

n. 公斤

▶She weighed eighty kilograms two year ago.
她兩年前八十公斤。

kilometer [`kɪlə‚mitɚ]　◀Track 1154

n. 公里

▶She walked one kilometer to school every morning.
她每天早上步行一公里去上學。

kind [kaɪnd]　◀Track 1155

adj. 親切的；有同情心的

▶She is kind and generous person.
她是很仁慈、大方的人。

n. 種類

▶What kind of clothes are you looking for?
你在找什麼種類的衣服？

kindergarten [`kɪndɚ‚gɑrtn]　◀Track 1156

n. 幼稚園

▶She is a kindergarten teacher.
她是幼稚園老師。

king [kɪŋ]　◀Track 1157

n. 國王；某領域中最有勢力的人；大王

▶The king led a tragic life and died young.
這名國王過著悲劇性的人生，後來英年早逝。

kingdom [`kɪŋdəm]　◀Track 1158

n. 王國

▶The United Kingdom has been a democracy although the royal family continues to attract the public's attention.
英國是民主國家，然而皇室仍持續吸引著大眾的目光。

初級

kiss [kɪs]
◀Track 1159

v. 親吻

▶ After the bedtime story, he kissed the children goodnight.
他說完床邊故事後,吻了孩子向他們說晚安。

n. 親吻

▶ She leaned forward and gave her little son a kiss.
她向前傾並親了兒子一下。

相關片語 **blow sb. a kiss**
給某人飛吻

▶ She blew him a kiss as she boarded the train.
她上火車時給他一個飛吻。

kitchen [ˋkɪtʃɪn]
◀Track 1160

n. 廚房

▶ What's she doing in the kitchen?
她在廚房做什麼?

kite [kaɪt]
◀Track 1161

n. 風箏

▶ The children were flying kites in the park.
孩子在公園放風箏。

kitten [ˋkɪtn]
◀Track 1162

n. 小貓

▶ We adopted two kittens from the animal shelter.
我們在動物收容所領養兩隻小貓。

kitty [ˋkɪtɪ]
◀Track 1163

n. 小貓;貓咪

▶ Come here, kitty.
過來,小貓咪。

knee [ni]
◀Track 1164

n. 膝蓋;膝關節

▶ He knelt down on one knee and proposed to his girlfriend.
他單膝跪下向女友求婚。

相關片語 **on one's knees**
下跪的;跪著的

▶ He was on his knees begging for forgiveness.
他跪著乞求得到饒恕。

knife [naɪf]
◀Track 1165

n. 刀;刀子

▶ I can't use chopsticks. May I have a knife and fork?
我不會用筷子,可以給我刀叉嗎?

knock [nɑk]
◀Track 1166

v. 敲;擊打

▶ Someone is knocking on the door.
有人在敲門。

know [no]
◀Track 1167

v. 知道;認識

▶ Do you know his name?
你知道他的名字嗎?

knowledge [ˋnɑlɪdʒ]
◀Track 1168

n. 知識;學問;了解

▶ I have only a limited knowledge of Japanese.
我對日語所知有限。

相關片語 **common knowledge**
常識;眾所周知的事

▶ It is common knowledge that trans fats are bad for health.
反式脂肪對健康有害是常識。

koala [ko`ɑlə]　　🔊 Track 1169
n. 無尾熊

▶Koalas eat mainly eucalyptus leaves.
無尾熊主食是尤加利樹葉。

Korea [ko`riə]　　🔊 Track 1170
n. 韓國

▶TWICE is a famous girl group in Korea.
TWICE是韓國知名的女子團體。

Korean [ko`riən]　　🔊 Track 1171
adj. 韓國的；韓語的；韓國人的

▶My mother likes to watch Korean dramas.
我媽媽喜歡看韓劇。

n. 韓語；韓國人

▶He can speak Korean fluently.
他能說流暢的韓語。

KTV [ke-ti-vi]　　🔊 Track 1172
n. 卡拉OK

▶We celebrated our friend's birthday at a KTV pub.
我們在KTV慶祝朋友的生日。

初級

▶ Ll

　　以下表格是全民英檢官方公告初級「聽、說、讀、寫」所須具備的能力，本書例句皆依此範疇特別設計，只要掃描右方QR code，就能搭配相對應的音軌，實現「眼耳並用」方式，刺激左腦的語言學習功能；同時也可使用本書附贈的紅膠片，將其置於單字上，一面記憶一面自我挑戰，達到雙倍的學習成果！

聽 ▶	能聽懂與日常生活相關的淺易談話，包含價格、時間及地點等。
說 ▶	能朗讀簡易文章、簡單地自我介紹，對熟悉的話題能以簡易英語對答，如問候、購物、問路等。
讀 ▶	可看懂與日常生活相關的淺易英文，並能閱讀路標、交通號誌、招牌、簡單菜單、時刻表及賀卡等。
寫 ▶	能寫簡單的句子及段落，如寫明信片、便條、賀卡及填表格等。對一般日常生活相關事物，能以簡短的文字敘述或說明。

lack [læk]　◀ Track 1173

n. 缺少；不足

▶His major problem is a lack of confidence.
他最大的問題是缺乏自信。

v. 缺乏，沒有

▶They lacked three staff members due to insufficient budget.
他們因為預算不足，短缺三名員工。

lady [`ledɪ]　◀ Track 1174

n. 女士；小姐

▶Ladies and gentlemen, welcome to the Disneyland.
各位女士先生，歡迎來到迪士尼樂園。

相關片語 **bag lady**
　　　　拾荒婦人；流浪婦女

▶She gave a few coins to the bag lady sleeping on the street.
她給一個睡在街頭的拾荒婦人一些銅板。

ladybird [`ledɪ,bɝd]　◀ Track 1175

n. 瓢蟲（英）

▶We found a ladybird in our school garden.
我們在學校庭園看到一隻瓢蟲。

ladybug [`ledɪ,bʌg]　◀ Track 1176

n. 瓢蟲（美）

▶The children were counting the spots on the back of a ladybug.
孩子們在數瓢蟲身上的斑點數目。

lake [lek]　◀ Track 1177

n. 湖

▶The hotel is situated near a lake.
旅館位在一座湖邊。

lamb [læm]　◀ Track 1178

n. 小羊；羔羊

▶They roasted some lamb for supper.
他們晚餐吃烤羊肉。

lamp [læmp]
◀ Track 1179

n. 燈

▶She just bought a desktop lamp.
她剛買了一個桌燈。

相關片語 **floor lamp**
落地燈

▶The floor lamp gives out the right amount of light.
這個落地燈的燈光很充足。

land [lænd]
◀ Track 1180

n. 陸地；土地

▶They bought a plot of land to build a house.
他們買了一塊土地蓋房子。

v. 登陸；降落

▶We will land in Frankfurt at 6:00 A.M.
我們將於早上六點飛抵法蘭克福。

lane [len]
◀ Track 1181

n. 小路；巷；車道；跑道

▶He lives on the Lark Lane in Liverpool.
他住在利物浦的雲雀街。

language
◀ Track 1182

[`læŋgwɪdʒ]

n. 語言

▶Audrey can speak five languages fluently.
奧黛莉能流暢地說五種語言。

相關片語 **first language**
母語

▶German is my first language.
德文是我的母語。

Lantern Festival
◀ Track 1183

[`læntən-`fɛstəv]

n. 元宵節

▶We eat sticky rice balls on Lantern Festival.
元宵節這天我們吃湯圓。

lap [læp]
◀ Track 1184

n. （操場的）一圈；（泳池的）一趟來回

▶He was passed by several runners in the final lap and finished sixth.
他在最後一圈被幾名選手超出，最終得了第六名。

large [lɑrdʒ]
◀ Track 1185

adj. 大的

▶He came from a large family. He has eight siblings.
他來自大家庭，有八個兄弟姊妹。

last [læst]
◀ Track 1186

adj. 最後的；上一個的

▶He was the last one to arrive at the seminar.
他是最後一個到研討會的人。

adv. 最後

▶Nick finished last in the race.
尼克在比賽中倒數第一。

n. 最後

▶He fought the disease to the last.
他一直到最後都在對抗病魔。

相關片語 **at last**
終於

▶I finished my dissertation at last.
我終於把論文寫完了。

初級

late [let]
🔊 Track 1187

adj. 晚的；遲的

▶I was late for work this morning due to traffic jam.
我今早因交通阻塞上班遲到。

adv. 晚地

▶She arrived late and was punished heavily.
她遲到而且被重重地懲罰。

later [`letə]
🔊 Track 1188

adv. 較晚地；以後

▶"See you later, alligator." "In a while, crocodile."
「待會見。」「再見了。」

補充片語 call back 回電話

latest [`letɪst]
🔊 Track 1189

adj. 最新的；最近的；最遲的

▶Her latest movie is remarkable.
她的最新電影真精彩。

laugh [læf]
🔊 Track 1190

v. 笑

▶People laugh at me when I sing.
我唱歌時，大家都會嘲笑我。

補充片語 laugh at 嘲笑

n. 笑；笑聲；樂趣；令人發笑的人事物

▶He gave a hearty laugh.
他爽朗地笑了。

law [lɔ]
🔊 Track 1191

n. 法律

▶Stealing is against the law.
偷竊是觸犯法律的。

lawyer [`lɔjə]
🔊 Track 1192

n. 法律

▶She hired a lawyer to start a divorce.
她雇了一名律師幫她處理離婚。

lay [le]
🔊 Track 1193

v. 放；鋪設；產卵

▶The diplomat laid a good foundation for the relations between the two countries.
外交官為兩國關係打下良好的基礎。

lazy [`lezɪ]
🔊 Track 1194

adj. 懶惰的；懶洋洋的

▶He's is such a lazy bone.
他真是個懶惰蟲。

相關片語 lazy Susan
餐桌上的圓轉盤

▶We bought a lazy Susan for our son and his family.
我們買了一個餐桌圓轉盤送給兒子一家人。

lead [lid]
🔊 Track 1195

v. 帶領；引導；導向；領先

▶He is the right person to lead the team.
他是帶領這個團隊的合適人選。

n. 指導；榜樣；帶領

▶We followed his lead and put his ideas into action.
我們跟隨他的帶領並把他的想法付諸實現。

補充片語 follow one's lead
效法某人；以某人為榜樣

leader [`lidə]
🔊 Track 1196

n. 領導者；領袖

▶Cathy is a cheer leader.
凱西是啦啦隊長。

相關片語 **class leader**
班長

▶He was the class leader and an excellent basketball player.
他是班長又是優秀的籃球員。

leadership [ˈlidəˌʃɪp] ◀Track 1197
n. 領袖特質

▶Under his outstanding leadership, the company has become a leader in the semi-conductor industry.
在他的傑出領導之下，公司已成為半導體業的龍頭。

leaf [lif] ◀Track 1198
n. 葉子

▶The tree is thick with leaves.
這顆樹木的葉子很濃密。

learn [lɝn] ◀Track 1199
v. 學習

▶I started learning English when I was in junior high school.
我在國中時開始學英文。

least [list] ◀Track 1200
adv. 最少；最不

▶Heavy metal is the kind of music she likes the least.
重金屬音樂是她最不喜歡的音樂類型。

adj. 最少的；最不重要的

▶He is the least racist person I know.
他是我認識的人中最沒有種族偏見的人。

pron. 最少；最少的東西

▶We got the least, but we share it.
我們得到的最少，但我們會互相分享。

n. 最少；最小

▶It's the least I can do.
我只是盡一點微薄之力。

相關片語 **at least** 至少

▶The ticket will cost at least two hundred dollars.
這張票最少要花二百元。

leave [liv] ◀Track 1201
v. 離開；留下

▶It's time to leave, or we'll miss the train.
我們該離開了，不然會錯過火車。

n. 休假

▶She's on maternity leave.
她請育嬰假。

補充片語 **on leave** 休假

left [lɛft] ◀Track 1202
adj. 左邊的

▶Your left eye just twitched.
你的左眼皮剛剛抽動了一下。

n. 左邊；左側

▶The guy sitting on my left is a model.
坐在我左邊的男生是個模特兒。

adv. 向左地

▶Turn left at the next intersection, and you'll see the metro station right there.
在下一個十字路口左轉，你就會看到捷運站。

leg [lɛg] ◀Track 1203
n. 腳

▶She broke her leg after falling down from the stairs.
她從樓梯摔下來跌斷了一條腿。

初級

相關片語 show a leg 起床

▶It's time to show a leg.
趕快起床。

legal [`lig!]
🔈Track 1204

adj. 合法的

▶Ivory trading is not legal in Taiwan.
象牙交易在台灣是不合法的行為。

lemon [`lɛmən]
🔈Track 1205

n. 檸檬

▶Squeeze the lemon to make some lemon juice.
擠顆檸檬來做檸檬汁。

lemonade
🔈Track 1206

[ˌlɛmən`ed]

n. 檸檬水

▶I'd like one glass of lemonade, please.
我要一杯檸檬水，麻煩了。

lend [lɛnd]
🔈Track 1207

v. 借予；借出

▶Could you lend me one hundred dollars? I forgot to bring my wallet.
我可以跟你借一百元嗎？我忘了帶錢包。

length [lɛŋθ]
🔈Track 1208

n. （距離或時間的）長度

▶The ship is 15 meters in length.
這艘船的長度有十五米。

leopard [`lɛpɚd]
🔈Track 1209

n. 花豹

▶I can't tell the difference between a jaguar and a leopard.
我分不清楚美洲豹和花豹的差別。

less [lɛs]
🔈Track 1210

adv. 較少地；不如

▶She walks less quickly than she usually dose.
她走的速度比平常慢。

adj. 較少的

▶We spent less time in the game.
我們玩遊戲的時間較少。

相關片語 more or less
或多或少；多少有一點；差不多

▶The luggage is sixteen kilos, more or less.
行李大約是十六公斤。

lesson [`lɛsn]
🔈Track 1211

n. 課；教訓

▶To become an actress, she took acting lessons during the weekend.
為了成為女演員，她週末去上表演課。

相關片語 learn one's lesson
學到教訓

▶Joel learned his lesson after taking a selfie at a voting station.
喬伊在投票所裡自拍後，學到教訓了。

let [lɛt]
🔈Track 1212

v. 使；讓

▶Who let the dog out?
誰把狗放出來的？

let's [lɛts]
🔈Track 1213

abbr. 讓我們來……（**let us**的縮寫）

▶Let's go grab a bite.
我們去吃個點心吧。

letter [`lɛtɚ] ◀Track 1214
n. 信

▶I sent a letter and some photos to my grandmother.
我寄了一封信和一些照片給祖母。

lettuce [`lɛtɪs] ◀Track 1215
n. 萵苣

▶She cooked the chicken soup with some tomato and lettuce.
她煮雞湯並加了番茄和萵苣在湯裡。

level [`lɛv!] ◀Track 1216
n. 水平面；程度；級別

▶She speaks English with a high level of fluency.
她的英文流暢度很高。

adj. 水平的；同高度的；同程度的；
　　　平穩冷靜的

▶She was in rage, but her voice remained level.
她生氣了，不過語氣保持很平緩。

library [`laɪˌbrɛrɪ] ◀Track 1217
n. 圖書館

▶I went to the library to check out some books.
我去圖書館借了一些書。

lick [lɪk] ◀Track 1218
v. 舔

▶She licked the honey off her fingers.
她把手指上的蜂蜜舔乾淨。

n. 舔一口

▶I let my son have a lick of the popsicle.
我讓我兒子舔一口冰棒。

lid [lɪd] ◀Track 1219
n. 蓋子

▶Can you put a lid on the fry pan for me?
你可以幫我給煎鍋蓋上蓋子嗎？

lie [laɪ] ◀Track 1220
v. 躺

▶He laid in bed and fell asleep.
他躺在床上睡著了。

n. 謊言

▶He told a lie when he said he liked my father.
他騙我說他喜歡我爸爸。

v. 說謊；欺騙

▶She's lying again.
她又在說謊了。

相關片語 **white lie**
　　　　善意的謊言

▶Telling white lies may not be a good solution to our problems.
善意的謊言可能不是解決我們問題最好的方式。

life [laɪf] ◀Track 1221
n. 生命；性命；生活（狀態）；人生

▶Life is transient.
人生是短暫的。

相關片語 **walk of life**
　　　　行業；階層

▶People from all walks of life are very concerned about the terrible incident.
各行各業的人都很關切這起可怕的事件。

初級

lift [lɪft]
v. 舉起；提高；升起
▶He lifted the table with ease.
他很輕鬆地抬起了桌子。

n. 提；升；振奮；（英）電梯；順便搭載
▶We took the lift to the tenth floor.
我們搭電梯到第十樓。

相關片語 **give sb. a lift**
順便搭載某人一程
▶Let me give you a lift to your office.
我順便載你去辦公室。

◀ Track 1222

light [laɪt]
n. 燈；光線
▶Turn off the lights before you go to sleep.
你睡覺前要把燈關掉。

v. 照亮；點燃
▶You light up my life.
你點亮了我的生命。

adj. 亮的；淺色的
▶It's not light enough to take a good photo here.
這裡光線不夠亮，拍照不好看。

adv. 輕便地；少負擔地
▶She always travels light.
她旅行總是很輕便。

◀ Track 1223

lightning [`laɪtnɪŋ]
n. 閃電
▶Lightning often occurs suddenly.
閃電通常發生得很突然。

◀ Track 1224

like [laɪk]
prep. 像；如；和……一樣
▶You look just like your father.
你長得跟你爸爸好像。

◀ Track 1225

v. 喜歡
▶I like Phoebe because she is a such darling.
我很喜歡菲比，因為她很討人喜歡。

likely [`laɪklɪ]
adj. 很可能的
▶It's highly likely that Leo will win the competition.
里歐非常有可能會贏得比賽。

adv. 很可能地
▶He will likely need surgery.
他有可能要動手術。

◀ Track 1226

lily [`lɪlɪ]
n. 百合；百合花
▶She planted lilies and a rowan tree in the garden.
她在庭院種了百合花和山梨樹。

◀ Track 1227

limit [`lɪmɪt]
v. 限制
▶Can you limit your speech to fifteen minutes?
你可以把演說時間控制在十五分鐘之內嗎？

n. 限制；界限；限度
▶The time limit of the test is one hour.
測驗時間限定為一小時。

◀ Track 1228

line [laɪn]
n. 線；排；路線；行列
▶He was very old, and his face was covered with lines and spots.
他年紀很大，臉上布滿皺紋和斑點。

v. 排隊
▶We lined up to buy the flaky scallion pancake.
我們排隊要買蔥抓餅。

◀ Track 1229

相關片語 **cut in line**
插隊

▶A young girl was trying to cut in line, and a middle-aged woman behind her was very upset.
一個年輕女孩想插隊,排在後面的女士感到很不高興。

link [lɪŋk]　　Track 1230

n. 環節;連結

▶Studies shows that there is a link between diet and diabetes.
研究顯示,飲食與糖尿病有關聯。

v. 結合;連接;勾住

▶The UN report explains how greenhouse gas emission is linked to climate change.
聯合國報告解釋溫室氣體的排放如何與氣候變遷有關。

lion [`laɪən]　　Track 1231

n. 獅子

▶Lions are social animals.
獅子是群居動物。

lip [lɪp]　　Track 1232

n. 嘴唇

▶The actress is famous for her bee-stung lips.
這名女演員以豐唇而聞名。

liquid [`lɪkwɪd]　　Track 1233

n. 液體

▶Juice is a kind of liquid.
果汁是液體的一種。

adj. 液體的;流動的

▶He had few liquid assets since most of his wealth was tied up in stock market.
他的流動資金很少,因為大部分財產都從投到股市裡了。

list [lɪst]　　Track 1234

n. 名冊;清單

▶My wife gave me a shopping list and asked me to buy some groceries for her.
我妻子給我一份購物單,要我幫她買些雜貨。

v. 列舉

▶The professor listed some reading materials on the slide.
教授在投影片上列出了一些的閱讀教材。

相關片語 **on the danger list**
病危

▶He was on the danger list, but is much better now.
他一度病危,不過現在好多了。

listen [`lɪsn]　　Track 1235

v. 聽

▶I like to listen to classical music.
我喜歡聽古典樂。

listener [`lɪsnɚ]　　Track 1236

n. 傾聽者;收聽者;(一位)聽眾

▶A psychiatrist needs be a good listener.
心理醫生必須是一個好的傾聽者。

liter [`litɚ]　　Track 1237
=litre （英式英文）

n. 公升

初級

▶The athlete drinks at least three liters of water each day due to his intensive training.
運動員因為密集訓練，每天至少要喝三公升的水。

little [ˈlɪtl̩]

adj. 小的；少的；年幼的 ◀≋Track 1238

▶It took him only a little while to finish his dissertation.
他只花了很少的時間，就完成了論文。

pron. 沒有多少；少許；一點（東西）

▶When she met Harry, she knew little about him.
她和哈利見面時，對他所知不多。

adv. 少；毫不

▶He was a little bit anxious about the exam result.
他有點擔心考試結果。

live [lɪv]

v. 居住；生活 ◀≋Track 1239

▶My parents live in the United States, and I live in Australia.
我的雙親住在美國，而我住在澳洲。

loaf [lof]

n. 一條 ◀≋Track 1240

▶I bought a loaf of bread and ate half of it.
我買了一條麵包，吃掉了半條。

local [ˈlokl̩]

adj. 地方性的；當地的；本地的 ◀≋Track 1241

▶We bought our produce from the local farmer's market.
我們在當地的農民市集買農產品。

n. 當地居民；本地人

▶The restaurant is very popular with both locals and tourists.
這家餐廳很受當地人和遊客的喜愛。

locate [loˈket]

v. 使……座落於；找出……所在位置；定居 ◀≋Track 1242

▶The Empire State Building is located in New York.
帝國大廈位於紐約。

lock [lɑk]

v. 鎖；鎖住 ◀≋Track 1243

▶He locked his car using a remote.
他用遙控器把車子鎖好。

n. 鎖

▶She put a gym bag in a locker and used a combination lock to secure it.
她把運動袋放進置物櫃並用號碼鎖把櫃子鎖起來。

log [lɔg]

n. 原木；木料 ◀≋Track 1244

▶He stumbled on a log and fell on the ground.
他被木頭絆倒，跌落在地上。

相關片語 **sleep like a log**
睡得很熟

▶After a busy day, she slept like a log.
她忙了一天，晚上睡得很熟。

London [ˈlʌndən]

n. 倫敦 ◀≋Track 1245

▶The company's headquarters is in London.
公司總部在倫敦。

lone [lon]　🔊 Track 1246

adj. 孤單的；無伴的；單一的

▶She was a lone voice arguing against the amendment of the law.
她是唯一反對修法的人。

相關片語 **lone wolf**
獨來獨往的人

▶The suspect is a lone wolf and lives a peripatetic life.
嫌犯是個獨行俠，過著居無定所的生活。

lonely [`lonlɪ]　🔊 Track 1247

adj. 孤單的；寂寞的

▶He felt very lonely after divorce.
他離婚後感到很孤單。

long [lɔŋ]　🔊 Track 1248

adj. 長的；長久的

▶It was a long movie.
這部電影好長。

adv. 長久地

▶The clearance sale was long due.
這個清倉拍賣早已過期。

相關片語 **long face**
臭臉；難過、失望、鬱悶的表情

▶What happened? Why do you have a long face?
發生什麼事了？你為什麼看起來很哀傷？

look [lʊk]　🔊 Track 1249

v. 看；看著；看起來

▶He looked at the photo and smiled.
他看著照片，露出微笑。

n. 看；臉色；外表；面容

▶He had another look for his cell phone, but still couldn't find it.
他又找了一遍手機，但還是沒找到。

相關片語 **look after**
照顧；照看

▶They looked after the baby under the doctor's supervision.
他們在醫師的監督之下照顧小寶寶。

lose [luz]　🔊 Track 1250

v. 丟；失去；輸掉；損失

▶He lost his laptop.
他遺失了筆電。

相關片語 **lose heart**
氣餒

▶Michael never loses heart when he is confronted with difficulties.
麥可面對困難時從不氣餒。

loser [`luzə]　🔊 Track 1251

n. 失敗者；失主

▶The loser of the game claimed he did not make a real effort when playing the game.
比賽的輸家表示他參賽過程並沒有全力衝刺。

相關片語 **bad loser**
輸不起的人

▶Alice was a bad loser. She lost her temper and blamed everyone except herself.
艾莉絲是個輸不起的人，她發脾氣而且到處責怪別人就是不怪自己。。

補充片語 **lose one's temper**
發脾氣

loss [lɔs]　🔊 Track 1252

n. 損失；喪失

▶His passing was a great loss to our nation.
他的離世對我們的國家是很大的損失。

初級

lot [lɑt]
◀€Track 1253

n. 很多；一塊地

▶She has a lot of friends because she is nice and thoughtful.
她因為個性善良體貼，而有很多的朋友。

pron. 很多

▶It cost a lot of money to raise a big family.
要養活一個大家庭要花很多錢。

adv. 很多地；非常

▶We like the movie a lot.
我們很喜歡這部電影。

loud [laʊd]
◀€Track 1254

adj. 大聲的

▶Could you turn down the volume? The TV is too loud.
電視太大聲了。可以把音量轉小聲一點嗎？

補充片語 turn down
轉小聲

adv. 大聲地

▶Could you speak a little louder? It's noisy here.
你可以說大聲一點嗎？這裡很吵雜。

love [lʌv]
◀€Track 1255

v. 愛；喜好

▶I love my children so much.
我好愛我的小孩。

n. 愛

▶His love for his wife is still strong after thirty years of marriage.
走過三十年的婚姻後，他對妻子的愛仍很堅定。

相關片語 in love
相愛

▶Although they said they were just friends, we could tell that they were obviously in love.
雖然他們說彼此只是朋友，我們都看得出來他們很明顯地是陷入愛河了。

lovely [ˋlʌvlɪ]
◀€Track 1256

adj. 可愛的；令人愉快的；美好的

▶She is a lovely girl with a beautiful heart.
她人美心也美。

lover [ˋlʌvɚ]
◀€Track 1257

n. 戀人；情人（尤指男性）；愛好者

▶They are avid animal lovers.
他們是強烈愛好動物的人士。

low [lo]
◀€Track 1258

adj. 低的；矮的；情緒低落的

▶The ceiling in the house is too low. I just hit my head on it.
房子的天花板太低了，我的頭剛撞到天花板。

相關片語 in low water
手頭拮据

▶He lost his money in the stock market, so he is in low water.
他在股市賠錢，所以手頭很拮据。

lower [ˋloɚ]
◀€Track 1259

adj. 較低的；下等的；下層的

▶Her lower lip was stung by a bee.
她的下唇被蜜蜂螫到了。

v. 放下；降低

▶They lowered the man into a wheelchair.
他們把男人放下到輪椅上。

luck [lʌk]
◀⧼ Track 1260

n. 運氣；好運

▶ The best of luck with your interview.
祝你面試順利。

相關片語 **hard luck**
真不走運

▶ He failed to turn the tide. Hard luck.
他沒能扭轉情勢。真是不走運。

....

lucky [`lʌkɪ]
◀⧼ Track 1261

adj. 幸運的

▶ He was lucky to be alive after the air crash.
他很幸運在空難中能倖存。

相關片語 **lucky man**
幸運兒

▶ When Jennifer said yes, he felt he was the luckiest man in the world.
珍妮佛答應他的求婚時，他覺得自己是全世界最幸運的男人了。

....

lunch [lʌntʃ]
◀⧼ Track 1262

n. 午餐

▶ I had spaghetti for lunch.
我午餐吃義大利麵。

....

初級

▶ Mm

以下表格是全民英檢官方公告初級「聽、說、讀、寫」所須具備的能力，本書例句皆依此範疇特別設計，只要掃描右方QR code，就能搭配相對應的音軌，實現「眼耳並用」方式，刺激左腦的語言學習功能；同時也可使用本書附贈的紅膠片，將其置於單字上，一面記憶一面自我挑戰，達到雙倍的學習成果！

聽 ▶	能聽懂與日常生活相關的淺易談話，包含價格、時間及地點等。
說 ▶	能朗讀簡易文章、簡單地自我介紹，對熟悉的話題能以簡易英語對答，如問候、購物、問路等。
讀 ▶	可看懂與日常生活相關的淺易英文，並能閱讀路標、交通號誌、招牌、簡單菜單、時刻表及賀卡等。
寫 ▶	能寫簡單的句子及段落，如寫明信片、便條、賀卡及填表格等。對一般日常生活相關事物，能以簡短的文字敘述或說明。

ma'am [ˋmæəm]　◀ Track 1263
n. 閣下；女士（對女性的禮貌稱謂）

▶How can I help you, ma'am?
女士好，有我可以幫忙的地方嗎？

machine [məˋʃin]　◀ Track 1264
n. 機器

▶I don't know how to use the new washing machine.
我不知道怎麼用這台新的洗衣機。

mad [mæd]　◀ Track 1265
adj. 發狂的；惱火的

▶He was quite mad when people laughed at his girlfriend.
別人嘲笑他的女友時，他感到很生氣。

magazine [ˌmægəˋzin]
n. 雜誌　◀ Track 1266

▶She's a columnist of a magazine.
她是一本雜誌的專欄作家。

magic [ˋmædʒɪk]　◀ Track 1267
adj. 魔術的；有魔力的；不可思議的

▶The performance is magic. I totally love it.
這場表演真是不可思議。我非常喜歡。

n. 魔法；巫術；神奇的力量

▶What's his magic to make the show so appealing?
他到底有什麼魅力，讓這個節目這麼受歡迎？

magician [məˋdʒɪʃən]　◀ Track 1268
n. 魔術師

▶There will be a magician at the dinner party.
晚宴派對會有一位魔術師。

mail [mel]
◀️Track 1269

n. 郵件

▶You've got mail.
　你有郵件。

v. 郵寄

▶I spent the entire morning mailing.
　我花了一個早上寄信。

相關片語 **junk mail**
　　大批寄出的廣告郵件；垃圾郵件

▶How much junk mail do you get each day?
　你每天都收到多少垃圾郵件？

mailman [`mel,mæn]
◀️Track 1270
=postman **n.** 郵差

▶My dog always growls at and chases the mailman.
　我的小狗總是對郵差亂叫而且追著他跑。

main [men]
◀️Track 1271

adj. 主要的

▶The main idea of the story is about the battle between good and evil.
　這個故事的主題是正義與邪惡之間的對抗。

maintain [men`ten]
◀️Track 1272

v. 維持；維修；保養；繼續

▶The president is keen to maintain her popularity, but she fails horribly.
　總統很積極要維持民調，但她徹底失敗了。

major [`medʒɚ]
◀️Track 1273

adj. 主要的；較多的；主修的

▶The castle is a major tourist destination in Germany.
　這座城堡是德國主要的觀光景點。

n. 主修科目；主修學生

▶My major is French.
　我的主修是法文。

v. 主修

▶He majored in economics at Stanford.
　他在史丹佛大學主修經濟學。

make [mek]
◀️Track 1274

v. 做；製造；使

▶She made a chocolate cake for her boyfriend.
　她為男友做了一個巧克力蛋糕。

相關片語 **make it**
　　成功；及時趕到

▶I have every confidence that you can make it.
　我非常有信心你能辦得到。

male [mel]
◀️Track 1275

adj. 男性的；雄的；公的

▶Male lions have mane.
　公獅有鬃毛。

n. 男子；雄性動物

▶The male of the species is not so aggressive.
　這個物種的雄性攻擊性沒有那麼強。

mall [mɔl]
◀️Track 1276

n. 大規模購物中心

▶The mall was teeming with shoppers during holidays.
　這間購物中心在假日人潮眾多。

相關片語 **shopping mall**
　　購物中心；大商場

▶The shopping mall is situated in the middle of town.
　購物商城位在市中心。

初級

man [mæn] ◀Track 1277
n. （成年的）男人；人

▶The man in the blue jacket is her husband.
穿藍夾克的男士是她的先生。

相關片語 **family man**
有家室的男人；愛家的男人

▶A famous chef, Steve is a family man.
身為名廚，史蒂夫是愛家的男人。

manager [`mænɪdʒɚ] ◀Track 1278
n. 經理；經理人；負責人

▶He is the general manager of an international company.
他是一間國際公司的總經理。

Mandarin ◀Track 1279
[`mændərɪn] **n.** 中文

▶He can speak Mandarin very well.
他的中文說得很好。

mango [`mæŋgo] ◀Track 1280
n. 芒果

▶Mango is my favorite fruit.
芒果是我最愛的水果。

manner [`mænɚ] ◀Track 1281
n. 態度；方式；禮貌；舉止

▶The lady has very good table manners.
這位淑女擁有良好的餐桌禮儀。

補充片語 **table manner**
餐桌禮儀

many [`mɛnɪ] ◀Track 1282
adj. 很多的；許多的

▶How many languages can you speak?
你會說幾種語言？

pron. 許多人；很多（事物）

▶They're not interested in acquiring new machines because they already got too many of them.
他們沒興趣添購新機器，因為他們已經有很多了。

map [mæp] ◀Track 1283
n. 地圖

▶You can use Google map to find out where the restaurant is.
你可以用谷歌地圖找到那家餐廳的位置。

相關片語 **on the map**
重要的；出名的

▶The ancient paintings found in the basement of the church put the village on the map.
這座教堂地下室因為發現了古畫，讓這個小村莊出名了。

mark [mɑrk] ◀Track 1284
v. 做記號；打分數

▶The teacher was busy marking exam papers.
老師忙著改考卷。

n. 記號；符號

▶She has a brown birth mark on her arm.
她的手臂上有個棕色的胎記。

補充片語 **birth mark**
胎記

marker [mɑrkɚ] ◀Track 1285
n. 記號筆；馬克筆

►He used a red marker to highlight the topic sentence of each paragraph.
他用紅色馬克筆標註每段的主題句。

market [`mɑrkɪt]
◀Track 1286
n. 市場;股票市場

►I bought a bangle from a flea market.
我在跳蚤市場買了一條手鐲。

補充片語 flea market
跳蚤夜市

v. 在市場上銷售

►The company is trying to market their new product in Asia.
公司試圖將新產品行銷到亞洲。

marriage [`mærɪdʒ]
◀Track 1287
n. 婚姻;婚姻生活

►Marriage is not all rainbows and happiness.
婚姻生活並不總是如意快樂的。

married [`mærɪd]
◀Track 1288
adj. 已婚的;婚姻的

►How long have you been married?
你結婚多久了?

marry [`mærɪ]
◀Track 1289
v. 嫁;娶;和……結婚;嫁女兒

►Mandy married Stephen five years ago.
曼蒂五年前嫁給史蒂芬。

相關片語 marry money
與有錢人結婚

►She married money but lived a miserable life.
她嫁給有錢人但日子過得很悲慘。

marvellous [`mɑrvələs]
◀Track 1290

=marvellous（英式英文）
adj. 令人驚歎的;極好的

►She is a marvelous chef.
她是令人驚歎的好主廚。

mask [mæsk]
◀Track 1291
n. 面具;口罩

►The doctor wore a surgical mask when performing an operation.
醫師戴上外科口罩幫病人進行手術。

相關片語 gas mask 防毒面具

►The soldiers wore gas masks and protective clothing in the war zone.
士兵在戰區戴著防毒面具和防護衣。

mass [mæs]
◀Track 1292
n. 團;塊;大量

►There were masses of people in the market.
市場裡有很多人。

adj. 大眾的

►Anti-gun groups staged mass demonstrations all over the country.
反槍團體在全國發起大規模遊行示威。

master [`mæstɚ]
◀Track 1293
n. 主人

►You are the master of your life.
你是自己生命的主人。

mat [mæt]
◀Track 1294
n. 草蓆

►I like to sleep on a straw mat in summer.
我夏天喜歡睡在草蓆上。

初級

match [mætʃ]
◀Track 1295

n. 火柴；配對

▶Stop playing with matches. It's dangerous.
不要玩火柴，這樣很危險。

v. 配對；搭配

▶Does the blouse match the skirt?
這件女用襯衫和這條裙子相配嗎？

mate [met]
◀Track 1296

n. 同伴；伙伴；配偶

▶Jim is my best friend and my soul mate.
吉姆是我最好的朋友，也是我的知己。

補充片語 soul mate
靈魂相契、性情相投的人

material [mə`tɪrɪəl]
◀Track 1297

n. 材料；材質

▶The chemical is used as the raw material to produce detergent.
這個化學物被用來做清潔劑的原料。

math [mæθ]
=mathematics
◀Track 1298

n. 數學

▶My homeroom teacher teaches math and mandarin.
我的級任老師教數學和國語。

matter [`mætɚ]
◀Track 1299

n. 事情；問題；毛病

▶We thank you for bringing this matter to our attention.
我們感謝你讓我們注意到這個問題。

v. 要緊；有關係；重要

▶I know you don't think it's a big deal, but it matters to me.
我知道你覺得這件事沒什麼大不了的，但這對我來說很重要。

相關片語 matter of opinion
見仁見智的問題

▶Both essays are well-written. It's just a matter of opinion as to which is better.
兩篇文章都寫得很好，哪一篇較好是見仁見智的事。

maximum
◀Track 1300

[`mæksəməm]

adj. 最大的

▶The maximum load for this elevator is 480 kilos.
這部電梯的最大承載重量是四百八十公斤。

n. 最大數；最大限度；最高極限

▶The temperature might reach a maximum of 39℃ today.
今天最高溫度可能達到攝氏三十九度。

adv. 最多

▶You'd better cut down to one cigarette a day maximum.
你最好減少到每天最多一根香烟。

may [me]
◀Track 1301

aux. （表示可能性）也許；
（表示允許）可以

▶May I have your e-mail address?
我可以跟你要電郵地址嗎？

n. 五月（首字大寫）

▶We will leave for Vienna this coming May.
我們即將在五月前往維也納。

maybe [ˋmebɪ]
◀Track 1302

adv. 大概；可能；或許

▶Maybe you should give it a try.
你或許可以放手一試。

me [mi] **pron.** 我
◀Track 1303

▶Excuse me. Anybody here?
不好意思，有人在嗎？

meal [mil]
◀Track 1304

n. 一餐；進餐

▶You should brush your teeth after meals.
吃完飯應該要刷牙。

meaning [ˋminɪŋ]
◀Track 1305

n. 意義；含義；重要性

▶The editorial has a hidden meaning.
這篇社論有隱含的意義。

means [minz]
◀Track 1306

n. 方法；手段；工具

▶He will achieve his goals by all means.
他會盡一切方法達成目標。

補充片語 by all means
一定；盡一切辦法

measurable
◀Track 1307

[ˋmɛʒərəb!]

adj. 可測量的；可預見的；重大的

▶Scientists are studying whether spending too much time on cell phone will cause any measurable differences in adolescent brain structure.
科學家正在研究太常使用手機是否會對青少年的腦部結構造成重大的影響。

measure [ˋmɛʒɚ]
◀Track 1308

n. 度量單位；尺寸；分量

▶A kilogram is a measure of weight.
公斤是重量的計量單位。

v. 測量；計量

▶The machine measures your muscle tension.
這台機器可測量你的肌力。

measurement
◀Track 1309

[ˋmɛʒɚmənt]

n. 測定；測量；尺寸、三圍；測量法

▶The device is used for the measurement of arterial blood pressure.
這台儀器用來測量動脈血壓。

meat [mit]
◀Track 1310

n. 肉

▶Can the Venus flytrap eat meat other than insects?
捕蠅草除了昆蟲，也吃肉嗎？

mechanic [məˋkænɪk]
◀Track 1311

n. 技工；修理工

▶The mechanic assured me that my car will be ready tomorrow.
修理工向我保證我的車子明天會修好。

medicine [ˋmɛdəsn]
◀Track 1312

n. 藥

▶He has high blood pressure and needs to take medicine everyday.
他有高血壓，每天都要吃藥。

medium [ˋmidɪəm]
◀Track 1313

n. 中間；媒介物；手段；工具；傳播媒介

初級

▶They told the story through the medium of pantomime.
他們透過默劇的方式講述這個故事。

adj. 中間的；中等的

▶The bank robber is a man of medium height.
銀行搶犯是個中等身材的男子。

meet [mit]　◀Track 1314

v. 遇見；認識；迎接

▶She met her fiancé through a blind date.
她是透過相親認識未婚夫的。

meeting [`mitɪŋ]　◀Track 1315

n. 會議；聚會

▶Honey, I'm in a meeting. I'll call you back later.
親愛的，我現在正在開會，等一下回你電話。

melody [`mɛlədɪ]　◀Track 1316

n. 旋律；悅耳的聲音；曲調

▶She played an old Scottish melody.
她奏了一首古老的蘇格蘭曲調。。

melon [`mɛlən]　◀Track 1317

n. 甜瓜

▶She put the cut-up melon in a covered container.
她把切好的甜瓜放進盒子密封起來。

member [`mɛmbɚ]　◀Track 1318

n. 成員；會員

▶She was a member of the sorority.
她是大學姊妹會的會員。

相關片語 **life member**
　　　　終身會員

▶If you pay $1,000, you'll become a life member of this organization.
如果你繳一千元，就能成為這個機構的終身會員。

memory [`mɛmərɪ]　◀Track 1319

n. 記憶；記憶力；回憶

▶He has a retentive memory.
他的記憶力很好。

相關片語 **in memory of**
　　　　以紀念

▶The entrepreneur built a hospital in memory of his father.
這位企業家蓋了一家醫院紀念他的父親。

menu [`mɛnju]　◀Track 1320

n. 菜單

▶The menu of this restaurant is invariable, but the food is great.
這家餐廳的菜單一成不變，但是食物很美味。

message [`mɛsɪdʒ]　◀Track 1321

n. 訊息；口信；消息

▶May I leave a message to Katie?
我可以留言給凱蒂嗎？

metal [`mɛt!]　◀Track 1322

n. 金屬

▶Gold is a kind of precious metal.
金屬是貴重金屬的一種。

meter [`mitɚ]　◀Track 1323
=metre （英式英文）

n. 公尺；米

▶This cable is 200 meters long.
這條纜線有二百米長。

method [`mɛθəd] ◀Track 1324

n. 方法；方式

▶This method of growing plants is called hydroculture.
這個種植物的方式叫做水耕法。

---

microwave ◀Track 1325

[`maɪkro͵wev]

n. 微波爐

▶Put a potato in a microwave and it'll be ready in three minutes.
把馬鈴薯放進波爐，只需三分鐘就煮熟了。

v. 微波

▶I microwaved a frozen pizza for dinner.
我微波冷凍比薩當晚餐。

---

middle [`mɪd!] ◀Track 1326

adj. 中間的；中等的

▶He lived in the middle forest.
他住在中間的森林。

n. 中部；中途

▶He grew up in the middle of nowhere in rural Arkansas.
他在阿肯色州的偏僻郊區長大。

補充片語 **the middle of nowhere**
偏僻的地方；雞不生蛋鳥不拉屎的地方

相關片語 **pig in the middle**
夾在爭執雙方中間的人

▶When his mother and wife have a fight, he is always the pig in the middle.
他的媽媽和妻子只要一吵架，他就夾在中間難做人。

---

midnight [`mɪd͵naɪt] ◀Track 1327

n. 午夜

▶She studied for her finals until midnight.
她為了準備期末考，一直到半夜才上床睡覺。

adj. 半夜的

▶I'm hungry. Let's have some midnight snacks.
我肚子餓了，我們來吃點宵夜吧。

---

might [maɪt] ◀Track 1328

aux. 可能；可以；

（與現實情況相反）會；能

▶It might rain this afternoon.
下午可能會下雨。

---

mightn't [`maɪtnt] ◀Track 1329

abbr. 可能不會（**might not**的縮寫）

▶You mightn't believe it, but I saw Hugh Jackman shooting a scene in Paris.
你可能不相信，但我看到休‧傑克曼在巴黎拍一個場景。

---

mile [maɪl] ◀Track 1330

n. 英里；哩

▶The speed limit is 90 kilometers per hour on the highway.
高速公路限速每小時九十公里。

---

military [`mɪlə͵tɛrɪ] ◀Track 1331

adj. 軍事的；軍用的；軍人的

▶The country is developing state-of-the-art weapons to enhance its military might.
這個國家正在研發尖端武器，來加強軍事力量。

初級

補充片語 military might
軍事力量

n. 軍人；軍隊
▶The president used to serve in the military when he was young.
總統年輕時曾經從軍。

milk [mɪlk] ◀Track 1332
n. 奶
▶She bought a carton of milk and put it in the fridge.
她買了一盒牛奶，把它放到冰箱裡。

相關片語 milk tea 奶茶
▶I don't drink milk tea.
我不喝奶茶。

million [`mɪljən] ◀Track 1333
pron. 百萬個
▶The toxic chemical killed hundreds of thousand people and maimed millions.
這個有毒化學物質殺死數十萬人，並且讓數百萬人成為殘廢。

n. 百萬；百萬元；無數
▶The city has a population over a million.
這個城市人口超過百萬。

adj. 百萬的
▶It cost me three million dollars to buy the house.
我花了三百萬元買這棟房子。

mind [maɪnd] ◀Track 1334
n. 頭腦；智力；意向；主意
▶Let's do it before he changes his mind.
在他改變心意之前，我們開始著手吧。

v. 在意；介意
▶Do you mind if I open the window?
你介意我打開窗戶嗎？

相關片語 keep in mind
記住
▶Currently, we don't have any job vacancies, but we'll keep your application in mind.
我們目前沒有職缺，但是會記住你的申請。

mine [maɪn] ◀Track 1335
pron. 我的
▶You are the same age as mine.
你的年紀和我一樣大。

n. 礦；礦井；寶庫
▶He used to work in the mines.
他以前曾在礦坑工作。

v. 採礦
▶They are mining copper in this area.
他們在這個地區採銅。

相關片語 mine of information
知識的寶庫
▶He is a mine of information about wine-making.
他懂得很多釀酒的知識。

minor [`maɪnɚ] ◀Track 1336
adj. 較少的；較少的；次要的；不重要的；年幼的；副修的
▶It was just a minor operation.
這只是個小手術。

n. 未成年人；副修科目
▶She was shot when protecting the safety of three minors.
她在保護三名未成年人的安全時被槍擊中。

v 副修；兼修

▶Dan majored in journalism and minored in history.
丹主修新聞，副修歷史。

相關片語 **minor subject**
副修科目

▶Biochemistry was his minor subject.
生物化學是他的副修科目。

---

minus [`maɪnəs]
◀ Track 1337

prep. 減去

▶Twenty minus seven equals thirteen.
廿減七等於十三。

adj. 負的

▶Temperatures could drop to minus ten today.
今天氣溫可能會降到零下十度。

n. 負號、減號；負數；不利

▶The minus of a plus is a minus.
負正得負。

---

minute [`mɪnɪt]
◀ Track 1338

n. 分鐘

▶Wait a minute. I'll be right back.
等一下，我待會就回來。

v. 將……記錄下來；將……記在會議紀錄

▶The conversation on the phone will be minuted.
電話裡的對話會被記錄下來。

---

mirror [`mɪrɚ]
◀ Track 1339

n. 鏡子

▶The toddler is looking at his reflection in the mirror.
這個學步的小孩正看著自己在鏡中的模樣。

---

miss [mɪs]
◀ Track 1340

v. 錯過；想念

▶He missed his girlfriend terribly.
他很想念女友。

n. （首字大寫）小姐；女士（對未婚女子的稱謂）

▶Miss Lin, may I go to the bathroom?
林老師，我可以去廁所嗎？

---

missing [`mɪsɪŋ]
◀ Track 1341

adj. 缺掉的；失蹤的

▶The woman has been missing since 2015.
這名女子自從二〇〇五年起即下落不明。

初級

---

mistake [mɪ`stek]
◀ Track 1342

n. 錯誤；失誤

▶I found a few mistakes in the article.
我發現文章裡有一些錯誤。

v. 弄錯；誤解

▶Sorry, I mistook you for Jenny.
抱歉，我誤以為你是珍妮。

相關片語 **by mistake**
錯誤地

▶She used my toothbrush by mistake.
她誤用了我的牙刷。

---

mix [mɪks]
◀ Track 1343

v. 混合；拌和

▶He mixed the mashed potatoes with butter and pepper.
他把奶油和胡椒拌入馬鈴薯泥裡。

n. 混合；混合物；調配好的材料

▶There was an interesting mix of people at Amber's birthday party.
安柏的生日派對上來了各式各樣的人。

model [ˋmɑd!] ◀ Track 1344
n. 模型；模範；模特兒
▶Catherine is a fashion model and has graced the cover of Time magazine.
凱瑟琳是名時裝模特兒，並上過《時代》雜誌的封面。

補充片語 fashion model
時裝模特兒

v. 做……的模型；當模特兒
▶Gemma models for famous designers such as Karl Lagerfeld and Tom Ford.
潔瑪為卡爾・拉格菲爾德和湯姆・福德等知名設計師擔任服裝模特兒。

modern [ˋmɑdɚn] ◀ Track 1345
adj. 現代的；近代的；現代化的
▶The furniture looks modern and lights up the house.
這些傢俱看起來很時尚，讓屋子都明亮了起來。

moment [ˋmomənt] ◀ Track 1346
n. 瞬間；片刻
▶I'll be there in a moment.
我稍後就到。

mommy [ˋmɑmɪ] ◀ Track 1347
n. 媽媽
▶Mommy, I'm hungry.
媽媽，我肚子餓了。

Monday [ˋmʌnde] =Mon. **n.** 星期一 ◀ Track 1348
▶I have an appointment with my dentist next Monday.
我下週一要去看牙醫。

money [ˋmʌnɪ] ◀ Track 1349
n. 錢；金錢
▶He donated a lot of money to the charity.
他捐很多錢給慈善機關。

相關片語 make money
賺錢
▶She made money in college by selling handmade crafts.
她大學時靠賣手工藝品賺錢。

monkey [ˋmʌŋkɪ] ◀ Track 1350
n. 猴子
▶The monkeys were grooming each other.
猴子們正彼此梳理身上的毛。

相關片語 monkey bars
攀爬架；單槓
▶Monkey bars are also called the jungle gym.
單槓又稱為攀爬架。

monster [ˋmɑnstɚ] ◀ Track 1351
n. 怪獸；怪物
▶The novel is about a group of monsters trying to destroy the earth.
這本小說是關於一群怪物試圖摧毀地球。

month [mʌnθ] ◀ Track 1352
n. 月；月份
▶I'm going to Osaka next month.
我下個月要到大阪。

monthly [ˋmʌnθlɪ] ◀ Track 1353
adj. 每月的；每月一次的
▶They will have a monthly meeting with the CEO.

他們將和執行長開月會。

adv. 每月;每月一次

▶The committee members will meet monthly to discuss this issue.
委員會成員每個月將聚會討論這個議題。

n. 月刊

▶The monthly is a magazine that includes a variety of topics.
這本月刊包含多元的主題。

moon [mun]   ◀€Track 1354

n. 月亮;月球

▶I have never seen the moon this big.
我從沒看過這麼大的月亮。

相關片語 **once in a blue moon**
千載難逢地;難得地

▶The opportunity comes once in a blue moon. Don't miss it.
這個機會很難得,別錯過了。

mop [mɑp]   ◀€Track 1355

n. 拖把

▶She used a dish mop to do the dishes.
她用洗碗刷洗碗。

v. 用拖把拖;擦乾

▶I mopped the bathroom floor after the shower.
我洗完澡後拖浴室地板。

more [mor]   ◀€Track 1356

adv. 更多;更大程度地;再

▶He needs to listen more and asks the right question.
他需要多聽並問對問題。

pron. 更多的數量;更多的人或事物

▶The chocolates taste like heaven. I want more of them.
這巧克力真是美味得不得了,我還要更多。

adj. 更多的

▶I'd like to add more milk into the tea.
我想要在茶裡加更多的牛奶。

morning [`mɔrnɪŋ]   ◀€Track 1357

n. 早晨;上午

▶She went to the gym this morning.
她今天早上去健身房了。

mosquito [məs`kito]   ◀€Track 1358

n. 蚊子

▶The bug spray can repel mosquitoes for up to six hours.
這個驅蟲液能驅趕蚊子長達六小時。

most [most]   ◀€Track 1359

adv. 最;最大程度地;非常

▶She is the most generous person I have ever met.
她是我遇過最慷慨的人。

pron. 最大量;最多數;大部分

▶She made most of the desserts herself.
大部分的甜點是她做的。

adj. 最多的;多數的

▶Do you know who ate the most ice cream this afternoon?
你知道今天下午誰吃了最多的冰淇淋嗎?

相關片語 **at most** 最多

▶The dress costs $1,000 at most.
這件洋裝最多要花一千元。

moth [mɔθ]   ◀€Track 1360

初級

n. 蛾；蠹，蛀蟲
▶The moth looks like a butterfly.
蛾看起來像蝴蝶。

---

mother [`mʌðɚ]
◀ Track 1361
=mommy=mom
=momma=mamma

n. 媽媽；母親
▶She became a mother when she was only 18.
她十八歲就當媽媽了。

v. 像母親般照料；生下
▶She mothered her niece and sent her to school every morning.
她像母親般照料姪女並每天早上送她上學。

相關片語 **mother tongue**
母語

▶My mother tongue is Chinese.
我的母語是中文。

Mother's Day
◀ Track 1362
[`mʌðɚ-z-de]
n. 母親節
▶She bought a necklace for her mother on Mother's Day.
她在母親節這天買了一條項鍊送給媽媽。

---

motion [`moʃən]
◀ Track 1363
n. （物體的）移動、運行；動作、姿態
▶The motion of the boat made her dizzy.
船隻搖晃讓她感到頭暈。

v. 打手勢；做動作示意
▶He motioned his dog to sit down.
他打手勢叫他的狗坐下。

相關片語 **go through the motions**
做做樣子

▶He went through the motions of apologizing without really feeling remorseful.
他道歉只是做做樣子，並不是發自內心的懊悔。

---

motorcycle
◀ Track 1364
[`motɚ͵saɪk!]
=motorbike （英式英文）
n. 摩托車
▶His father had a cow when he bought a motorcycle.
他買摩托車時，他的爸爸非常不安。

補充片語 **have a cow**
心慌意亂

---

mountain [`maʊntn]
◀ Track 1365
n. 山
▶He plans to climb the Jade Mountain in summer.
他計畫夏天要去爬玉山。

相關片語 **go to the mountains**
上山

▶I went to the mountains to ski last week.
我上週上山去滑雪。

---

mouse [maʊs]
◀ Track 1366
n. 鼠；膽小如鼠的人
▶There's a mouse in the attic.
閣樓裡有一隻老鼠。

相關片語 **as quiet as a mouse**
無聲無響地

▶Irene was as quiet as a mouse yesterday. It wasn't like her.
艾琳昨天靜悄悄的,不像平時的她。

mouth [maʊθ] ◀€Track 1367
n. 嘴

▶Alice has a big mouth, and she speaks ill of people all the time.
艾莉絲有張大嘴巴,而且一天到晚在背後說別人的壞話。

相關片語 **down in the mouth**
　　　　垂頭喪氣的

▶Robert has been down in the mouth.
羅伯特最近垂頭喪氣的。

movable [`muvəb!] ◀€Track 1368
adj. 可動的;可移動的

▶The toy soldiers have arms and legs that are movable.
這些玩具士兵的手和腳是可以動的。

move [muv] ◀€Track 1369
v. 移動;搬動;遷移;搬家

▶He moved to Silicon Valley to pursue his career in venture capital.
他搬家到矽谷去從事創投。

補充片語 **venture capital**
　　　　創業投資

n. 移動;措施

▶Alice is very nosy and watches people's every move.
艾莉絲很愛管別人的閒事,總是監視別人的一舉一動。

movement ◀€Track 1370
[`muvmənt]
n. 運動;活動;行動

▶The boy made a sudden movement and frightened the cat away.
男孩突然動了一下,貓受到驚嚇跑走了。

movie [`muvɪ] ◀€Track 1371
=film=cinema=picture
n. 電影

▶I enjoy watching movies on Saturday afternoon.
我喜歡星期六下午看些電影。

Mr. [`mɪstə] ◀€Track 1372
=Mr
n. 先生(用於男士稱謂)

▶Mr. Brown looks like a Santa Claus.
布朗先生看起來很像聖誕老人。

Mrs. [`mɪsɪz] ◀€Track 1373
=Mrs
n. 太太;夫人(用於已婚女性稱謂)

▶Mrs. Musk is a certified dietician.
馬斯克太太是位經過認證的營養師。

MRT [ɛm-ɑr-ti] ◀€Track 1374
=mass rapid transit
=subway=underground
=metro
n. 大眾捷運系統

▶Taipei's MRT is one of the best metro systems in the world.
台北捷運是全球最好的大眾捷運系統之一。

Ms. [mɪs] =Ms ◀€Track 1375
n. 女士(用於婚姻狀態不明的女性稱謂)

▶Ms. Riley is a project manager.
萊莉女士是專案經理。

初級

MTV [ɛm-ti-vi]
◀ Track 1376

n. 音樂電視

▶ The singer won the 2018 MTV Video Music Award.
這名歌手獲得MTV音樂錄影帶 。

much [mʌtʃ]
◀ Track 1377

pron. 許多；大量的事物

▶ There was not much on TV last night.
昨晚電視沒什麼好看的。

adv. 非常；很

▶ Thank you so much.
很感謝你。

adj. 許多；大量的

▶ He doesn't earn much money.
他賺錢不多。

mud [mʌd]
◀ Track 1378

n. 泥；泥漿

▶ My bike is stuck in the mud.
我的腳踏車陷入泥巴裡了。

mug [mʌg]
◀ Track 1379

n. 大杯子；馬克杯

▶ She poured some coffee into the mug.
她倒了一些咖啡到馬克杯裡。

mule [mjul]
◀ Track 1380

n. 騾子；固執的人

▶ The mule was stuck in a freezing pool.
這頭騾子被困在冰冷的池子裡。

multiply [`mʌltəplaɪ]
◀ Track 1381

v. 乘；相乘；使成倍增加；繁殖

▶ If you multiply three by 10, you get 30.
用10乘以3等於30。

museum [mju`zɪəm]
◀ Track 1382

n. 博物館

▶ We went to the museum to see an exhibit.
我們去博物館參觀展覽。

music [`mjuzɪk]
◀ Track 1383

n. 音樂

▶ That's a beautiful piece of music.
那首樂曲好美。

相關片語 **face the music**
接受批評；承擔後果

▶ You must face the music if you make the wrong decision.
你若做錯誤的決定，要自行承擔後果。

musician [mju`zɪʃən]
◀ Track 1384

n. 音樂家

▶ Mozart is one of my favorite musicians.
莫札特是我最喜愛的音樂家之一。

must [mʌst]
◀ Track 1385

aux. 必定；必須；一定要

▶ I must finish my essay by Friday.
我在星期五前一定要寫好論文。

mustn't [`mʌsnt]
◀ Track 1386

abbr. 不可（**must not**的縮寫）

▶ You mustn't drive after drinking.
喝完酒後一定不能開車。

my [maɪ]
det. 我的

▶He is my father.
他是我的爸爸。

◀Track 1387

myself [maɪˋsɛlf]
pron. 我自己

▶I bought myself a new skirt.
我為自己買了一件新的裙子。

◀Track 1388

初級

▶ Nn

　　以下表格是全民英檢官方公告初級「聽、說、讀、寫」所須具備的能力，本書例句皆依此範疇特別設計，只要掃描右方QR code，就能搭配相對應的音軌，實現「眼耳並用」方式，刺激左腦的語言學習功能；同時也可使用本書附贈的紅膠片，將其置於單字上，一面記憶一面自我挑戰，達到雙倍的學習成果！

聽	▶	能聽懂與日常生活相關的淺易談話，包含價格、時間及地點等。
說	▶	能朗讀簡易文章、簡單地自我介紹，對熟悉的話題能以簡易英語對答，如問候、購物、問路等。
讀	▶	可看懂與日常生活相關的淺易英文，並能閱讀路標、交通號誌、招牌、簡單菜單、時刻表及賀卡等。
寫	▶	能寫簡單的句子及段落，如寫明信片、便條、賀卡及填表格等。對一般日常生活相關事物，能以簡短的文字敘述或說明。

nail [nel]　　🔊 Track 1389

n. 釘子；指甲

▶She clipped her nails and then polished them.
她剪指甲後把指甲拋光。

v. 釘；釘牢；固定；集中於

▶He nailed a painting into the wall.
他在牆上釘了一幅畫。

相關片語 **hit the nail on the head**
一針見血；正中要害

▶She hit the nail on the head when she mentioned that our society is morally bankrupt.
她提到現代社會道德淪亡，真是一針見血。

naked [`nekɪd]　　🔊 Track 1390

adj. 裸身的；光禿禿的；赤裸裸的

▶He stripped naked when he got drunk.
他喝醉酒就脫光衣服了。

相關片語 **get naked**
開心地玩

▶They got naked at the prom.
他們在畢業舞會玩得很開心。

name [nem]　　🔊 Track 1391

n. 名字

▶His name is Timothy.
他的名字是提摩西。

v. 命名；為……取名

▶We named our daughter Harper.
我們把女兒取名為哈珀。

相關片語 **last name** 姓

▶Her last name is Lopez.
她姓羅培茲。

napkin [`næpkɪn]　　🔊 Track 1392

n. 餐巾

▶I handed him a napkin.
我遞給他一條餐巾。

相關片語 **paper napkin**
餐巾紙

▶Are these paper napkins made from recycled paper?
這些餐巾紙是用回收紙做的嗎？

narrow [`næro] 　　　🔊 Track 1393
adj. 窄的；狹窄的

▶His hometown has many narrow streets.
他的家鄉有很多狹小的街道。

v. 使變窄；縮小、限制（範圍等）

▶We must narrow the digital divide in our country if we want to give our children a future.
如果我們要給孩子未來，就一定要努力縮小數位落差。

nation [`neʃən] 　　　🔊 Track 1394
n. 國家

▶The whole nation was very concerned about the outbreak of Ebola.
全國都很擔心伊波拉疫情的爆發。

national [`næʃən!] 　　　🔊 Track 1395
adj. 全國性的；國家的；國有的

▶Dragon Boat Festival is a national holiday here.
端午節在這裡是國定假日。

相關片語 **National Park**
國家公園

▶We went to the Taroko National Park last summer.
我們去年暑假去太魯閣國家公園玩。

natural [`nætʃərəl] 　　　🔊 Track 1396
adj. 自然的

▶Typhoons and earthquakes are natural disasters.
颱風和地震都是天然災害。

相關片語 **natural enemy**
天敵

▶Venus flytraps are the natural enemies of insects.
捕蠅草是昆蟲的天敵。

nature [`netʃɚ] 　　　🔊 Track 1397
n. 自然（狀態）；自然界；天性、本質

▶The photographer shared how her love for nature influenced her career.
攝影師分享她對自然界的熱愛如何影響了她的職業生涯。

相關片語 **answer the call of nature**
上洗手間

▶He went to the restroom to answer the call of nature.
他去上洗手間。

naughty [`nɔtɪ] 　　　🔊 Track 1398
adj. 頑皮的；淘氣的

▶My dog is very playful and naughty.
我的狗很愛玩耍又調皮。

near [nɪr] 　　　🔊 Track 1399
prep. 在……附近

▶I live near the Empire State Building.
我住在帝國大廈附近。

adj. 近的

▶Where is the nearest metro station?
離這裡最近的捷運站在哪裡？

初級

adv. 近；接近；幾乎

▶As her wedding was drawing near, she became more and more anxious.
隨著她的婚禮日期的到來，她變得越來越焦慮。

v. 靠近

▶The project is nearing completion.
這項計畫快要完成了。

nearby [`nɪr‚baɪ] ◀ Track 1400
adj. 附近的

▶They stopped at a nearby shop to buy some beverages.
他們順路在附近的一家商店買了一些飲料。

adv. 在附近

▶There was a handsome guy standing nearby.
有個俊俏的男生站在附近。

nearly [`nɪrlɪ] ◀ Track 1401
adv. 幾乎；差不多

▶My son is nearly as tall as my husband.
我兒子現在幾乎和我先生一樣高。

neat [nit] ◀ Track 1402
adj. 整齊的；工整的；整潔的

▶His apartment is always neat.
他的公寓總是很整潔。

necessary [`nɛsə‚sɛrɪ] ◀ Track 1403
adj. 必須的；必要的

▶It is necessary for all of us to attend the meeting.
我們全體都必須參加這個會議。

neck [nɛk] ◀ Track 1404
n. 脖子；頸

▶She wore a pearl necklace around her neck.
她在脖子上戴了一條珍珠項鍊。

相關片語 **break one's neck** 拚命（做某事）

▶He broke his neck and finished the work before deadline.
他拚了命在期限前將工作完成。

necklace [`nɛklɪs] ◀ Track 1405
n. 項鍊

▶She wore a diamond necklace at the party.
她戴著鑽石項鍊參加派對。

need [nid] ◀ Track 1406
v. 需要

▶I need to take a break.
我需要休息。

n. 需要；貧窮；困窘

▶Is he in need of help?
他需要幫忙嗎？

相關片語 **in need** 在窮困中

▶They donated money to those who are in need.
他們捐錢給生活貧困的人。

aux. 必須

▶You need not come.
你不需要來。

needle [`nid!] ◀ Track 1407
n. 針；指針

▶I helped my grandmother thread the needle.
我幫祖母把線穿進針裡。

v. 用針縫；用針刺；用話刺激

▶She always needled her husband and chastised him.
她總用話刺激丈夫生氣並斥責他。

相關片語 **as sharp as a needle**
非常機靈的

▶The boy is not stupid at all. He is as sharp as a needle.
那男孩一點也不笨，他非常機靈。

negative [`nɛɡətɪv] ◀Track 1408
adj. 否定的；負面的、消極的

▶Her negative reply dashed his hope.
她的負面回應打破了他的希望。

n. 否定；否定的回答；拒絕

▶Her reply was in the negative.
她的回應是否定的。

neighbour [`nebɚ] =neighbor ◀Track 1409
n. 鄰居

▶We get along with our neighbors.
我們和鄰居相處和睦。

v. 住在附近；與……為鄰

▶Our dorm neighbors a lake.
我們的宿舍與一座湖毗鄰。

neither [`niðɚ] ◀Track 1410
adv. 也不

▶He won't attend the meeting, and neither will I.
他不會參加會議，我也不會。

pron. 兩個中沒有一個

▶I want neither of them.
這兩者我都不要。

adj. 兩者都不

▶Neither novels is appealing for me.
我對這兩本小說都沒興趣。

conj. 既不……，也不……

▶She neither sleeps nor eats.
她不睡也不吃。

nephew [`nɛfju] ◀Track 1411
n. 姪兒；外甥

▶My nephew lives in Mexico.
我的姪兒住在墨西哥。

nervous [`nɝvəs] ◀Track 1412
adj. 緊張的

▶Stop fidgeting. You're too nervous.
不要扭來扭去的，你太緊張了。

nest [nɛst] ◀Track 1413
n. 巢；窩；穴

▶There's a wasps' nest in the attic.
閣樓有一個蜂窩。

v. 築巢

▶Some swallows are nesting in our roof.
有些燕子在我們的屋頂下築巢。

net [nɛt] ◀Track 1414
n. 網狀物；網

▶We caught some dragonflies with the nets.
我們用網子抓到一些蜻蜓。

v. 用網捕

▶He netted a lot of fish this afternoon.
他下午用網子撈到很多魚。

never [`nɛvɚ] ◀Track 1415
adv. 從不；永不；絕不

初級

▶She's never been to Paris before.
她從未去過巴黎。

相關片語 **never mind**
沒關係；不要介意

▶He didn't mean to hurt you. Never mind.
他沒有傷害你的意思，別介意。

---

new [nju]
Track 1416

adj. 新的

▶I bought myself a new purse.
我買了一個新錢包。

相關片語 **new face** 新面孔

▶She's a new face in the fashion industry.
她是時尚界的新面孔。

New Year's Day
Track 1417

[nju-jɪrz-de] **n.** 元旦

▶How are we going to celebrate the New Year's Day?
我們要怎麼慶祝元旦？

New Year's Eve
Track 1418

[nju-jɪrz-iv] **n.** 除夕

▶We will have a party on New Year's Eve.
我們除夕要開派對。

New York [nju-jɔrk]
Track 1419

n. 紐約

▶New York is one of the fashion capitals in the world.
紐約是世界時尚之都的其中之一。

---

news [njuz]
Track 1420

n. 新聞；消息

▶People were saddened by the terrible news.
人們對這個壞消息感到很難過。

相關片語 **in the news**
上新聞；被報導

▶Our teacher was in the news.
我們的老師上新聞了。

---

newspaper
Track 1421

[`njuzˌpepɚ]

n. 報紙

▶I read a daily newspapers.
我每天看日報。

---

next [`nɛkst]
Track 1422

adj. 緊鄰的；接下來的；居次的

▶Who's next?
誰是下一個？

adv. 接下來；次於

▶What happened next?
接下來發生什麼事？

---

nice [naɪs]
Track 1423

adj. 好的；美好的；好心的

▶Is he nice?
他為人好嗎？

---

niece [nis]
Track 1424

n. 姪女；外甥女

▶My niece is an English tutor.
我的外甥女是英文家教。

---

night [naɪt]
Track 1425

n. 夜晚

▶We heard wolves crying in the still of the night.
我們在深夜聽到狼叫聲。

相關片語 **night owl** 夜貓子

▶My husband has been a night owl for as long as I can remember.
在我的記憶裡，我先生一向是個夜貓子。

nine [naɪn]　◀€Track 1426

pron. 九個

▶My sister has ten skirts, and I like nine of them.
我姊姊有十件裙子，我喜歡其中九件。

n. 九

▶Seven plus two equals nine.
七加二等於九。

adj. 九的；九個的

▶He bought nine eggs in the market.
他在市場買了九個雞蛋。

相關片語 **on cloud nine** 直上雲霄；極快樂

▶She was on cloud nine when she got the admission letter from Cambridge University.
她收到劍橋大學的入學通知時，高興得不得了。

nine·teen [`naɪn`tin]　◀€Track 1427

pron. 十九個

▶Nineteen of the passengers were seriously injured.
有十九名乘客受到重傷。

n. 十九；十九歲

▶She was Miss USA when she was at the age of nineteen.
她在十九歲時選上美國小姐冠軍。

adj. 十九的；十九個的

▶The textbook has been translated into nineteen languages.
這本教科書被翻譯成十九國語言。

ninety [`naɪntɪ]　◀€Track 1428

pron. 九十；九十個

▶Ninety of the children died of malaria.
這群孩子中，有九十名死於虐疾。

n. 九十；九十歲

▶He is ninety, but he's still young at heart.
他九十歲了，不過心理仍然很年輕。

adj. 九十的；九十個的

▶We invited ninety students to the seminar.
我們邀請九十個學生參加研討會。

no [no]　◀€Track 1429

adv. 不；不是；沒有；並無

▶Math is no more difficult than any other subject.
數學並不比其它科目難。

adj. 沒有

▶I have no homework today.
我今天沒有作業。

n. 不；沒有

▶We sent twenty invitation letters. So far, we have seventeen yeses and three noes.
我們寄出了二十封邀請函，目前為止獲覆十七人願意參加，三人不參加。

相關片語 **no more** 不再

▶I can't take it no more.
我再也受不了了。

nobody [`nobɑdɪ]　◀€Track 1430

pron. 沒有人；無人

▶Nobody is home.
家裡沒有人。

初級

n. 無足輕重的小人物

▶Cheryl is just a nobody trying to get more attention from her boss.
雪若只不過是個想引起老闆注意的無名之輩。

相關片語 **be nobody's fool**
相當精明，不易受騙

▶I'm nobody's fool.
我沒那麼容易上當。

---

nobody's [`nobadız] ◀╣Track 1431

abbr. 沒有人的、沒有人是（**nobody**的所有格，或**nobody is**的縮寫）

▶Nobody's perfect.
沒有人是完美的。

---

nod [nad] ◀╣Track 1432

v. 點頭；打盹

▶My teacher nodded for me to come in.
老師點頭示意要我進來。

n. 點頭；打瞌睡

▶My boss gave me his nod about my proposal.
我的老闆同意我的提案。

相關片語 **nod off**
打盹，打瞌睡

▶He nodded off during the class.
他上課打瞌睡。

---

noise [nɔɪz] ◀╣Track 1433

n. 噪音

▶She was woken by the sudden noise.
她被突如其來的噪音吵醒。

相關片語 **noise pollution**
噪音污染

▶Noise pollution can cause many health problems.
噪音污染會引起很多健康問題。

---

noisy [`nɔɪzɪ] ◀╣Track 1434

adj. 吵鬧的；喧鬧的；充滿噪聲的；嘈嚷的

▶Be quiet. You've been noisy all this morning.
安靜點，你今天早上吵死人了。

---

none [nʌn] ◀╣Track 1435

pron. 一個也無；沒有任何人或物；無一人

▶None of their children have blue eyes.
他們的孩子眼珠都不是藍色的。

adv. 毫不；絕不；一點也不

▶She has been hospitalized for three weeks, but she's none the better for it.
她已住院三個星期，但情況沒有起色。

相關片語 **second to none**
最佳的；不亞於任何人

▶My mother's chocolate cake is second to none.
我媽媽做的巧克力蛋糕無人能出其右。

---

noodle [`nud!] ◀╣Track 1436

n. 麵

▶His favorite food is beef noodles.
他最愛吃牛肉麵。

補充片語 **beef noodles**
牛肉麵

---

noon [nun] ◀╣Track 1437

n. 中午；正午

▶I must finish the work by noon.
我在中午前一定要完成這個工作。

nor [nɔr]
◀ Track 1438

conj. 也不

▶Neither Henry nor Ben knew what happened.
亨利和班恩都不知道發生了什麼事。

補充片語 neither... nor...
既不……，也不……

---

north [nɔrθ]
◀ Track 1439

n. 北方

▶Most of Taiwan's population is concentrated in the north.
台灣大部分的人口集中在北部。

adj. 北部的；北方的

▶The United States is a country located in North America.
美國是位在北美洲的國家。

adv. 向北；在北方；自北方

▶The bedroom faces north and is quite cold and dark.
臥室朝北，裡面又冷又陰暗。

---

northern [`nɔrðən]
◀ Track 1440

adj. 北方的

▶Taipei is a northern city with a very comtemporary and modern feel.
台北是一座北部的城市，融合了當代和現代化的感覺。

相關片語 northern lights
北極光

▶Thousands of tourists flock to Canada to watch the northern lights each year.
每年都有數千名遊客到加拿大看北極光。

---

nose [noz]
◀ Track 1441

n. 鼻子

▶I had a runny nose.
我流鼻涕。

相關片語 a nose job
隆鼻手術

▶She admitted that she had a nose job.
她承認動過隆鼻手術。

---

not [nɑt]
◀ Track 1442

adv. 不

▶Alice is not trustworthy.
艾莉絲是個不值得信任的人。

相關片語 not at all 一點也不

▶She is not nice at all.
她為人一點也不好。

---

note [not]
◀ Track 1443

n. 筆記；便條

▶There's a note on the fridge.
冰箱上貼著一張便條。

v. 注意；提到；記下

▶He noted that the company is facing a financial crisis.
他提到公司正面臨金融危機。

相關片語 take notes 記筆記

▶He took notes during the class.
他在課堂寫筆記。

---

notebook [`notˌbʊk]
◀ Track 1444

n. 筆記本；筆記型電腦

▶She brought a notebook to the meeting.
她帶了一本筆記本參加會議。

相關片語 notebook computer
筆記型電腦

初級

▶He made a diagram in his notebook computer.
他用筆記型電腦做了一個圖表。

nothing [`nʌθɪŋ]　◀€Track 1445

pron. 沒什麼；什麼事物都沒有

▶There's nothing in the carton. It's totally empty.
紙箱裡什麼都沒有，完全是空的。

n. 微不足道的事或物

▶He felt he was a nothing and an useless nobody.
他覺得自己是個微不足道、一無是處的人。

相關片語 **go for nothing**
白費；沒有結果

▶The teacher felt her efforts went for nothing because the students didn't pay attention.
老師覺得努力都白費了，因為學生不注意聽課。

notice [`notɪs]　◀€Track 1446

n. 公告；通知；注意；察覺

▶They put a notice in the paper announcing when the audition will take place.
他們在報紙刊登試鏡舉辦的時間。

v. 注意；注意到

▶I noticed that a dog was staring at me.
我注意到有隻狗在盯著我看。

相關片語 **without notice**
不預先或另行通知地

▶His boss was a jerk. He was fired without notice.
他的老闆很壞，他沒被事先告知就被裁員了。

novel [`nɑvl]　◀€Track 1447

n. （長篇）小說

▶This is the best novel I have ever read.
這是我讀過最棒的小説。

adj. 新奇的；新穎的

▶He came up with a novel idea.
他想到了一個很新穎的點子。

November　◀€Track 1448
[no`vɛmbɚ]

n. 十一月

▶The meeting will take place in November.
會議將在十一月舉行。

now [naʊ]　◀€Track 1449

adv. 現在；此刻；馬上

▶Smart phones are very common now.
智慧型手機現在很普及。

n. 現在；目前；此刻

▶She said she will take care of Eric from now on.
她説從現在起，她會照顧艾利克。

補充片語 **from now on**
從現在起

相關片語 **up to now**
到現在為止

▶He has done so much for us up to now.
到目前為止，他為我們做了好多的事。

number [`nʌmbɚ]　◀€Track 1450

n. 數字；數量

▶Our flight number is MU734.
我們的航班號碼是MU734。

v. 編號；給號碼；算入

▶The folders were numbered and filed away.
這些檔案都經過編號存檔。

------

nurse [nɝs]

◀ Track 1451

n. 護士

▶My wife is a nurse.
我的妻子是護士。

v. 看護；護理

▶He nursed the injured dog until it was well again.
他照料受傷的小狗，直到牠恢復健康。

相關片語 **put sb. to nurse**
請人照料

▶They put their baby to nurse.
他們請人照料寶寶。

------

nut [nʌt]

◀ Track 1452

n. 堅果；核果；難事；難對付的人；腦袋

▶She is allergic to nuts.
她吃堅果會過敏。

相關片語 **do one's nut**
發怒；氣炸

▶Jack will do his nut if I'm late again.
如果我再遲到，傑克會翻臉的。

初級

▶ Oo

　　以下表格是全民英檢官方公告初級「聽、説、讀、寫」所須具備的能力，本書例句皆依此範疇特別設計，只要掃描右方QR code，就能搭配相對應的音軌，實現「眼耳並用」方式，刺激左腦的語言學習功能；同時也可使用本書附贈的紅膠片，將其置於單字上，一面記憶一面自我挑戰，達到雙倍的學習成果！

聽	▶ 能聽懂與日常生活相關的淺易談話，包含價格、時間及地點等。
説	▶ 能朗讀簡易文章、簡單地自我介紹，對熟悉的話題能以簡易英語對答，如問候、購物、問路等。
讀	▶ 可看懂與日常生活相關的淺易英文，並能閱讀路標、交通號誌、招牌、簡單菜單、時刻表及賀卡等。
寫	▶ 能寫簡單的句子及段落，如寫明信片、便條、賀卡及填表格等。對一般日常生活相關事物，能以簡短的文字敘述或説明。

obey [ə`be]　◀╡Track 1453
v 遵守；服從

▶Some countires do not bey the rules of international law.
有些國家不遵守國際法。

object [`abdʒɪkt]　◀╡Track 1454
n 物體；對象；目標；目的

▶The museum is exhibiting a collection of precious objects from ancient China.
這間博物館正在展示一系列來自古代中國的珍貴收藏。

v 反對；反對説

▶Nobody objected when the teacher said there would be no homework today.
老師説今天沒有回家作業時，沒有人反對。

occur [ə`kɝ]　◀╡Track 1455
v 發生

▶The accident occurred ten mintues ago.
意外是在十分鐘前發生的。

ocean [`oʃən]　◀╡Track 1456
n 海洋

▶The Titanic sank in the Atlantic Ocean.
鐵達尼號沉到大西洋。

補充片語 the Atlantic Ocean
大西洋

o'clock [ə`klɑk]　◀╡Track 1457
adv ……點鐘

▶It's seven o'clock. Rise and shine.
七點了，起床吧。

October [ak`tobɚ]　◀╡Track 1458
=Oct. **n** 十月

▶Her birthday is in October.
她的生日在十月。

of [ɑv]
◀ Track 1459

prep. 屬於；……的；因為

▶He is a good friend of mine.
他是我的好友。

off [ɔf]
◀ Track 1460

adv. 離開；隔開；關掉

▶It's time to go to bed. Turn off the TV.
該睡覺了，把電視關掉。

prep. 在……下方；移開；離開

▶The horse hopped off the fence.
這隻馬跳躍過了圍籬。

adj. 偏離的；較遠的；不正常的

▶Give him a break. He's having an off day today.
不要為難他，他今天狀態不佳。

offer [ˈɔfɚ]
◀ Track 1461

v. 提供；提議；給予

▶He was offered a job in Sweden.
他在丹麥得到一份工作。

n. 提議；機會

▶They made an offer that we couldn't refuse.
他們的提議讓我們無法拒絕。

office [ˈɔfɪs]
◀ Track 1462

n. 辦公室；公司

▶Excuse me, where is Prof. Smith's office?
不好意思，史密斯教授的辦公室在哪裡？

相關片語 **office worker**
上班族

▶My father is a nine-to-five office worker.
我爸爸是朝九晚五的上班族。

補充片語 **nine-to-five**
朝九晚五的

officer [ˈɔfəsɚ]
◀ Track 1463

n. 官員（軍官；警官）；公務員；高級職員

▶Two police officers came here to investigate a crime.
兩名警官來這裡調查一件刑案。

official [əˈfɪʃəl]
◀ Track 1464

n. 官員；公務員

▶He is a high-ranking official in the US Department of State.
他是美國國務院的高階官員。

adj. 官方的；正規的

▶White House is the official residence of the president of the United States.
白宮是美國總統的官邸。

often [ˈɔfən]
◀ Track 1465

adv. 時常

▶She doesn't eat meat very often.
她不是很常吃肉。

oil [ɔɪl]
◀ Track 1466

n. 油

▶I use olive oil when I cook.
我用橄欖油煮菜。

v. 給……上油；塗油

▶She oiled her bike before riding it to school.
她騎腳踏車上學前給車子上了油。

相關片語 **burn the midnight oil**
開夜車

初級

▶She burned the midnight oil preparing for her daughter's wedding.
她為了準備女兒的婚禮而熬夜。

OK [ˋoˋke]　◀Track 1467
=O.K.=ok=o.k.=Okay
adj. 可以的；不錯的

▶Is it OK if I bring my children to work?
我帶著孩子來上班，可以嗎？

adv. 尚可

▶I slept OK last night.
我昨晚睡得還可以。

n. 認可

▶We got the OK from our boss to go ahead with our proposal.
我們的老闆同意我們實施提案。

v. 批准；認可

▶The chairman has OK'd our suggestions.
主席批准我們的建議。

old [old]　◀Track 1468
adj. 老的；舊的

▶It's never too old to learn.
活到老，學到老。

omit [oˋmɪt]　◀Track 1469
v. 遺漏；省略；忽略不做

▶The textbook omitted the slaughter that happened in World War II.
教科書省略掉第二次世界大戰發生的大屠殺。

on [ɑn]　◀Track 1470
prep. 在……上

▶There is a book on the desk.
書桌上有一本書。

adv. 繼續；（穿）上；開著

▶Turn on the TV. I want to watch a Korean drama.
打開電視，我要看一齣韓劇。

once [wʌns]　◀Track 1471
adv. 一次；曾經

▶I went mountain climbing once.
我去爬過一次山。

conj. 一旦；一……便……

▶Once you sign the contract, you can't make any changes.
你一旦簽了合約，就不能做更改了。

相關片語 **all at once**
突然

▶She lost her parents all at once.
她突然喪失雙親。

one [wʌn]　◀Track 1472
pron. 一個

▶He had two pieces of paper, and I had one.
他有兩張紙，我有一張。

n. 一；一歲

▶The toddler will be one next week.
這名幼兒下週就滿一歲了。

adj. 一的；一個的

▶I have one telescope.
我有一個望眼鏡。

相關片語 **one and only**
唯一的

▶He is the one and only person that both sides can trust.
他是雙方唯一可以信賴的人。

onion [`ʌnjən]
🔊 Track 1473

n. 洋蔥

▶He doesn't like the smell of oinions.
他不喜歡洋蔥的味道。

相關片語 **spring onion**
青蔥

▶Mom is chopping spring onions in the kitchen.
媽媽正在廚房切青蔥。

only [`onlɪ]
🔊 Track 1474

adv. 僅；只

▶He was only joking.
他只是在開玩笑。

adj. 唯一的

▶He was the only passenger on the bus.
他是巴士上唯一的乘客。

conj. 可是；不過

▶The fabric is similar to cotton, only it is a lot cheaper.
這種布料跟棉料類似，只不過價格便宜多了。

open [`opən]
🔊 Track 1475

v. 開；打開

▶Open your book and turn to page 30.
打開書並翻到三十頁。

adj. 開放的；打開的

▶He left his luggage open.
他把行李箱打開。

相關片語 **open secret**
公開的秘密

▶It's an open secret that Emily is looking for a new job.
艾蜜莉正在找新工作，這是個公開的秘密。

operate [`ɑpə͵ret]
🔊 Track 1476

v. 運轉；營運；操作；動手術

▶Could you show me how to operate the remote control?
你可以教我怎麼操作這個遙控器嗎？

operation [͵ɑpə`reʃən]
🔊 Track 1477

n. 操作；運轉；經營；手術

▶The operation was very successful.
手術很順利。

opinion [ə`pɪnjən]
🔊 Track 1478

n. 意見；看法

▶Everybody has different opinions on euthanasia.
每個人對安樂死都有不同的看法。

相關片語 **in one's opinion**
依某人所見

▶In my opinion, it is necessary to employ stricter gun control laws.
依我的見解，應該要實施更嚴格的法律來進行槍枝管制。

opportunity
🔊 Track 1479
[͵ɑpə`tjunətɪ]

n. 機會

▶He didn't have the opportunity to go to college.
他以前沒機會上大學。

or [ɔr]
🔊 Track 1480

conj. 或者；否則

▶Shape up or ship out.
不改進就開除你。

初級

orange [ˋɔrɪndʒ] ◀Track 1481

n. 柳橙；橙色

▶My favorite fruit is orange.
我最喜愛的水果是柳橙。

adj. 橙色的；柳橙的

▶Your foundation is a bit too orange.
你的粉底有點太橘了。

order [ˋɔrdə] ◀Track 1482

n. 次序；命令；訂購

▶He placed an order for a kitchen cabinet.
他訂了一個廚櫃。

相關片語	out of order
	發生故障

▶Our TV is out of order.
我們的電視故障了。

v. 命令；訂購；點菜

▶I ordered a spaghetti and a salad.
我點了一份義大利麵和沙拉。

ordinary [ˋɔrdn͵ɛrɪ] ◀Track 1483

adj. 平凡普通的；平常的

▶The movie star longs to live an ordinary life.
這名影星渴望過著平凡的生活。

organ [ˋɔrgən] ◀Track 1484

n. 器官

▶He donated his organs before he passed away.
他過世前捐贈了身上的器官。

organization [͵ɔrgənəˋzeʃən] ◀Track 1485
=organisation （英式英文）

n. 組織；機構

▶The Red Cross is a non-profit organization.
紅十字會是非營利組織。

organize [ˋɔrgə͵naɪz] ◀Track 1486
=organise （英式英文）

v. 組織；安排；籌劃；使有條理

▶The meeting was organized by UNESCO.
這個會議是由聯合國教科文組織籌劃的。

other [ˋʌðə] ◀Track 1487

adj. 其他的；其餘的；（兩者中）另一個的

▶She was standing on the other side of the street.
她站在街道的另一端。

pron. （兩者中的）另一方；其餘的人或事物

▶You shouldn't ask others to do your work for you.
你不應該叫別人替你做你的工作。

相關片語	every other day
	每隔一天；每兩天一次

▶I have ballet class every other day.
我每兩天有一堂芭蕾課。

our [ˋaʊr] ◀Track 1488

det. 我們的

▶We finished our homework at school.
我們在學校就寫完功課了。

ours [ˋaʊrz] ◀Track 1489

pron. 我們的（東西）

▶Which house is ours?
哪一間是我們的房子？

out [aʊt] ◀Track 1490

adv. 出外；向外；在外

▶She doesn't cook, so she always eats out.
她不煮飯，所以總是在外食。

adj. 外側的；向外的；用完的；不流行的

▶Mini skirts are out of fashion now.
迷你裙現在不流行了。

prep. 通過……而出

▶The cat jumped out of the window.
貓咪從窗口跳出去。

outside [`aʊt`saɪd] ◀€Track 1491
prep. 在……之外

▶We saw a strange person outside the window.
我們看見一個怪異的人在窗外。

adv. 在外面

▶It was hot outside.
外面很熱。

adj. 外面的；外部的

▶They called in an outside expert to help them restructure the company.
他們外請專家，協助重整公司。

n. 外面；外部；外觀

▶The outside of the hotel was painted pink.
飯店外部漆成了粉紅色。

oven [`ʌvən] ◀€Track 1492
n. 爐；烤箱

▶The chef roasted the beef in the oven.
主廚用烤箱烤牛肉。

over [`ovə] ◀€Track 1493
adv. 在上方；在上空；超過；遍及

▶He fell over and strained his ankle.
他跌倒並扭傷了腳踝。

adj. 結束了的

▶It was over between the two of us.
我們兩人之間的關係結束了。

prep. 在上方；在上空；越過上方

▶She put her hands over her ears because she couldn't bear to listen to the big noise.
她用手捂住耳朵，因為她無法忍受這麼大的噪音。

overpass [ˌovə`pæs] ◀€Track 1494
n. 天橋

▶He walked along this overpass on his way to school.
他沿著這座天橋走到學校。

overseas [`ovə`siz] ◀€Track 1495
adj. 海外的

▶The company is trying to break into the overseas markets.
這家公司正在努力打進海外市場。

adv. 在海外

▶She has been living overseas for over twenty years.
她在國外已住了超過二十年。

相關片語 **overseas student**
留學生

▶The school provides accommodations for overseas students.
學校有提供留學生宿舍。

owl [aʊl] ◀€Track 1496
n. 貓頭鷹；常熬夜的人

▶My husband is a night owl. He just feels more energetic at night.
我先生是個夜貓族，他晚上精神特別好。

own [on]
 Track 1497

pron. 自己的（東西）

▶He is planning to buy a house of his own.
他打算買一間屬於自己的房子。

v. 擁有

▶My parents own a Chinese restaurant in China Town.
我父母在中國城有一間中式餐廳。

adj. 自己的

▶She wants to have her own apartment.
她想擁有自己的公寓。

相關片語 **on one's own**
靠自己

▶He was on his own when he turned sixteen.
他十六歲就開始靠自己生活了。

owner [`onɚ]
 Track 1498

n. 所有人；物主

▶She is the owner of this cute puppy.
她是這隻可愛小狗的主人。

ox [ɑks]
 Track 1499

n. 牛；閹牛

▶He is as strong as an ox.
他壯得像頭牛。

▶ Pp

　　以下表格是全民英檢官方公告初級「聽、說、讀、寫」所須具備的能力，本書例句皆依此範疇特別設計，只要掃描右方QR code，就能搭配相對應的音軌，實現「眼耳並用」方式，刺激左腦的語言學習功能；同時也可使用本書附贈的紅膠片，將其置於單字上，一面記憶一面自我挑戰，達到雙倍的學習成果！

聽	▶ 能聽懂與日常生活相關的淺易談話，包含價格、時間及地點等。
說	▶ 能朗讀簡易文章、簡單地自我介紹，對熟悉的話題能以簡易英語對答，如問候、購物、問路等。
讀	▶ 可看懂與日常生活相關的淺易英文，並能閱讀路標、交通號誌、招牌、簡單菜單、時刻表及賀卡等。
寫	▶ 能寫簡單的句子及段落，如寫明信片、便條、賀卡及填表格等。對一般日常生活相關事物，能以簡短的文字敘述或說明。

初級

P.M. [ˋpiˋɛm]　　　　◀Track 1500
=p.m.=PM
adv. 下午；午後

▶The cocktail party began at 7:00 P.M.
　雞尾酒在晚上七點舉行。

----

pack [pæk]　　　　◀Track 1501
v. 裝箱；打包

▶We'll go to the United States tomorrow. Have you packed?
　我們明天要去美國，你打包了嗎？

n. 包；綑；包裹；背包

▶What she said was a pack of lies.
　她說的話是一堆謊言。

----

package [ˋpækɪdʒ]　　　　◀Track 1502
n. 包裹

▶The courier delivered a package for you about an hour ago.
　快遞約一小時前送來一個包裹給你。

| 相關片語 | **package tourist** 跟團遊客 |

▶Do you prefer to be a package tourist or a backpacking traveler?
　你喜歡跟團旅遊還是自助旅行？

----

page [pedʒ]　　　　◀Track 1503
n. 頁

▶There's a diagram on page 20.
　第二十頁有一張示意圖。

----

pain [pen]　　　　◀Track 1504
n. 疼痛、痛苦；辛苦

▶I feel a lot of pain on my back.
　我的背部很疼痛。

相關片語 **pain in the neck**
令人討厭的人事物

▶Lucy is a trouble maker. She is a pain in the neck.
露西是個麻煩製造者，很令人討厭。

painful [`penfəl]   ◀≣Track 1505
adj. 疼痛的；令人不快的

▶The news article brought back painful memories.
這篇新聞喚起了痛苦的回憶。

paint [pent]   ◀≣Track 1506
v. 油漆；漆上顏色；畫

▶She painted a mountain and a rainbow on the canvas.
她在油畫布畫了一座山和一條彩虹。

n. 油漆；塗料

▶The paint on the wall is starting to peel.
牆上的油漆正在剝落。

painter [`pentɚ]   ◀≣Track 1507
n. 油漆工；畫家

▶Monet was an impressionist painter.
莫內是印象派畫家。

相關片語 **Sunday painter**
業餘畫家

▶It is said that Hitler used to be a Sunday painter.
聽說希特勒曾是業餘畫家。

painting [`pentɪŋ]   ◀≣Track 1508
n. 上油漆；繪畫

▶I bought a painting to decorate the living room.
我買一幅畫來裝飾客廳。

pair [pɛr]   ◀≣Track 1509
n. 一對；一雙

▶She wore a pair of high heels.
她穿著一雙高跟鞋。

pajamas   ◀≣Track 1510
[pə`dʒæməs]
=pyjamas （英式英文）
n. 睡衣

▶Are you coming to my pajama party?
你要來參加我的的睡衣派對嗎？

pale [pel]   ◀≣Track 1511
adj. 蒼白的

▶He looked pale and gaunt.
他看起來很蒼白憔悴。

palm [pɑm]   ◀≣Track 1512
n. 手掌；手心

▶He held a five-dollar coin in the palm of his hand.
他的手掌握著一枚五元硬幣。

pan [pæn]   ◀≣Track 1513
n. 平底鍋

▶He heated the milk in a pan.
他用平底鍋熱牛奶。

panda [`pændə]   ◀≣Track 1514
n. 貓熊

▶Pandas eat bamboos.
貓熊吃竹子。

pants [pænts]   ◀≣Track 1515
=trousers （英式英語）
n. 褲子

▶ You look great in the new pants.
你穿這條新褲子很好看。

相關片語 **have ants in one's pants**
坐立難安

▶ He had ants in his pants. He couldn't wait to fly to Italy.
他坐立難安，等不及要飛行到義大利了。

---

papaya [pə`paɪə]　◀€Track 1516
n. 木瓜

▶ She grew a papaya tree in the garden.
她在庭院種了一顆木瓜樹。

---

paper [`pepɚ]　◀€Track 1517
n. 紙；報紙；試卷；報告；論文

▶ His paper has been constantly cited by researchers and students.
他的論文經常被研究員和學生引用。

相關片語 **paper tiger**
紙老虎；外強中乾的人或事物

▶ Pay no attention to what she said. She's a paper tiger.
不用理她說的話，她是一隻紙老虎。

---

pardon [`pardn]　◀€Track 1518
n. 原諒；寬恕

▶ I beg your pardon. What did you just say?
請重複一遍，你剛剛說什麼？

v. 原諒；寬恕

▶ Pardon me. I need to go home now.
不好意思，我現在得趕回家了。

---

parent [`pɛrənt]　◀€Track 1519
n. 父親；母親

▶ My parents owned a supermarket.
我的父母親擁有一家超市。

相關片語 **single parent**
單親

▶ A single parent, she brought up five children.
她是單親媽媽，帶大五個小孩。

Paris [`pærɪs]　◀€Track 1520
n. 巴黎

▶ Paris fashion week will begin next Monday.
巴黎時尚週將在下週一展開。

---

park [park]　◀€Track 1521
n. 公園；遊樂場

▶ Children are playing frisbee in the park.
孩子正在公園玩飛盤。

v. 停車

▶ I forgot where I parked my car.
我忘了我把車停在哪裡。

---

parrot [`pærət]　◀€Track 1522
n. 鸚鵡

▶ His parrot can speak three languages.
他的鸚鵡會說三種語言。

---

part [part]　◀€Track 1523
n. 部分；一部份

▶ Practicing calligraphy is a part of her daily routine.
練書法是她日常的一部份。

v. 分別；使分開；分成幾部分
► Jamie and Nicole parted on very bad terms.
傑米和妮可不歡而散。

particular [pəˋtɪkjələ] ◀Track 1524
adj. 特殊的；特定的
► She developed a particular interest in photography.
她對攝影有特殊的興趣。

partner [ˋpɑrtnə] ◀Track 1525
n. 夥伴；拍檔；合夥人
► He is a partner in a law firm.
他是律師事務所的合夥人。

party [ˋpɑrtɪ] ◀Track 1526
n. 派對；聚會；政黨
► They're going to Nick's birthday party.
他們正要去尼克的生日派對。

相關片語 **home party**
家庭派對；轟趴

► My family had a home party last weekend.
我們家上週舉辦了家庭派對。

pass [pæs] ◀Track 1527
v. 前進；通過；死亡；（考試）及格
► He passed his calculus exam.
他的微積分考試及格了。

n. 通行證
► You need a pass to visit the White House.
你參觀白宮時需通行證。

相關片語 **pass away**
去世

► My grandmother passed away five years ago.
我祖母五年前去世了。

passenger [ˋpæsndʒə] ◀Track 1528
n. 乘客；旅客
► Five passengers were injured in the random killing.
在這起隨機殺人事件中，有五名乘客受傷。

past [pæst] ◀Track 1529
prep. 經過；通過；超過
► It's four past three.
現在是三點四分。

adv. 經過；越過
► He walked right past us without saying anything.
他從我們身邊直接走過，什麼也沒說。

n. 過去；昔日；往事
► People used feathers to write and draw in the past.
從前人們用羽毛書寫和繪畫。

adj. 過去的；以前的
► The company has made a lot of profits over the past few years.
這間公司在過去幾年獲利很多。

paste [pest] ◀Track 1530
n. 漿糊；麵糰
► Mix the flour and egg into a paste.
把麵粉和蛋合成麵糰。

v. 用漿糊黏貼
► She cut the article and pasted it in her notebook.
她把文章剪下來，貼在她的筆記本裡。

pat [pæt]
🔊 Track 1531

v 輕拍；輕撫

▶The teacher patted his shoulder and told him to be brave.
老師拍了他的肩膀，叫他要勇敢。

n 輕拍；輕打

▶She gave the puppy a pat.
她輕輕拍了那隻幼犬。

path [pæθ]
🔊 Track 1532

n 小徑；小路

▶We walked along the path through the park.
我們沿著公園的小路走著。

patient [`peʃənt]
🔊 Track 1533

adj 有耐心的；有耐性的

▶The teacher is very patient with children.
老師對孩子很有耐心。

n 病人

▶Several patients were successfully treated with the new drug.
有幾位病人服用新藥的療效很好。

pattern [`pætən]
🔊 Track 1534

n 花樣；圖案

▶Our lifestyles have caused a change in weather patterns.
我們的生活方式已改變氣候型態。

pause [pɔz]
🔊 Track 1535

v 停頓；暫停

▶She paused and drank some water.
她停頓下來喝點水。

n 停頓；中斷

▶After a long pause, someone finally started a conversation.
在一段很長的停頓後，終於有人開啟對話了。

pay [pe]
🔊 Track 1536

v 支付；付錢；償還

▶She paid one hundred dollars for the ticket.
她花一百元買了這張票。

n 薪水；報酬

▶It was a stressful job, and the pay was low.
這份工作壓力很大，薪水又低。

初級

payment [`pemənt]
🔊 Track 1537

n 支付；付款；支付的款項

▶Payment will be made upon delivery.
貨到付款。

PE [pi-i]
🔊 Track 1538
=physical education

n 體育；體能教育

▶They played dodge ball in PE class this afternoon.
他們今天下午的體育課打躲避球。

peace [pis]
🔊 Track 1539

n 和平；平靜；治安

▶Although they have different religions, they live in peace with each other.
他們雖有不同的宗教，但彼此相處和睦。

補充片語 **live in peace with sb.**
與某人和睦相處

205

peaceful [`pisfəl]
Track 1540
adj. 平靜的；和平的；寧靜的；安詳的

▶The two countries found a peaceful solution.
這兩國找到和平的解決之道。

peach [pitʃ]
Track 1541
n. 桃子；桃樹；桃色

▶The peach had bruises on it.
這顆桃子有瘀痕。

peanut [`pi͵nʌt]
Track 1542
n. 花生

▶Who invented peanut butter?
花生醬是誰發明的？

補充片語 peanut butter
花生醬

pear [pɛr]
Track 1543
n. 洋梨；洋梨樹

▶The pear is too firm to eat.
這顆洋梨太硬，還不能吃。

pen [pɛn]
Track 1544
n. 筆；鋼筆

▶No matter where he goes, he always brings a pen with him.
不管他到哪裡，他總是帶著一枝筆。

pencil [`pɛns!]
Track 1545
n. 鉛筆

▶He wrote his homework with a pencil.
他用鉛筆寫作業。

penguin [`pɛngwɪn]
Track 1546
n. 企鵝

▶Penguins are aquatic birds.
企鵝是水棲動物。

people [`pip!]
Track 1547
n. 人們；人民；民族

▶There are billions of people all over the world.
全球有數十億人口。

相關片語 street people
在街頭流浪的人

▶The charity offered food to street people on New Year's Eve.
慈善機構在除夕夜提供街友食物。

pepper [`pɛpɚ]
Track 1548
n. 胡椒

▶I like to put some pepper in my corn chowder.
我喜歡在玉米濃湯裡放一些胡椒。

per [pɚ]
Track 1549
prep. 每

▶The dinner is $50 per person.
晚餐費用每人五十元。

perfect [`pɝfɪkt]
Track 1550
adj. 完美的；理想的

▶Practice makes perfect.
熟能生巧。

perhaps [pɚ`hæps]
Track 1551
adv. 也許；大概

▶Perhaps all she wanted was a big hug.
也許她需要的是一個大大的擁抱。

period [`pɪrɪəd]
n. 時期；時代；週期；生理期
◀€Track 1552

▶He bought the house during the SARS period.
嚴重急性呼吸道症候群爆發期間他買了這間房子。

person [`pɝsn]
n. 人
◀€Track 1553

▶He's a very generous person.
他是很大方的人。

personal [`pɝsn!]
adj. 個人的；私人的；涉及私事的
◀€Track 1554

▶Please don't forget your personal belongings when you leave the plane.
下機時請勿忘了攜帶個人物品。

相關片語	personal leave
	事假

▶I was on personal leave for two days.
我請事假兩天。

pet [pɛt]
n. 寵物
◀€Track 1555

▶She has three pets, a dog and two cats.
她有三隻寵物：一隻狗和兩隻貓。

相關片語	teacher's pet
	老師的寵兒

▶She is the teacher's pet, and she always gets straight A.
她是老師喜歡的學生，總是所有科目都得到優等。

Philippines [`fɪlə,pinz]
n. 菲律賓
◀€Track 1556

▶I have been to the Philippines.
我曾去過菲律賓。

phone [fon] =telephone
n. 電話
◀€Track 1557

▶May I have your phone number?
我能跟你要電話號碼嗎？

v. 打電話

▶Please phone him to get your book back.
請打電話給他，把你的書拿回來。

photo [`foto]
n. 相片；照片
◀€Track 1558

▶She took a lot of photos when she was young.
她年輕時拍了很多照片。

photograph [`fotə,græf]
=photo **n.** 相片；照片
◀€Track 1559

▶The woman in the photograph is a New York socialite.
照片中的女人是紐約名媛。

photographer [fə`tɑgrəfɚ]
n. 攝影師
◀€Track 1560

▶He is a fashion photographer.
他是時尚攝影師。

初級

phrase [frez]
◀ᴱ Track 1561
n. 片語；詞組

▶His pet phrase is "live your dream."
他的口頭禪是「築夢踏實」。

補充片語 pet phrase
口頭禪

physics [`fɪzɪks]
◀ᴱ Track 1562
n. 物理學

▶He majored in physics when he was in college.
他大學主修物理學。

piano [pɪ`æno]
◀ᴱ Track 1563
n. 鋼琴

▶He can play the piano beautifully.
他的鋼琴彈得很美妙動人。

pick [pɪk]
◀ᴱ Track 1564
v. 挑；撿；選；摘

▶He picked up the pencil from the floor.
他從地板撿起一枝鉛筆。

補充片語 pick up 撿起

相關片語 pick on sb.
找某人的碴

▶Stop picking on me. Pick on someone your own size.
別找我麻煩，有種去單挑跟你同類的人。

picnic [`pɪknɪk]
◀ᴱ Track 1565
n. 野餐

▶We had a picnic in the park today.
我們今天在公園野餐。

v. 野餐

▶They are picnicking on the river bank.
他們正在河岸上野餐。

picture [`pɪktʃɚ]
◀ᴱ Track 1566
n. 圖片；照片

▶He drew a picture of his girlfriend.
他畫了一張女友的畫像。

v. 想像；畫；拍攝

▶Can you picture a world without wars?
你能想像沒有戰爭的世界嗎？

pie [paɪ]
◀ᴱ Track 1567
n. 餡餅；派（有餡的酥餅）

▶Mom made a peach pie this morning.
媽媽早上做了一個桃子派。

相關片語 as easy as pie
極容易

▶Playing the violin is as easy as pie for him.
拉小提琴對他來說易如反掌。

piece [pis]
◀ᴱ Track 1568
n. 一片；一塊；一張；一件；破片

▶The teach gave each student a piece of paper.
老師給每個學生一張紙。

相關片語 piece of cake
極容易的事

▶The exam was a piece of cake to him.
這次考試對他來說容易得不得了。

pig [pɪg]
n. 豬

►You live like a pig. You really need to make a change.
你過著好邋遢的生活，你應該做個改變。

補充片語 live like a pig
過著邋遢的生活

相關片語 when pigs fly
絕不可能

►She will help the poor when pigs fly.
要她幫助窮人是絕不可能的事。

◄Track 1569

pigeon [`pɪdʒɪn]
n. 鴿子；鴿肉

►Spring is coming. Birds are singing and pigeons are cooing.
春天來了，鳥兒在唱歌，鴿子在咕咕叫。

◄Track 1570

pile [paɪl]
v. 堆積；堆放

►She piled the magazines on the coffee table.
她把雜誌堆放在咖啡桌上。

n. 堆；一堆；大量

►She put a pile of dirty clothes into the washing machine.
她把一大堆的髒衣服放進洗衣機。

相關片語 make one's pile
發財

►He made his pile from making cars.
他以製造汽車致富。

◄Track 1571

pillow [`pɪlo]
n. 枕頭

►I bought myself a new pillow.
我幫自己買了一個新枕頭。

◄Track 1572

pin [pɪn]
n. 大頭針；別針；胸針

►She stuck up a note on the board with a pin.
她在公告欄用大頭針釘了一個紙條。

v. （用別針）別住；（用大頭針）釘住

►He pinned a picture of galaxy on the bedroom wall.
他釘了一張銀河的海報在臥室的牆上。

◄Track 1573

pineapple [`paɪnˌæp!]
n. 鳳梨

►Pineapples are tropical fruit.
鳳梨是熱帶水果。

◄Track 1574

ping-pong [`pɪŋˌpɑŋ]
n. 乒乓球；桌球

►She is a professional ping-pong player.
她是職業乒乓球選手。

◄Track 1575

pink [pɪŋk]
adj. 粉紅的；桃紅的

►You look good in the pink dress.
你穿這件粉紅色的洋裝很好看。

n. 粉紅色；桃紅色

►My daughter's favorite color is pink.
我女兒最喜歡的顏色是粉紅色。

◄Track 1576

pipe [paɪp]
n. 管；煙斗；管樂器

►He repaired the damaged pipe.
他把壞掉的水管修好了。

◄Track 1577

初級

pitch [pɪtʃ] ◀Track 1578
n. 投球；音樂聲調

▶His voice dropped to a much lower pitch.
他的聲調降低了許多。

v. 投球

▶He pitched the ball as far as he could.
他盡力把球投得遠一些。

pizza [`pitsə] ◀Track 1579
n. 比薩；義大利肉餡餅

▶I'd like to have a pepperoni pizza.
我想點一份義大利香腸比薩。

place [ples] ◀Track 1580
n. 地方；居住的地方

▶He was looking for a place to live.
他在找住的地方。

v. 放置

▶She placed the old furniture in the basement.
她把舊家具放在地下室。

相關片語 **out of place**
不適合

▶It was out of place for you to laugh when the teacher said she was going to retire.
老師說要退休時，你笑了出來很不恰當。

plain [plen] ◀Track 1581
n. 平原；曠野

▶His photos successfully captured the beauty of the Mongolian plains.
他拍的照片成功捕捉了蒙古草原之美。

adj. 簡樸的；不攙雜的；清楚的；坦白的

▶He usually wears plain black shirt.
他常穿著樸素的黑襯衫。

adv. 清楚地；平易地；完全地

▶It's just plain silly to think that the world should revolve around you.
你以為世界應該要繞著你轉，簡直傻透了。

plan [plæn] ◀Track 1582
n. 計劃

▶Do you have any plan for the weekend?
你週末有什麼計畫嗎？

v. 做計劃；規劃

▶They plan to get married next month.
他們計畫下個月結婚。

plane [plen] ◀Track 1583
n. 飛機

▶The plane took off as normal on Monday evening.
飛機在星期一晚間正常起飛。

補充片語 **take off**
起飛

planet [`plænɪt] ◀Track 1584
n. 行星

▶Many people wonder if there are any intelligent life on other planets.
許多人都很好奇其他星球上是否有其他智慧生物的存在。

plant [plænt] ◀Track 1585
v. 種植

▶The farmer planted crops and vegetables.
農民種了稻穀和蔬菜。

n. 植物;植栽

▶This plant grows well and needs little water.
這種植物不用澆很多的水就能長得很好。

plate [plet]

n. 盤子

▶Can we stop using plastic plates and cups?
我們可以不要用塑膠盤和杯子嗎?

相關片語 **fashion plate**
穿著時髦的人

▶There's no denying that Lady Gaga is a fashion plate.
無可否認地,女神卡卡是個穿著時髦的人。

platform [ˈplætˌfɔrm]

n. 講台;月台

▶We are waiting for our train on the platform.
我們正在月台上等候火車。

play [ple]

v. 玩;遊戲;彈奏(樂器);
打(球類運動);扮演(角色)

▶The students played dodge ball during recess.
學生在下課時間玩躲避球。

n. 遊戲;戲劇;活動

▶We saw a wonderful play last night.
我們昨晚看了一場很棒的劇。

player [ˈpleɚ]

n. 選手;玩家

▶Beckham is a famous soccer player.
貝克漢是知名的足球員。

playful [ˈplefəl]

adj. 愛玩耍的;開玩笑的

▶The puppy is very playful.
幼犬很愛玩耍。

playground

[ˈpleˌgraʊnd]

n. 遊樂場;操場

▶Children are playing soccer on the playground.
孩子們在操場踢足球。

pleasant [ˈplɛzənt]

adj. 愉快的;欣喜的

▶Welcome to Taipei. We hope you'll have a pleasant stay.
歡迎來到台北,祝你們旅途愉快。

please [pliz]

v. 使滿意

▶Her mother is very hard to please.
她的媽媽很難取悅。

adv. 請

▶Please let me know if you need further information.
若你需要更進一步的資訊,請不吝告知。

相關片語 **please oneself**
請便

▶Please yourself if you are leaving the party.
若你要離開派對,請便囉。

pleased [plizd]

adj. 高興的;滿意的

▶My father was pleased to know that I got a promotion.
我爸爸很高興得知我升遷了。

初級

pleasure [`plɛʒɚ] ◀Track 1595
n. 愉快；高興；樂事

▶Her visits gave her parents great pleasure.
她去探望雙親，讓他們很開心。

plus [plʌs] ◀Track 1596
prep. 加上

▶Two plus two is four.
二加二是四。

adj. 正的，好處，高一點

▶The dress cost $1,000 plus.
這件洋裝要價一千元以上。

n. 好處，附加物

▶Your education background is a plus for the job.
你的學歷背景對於從事這份工作有加分的效果。

pocket [`pɑkɪt] ◀Track 1597
n. 口袋；財力

▶He is a man with deep pockets.
他是財力很雄厚的男人。

adj. 袖珍的；小型的；零星花用的

▶He delivered newspapers to earn some pocket money.
他送報紙賺取一些零用錢。

v. 把……裝入口袋內；侵吞；盜用

▶She carefully pocketed her money.
她小心地把錢放入口袋。

poem [`poɪm] ◀Track 1598
n. 詩

▶The pastoral poem is beautifully-written.
這首田園詩寫得真美。

poet [`poɪt] ◀Track 1599
n. 詩人

▶Robert Frost is my favorite poet.
羅伯特‧佛洛斯特是我最喜歡的詩人。

poetry [`poɪtrɪ] ◀Track 1600
n. （總稱）詩；詩歌；詩意

▶Shakespeare was a great master of English poetry.
莎士比亞是英國詩歌的大師級人物。

point [pɔɪnt] ◀Track 1601
v. 指；指出

▶He pointed out my mistakes.
他指出我的錯誤。

n. 尖端；要點；中心思想；得分

▶He made some interesting points in his essay.
他的文章中有些觀點很有意思。

相關片語 **point of view**
看法；觀點

▶From a political point of view, this policy won't work.
從政治的觀點來看，這項政策不會成功。

poison [`pɔɪzn] ◀Track 1602
n. 毒；毒藥；有害之物

▶We put some rat poison in the attic.
我們在閣樓放了一些老鼠藥。

v. 毒害；下毒

▶The police confirmed that the double agent was poisoned to death.
警方證實這位雙面間諜是被下毒害死的。

police [pə`lis] ◀Track 1603
n. 警察；警方

▶The police is investigating the heinous crime.
警方正在調查這起駭人的刑案。

相關片語 **police station**
警察局

▶Where is the nearest police station?
離這裡最近的警察局在哪裡？

policeman
◀ Track 1604
[pə`lismən]

=cop n. 警員；警察

▶My father is a policeman.
我爸爸是警察。

policy [`paləsɪ]
◀ Track 1605
n. 政策；方針

▶He advises the president on Asian policy.
他給總統有關亞洲政策的建議。

polite [pə`laɪt]
◀ Track 1606
adj. 禮貌的；有理的

▶You should be polite to your supervisors.
你應該要對上司有禮貌。

pollute [pə`lut]
◀ Track 1607
v. 污染

▶The toxic chemical has polluted the entire river.
有毒的化學物已污染了這條河流。

pollution [pə`luʃən]
◀ Track 1608
n. 污染

▶Noise pollution is a problem that has long been neglected.
噪音污染是個長期被忽視的問題。

pond [pɑnd]
◀ Track 1609
n. 池塘

▶Several frogs and fish live in the pond.
池塘裡住了幾隻青蛙和魚。

相關片語 **big fish in a little pond**
小地方的大人物；大材小用

▶He prefers to be a big fish in a little pond.
他寧為雞首，不為牛後。

pool [pul]
◀ Track 1610
n. 池；水池

▶The boy was swimming in a pool.
男孩在池裡游泳。

相關片語 **swimming pool**
游泳池

▶We have a swimming pool in the backyard.
我們在後院有個游泳池。.

poor [pʊr]
◀ Track 1611
adj. 可憐的；不幸的；貧窮的；粗劣的

▶He lived a poor life.
他過著貧窮的生活。

pop [pɑp]
◀ Track 1612
v. 突然出現；迅速行動；開槍

▶The children were popping all the balloons.
孩子們把所有的氣球弄爆了。

popcorn [`pɑp͵kɔrn]
◀ Track 1613
n. 爆米花

▶We bought a tub of popcorn.
我們買了一桶爆米花。

初級

popular [`pɑpjələ]　◀Track 1614

adj. 流行的；普遍的；受歡迎的

▶She is very popular at school.
她在學校很受歡迎。

population　◀Track 1615
[,pɑpjə`leʃən]

n. 人口

▶The population in Taiwan is decreasing.
台灣的人口正在減少中。

pork [pɔrk]　◀Track 1616
n. 豬肉

▶I'd like a pork steak, please.
我要一份豬排，麻煩了。

port [port]　◀Track 1617
n. 港；港市；口岸

▶Kiribati used to be the 17th busiest fishing port in the world.
吉里巴斯曾是全球第十七個最繁忙的漁港。

pose [poz]　◀Track 1618
v. 擺姿勢；裝腔作勢；使擺好姿勢

▶He posed for photographs in front of the Eiffel Tower.
他在艾菲爾鐵塔前面擺好了姿勢拍照。。

n. 姿勢；姿態

▶The model struck poses for cameras.
模特兒在相機前擺姿勢。

position [pə`zɪʃən]　◀Track 1619
n. 位置；地方；姿勢；地位；身份；立場；職務

▶I'm not in the position to make any comments on this issue.
針對這個議題，我沒有立場做出任何評論。

v. 把……放在適當位置

▶The army was positioned in the south of the city.
軍隊駐紮在城市的南邊。

positive [`pɑzətɪv]　◀Track 1620
adj. 確定的；確信的；積極的；
　　　肯定的；正面的

▶She has a positive attitude toward life.
她對生命抱持正面的態度。

possibility　◀Track 1621
[,pɑsə`bɪlətɪ]

n. 可能性

▶There is still a possibility that the team will win.
這支隊伍仍有獲勝的可能性。

possible [`pɑsəb!]　◀Track 1622
adj. 可能的；有可能的

▶Anything is possible.
任何事都有可能發生的。

相關片語 **as soon as possible**
　　盡快

▶We will fix the problem as soon as possible.
我們會盡快解決這個問題。

post [post]　◀Track 1623
n. 崗位；哨所；職守；郵政；郵寄；郵件

▶He works at the post office.
他在郵局上班。

v. 佈置（崗哨）

▶The diplomat was posted to Japan for two years.
外交官被外派到日本兩年。

postcard [`post͵kɑrd] ◀Track 1624
n. 明信片

▶Could you send me a postcard when you are in Botswana?
你到波紮那可以寄給我一張明信片嗎？

pot [pɑt] ◀Track 1625
n. 鍋子；一鍋

▶We made a pot of chicken soup.
我們做了一鍋雞湯。

potato [pə`teto] ◀Track 1626
n. 馬鈴薯

▶I like mashed potatoes with Parmesan cheese.
我喜歡馬鈴薯泥加巴馬臣芝士。

相關片語 **hot potato**
燙手山芋；棘手的問題

▶The ethics case is a hot potato.
這個跟倫理有關的案子是個燙手山芋。

pound [paʊnd] ◀Track 1627
n. 磅

▶The tomatoes weigh three pounds.
這番茄有三磅重。

powder [`paʊdɚ] ◀Track 1628
n. 粉；粉狀物；化妝用粉

▶She bought some chili powder and spices in the grocery store.
她在雜貨店買了一些辣椒粉和香料。

v. 擦粉；把粉撒在……上

▶Amy disappeared to powder her nose. 艾咪不在，她去補妝。

補充片語 **powder one's nose**
補粉

相關片語 **powder room**
（女用）化妝室

▶Where is the powder room?
化妝室在哪裡？

power [`paʊɚ] ◀Track 1629
n. 力量；能力；職權

▶The prime minister had more power than the president in that country.
那個國家總理的權力比總統還大。

相關片語 **come to power**
掌權；上任

▶When he came to power in 2017, the president and his cabinet tried hard to overcome economic stagnation.
二〇一七年上任後，總統和內閣致力克服經濟的停滯。

powerful [`paʊɚfəl] ◀Track 1630
adj. 強而有力的；有權威的；有影響的

▶Lions are powerful animals.
獅子是強而有力的動物。

practice [`præktɪs] ◀Track 1631
n. 練習

▶He has a talent for music, but he still needs a lot of practice.
他有音樂的天賦，但仍需要多加練習。

v. 練習

▶She practices playing the piano regularly.
她經常練鋼琴。

初級

praise [prez]
◀ Track 1632

v. 讚美；表揚

▶The scientist was highly praised for his research findings.
這名科學家因他的研究發現獲得高度讚揚。

n. 讚揚；稱頌

▶She deserved praise for her hard work and contributions.
她如此辛勤工作和奉獻，理應獲得表揚。

pray [pre]
◀ Track 1633

v. 祈禱；祈求

▶Let's pray that the children will be rescued safely.
我們祈求孩子能被安全救出。

presence ['prezns]
◀ Track 1634

n. 出席；在場；面前

▶The company has presence in four continents.
這家公司在四大洲都有事業版圖。

precious ['preʃəs]
◀ Track 1635

adj. 貴重的；珍貴的

▶My children are very precious to me.
我的小孩對我來說很寶貴。

prefer [prɪ`fɚ]
◀ Track 1636

v. 寧願；更喜歡

▶I prefer cold weather to hot weather.
比起熱天，我更喜歡冷天。

prepare [prɪ`pɛr]
◀ Track 1637

v. 準備

▶He burned the midnight oil to prepare for his presentation.
他熬夜準備他的報告。

present ['prɛznt]
◀ Track 1638

adj. 出席的；在場的；現在的；當前的

▶Tom Cruise will be present at the movie premiere in Los Angeles.
湯姆‧克魯斯將出席洛衫磯的電影首映會。

n. 禮物；現在

▶She gave me a present on my birthday.
我生日時，她給我一份禮物。

president
◀ Track 1639

['prɛzədənt]

n. 總統

▶Donald Trump is the current president of the United States.
唐納‧川普是現任美國總統。

press [prɛs]
◀ Track 1640

n. 新聞界；新聞輿論；壓、按；熨平、燙平

▶Unfortunately, freedom of the press is sometimes abused.
令人遺憾的是，新聞自由有時被濫用了。

v. 按；擠；壓；催促

▶Press the button to turn on the air conditioner.
按這個鈕來開冷氣。

pretty ['prɪtɪ]
◀ Track 1641

adj. 漂亮的

▶Amy is one of the prettiest girls at school.
艾咪是學校裡最漂亮的女孩之一。

adv. 非常；蠻；頗

▶He was pretty sad to know that he didn't pass the exam.
他得知考試不及格時，感到很難過。

price [praɪs] ◀ Track 1642

n. 價錢；價格

▶ I don't think the current housing prices are reasonable.
我不認為現在的房價是合理的。

v. 給……定價；為……標價

▶ The diamond was priced at $100,000.
這顆鑽石要價為十萬元。

pride [praɪd] ◀ Track 1643

n. 自豪；得意；引以為傲的人或事物；自尊心

▶ He felt a great sense of pride when his daughter was admitted to Harvard University.
他的女兒被哈佛大學錄取時，他感到很自豪。

priest [prist] ◀ Track 1644

n. 牧師

▶ He was ordained a priest in 1989.
他在一九八九年被授予牧師的職務。

prince [prɪns] ◀ Track 1645

n. 王子

▶ Prince Harry got married in 2018.
哈利王子在二〇一八年結婚。

princess [`prɪnsɪs] ◀ Track 1646

n. 公主

▶ The Little Princess is a famous children's novel.
小公主是著名的兒童讀物。

principle [`prɪnsəp!] ◀ Track 1647

n. 原則；原理；道德；信條

▶ The man doesn't have any principles.
這個男人毫無道德可言。

print [prɪnt] ◀ Track 1648

v. 印；印刷；發行；出版

▶ The magazine refuses to print swear words.
這家雜誌拒絕刊登髒話。

n. 印刷字體；印記；拷貝；印刷業

▶ The sentence is in italic print.
這個句子是斜體字。

相關片語 **out of print**
已絕版

▶ The textbook is outdated and therefore it's out of print.
這本教科書已跟不上時代了，所以已經絕版。

printer [`prɪntɚ] ◀ Track 1649

n. 印表機

▶ The print quality of the laser printer is superb.
這台雷射印表機的列印品質是上等的。

補充片語 **laser printer**
雷射印表機

prison [`prɪzn] ◀ Track 1650

n. 監獄；拘留所

▶ He was sent to prison for smuggling ivory.
他因為走私象牙而被送進牢房。

補充片語 **send sb. to prison**
送某人進牢房；將某人關進監獄

prisoner [`prɪznɚ] ◀ Track 1651

n. 犯人；囚犯

▶ The prisoner was tortured by electrical charges.
囚犯被用電擊折磨。

初級

pri·vate [`praɪvɪt] ◀≣Track 1652
adj. 個人的；私下的

▶She studied at a private high school.
她在私立高中就讀。

prize [praɪz] ◀≣Track 1653
n. 獎；獎品；獎金

▶I won the first prize in the raffle.
我摸彩得了最大獎。

probably [`prɑbəblɪ] ◀≣Track 1654
adv. 可能；有可能地

▶This is probably fake news again.
這可能又是假新聞。

problem [`prɑbləm] ◀≣Track 1655
n. 問題；難題

▶He had financial problems three years ago.
他在三年前面臨財務危機。

相關片語 **sleep over a problem**
把問題留到第二天再解決

▶Kevin is not the kind of man who sleeps over a problem.
凱文不是會把問題留到第二天再解決的人。

produce [prə`djus] ◀≣Track 1656
v. 生產；出產

▶Our company produces skin care products.
我們的公司生產保養品。

producer [prə`djusə] ◀≣Track 1657
n. 生產者；製作人

▶The famous producer was involved in a number of sex scandals.
這名製片人涉及多起性醜聞。

product [`prɑdəkt] ◀≣Track 1658
n. 產品

▶We came up with new ideas to market our new product.
我們想了一些新點子來行銷我們的新產品。

production [prə`dʌkʃən] ◀≣Track 1659
n. 生產；製作；產量；產物

▶The new car will go into production next month.
這款新車下個月將開始生產。

professor [prə`fɛsə] ◀≣Track 1660
n. 教授

▶Professor Nye is an expert in economics.
奈伊教授是經濟學的專家。

program [`progræm] ◀≣Track 1661
=programme （英式英文）
n. 節目；節目單；計劃；方案

▶My favorite TV program is Britain's Got Talent.
我最喜歡的電視節目是《英國達人秀》。

v. 為……安排節目；為（電腦）設計程式；為……制定計劃

▶The company programmed the Falcon 9 rocket's first stage.
這家公司負責設計獵鷹九號火箭第一階段的發射任務。

progress [prə`grɛs] ◀≣Track 1662
n. 前進；進步；進展

▶The country has made a lot of progress on human rights.
這個國家在人權取得很大的進展。

v. 前進；進步

▶My French hasn't progressed much. I really need to study hard to catch up with the rest of the class.
我的法文進步不多，我實在要好好用功趕上班上其他同學。

補充片語 catch up with
趕上

project [prə`dʒɛkt]
◀ Track 1663

n. 計劃；企劃

▶The project was completed successfully.
這個企劃案已成功完成了。

promise [`prɑmɪs]
◀ Track 1664

v. 承諾；答應；保證

▶I promised her that I will not spill the beans.
我向她承諾不會洩密。

補充片語 spill the beans
洩密

n. 承諾；諾言

▶He kept his promise to renegotiate the deal.
他遵守承諾重新協議這筆交易。

pronounce
◀ Track 1665

[prə`naʊns]

v. 發音

▶Could you tell me how to pronounce the word?
你可以告訴我這個字要怎麼發音嗎？

propose [prə`poz]
◀ Track 1666

v. 提議；建議；求婚

▶Josh proposed to his girlfriend last night.
喬許昨晚向女友求婚。

相關片語 propose a toast
提議祝酒

▶Before we start the meal, I want to propose a toast to my parents.
開飯前，我提議向我的父母舉杯祝賀。

protect [prə`tɛkt]
◀ Track 1667

v. 保護

▶The secret service agents are responsible for protecting the president's safety.
密勤人員負責保護總統的安全。

protection
◀ Track 1668

[prə`tɛkʃən]

n. 保護；防護

▶Construction workers wore hard hats for protection.
建築工人為了防護而帶工地帽。

proud [praʊd]
◀ Track 1669

adj. 驕傲的；得意的

▶He is very proud of his daughter.
他很以女兒為榮。

prove [pruv]
◀ Track 1670

v. 證明；結果是

▶The experiment proved a success.
這個實驗結果是大成功。

provide [prə`vaɪd]
◀ Track 1671

v. 提供

▶The soup kitchen provides food for the homeless.
這個施食處提供流浪者食物。

初級

補充片語 **soup kitchen**
施食處

public [`pʌblɪk]
🔊 Track 1672

adj. 大眾的；公共的；民眾的

▶Diana used her fame to raise public awareness of a number of important humanitarian issues.
黛安娜利用她的知名度喚起大眾對許多人道議題的重視。

n. 公眾；民眾

▶The library welcomed the public to attend a community meeting there.
圖書館歡迎民眾前往參加社區大會。

pudding [`pʊdɪŋ]
🔊 Track 1673

n. 布丁

▶The butterscotch pudding is so delicious.
牛油糖果布丁真是美味啊。

pull [pʊl]
🔊 Track 1674

v. 拉；拖；牽；拽；拔

▶She pulled the curtain open.
她把窗簾拉開。

n. 拉；拖；拉力

▶The little girl gave her father's tie a pull, and he made a face in return.
小女孩拉了一下她爸爸的領帶，爸爸做了鬼臉回應。

相關片語 **give sth. a pull**
拉某物

pump [pʌmp]
🔊 Track 1675

n. 泵，唧筒；幫浦

▶The pump is powered by solar energy.
這個幫浦是用太陽能驅動的。

v. 用唧筒抽；打氣；灌注

▶He is pumping air into the flat tire.
他正在幫沒氣的輪胎打氣。

pumpkin [`pʌmpkɪn]
🔊 Track 1676

n. 南瓜

▶Cinderella rode in a carriage made from a pumpkin to meet her prince.
灰姑娘乘南瓜變成的馬車去見她的王子。

punish [`pʌnɪʃ]
🔊 Track 1677

v. 處罰

▶He was punished for not doing his homework.
他因沒做回家作業而被處罰。

punishment
🔊 Track 1678

[`pʌnɪʃmənt] **n.** 懲罰

▶Some people are for capital punishment while others are not.
有些人支持死刑，有些人則否。

補充片語 **capital punishment**
死刑

pupil [`pjup!]
🔊 Track 1679

n. 小學生，學生；未成年人

▶They are third-year pupils.
他們是小學三年級的學生。

puppet [`pʌpɪt]
🔊 Track 1680

n. 木偶，玩偶；傀儡

▶The emperor became a puppet of military generals.
皇帝變成將軍們的傀儡。

puppy [ˋpʌpɪ]　◀€ Track 1681

n. 小狗

▶We found a stray puppy in the garage.
我們在車庫發現一隻流浪的幼犬。

相關片語 **puppy love**
少男少女的短暫戀愛

▶My grandfather still remembers his puppy love with pleasure.
我祖父想起年輕時的青澀戀愛，仍感到歡喜。

purchase [ˋpɝtʃəs]　◀€ Track 1682

n. 購買；購買之物

▶The system is a wise purchase.
購買這個系統是明智的。

v. 購買

▶You can purchase the goods online.
你可以在網路上買到這些商品。

purple [ˋpɝp!]　◀€ Track 1683

adj. 紫色的；紫的

▶You look gorgeous in the purple gown.
你穿這件紫色晚禮服真美。

n. 紫色

▶His favorite color is purple.
他最喜歡的顏色是紫色。

相關片語 **born in the purple**
生於顯貴家庭

▶From an early age, the princess knew she was born in the purple.
公主很小的時候就知道自己出生於顯貴家庭。

purpose [ˋpɝpəs]　◀€ Track 1684

n. 目的；意圖；用途

▶The money should be used to good purpose.
這筆錢應用在該用的地方。

相關片語 **answer sb.'s purpose**
適合某人的需要

▶This expedient answered her purpose.
這個權宜之計符合她的需求。

purse [pɝs]　◀€ Track 1685

n. 錢包；女用手提包

▶She bought a leather purse.
她買了一個皮革錢包。

push [pʊʃ]　◀€ Track 1686

v. 推；催促

▶The teacher pushed his students to study hard.
老師督促他的學生用功讀書。

n. 推進；努力；衝進

▶She is a bright kid. All we need to do is to give her a push and she will excel.
她是個聰明的孩子。我們要做的就是推她一把，她就會表現得很卓越。

補充片語 **give sb. a push**
推某人一把

put [pʊt]　◀€ Track 1687

v. 放；擺；使處於……狀態

▶He put his keys on the desk.
他把鑰匙放在書桌上。

初級

puzzle [`pʌz!]

◀⊱Track 1688

n. 謎;難題

▶The case has remained a puzzle for centuries.
這個案子長達數世紀仍是個謎團。

v. 迷惑;為難;使迷惑不解

▶We were puzzled about how the incident could have happened.
我們對於這個事件發生的原因感到很困惑。

▶ Qq

　　以下表格是全民英檢官方公告初級「聽、說、讀、寫」所須具備的能力，本書例句皆依此範疇特別設計，只要掃描右方QR code，就能搭配相對應的音軌，實現「眼耳並用」方式，刺激左腦的語言學習功能；同時也可使用本書附贈的紅膠片，將其置於單字上，一面記憶一面自我挑戰，達到雙倍的學習成果！

聽 ▶	能聽懂與日常生活相關的淺易談話，包含價格、時間及地點等。
說 ▶	能朗讀簡易文章、簡單地自我介紹，對熟悉的話題能以簡易英語對答，如問候、購物、問路等。
讀 ▶	可看懂與日常生活相關的淺易英文，並能閱讀路標、交通號誌、招牌、簡單菜單、時刻表及賀卡等。
寫 ▶	能寫簡單的句子及段落，如寫明信片、便條、賀卡及填表格等。對一般日常生活相關事物，能以簡短的文字敘述或說明。

初級

quality [ˋkwɑlətɪ] ◀ Track 1689
n. 品質

▶ The quality of the company's products is excellent.
這家公司的產品品質很優。

相關片語 quality time
（與家人相處的）珍貴時光

▶ She spent quality time with her mother during family holidays.
她在家族渡假期間享受與母親共度的珍貴時光。

quantity [ˋkwɑntətɪ] ◀ Track 1690
n. 量；數量；分量；大量；音量

▶ It's quality not quantity that matters.
重要的是質量而非數量。

quarter [ˋkwɔrtɚ] ◀ Track 1691
n. 四分之一；一刻鐘

▶ It's a quarter after seven.
現在是七點十五分。

queen [ˋkwin] ◀ Track 1692
n. 皇后

▶ Meghan's mother was invited by Queen Elizabeth to spend Christmas with the royal family.
梅根的媽媽獲伊麗莎白女皇的邀請和皇室共度耶誕節。

question [ˋkwɛstʃən] ◀ Track 1693
n. 問題；詢問

▶ After a long pause, someone finally asked a question.
停頓了很久，終於有人提問了。

v. 質疑；詢問

▶After the food scandal, the public began to question the company's integrity.
食品醜聞爆發之後，大眾開始質疑這家公司的誠信度。

相關片語 pop the question 求婚

▶Grace was overjoyed when her boyfriend popped the question.
當葛麗絲的男友向她求婚時，她樂不可支。

quick [kwɪk] ◀ Track 1694
adj. 快的

▶He had a quick breakfast and then rushed to the office.
他匆忙吃完餐，然後衝去辦公室。

相關片語 quick-tempered
性急的；易怒的

▶She is arrogant and quick-tempered.
她很傲慢又易怒。

quiet [`kwaɪət] ◀ Track 1695
adj. 安靜的

▶Be quiet. The baby is sleeping.
安靜點，寶寶正在睡覺。

quit [kwɪt] ◀ Track 1696
v. 戒除；離開；退出；停止

▶He quit his job because of health problems.
他因健康因素而辭掉工作。

quite [kwaɪt] ◀ Track 1697
adv. 相當

▶The twin sisters have quite different personalities.
這對雙胞胎姊妹個性相當迥異。

相關片語 quite some time
相當長的時間

▶She has been a fan of the boy band for quite some time.
她已是這個男子團體的粉絲一段時間了。

quiz [kwɪz] ◀ Track 1698
n. 測驗；隨堂小考

▶I have a math quiz tomorrow.
我明天有數學隨堂考。

相關片語 pop quiz
突擊測驗

▶Our science teacher gave us a pop quiz.
我們的自然老師給我們臨時測驗。

▶ **Rr**

　　以下表格是全民英檢官方公告初級「聽、說、讀、寫」所須具備的能力，本書例句皆依此範疇特別設計，只要掃描右方QR code，就能搭配相對應的音軌，實現「眼耳並用」方式，刺激左腦的語言學習功能；同時也可使用本書附贈的紅膠片，將其置於單字上，一面記憶一面自我挑戰，達到雙倍的學習成果！

聽	▶ 能聽懂與日常生活相關的淺易談話，包含價格、時間及地點等。
說	▶ 能朗讀簡易文章、簡單地自我介紹，對熟悉的話題能以簡易英語對答，如問候、購物、問路等。
讀	▶ 可看懂與日常生活相關的淺易英文，並能閱讀路標、交通號誌、招牌、簡單菜單、時刻表及賀卡等。
寫	▶ 能寫簡單的句子及段落，如寫明信片、便條、賀卡及填表格等。對一般日常生活相關事物，能以簡短的文字敘述或說明。

初級

---

rabbit [ˋræbɪt]　◀ᔒ Track 1699

n. 兔子

▶ We have a pet rabbit in the backyard.
我們的後院養了一隻家兔。

---

race [res]　◀ᔒ Track 1700

v. 比速度；參加競賽；使全速行進；使疾走

▶ He raced down the stairs and shouted at the man who killed his wife.
他飛奔走下樓梯對著殺害他妻子的男子咆哮。

n. 賽跑；競賽；人種；民族

▶ Let's have a ping-pong race.
我們來場桌球比賽吧。

---

radio [ˋredɪˌo]　◀ᔒ Track 1701

n. 收音機；無線電廣播

▶ He switched on the radio to listen to some music.
他打開收音機聽音樂。

---

railroad [ˋrelˌrod]　◀ᔒ Track 1702
=railway（英式英文）

n. 鐵路

▶ Two new railroads are under constructions.
兩條新鐵路正在興建中。

---

rain [ren]　◀ᔒ Track 1703

n. 雨

▶ According to weather forecast, there will be rain tomorrow.
根據氣象預測，明天會下雨。

v. 下雨

▶ It never rains but it pours.
屋漏偏逢連夜雨。

相關片語 **rain cats and dogs**
下傾盆大雨

▶It was raining cats and dogs an hour ago.
一小時前，外頭正下著傾盆大雨。

rainbow [`ren͵bo]　◀ Track 1704
n. 彩虹

▶There was a beautiful rainbow in the afternoon.
下午有道很美麗的彩虹。

rainy [`renɪ]　◀ Track 1705
adj. 下雨的；多雨的

▶Yesterday was a rainy day.
昨天是下雨天。

raise [rez]　◀ Track 1706
v. 舉起；提高；養育；豎起

▶Journalists raised their hands to ask questions in the press conference.
記者們在記者招待會舉手提問。

n. 加薪；提高

▶He was promoted and given a raise.
他獲得升遷及加薪。

range [rendʒ]　◀ Track 1707
n. 範圍；區域

▶They offered us a range of options.
他們給了我們各種選擇。

v. 排列；使並列；把……分類；範圍涉及……

▶The price ranges between $15 and $20.
價格在十五到二十元之間。

rapid [`ræpɪd]　◀ Track 1708
adj. 快的；快速的

▶She made a rapid recovery after the operation.
她手術後復原很迅速。

rare [rɛr]　◀ Track 1709
adj. 很少的；罕見的

▶These plants are rare.
這些植物很罕見的。

rat [ræt]　◀ Track 1710
n. 老鼠

▶I hate rats.
我討厭老鼠。

rather [`ræðɚ]　◀ Track 1711
adv. 相當；頗；寧可；倒不如

▶She felt rather uncomfortable.
她感到很不舒服。

reach [ritʃ]　◀ Track 1712
v. 抵達；到達；伸手及到；與……取得聯繫

▶You can reach me by e-mail.
你可以用電郵聯絡我。

n. 可及的範圍

▶The rat poison was put out of children's reach.
老鼠藥放在孩子拿不到的地方。

補充片語 **out of one's reach**
某人拿不到的地方

read [rid]　◀ Track 1713
v. 閱讀

▶I like to read novels and poems.
我喜歡讀小說和詩。

ready [`rɛdɪ]
◀€ Track 1714

adj. 準備好的

▶Are you ready? Get set, and go!
你準備好了嗎？預備，開始！

real [`riəl]
◀€ Track 1715

adj. 真的；真實的

▶My love for you is real.
我對你的愛是真實的。

reality [ri`ælətɪ]
◀€ Track 1716

n. 真實；現實

▶She is out of touch with reality.
她脫離現實。

realize [`rɪə͵laɪz]
=realise （英式英文）
◀€ Track 1717

v. 領悟；理解

▶Do you realize what you have done?
你意識到你做了什麼事了嗎？

really [`rɪəlɪ]
◀€ Track 1718

adv. 很；確實地；真的

▶Gary is really nice.
蓋瑞人真的很好。

reason [`rizn]
◀€ Track 1719

n. 理由；原因

▶He credited his wife as the reason why he became a better man.
他把自己成為一個更好男人的原因，歸功給他的妻子。

receive [rɪ`siv]
◀€ Track 1720

v. 收到；獲得

▶Have you received my wedding invitation?
你收到我的婚禮邀請函了嗎？

recent [`risnt]
◀€ Track 1721

adj. 最近的；不久前的

▶There has been too much violent content on TV in recent years.
最近幾年電視有太多的暴力內容。

recently [`risntlɪ]
◀€ Track 1722

adv. 最近；近來；不久前

▶We just met recently.
我們最近才認識彼此。

record
◀€ Track 1723

[`rɛkəd] [rɪ`kɔrd]

n. 記載；紀錄；前科紀錄；成績；最高紀錄

▶She keeps a record of her daily expenses.
她每天都把花費記錄下來。

v. 記錄；錄音

▶I recorded the song from the radio.
我從收音機把這首歌錄下來了。

recover [rɪ`kʌvə]
◀€ Track 1724

v. 重新獲得；恢復（原狀）；挽回；彌補

▶He hasn't recovered from pneumonia.
他的肺炎還沒康復。

rectangle
◀€ Track 1725

[rɛk`tæŋg!]

n. 矩形；長方形

▶She folded a piece of paper into a rectangle.
她把紙摺成了一個長方形。

初級

recycle [ri`saɪk!] ◀ Track 1726

v. 使再循環;使再利用;回收

▶Paper, bottle, and metal can be recycled.
紙張、瓶子、金屬都是可以回收利用的。

red [rɛd] ◀ Track 1727

adj. 紅的;紅色的

▶Children receive red envelopes during the Chinese New Year.
小孩過農曆年能拿到紅包。

n. 紅;紅色;紅色的衣服

▶He used a lot reds and blacks in his paintings .
他的畫作大量使用紅色和黑色。

相關片語 **see red**
　　　　生氣;盛怒

▶He saw red when he was turned away from seeing his son.
他被拒絕探視兒子而感到很氣憤。

refrigerator
[rɪ`frɪdʒə͵retə] ◀ Track 1728
=fridge=icebox

n. 冰箱

▶She put all her food in the refrigerator.
她把所有食物都放在冰箱裡。

refuse [rɪ`fjuz] ◀ Track 1729

v. 拒絕

▶She refused her boyfriend's proposal.
她拒絕男友的求婚。

regard [rɪ`gɑrd] ◀ Track 1730

v. 把……看作;看待;注重

▶She is regarded as the best teacher at the school.
她被公認是學校最好的老師。

n. 注意;關心;問候;敬意

▶I hold Einstein in high regard.
我很尊敬愛因斯坦。

region [`ridʒən] ◀ Track 1731

n. 地區;行政區域;部位;領域

▶We live in the sub-tropical region.
我們住在亞熱帶。

regret [rɪ`grɛt] ◀ Track 1732

v. 後悔;懊悔;感到遺憾

▶I believe you won't regret it.
我相信你不會後悔的。

n. 遺憾;悔恨;哀悼

▶She had no regrets for what she had done.
她對自己所做的事一點都沒有悔意。

regular [`rɛgjələ] ◀ Track 1733

adj. 固定的;規律的

▶She made a regular visit to her mother.
她定期探望媽媽。

reject [rɪ`dʒɛkt] ◀ Track 1734

v. 拒絕;抵制;駁回;排斥

▶He rejected her help.
他拒絕她的幫助。

relation [rɪ`leʃən] ◀ Track 1735

n. 關係;關聯;血親關係;親屬

▶They seem to have bad relations with their neighbors.
他們看起來和鄰居關係很不好。

relationship
◀€Track 1736

[rɪˋleʃənˋʃɪp]

n. 關係；人際關係；親屬關係；婚姻關係；戀愛關係

▶The golden couple ended their relationship last month.
這對金童玉女上個月結束了婚姻關係。

相關片語 **parent-child relationship**
親子關係

▶Reading with your children can foster parent-child relationship.
和孩子一同閱讀有助發展良好的親子關係。

relative [ˋrɛlətɪv]
◀€Track 1737

adj. 相對的；比較的；與……有關的

▶She has been living in relative comfort since she worked in the new company.
她自從在新公司工作後，日子過得相對舒適了些。

n. 親戚；親屬

▶My parents are my immediate relatives.
我父母是我的直系親屬。

remember
◀€Track 1738

[rɪˋmɛmbɚ]

v. 記得；記住

▶He couldn't remember my phone number.
他不記得我的電話號碼。

remind [rɪˋmaɪnd]
◀€Track 1739

v. 提醒；使記起

▶The movie reminds me of an old friend of mine.
這部電影使我想起一位老友。

rent [rɛnt]
◀€Track 1740

n. 租；租借；租金

▶The apartment is for rent.
這間公寓待出租。

v. 租；租用

▶The company rented the building as its headquarters.
公司租了這棟大樓做為總部。

repair [rɪˋpɛr]
◀€Track 1741

n. 修理；修補；修理工作；維修狀況；修理部位

▶The trousers have several repairs.
這件褲子有幾處修補過的地方。

v. 修理；修補；補救

▶I had my scooter repaired yesterday.
我昨天把機車送修。

repeat [rɪˋpit]
◀€Track 1742

v. 重複；重做；重讀

▶Repeat after me.
跟著我一起唸。

相關片語 **repeat a year**
留級

▶He flunked several exams and had to repeat a year.
他很多考試都不及格，必須留級。

reply [rɪˋplaɪ]
◀€Track 1743

v. 回答；答覆；回應

▶He didn't reply to my question.
他沒回答我的問題。

n. 回覆；答覆

初級

▶The company gave me a prompt reply after I made a complaint about their service.
我向公司抱怨他們的服務後，得到了迅速的回覆。

---

report [rɪ`port] 🔊 Track 1744

n. 報告；報導；成績單

▶According to the weather report, there will be a cold air mass coming next week.
根據氣象預報，下週將有一波冷氣團報到。

v. 報告；報導；告發

▶The candidate was reported to the police for bribery.
候選人被檢舉賄選。

相關片語	report for duty
	報到上班

▶The newcomer has reported for duty this morning.
新進人員早上已報到上班。

---

reporter [rɪ`portɚ] 🔊 Track 1745

n. 記者

▶My uncle is a reporter.
我叔叔是位記者。

---

require [rɪ`kwaɪr] 🔊 Track 1746

v. 需要；要求；命令

▶Visitors are required to take off their shoes when entering the temple.
訪客進入廟宇需要脫鞋。

---

requirement 🔊 Track 1747

[rɪ`kwaɪrmənt]

n. 需要；必需品；必要條件；要求

▶He failed to meet the requirements of the course and was flunked.
他沒達到這門課程的要求而被當掉。

---

respect [rɪ`spɛkt] 🔊 Track 1748

n. 尊敬；尊重；注重

▶I have great respect for Prof. Yang.
我非常敬重楊教授。

v. 尊敬；尊重

▶Her parents respected her choice to be an actress.
她的父母尊重她要成為女演員的決定。

---

responsible 🔊 Track 1749

[rɪ`spɑnsəb!]

adj. 有責任的；負責任的

▶We all need to be responsible for our behavior.
我們都要對自己的行為負責。

---

rest [rɛst] 🔊 Track 1750

v. 休息

▶She rested for half an hour before picking up her son.
她休息了半小時後，再去接兒子。

n. 休息

▶You really need to take a rest.
你真的該休息了。

---

restaurant 🔊 Track 1751

[`rɛstərənt]

n. 餐廳

▶The food at that restaurant is very tasty.
那間餐廳的食物很美味。

restroom [ˈrɛstrum] ◀Track 1752

n. 洗手間；廁所；盥洗室

▶ He went to the restroom about five minutes ago.
他大概五分鐘前去洗手間了。

result [rɪˈzʌlt] ◀Track 1753

n. 結果；後果

▶ She was anxious about the exam result.
她對於考試結果感到很焦慮。

v. 產生；發生；導致……結果

▶ Their failure resulted from their recklessness.
他們的失敗是魯莽所致。

補充片語 result from
因……所造成

相關片語 without result
徒勞無功；毫無結果

▶ The meeting concluded without result.
會議結束卻毫無成果。

return [rɪˈtɜ˞n] ◀Track 1754

v. 返回；歸；回復；歸還

▶ He left Sierra Leone at the age of 14 and had never returned.
他十四歲離開獅子山以後就再也沒回去過。

n. 返回；歸；回報；報答

▶ After her return, you two can discuss the problem together.
在她回來之後，你們兩個可以一起討論這個問題。

review [rɪˈvju] ◀Track 1755

n. 複習；溫習；再檢查；複審；評論

▶ The new film got mixed reviews.
這部新片毀譽參半。

v. 複習

▶ He reviewed his notes before the exam.
他在考試前複習筆記。

revise [rɪˈvaɪz] ◀Track 1756

v. 修訂；校訂；修改

▶ The editor-in-chief revised the news article before it was released online.
總編修改新聞稿後，才讓它發布在網路上。

rice [raɪs] ◀Track 1757

n. 米；米飯

▶ I prefer rice to noodles.
比起麵，我更喜歡吃米飯。

相關片語 rice milk
米漿

▶ The rice milk is so creamy and mellow.
這米漿非常濃郁順口。

rich [rɪtʃ] ◀Track 1758

adj. 富裕的；豐富的；有錢的

▶ The country is rich in natural resources.
這個國家天然資源豐富。

n. 有錢人

▶ The economy in this particular area is mainly supported by the rich living here.
這個特殊地區的經濟主要是由住在這裡的有錢人支撐起來的。

相關片語 new rich
最近致富的人；
暴發戶（源自法文neuvo riche）

▶ He sells cars to India's new rich.
他賣車給印度的新富。

初級

ride [raɪd]
🔊 Track 1759

v. 騎馬；乘車；乘車旅行；乘坐；搭乘

▶ I ride a scooter to work everyday.
我每天騎機車上班。

n. 騎；乘坐；搭乘；乘車旅行；兜風

▶ She asked me for a ride into the city.
她要求搭我的便車去城市裡。

相關片語 **give sb. a ride**
讓某人搭車；搭載某人

▶ It's midnight. Let me give you a ride.
已經半夜了，讓我送你回家。

right [raɪt]
🔊 Track 1760

adj. 對的；正確的；右邊的

▶ You're right. I should've kept her at bay.
你是對的，我早該離她遠一點。

adv. 對；正確地；向右

▶ Go straight ahead along the street and then turn right.
沿著街道直走，然後右轉。

n. 右邊；右側；權利

▶ They defended human rights by peaceful means.
他們以和平的方式捍衛人權。

ring [rɪŋ]
🔊 Track 1761

v. 按鈴；敲鐘；打電話；（鐘或鈴）響

▶ The children rang the doorbell and chanted "trick-or-treat."
孩子們按門鈴並呼喊「不給糖就搗蛋」。

n. 戒指

▶ She is showing off her diamond ring again.
她又在炫耀她的鑽石戒指了。

rise [raɪz]
🔊 Track 1762

v. 上昇；升起；上漲；增加

▶ The consumption of milk has risen lately in urban areas.
最近市區的牛奶消費量有增加的趨勢。

n. 增加；上漲；上升；提升；發跡

▶ Juvenile delinquency is on the rise again.
青少年犯罪率再度增長。

river [`rɪvɚ]
🔊 Track 1763

n. 河；河流

▶ There is a river in front of the house.
房子前面有一條河流。

roach [rotʃ]
🔊 Track 1764

n. 蟑螂

▶ I hate roaches, especially those that can fly.
我討厭蟑螂，特別是會飛的。

road [rod]
🔊 Track 1765

n. 馬路

▶ There is no royal road for learning.
學習沒有捷徑。

rob [rɑb]
🔊 Track 1766

v. 搶劫；盜取；非法剝奪

▶ The military regime robbed the people of their freedom and democracy.
軍政府剝奪了人民的自由與民主。

補充片語 **rob sb. of sth.**
從某人身上搶劫某物

robot [`robət]
◀Track 1767

n. 機器人

▶The AI robot can make you a better ping-pong player.
這部人工智慧機器人能幫助你成為更好的桌球選手。

---

rock [rɑk]
◀Track 1768

n. 岩石；石塊

▶Her faith remains as firm as a rock.
她的信心堅若磐石。

v. 搖動；使搖晃

▶The babysitter rocked the baby to sleep.
保姆輕輕搖著寶寶哄他入睡。

相關片語 **rock the boat**
無風起浪；惹是生非

▶Things are going pretty well, so don't rock the boat.
事情進展得很順利，所以別無風起浪。

相關片語 **on the rocks**
加冰塊

▶I'll have a champagne on the rocks.
我的香檳要加冰塊。

---

rocky [`rɑkɪ]
◀Track 1769

adj. 岩石的；多岩石的；岩石構成的

▶They rode scooters carefully through the rocky lane.
他們沿著石子小徑小心騎著機車。

---

role [rol]
◀Track 1770

n. 角色；作用

▶The famous actor played the leading role in the blockbuster.
那位知名的男演員在這部賣座強片扮演主角。

---

roll [rol]
◀Track 1771

v. 滾動；轉動；搖擺；搖晃

▶A dice rolled under the table.
骰子滾到桌子底下去了。

n. 滾動；一捲；捲餅

▶Mom made some egg rolls and cakes for desserts.
媽媽做了一些蛋捲和蛋糕做為甜點。

補充片語 **egg roll**
蛋捲

相關片語 **roll one's eyes**
翻白眼

▶Simon rolled his eyes at Amy because he knew she was lying again.
賽門對艾咪翻了個白眼，因為他知道她又在說謊了。

---

roof [ruf]
◀Track 1772

n. 屋頂

▶We heard a cat meowing atop our roof.
我們聽到屋頂有隻貓在喵喵叫。

相關片語 **hit the roof**
勃然大怒

▶Mom hit the roof when she heard Peter cheat on his exam.
媽媽聽到彼得考試作弊，氣得不得了。

---

room [rum]
◀Track 1773

n. 房間；室；空間；場所

▶He never had a room of his own until now.
他直到現在之前，從來沒有自己的房間。

相關片語 **living room** 客廳

初級

▶We have a bean bag chair in the living room.
我們的客廳有個豆袋椅。

rooster [`rustɚ]　◀≋Track 1774
n. 公雞；狂妄自大的人

▶My grandfather raised a lot of roosters and hens in his chicken farm.
我祖父在養雞場養了很多公雞和母雞。

root [rut]　◀≋Track 1775
n. 根；根部；根基；根源

▶The roots of the tree go down at least two meters.
樹根至少深至二公尺以下。

v. 使紮根；使固定；生根；根源於

▶Ivies root easily in water.
常春藤很容易在水中生根。

rope [rop]　◀≋Track 1776
n. 繩子；繩索

▶He was at the end of his rope.
他已黔驢技窮了。

rose [roz]　◀≋Track 1777
n. 玫瑰

▶He gave his girlfriend 99 roses.
他送給女友九十九朵玫瑰。

round [raʊnd]　◀≋Track 1778
adv. 環繞地；在周圍；在附近；到各處

▶He looked round and saw no one.
他環顧四方，沒看到任何人。

prep. 環繞；在……周圍；去……四處

▶We sat round the pool in the evening.
我們晚上圍著水池坐著。

n. 一輪；一回合；循環

▶She won a round of applause after she finished her singing.
她唱完歌以後，得到一陣掌聲。

adj. 圓的；圓形的

▶The hairstyle suits people with round faces.
這種髮型適合圓臉的人。

row [raʊ]　◀≋Track 1779
n. 一列；一排

▶They had seats in the back row of the theater.
他們坐在戲院後排。

v. 划船

▶We rowed the boat gently down the stream.
我們從容划船過小河。

royal [`rɔɪəl]　◀≋Track 1780
adj. 王室的；皇家的

▶Meghan is a new member of the royal family.
梅根是皇室的新成員。

rub [rʌb]　◀≋Track 1781
v. 擦；摩擦

▶She rubbed her hands together with embarrassment.
她尷尬地摩擦雙手。

相關片語 **rub sb. the wrong way**
惹惱某人

▶He rubbed Peter the wrong way by characterizing Betty as evil.
他形容貝蒂是邪惡的，而惹惱了彼得。

補充片語 **in a bad mood**
心情很差

rubber [`rʌbɚ]
◀≋ Track 1782

adj. 橡膠製成的

▶She wore a pair of rubber slippers.
她穿了一雙橡膠拖鞋。

n. 橡膠

▶She worked in a rubber factory.
她在橡膠工廠工作。

rude [rud]
◀≋ Track 1783

adj. 魯莽的；無禮的

▶Don't be rude to your sister.
你對妹妹不能無禮。

ruin [`rʊɪn]
◀≋ Track 1784

n. 毀滅；毀壞；廢墟、遺跡

▶They visited the ruins of Roman amphitheater.
他們參觀羅馬競技場的遺跡。

v. 毀壞

▶My mother ruined my life.
我媽媽毀了我的生命。

rule [rul]
◀≋ Track 1785

n. 規則；規定；慣例

▶Diplomats have immunity against the rule of law in the country they are serving.
外派他國的外交官在當地擁有刑事免責權。

v. 統治；管轄；支配

▶The king ruled his country for more than 30 years.
國王統治他的國家逾三十年。

ruler [`rulɚ]
◀≋ Track 1786

n. 尺；統治者

▶She used a ruler to draw a triangle.
她用尺畫出一個三角形。

run [rʌn]
◀≋ Track 1787

v. 跑；奔馳；經營

▶He can run very fast.
他跑得很快。

n. 跑；奔馳

▶The train station is a ten minutes' run from the museum.
從火車站到博物館跑步需十分鐘。

runner [`rʌnɚ]
◀≋ Track 1788

n. 跑步者；賽跑者

▶She is a marathon runner.
她是馬拉松跑者。

rush [rʌʃ]
◀≋ Track 1789

v. 衝；闖；趕緊；急速行動

▶The injured man was rushed to the hospital by his wife.
受傷的男子被妻子火速送到醫院。

n. 衝；奔；急速行動；匆忙；緊急

▶There was a rush for the train tickets before Chinese New Year.
農曆年前出現了搶購火車票的熱潮。

Russia [`rʌʃə]
◀≋ Track 1790

n. 蘇俄

▶She used to study in Russia in her youth.
她年輕時曾在蘇俄留學。

初級

Russian [ˋrʌʃən]

◀€ Track 1791

adj. 蘇俄的；俄語的

▶The Russian girl is a supermodel, who has many followers on her Facebook page.

這個俄國女孩是名超模，在臉書有很多追蹤者。

n. 俄國人；俄語

▶He can speak Russian, Spanish, and English.

他能說俄語、西班牙語和英語。

▶ Ss

以下表格是全民英檢官方公告初級「聽、說、讀、寫」所須具備的能力，本書例句皆依此範疇特別設計，只要掃描右方QR code，就能搭配相對應的音軌，實現「眼耳並用」方式，刺激左腦的語言學習功能；同時也可使用本書附贈的紅膠片，將其置於單字上，一面記憶一面自我挑戰，達到雙倍的學習成果！

聽 ▶	能聽懂與日常生活相關的淺易談話，包含價格、時間及地點等。
說 ▶	能朗讀簡易文章、簡單地自我介紹，對熟悉的話題能以簡易英語對答，如問候、購物、問路等。
讀 ▶	可看懂與日常生活相關的淺易英文，並能閱讀路標、交通號誌、招牌、簡單菜單、時刻表及賀卡等。
寫 ▶	能寫簡單的句子及段落，如寫明信片、便條、賀卡及填表格等。對一般日常生活相關事物，能以簡短的文字敘述或說明。

初級

sad [sæd] ◀Track 1792
adj. 悲傷的；悲哀的

▶He has been very sad since his girlfriend passed away.
他的女友過世後，他至今仍悲傷不已。

safe [sef] ◀Track 1793
adj. 安全的；平安的

▶It's not safe going out alone in this city.
在這座城市晚上單獨出門是不安全的。

n. 保險箱；冷藏櫃

▶She kept her jewelry in the safe.
她把珠寶存放在保險箱裡。

相關片語 **safe and sound**
安然無恙地

▶The child came back safe and sound.
孩子平安無事地回來。

safety [`seftɪ] ◀Track 1794
n. 安全；平安

▶For your safety, please observe the following rules.
為了你的安全，請遵守以下規則。

sail [sel] ◀Track 1795
v. 航行；開船；駕駛（船）

▶My grandfather can sail a boat.
我祖父會駕船。

n. 乘船航行；船隻；船帆

▶They set sail from Norway.
他們從挪威啟航。

sailor [`selɚ] ◀Track 1796
n. 船員；水手

▶He was a sailor on the USS Oklahoma.
他是奧克拉荷馬號戰艦的手水。

salad [ˋsæləd]
🔊 Track 1797

n. 沙拉

▶Caesar salad is one of my all-time favorite salads.
凱撒沙拉是我最喜愛的沙拉之一。

相關片語	salad days
	少不更事的時期

▶I was silly and immature during my salad days.
我年輕不懂事時既愚蠢又不成熟。

sale [sel]
🔊 Track 1798

n. 出售;銷售額;拍賣

▶The apartment is for sale.
這棟公寓要出售。

相關片語	on sale
	廉售中;特賣中

▶The clothes are on sale for $100.
這些衣服特價一百元。

salesman [ˋselzmən]
🔊 Track 1799

n. 推銷員;男店員

▶He's a car salesman.
他是汽車推銷員。

salt [sɔlt]
🔊 Track 1800

n. 鹽

▶Don't rub salt into my wound.
不要在我的傷口上撒鹽。

salty [ˋsɔltɪ]
🔊 Track 1801

adj. 鹹的

▶Sea water tastes salty.
海水嘗起來是鹹的。

same [sem]
🔊 Track 1802

pron. 相同的事物

▶Your zodiac sign is just the same as mine.
你和我的星座是同一個。

adj. 一樣的;相同的

▶She wore the same dress at two different locations.
她在兩個場合都穿一樣的洋裝。

sample [ˋsæmp!]
🔊 Track 1803

n. 樣品;試用品;例子

▶I got a free sample of the skin care product.
我拿到護膚品的免費試用品。

v. 抽樣檢查;品嘗;體驗

▶She sampled the tea and then added more tea leaves.
她試喝了一下茶,接著加了更多的茶葉。

sand [sænd]
🔊 Track 1804

n. 沙

▶They walk barefoot on the sand.
他們赤腳走在沙子上。

sandwich [ˋsændwɪtʃ]
🔊 Track 1805

n. 三明治

▶I had a tuna sandwich for breakfast.
我早餐吃了一個鮪魚三明治。

satisfy [ˋsætɪsˌfaɪ]
🔊 Track 1806

v. 使滿意;使滿足;滿足

▶His answer didn't satisfied her.
他的回應並未讓她感到滿意。

Saturday [ˋsætɚde] =Sat.
🔊 Track 1807

n. 星期六

▶I usually get up late on Saturdays.
我通常星期六都很晚起。

sauce [sɔs]
🔊 Track 1808
n. 醬；醬汁

▶Mom used soy bean sauce to cook beef stew.
媽媽用醬油燉牛肉。

saucer [ˋsɔsɚ]
🔊 Track 1809
n. 茶托；淺碟

▶The restaurant served the tea in cups and saucers.
餐廳用茶杯和茶碟裝茶。

相關片語 **saucer eyes**
睜得又圓又大的眼睛

▶The kitten looked at fish with her saucer eyes.
小貓睜著又圓又大的眼睛看著魚。

save [sev]
🔊 Track 1810
v. 救；挽救；節省；儲蓄；保留

▶She saved money every month in order to buy a house.
她為了買房子，每個月都存錢。

相關片語 **save face**
保留面子

▶Both parties saved face with the compromise.
兩個政黨因為妥協而都保足了面子。

saw [sɔ]
🔊 Track 1811
v. 鋸；鋸開

▶He sawed off the dead branches.
他把枯枝鋸掉。

n. 鋸子

▶He used a hand saw to cut up the firewood。
他用手鋸砍柴火。

say [se]
🔊 Track 1812
v. 說；講述

▶Mom said you should study harder.
媽媽說你應該用功一點。

scale [skel]
🔊 Track 1813
n. 刻度；比例；規模；磅秤

▶Social workers are not on the high social scale in that country.
那個國家的社工地位不高。

scared [skɛrd]
🔊 Track 1814
adj. 害怕的；不敢的

▶She is scared of darkness.
她害怕黑漆漆的一片。

scarf [skɑrf]
🔊 Track 1815
n. 圍巾

▶I bought a knitted scarf.
我買了一條針織圍巾。

scene [sin]
🔊 Track 1816
n. 場面；景色；（事件發生的）地點；（戲劇的）場景

▶The scene of the film was set in London.
這部電影在倫敦取景。

school [skul]
🔊 Track 1817
n. 學校

▶He went to school at seven o'clock.
他七點鐘去上學 。

初級

science [`saɪəns] ◀Track 1818
n. 科學

▶She majored in computer science in college.
她大學主修電腦科學。

scientist [`saɪəntɪst] ◀Track 1819
n. 科學家

▶He is a climate scientist.
他是氣候科學家。

scissors [`sɪzɚz] ◀Track 1820
n. 剪刀

▶She used the scissors to cut the ribbon at the opening of the new museum.
她在新博物館的落成典禮中用剪刀剪綵。

scooter [`skutɚ] ◀Track 1821
n. 踏板車；小輪摩托車

▶Brad loved his scooter, and he rode it around and about.
布萊德很愛他的摩托車，騎著它到處趴趴走。

score [skor] ◀Track 1822
v. 得分

▶The New York Yankees scored three in the ninth.
紐約洋基棒球隊在第九局得了三分。

n. 分數；比數

▶She got the score of eighty-five on the exam.
她考試得了八十五分。

screen [skrin] ◀Track 1823
n. 屏；幕；簾；螢幕；紗窗、門

▶He bought a television with a 40-inch screen.
他買了一部四十吋的電視。

v. 遮蔽；掩護；放映（電影）

▶The show will be screened on PBS.
這個節目將在美國公共電視放映。

sea [si] ◀Track 1824
n. 海

▶I sent the cargo by sea.
我用海運寄送貨物。

search [sɝtʃ] ◀Track 1825
n. 搜查；搜尋；調查

▶After a long search, she finally found her birth certificate.
她找了很久才找到她的出生證明。

v. 搜查；細看；探查

▶He searched his memory for the woman's face, but he couldn't remember it.
他拼命想起這個女人的長相，卻怎麼也記不起來。

season [`sizn] ◀Track 1826
n. 季節

▶New York's fashion season begins in March.
紐約時尚季在三月開始。

v. 為……調味

▶The chef seasoned the dish with rosemary.
主廚用迷迭香幫這道菜調味。

相關片語 **rainy season**
雨季

▶He avoids traveling during rainy season.
他避免在雨季外出旅行。

seat [sit] n. 座位 ◀Track 1827

▶Please keep my seat for me while I'm in the bathroom.
我去上廁所時，請幫我看著我的座位。

v. 就座

▶The theater seats 100 people.
戲院可坐一百人。

second [`sɛkənd] ◀Track 1828

n. 秒；瞬間；片刻；第二名

▶Do you have a second? I need to talk to you.
你有時間嗎？我需要跟你談一下。

adj. 第二的；次要的

▶Jamie is their second child.
傑米是他們的第二個孩子。

adv. 其次；居次地

▶Aron won the race and Kevin finished second.
艾倫得了賽跑冠軍，凱文得了第二名。

相關片語 second banana
在戲裡演配角的人

▶She was sick and tired of playing second banana in the play.
她很厭倦在戲裡擔任配角。

secret [`sikrɪt] ◀Track 1829

adj. 秘密的；私下的；神秘的

▶The prisoner was kept in a secret cell.
戰俘被藏在祕密的牢房裡。

n. 秘密

▶Your secret is safe with me.
我會守口如瓶的。

secretary [`sɛkrə,tɛrɪ] ◀Track 1830

n. 秘書

▶She was seeking for a job as a secretary.
她在找秘書的工作。

section [`sɛkʃən] ◀Track 1831

n. 部分；地段；切下的部分

▶She is reading the entertainment section in the newspaper.
她正在閱讀報紙的娛樂版。

see [si] ◀Track 1832

v. 看到；看見；理解；將……看作；目睹

▶Have you seen the woman before?
你見過這名女子嗎？

相關片語 see sb. off
為某人送行

▶She went to the airport to see her boyfriend off.
她到機場站為男友送機。

seed [sid] ◀Track 1833

n. 種子；籽；根源

▶Pumpkin seeds are nutritious.
南瓜籽很營養。

seek [sik] ◀Track 1834

v. 尋找；探索；追求

▶He has been seeking medical help for sleep problems.
他為了改善睡眠問題，一直在尋求醫療協助。

相關片語 hide-and-seek
捉迷藏

▶Children are playing hide-and-seek in the house.
孩子們正在屋裡玩捉迷藏。

初級

seem [sim]
v. 看起來好像；似乎
▶She seemed very happy.
她看起來很快樂。

Track 1835

seesaw [`si,sɔ]
n. 翹翹板
▶Let's play on the seesaw.
我們去玩翹翹板吧。

Track 1836

seldom [`sɛldəm]
adv. 很少
▶I seldom go to the movie theater.
我很少到電影院看電影。

Track 1837

select [sə`lɛkt]
v. 挑選
▶She selected a white shirt to match her black skirt.
她選了一件白襯衫搭配黑裙子。

Track 1838

selection [sə`lɛkʃən]
n. 選擇；選拔；挑選
▶These are the selections from Hemingway.
這些是海明威的作品選集。

Track 1839

self [sɛlf]
n. 自身；自己；自我
▶She isn't her usual cheerful self.
她不像平時那麼開朗。

Track 1840

selfish [`sɛlfɪʃ]
adj. 自私的
▶The man is selfish and ego-centric.
這個男人既自私又自我中心。

Track 1841

sell [sɛl]
v. 賣；出售
▶The online store sells everything you can think of.
這家網路商店賣的東西應有盡有。

Track 1842

相關片語 **sell sb. out**
出賣某人
▶She was sold out by her boss.
她被她的老闆出賣了。

semester [sə`mɛstɚ]
n. 學期
▶We will have a new homeroom teacher next semester.
我們下學期會有新的級任老師。

Track 1843

send [sɛnd]
v. 發送；派遣；寄
▶He sent me a love letter.
他送給我一封情書。

Track 1844

sense [sɛns]
n. 感覺；感官；意識；意義
▶She doesn't have any common sense at all.
她一點常識都沒有。

v. 感覺到；意識到；了解
▶I could sense that something went terribly wrong.
我能感覺到事情非常不對勁。

相關片語 **make sense**
講得通；具有意義
▶Your logic doesn't make sense to me.
你的邏輯對我來說講不通。

Track 1845

sentence [`sɛntəns]
n. 句子

Track 1846

▶There are two typos in this sentence.
這個句子中有兩個打字錯誤。

separate [`sɛpəˌret]
◀Track 1847

adj. 分開的；單獨的；個別的

▶They were interviewed in separate rooms.
他們在個別的房間裡接受面試。

v. 分割；分離

▶The couple separated and shared custody.
這對夫妻分居並共同享有監護權。

September
◀Track 1848

[sɛp`tɛmbə]

=Sept. **n.** 九月

▶The president will visit Japan in September.
總統九月將訪日。

serious [`sɪrɪəs]
◀Track 1849

adj. 嚴重的；嚴肅的；認真的

▶Climate change is a serious problem.
氣候變遷是很嚴重的問題。

servant [`sɝvənt]
◀Track 1850

n. 僕人

▶My father is a public servant.
我爸爸是公務員。

serve [sɝv]
◀Track 1851

v. 為……服務；供應（飯菜）；端上；任職；服刑

▶He served in the navy for 10 years.
他在海軍服役十年。

service [`sɝvɪs]
◀Track 1852

n. 服務

▶The service of the hotel was excellent.
這家餐廳的服務很棒。

set [sɛt]
◀Track 1853

n. 一套；一組；一部

▶A set of commemorative stamps has been issued recently in tribute to the former president.
最近有一套紀念郵票即將發行以紀念前任總統。

v. 放；置；設置；調整

▶She cooked while her husband set the table.
她在做飯，先生幫忙擺碗盤。

adj. 固定的；下定決心的；準備好的

▶Everything was set for the party.
派對一切都準備妥當了。

settle [`sɛt!]
◀Track 1854

v. 安頓；安排；安放；確定；使安下心來；解決

▶She arrived precisely at rehearsal time, and had not settled herself after hurrying to make it.
她在彩排的那一刻準時抵達，並因匆忙趕來而沒能平靜下來。

settlement
◀Track 1855

[`sɛt!mənt]

n. 解決；協議；安頓；安身

▶So far, it's not likely to negotiate a peaceful settlement between the two countries.
至今看來，兩國要達成和平協議還不太可能。

初級

seven [ˋsɛvn]
🔊 Track 1856

pron. 七個

▶Seven of the students failed the exam.
這群學生中有七個考試不及格。

n. 七;七歲

▶Seven plus two is nine.
七加二等於九。

adj. 七的;七個的

▶There are seven people in my family.
我家有七個人。

seventeen
🔊 Track 1857

[͵sɛvnˋtin]

pron. 十七個

▶Seventeen of the thirty chairs were occupied.
三十張椅子中,有十七張已有人坐了。

n. 十七

▶She became a mother at the age of seventeen.
她在十七歲當了媽媽。

adj. 十七的;十七個的

▶There are seventeen students in my class.
我的班上有十七個學生。

seventy [ˋsɛvntɪ]
🔊 Track 1858

pron. 七十個

▶He bought one hundred apples, and I bruised seventy of them.
他買了一百個蘋果,我弄傷了其中七十個。

n. 七十

▶At seventy, she was still very energetic.
她七十歲仍精力充沛。

adj. 七十的;七十個的

▶The incident happend seventy years ago.
這起事件是在七十年前發生的。

several [ˋsɛvərəl]
🔊 Track 1859

adj. 幾個的

▶I have several friends that I completely trust.
我有幾個朋友是我完全可以信任的。

pron. 幾個

▶Several of the students were late for class.
有好幾個學生上課遲到。

shake [ʃek]
🔊 Track 1860

v. 震動;搖動;動搖

▶The two leaders shook hands when they met.
兩國領袖見面時握手。

n. 搖動;震動;握手;地震

▶He gave the box a shake before opening it.
他在打開箱子之前,搖了一下箱子。

shall [ʃæl]
🔊 Track 1861

aux. 將;會(用於第一人稱、亦可用於問句第一和第三人稱)

▶Shall we go now?
我們現在要出發了嗎?

shape [ʃep]
🔊 Track 1862

n. 形狀;形式;(健康的)情況

▶She eats organic food and does yoga to stay in shape.
她吃有機食物並做瑜珈來保持健康。

補充片語 stay in shape
保持健康

v. 形成；塑造；使成形

▶Young people play an important role in shaping our future.
年輕人在塑造我們的未來方面扮演著重要的角色。

補充片語 play an important role
扮演重要角色

share [ʃɛr]
◀ Track 1863

n. 一份；（分擔的）一部份；分攤

▶He didn't do his share of the work.
他沒盡到分內的工作。

v. 分擔；分享

▶Tiffany and her sister share some common characteristics.
蒂芬妮和她妹妹有一些共同的特徵。

shark [`ʃɑrk]
◀ Track 1864

n. 鯊魚；貪婪狡猾的人；詐騙者

▶That man is like a shark.
那個男人很狡猾。

sharp [ʃɑrp]
◀ Track 1865

adj. 尖銳的；鋒利的；急劇的；急轉的

▶He's got a sharp tongue.
他說話很刻薄。

she [ʃi]
◀ Track 1866

pron. 她

▶She is a super model.
她是名模。

she'd [ʃid]
◀ Track 1867

abbr. 她會、她已（**she had**或**she would**的縮寫）

▶She'd chatted online for three hours.
她已在網路聊天長達三個小時了。

sheep [ʃip]
◀ Track 1868

n. 羊；綿羊

▶My grandparents kept a flock of sheep in their farm.
我的祖父母在農場養了一群羊。

相關片語 black sheep
害群之馬；敗類；敗家子

▶Born in a wealthy family, he is the black sheep of his family.
他出生富裕，卻是家中的敗家子。

sheet [ʃit]
◀ Track 1869

n. 床單；（一張）紙

▶He wrote his e-mail on a sheet of paper.
他把電郵寫在一張紙上。

shelf [ʃɛlf]
◀ Track 1870

n. 架子；擱板

▶She put the old magazines on the bottom shelf.
她把舊雜誌放在底層書架。

相關片語 shelf life
保存期限；耐儲時間

▶The shelf life of the canned tuna is six months.
這個鮪魚罐頭的保存期限是六個月。

shell [ʃɛl]
◀ Track 1871

n. 殼；外殼；甲殼

▶Turtles all have shells.
烏龜都有甲殼。

she'll [ʃil]
◀ Track 1872

abbr. 她會（**she will**的縮寫）

▶She'll visit us tomorrow.
她明天會來看我們。

初級

she's [ʃiz] ◀Track 1873
abbr. 她是（**she is** 的縮寫）

▶She's taking a selfie.
她正在自拍。

shine [ʃaɪn] ◀Track 1874
v. 發光；照耀

▶The sun shone brightly while I walked out of the office.
我走出辦公室時，陽光正發出耀眼的光芒。

ship [ʃɪp] ◀Track 1875
n. 船

▶The ship struck a rock and sank deep into the ocean.
船撞到一座岩石，沉入海底中。

v. 船運；運送

▶The goods will be shipped to the US by Friday.
貨物在星期五以前將以海運送到美國。

shirt [ʃɝt] ◀Track 1876
n. 襯衫；男式襯衫

▶There is a stain on your shirt.
你的襯衫有污漬。

相關片語 **keep one's shirt on**
不發脾氣

▶Keep your shirt on. Let me handle it.
別發脾氣，交給我來處理。

shock [ʃɑk] ◀Track 1877
n. 衝擊；震驚；打擊；中風

▶The new kind of terrorism came as a shock to everyone.
新型態的恐怖主義對大家來說是個很大的衝擊。

shocked [ʃɑkt] ◀Track 1878
adj. 使人感到震驚的

▶I was shocked to see how ill she was.
看到她病得這麼重，我感到很震驚。

shoe [ʃu] ◀Track 1879
n. 鞋子

▶She wore a pair of ballet shoes.
她穿著一雙芭蕾舞鞋。

相關片語 **in sb's shoes**
處於某人的境地

▶Maybe you should put yourself in his shoes.
或許你應該站在他的立場想一下。

shoot [ʃut] ◀Track 1880
v. 放射；開槍；射中

▶The politician was shot by an assassin.
這名政治人物遭到刺客開槍射中。

n. 射擊；拍攝；狩獵會

▶The super model did a fashion shoot in the garden.
超模在花園拍攝時裝照。

shop [ʃɑp] ◀Track 1881
=store
n. 商店

▶I bought a new hat in the shop.
我在商店買了一頂新帽子。

v. 購物；逛商店

▶We're going shopping tomorrow.
我們明天要去購物。

shore [ʃɔr] ◀Track 1882
n. 岸；濱

▶The yacht was about two miles off the shore.
遊艇離岸邊有兩英里左右的距離。

---

short [ʃɔrt] ◀ Track 1883
adj. 矮的；短的

▶She is shorter than her brother.
她比弟弟矮。

---

shorts [ʃɔrts] ◀ Track 1884
n. 短褲；寬鬆運動短褲

▶He wore a T-shirt and tennis shorts to the class.
他穿著汗衫和網球短褲去上課。

---

shot [ʃɑt] ◀ Track 1885
n. 射擊；射門；嘗試

▶The police fired two shots at the terrorist's van.
警方向恐怖份子的箱形車開了兩槍。

相關片語 **have a shot**
試試看

▶Why don't you have a shot at making your own grape wine?
你何不嘗試自製葡萄酒呢？

---

should [ʃʊd] ◀ Track 1886
aux. 應該

▶You should do your homework.
你應該要做功課。

---

shoulder [`ʃoldɚ] ◀ Track 1887
n. 肩膀

▶My dog rested his head on my shoulder when we took a selfie together.
我和我的小狗自拍時，牠把頭靠在我的肩上。

相關片語 **give sb. the cold shoulder** 故意冷落某人

▶I don't understand why he gave me the cold shoulder in the party.
我不明白他為何在派對上對我那麼冷淡。

---

shouldn't [`ʃʊdnt] ◀ Track 1888
abbr. 不該（should not的縮寫）

▶You shouldn't cross the line.
你不應該撈過界。

---

shout [ʃaʊt] ◀ Track 1889
v. 呼喊；喊叫

▶The man is shouting at his wife.
男人正在對妻子大聲吼叫。

n. 呼喊；喊叫聲

▶Did you hear any shouts last night?
你昨晚有聽到喊叫聲嗎？

---

show [ʃo] ◀ Track 1890
v. 顯示；顯露；展示；演出；出示；帶領

▶She showed me around the company.
她帶我參觀公司。

n. 展覽；表現；表演；演出節目；顯示

▶The radio show will be on at 10 A.M.
收音機節目是早上十點開始。

相關片語 **show up**
出現；露面；出席

▶Don't worry. He will show up soon.
別擔心，他很快就會到了。

---

shower [`ʃaʊɚ] ◀ Track 1891
n. 陣雨；淋浴

▶He was in the shower when the door bell rang.
門鈴響時，他正在淋浴。

初級

v. 下陣雨；沖澡

▶He showered quickly and returned to his room.
他很快洗完澡就回房間了。

shrimp [ʃrɪmp] 🔊Track 1892
n. 蝦

▶I can't tell the difference between shrimps and prawns.
我分不清楚蝦和對蝦的差異。

shut [ʃʌt] 🔊Track 1893
v. 關閉

▶He shut himself in his room for two weeks.
他把自己關在房間兩個星期了。

shy [ʃaɪ] 🔊Track 1894
adj. 害羞的；靦腆的

▶She is a shy girl.
她是害羞的女孩。

sick [sɪk] 🔊Track 1895
adj. 病的；想吐的；對……厭煩的

▶I'm sick of their gossips.
我對他們的八卦感到很厭煩。

side [saɪd] 🔊Track 1896
n. 邊；面；一方

▶He sat on the side of the bed while talking to his friend on the phone.
他坐在床邊和朋友講電話。

sidewalk [`saɪd͵wɔk] 🔊Track 1897
=pavement （英式英文）
n. 人行道

▶She walked on the sidewalk with her grandmother.
她和祖母走在人行道上。

sight [saɪt] 🔊Track 1898
n. 視覺；看見；視界

▶He has lost his sight.
他已經失明了。

sign [saɪn] 🔊Track 1899
v. 簽名

▶Tom Cruise signed his name on my T-shirt.
湯姆・克魯斯在我的汗衫上簽名。

n. 記號；標牌；手勢

▶The sign says "No Fishing."
標牌上寫著「請勿釣魚」。

silence [`saɪləns] 🔊Track 1900
n. 沉默；無聲

▶The politician finally broke silence.
這名政治人物終於打破沉默。

silent [`saɪlənt] 🔊Track 1901
adj. 沈默的；默不作聲的；寂靜無聲的

▶She was silent for quite a while.
她沉默了很久。

silk [sɪlk] 🔊Track 1902
n. 絲

▶She wore a dress made from silk.
她穿了一件用絲綢做的洋裝。

adj. 絲的；絲織的

▶He wore a silk shirt.
他穿了一件絲質襯衫。

silly [`sɪlɪ]
🔊 Track 1903

adj. 糊塗的；愚蠢的

▶Don't be silly. I know you can do it.
別傻了，我知道你辦得到。

silver [`sɪlvɚ]
🔊 Track 1904

n. 銀；銀色；銀牌

▶She won a silver in the 200 meter freestyle.
她在兩百公尺自由式項目中奪得銀牌。

adj. 銀的；銀色的

▶He was born with a silver spoon.
他是含著銀湯匙出生的。

similar [`sɪmələ]
🔊 Track 1905

adj. 相似的；相像的

▶Cathy and I have similar interests.
凱西和我的興趣很相似。

simple [`sɪmp!]
🔊 Track 1906

adj. 簡單的；簡樸的；單純的

▶She enjoys living a simple life.
她喜歡過著簡樸的生活。

simply [`sɪmplɪ]
🔊 Track 1907

adv. 簡單地；樸素地；僅僅；簡直

▶You look simply gorgeous in these pictures.
妳在照片中美極了。

since [sɪns]
🔊 Track 1908

conj. 自從；既然；因為

▶He's been on his own since his parents died.
他的父母過世後，他就自力更生了。

prep. 自……以來

▶He hasn't heard from Julia since last month.
他自上個月以來沒聽到茱麗亞的消息。

adv. 此後；之前

▶She started smoking two years ago, and has been coughing ever since.
她兩年前開始抽烟，從此就咳嗽至今。

sincere [sɪn`sɪr]
🔊 Track 1909

adj. 誠摯的；衷心的

▶She is a decent and sincere girl.
她是正派真誠的女孩。

sing [sɪŋ]
🔊 Track 1910

v. 唱；唱歌

▶I sang in the choir when I was in elementary school.
我國小時是合唱團員。

Singapore [`sɪŋgəˌpor]
🔊 Track 1911

n. 新加坡

▶Have you been to Singapore?
你去過新加坡嗎？

singer [`sɪŋɚ]
🔊 Track 1912

n. 歌手；歌唱家

▶Céline Dion is a great singer.
席琳·狄翁是一位很棒的歌手。

single [`sɪŋg!]
🔊 Track 1913

adj. 單一的；單身的

▶He has been single for three years.
他已單身三年了。

n. 單個；單身者；單打比賽

▶I'd like to reserve a single, please.
我想預訂一間單人房，麻煩了。

初級

sink [sɪŋk]
◀ Track 1914

n. 流理台；水槽

▶ She always keeps the kitchen sink clean.
她總是保持廚房流理台清潔。

v. 下沉；沒落；下陷

▶ The ship sank after hitting an iceberg.
船撞到冰山後沉下去了。

sir [sɝ]
◀ Track 1915

n. 先生；老師；長官

▶ How can I help you, sir?
先生您好，有什麼可以為您效勞的地方嗎？

sister [`sɪstɚ]
◀ Track 1916

n. 姐妹

▶ I have two sisters.
我有兩個妹妹。

sit [sɪt]
◀ Track 1917

v. 坐

▶ He gestured his dog to sit down.
他以手勢叫小狗坐下。

six [sɪks]
◀ Track 1918

pron. 六個

▶ He said he liked the cupcakes I made, so I gave him six of them.
他說他喜歡我做的杯子蛋糕，所以我給他六個。

n. 六

▶ His son turned six last month.
他的兒子上個月滿六歲。

adj. 六的；六個的

▶ I have six apples.
我有六顆蘋果。

sixteen [`sɪks`tin]
◀ Track 1919

pron. 十六個

▶ She has twenty dresses, and I hate sixteen of them.
她有二十件洋裝，我不喜歡其中十六件。

n. 十六

▶ He dropped out of school at the age of sixteen.
他十六歲輟學。

adj. 十六的；十六個的

▶ My grandparents have sixteen grandchildren.
我祖父母有十六個孫子女。

sixty [`sɪkstɪ]
◀ Track 1920

pron. 六十；六十個

▶ Sixty of them arrived this evening.
他們其中六十人今晚到達。

n. 六十

▶ I plan to retire at sixty.
我打算六十歲時退休。

adj. 六十的；六十個的

▶ There are sixty boys in the club.
俱樂部有六十個男孩。

size [saɪz]
◀ Track 1921

n. 尺寸；大小

▶ The dress is not my size.
這件洋裝不是我的尺寸。

skate [sket]
◀ Track 1922

n. 冰鞋；四輪溜冰鞋

▶ He bought a pair of skates for his son as a Christmas gift.
他買了一雙溜冰鞋送兒子當耶誕禮物。

v. 溜冰

▶ She skates beautifully and elegantly.

她溜冰很美又優雅。

ski [ski]
🔊 Track 1923

n. 滑雪板

▶He broke one of his skis.
他摔壞了其中一個滑雪板。

v. 滑雪

▶I went skiing in Switzerland last winter.
我去年冬天去瑞士滑雪。

skill [`skɪl]
🔊 Track 1924

n. （專門）技術；技巧；技能

▶He has excellent writing skills.
他的寫作技巧很高。

skilled [skɪld]
🔊 Track 1925

adj. 熟練的；有技能的

▶Interpreting is a highly skilled job.
口譯是高度技能的工作。

skillful [`skɪlfəl]
=skilful （英式英文）
🔊 Track 1926

adj. 有技術的；熟練的

▶She is a skillful songwriter.
她是個純熟的作曲家。

skin [skɪn]
🔊 Track 1927

n. 皮；皮膚

▶Skin is the largest organ in human body.
皮膚是身體最大的器官。

skinny [`skɪnɪ]
🔊 Track 1928

adj. 皮的；皮包骨的、極瘦的

▶The girl who has anorexia is very skinny.
這名有厭食症的女孩極瘦。

skirt [skɝt]
🔊 Track 1929

n. 裙；裙子

▶The model was dressed in a mini skirt.
模特兒穿著一件迷你裙。

v. 位於……邊緣；繞過……的邊緣

▶We took the road which skirted round the town.
我們沿著鎮邊的路走過去。

sky [skaɪ]
🔊 Track 1930

n. 天空

▶I saw an eagle flying in the sky.
我看到一隻老鷹在天空中翱翔。

相關片語 **a pie in the sky**
遙不可及的夢想

▶His dream seems to be a pie in the sky.
他的夢想似乎遙不可及。

sleep [slip]
🔊 Track 1931

v. 睡覺

▶She slept like a baby last night.
她昨晚睡得很熟。

n. 睡眠

▶He didn't get enough sleep the night before.
他前晚睡眠不足。

sleepy [`slipɪ]
🔊 Track 1932

adj. 昏昏欲睡的；想睡的

▶I suddenly felt very sleepy in the meeting.
我在開會時突然覺得很想睡。

初級

slender [`slɛndɚ]
🔊 Track 1933

adj. 修長的；苗條的；纖細的；微薄的

▶ The model has a beautiful slender figure.
模特兒身材曼妙苗條。

---

slide [slaɪd]
🔊 Track 1934

v. 滑；滑落；悄悄地走

▶ He slid out of the conference room.
他悄悄地溜出了會議室。

n. 溜滑梯

▶ Two cute pandas are playing on the slide.
兩隻可愛的貓熊在玩溜滑梯。

---

slim [slɪm]
🔊 Track 1935

adj. 苗條的；微薄的；少的

▶ The model is much slimmer in person.
模特兒本人更苗條。

---

slip [slɪp]
🔊 Track 1936

v. 滑動；滑跤；滑落；遺忘

▶ Her e-mail has slipped my mind.
我忘了她的電郵。

n. 滑動；下降；失足；紙條

▶ His assistant gave him a slip of paper during the meeting.
他的助理在會議中遞了一張紙條給他。

---

slippers [`slɪpɚz]
🔊 Track 1937

n. 室內便鞋；淺口拖鞋

▶ She wore a pair of slippers to the supermarket.
她穿著拖鞋到超市。

---

slow [slo]
🔊 Track 1938

adj. 慢的；緩緩的；耗時的；慢了的

▶ She is a slow driver.
她開車很慢。

v. 放慢；使慢；變慢

▶ He slowed his pace a little to walk beside his wife.
他放慢腳步和妻子走在一起。

adv. 慢了地；慢慢地

▶ My watch runs slow.
我的手錶走得很慢。

---

small [smɔl]
🔊 Track 1939

adj. 小的；少量的；瘦小的；低微的

▶ He lives in a small village.
他住在小村莊。

相關片語 **small talk** 閒聊

▶ The two leaders made some polite small talk before the negotiation.
兩國領袖在協商前禮貌性地寒暄了一下。

---

smart [smɑrt]
🔊 Track 1940

adj. 聰明的

▶ My dog is very smart.
我的狗很聰明。

相關片語 **book smart**
書呆子氣的

▶ Is it better to be book smart or street smart?
很會唸書的人和深諳人情事故的人，兩者哪一種比較好？

---

smell [smɛl]
🔊 Track 1941

n. 氣味；嗅覺

▶ I like the smell of grass.
我喜歡小草的味道。

v. 聞；嗅；聞出；發出氣味；有氣味；

▶ The fish smells terrible.
魚聞起來發臭了。

smile [smaɪl] ◀Track 1942

v. 微笑

▶He smiled at me.
他向我露出笑容。

n. 微笑

▶Diane has a radiant smile.
黛安有著燦爛的笑容。

smoke [smok] ◀Track 1943

n. 煙；煙霧；一口煙

▶Tobacco smoke is carcinogenic.
香菸的煙霧是致癌的。

v. 抽菸；冒煙；煙燻

▶He still smokes after his daughter was born.
他的女兒出生後，他仍沒戒菸。

snack [snæk] ◀Track 1944

n. 小吃；點心

▶Would you like some midnight snacks?
你要不要吃點宵夜？

v. 吃快餐；吃點心

▶He often snacks on chocolates.
他常常把巧克力糖當點心吃。

snail [snel] ◀Track 1945

n. 蝸牛

▶Their research is moving at a snail's pace.
他們的研究進展很緩慢。

snake [snek] ◀Track 1946

n. 蛇

▶I watched a snake slither away.
我看到一隻蛇滑行過去。

sneakers [`snikɚz] ◀Track 1947

n. 運動鞋

▶He wears sneakers to work everyday.
他每天都穿運動鞋上班。

sneaky [`snikɪ] ◀Track 1948

adj. 鬼鬼祟祟的

▶He came up with a sneaky plan to win the contest.
他想出一個能贏得比賽的狡詐計畫。

snow [sno] ◀Track 1949

n. 雪

▶Children played in snow and made a snowman.
孩子在玩雪並堆了一個雪人。

v. 下雪

▶It's snowing outside.
現在外面正在下雪。

snowy [snoɪ] ◀Track 1950

adj. 下雪的

▶Remember to keep warm on a snowy day.
下雪天要記得保暖。

so [so] ◀Track 1951

adv. 這麼；多麼；如此地；因此

▶The kitten is so cute.
小貓真可愛。

conj. 所以；因此

▶He was bored at home, so he watched TV to kill time.
他在家感到很無聊，所以他看電視打發時間。

相關片語 **so so**
馬馬虎虎；還好

初級

▶"How have you been?" "So so."
「你最近好嗎？」「馬馬虎虎。」

soap [sop] 🔊 Track 1952
n. 肥皂

▶She gave me a box of handmade soaps.
她送我一盒手工肥皂。

v. 用肥皂洗

▶The mother soaped the baby all over.
媽媽幫寶寶全身抹上肥皂。

soccer [`sʌkɚ] 🔊 Track 1953
n. 足球；足球運動

▶He is one of the best soccer players in the team.
他是球隊最好的足球員之一。

social [`soʃəl] 🔊 Track 1954
adj. 社會的；社交的

▶Doris is a social worker.
桃樂絲是一名社工。

society [sə`saɪətɪ] 🔊 Track 1955
n. 社會；社團；交際；交往

▶Our society has not reached a consensus on same-sex marriage.
我們的社會針對同婚還沒達成共識

socks [sɑks] 🔊 Track 1956
n. 襪子

▶Take off your dirty socks before you go to bed.
睡覺前把你的髒襪子脫掉。

soda [`sodə] 🔊 Track 1957
n. 蘇打；蘇打水；汽水

▶May I have a soda, please?
請給我一杯汽水，麻煩了。

sofa [`sofə] 🔊 Track 1958
n. 沙發

▶My brother is sitting on the sofa and watching a movie.
我弟弟坐在沙發上看電影。

soft [sɔft] 🔊 Track 1959
adj. 柔軟的；輕柔的；柔和的；不含酒精的

▶Her hair is soft and slightly curly.
她的頭髮很柔軟而且有點微捲。

soldier [`soldʒɚ] 🔊 Track 1960
n. 軍人；士兵

▶Many soldiers died in the long and bloody battle.
許多士兵在這場漫長血腥的戰爭中喪生。

solution [sə`luʃən] 🔊 Track 1961
n. 解答；解決辦法

▶I can't think of any solution to this problem.
我想不出這個問題的任何解決方法。

solve [sɑlv] 🔊 Track 1962
v. 解決

▶The child prodigy solved the difficult math problem.
這名天才兒童解開了這個數學問題。

some [sʌm] 🔊 Track 1963
pron. 一些

▶I bought a bottle of grape wine. Would you like to try some of it?
我買了一瓶葡萄酒，你要不要嘗一些？

adj. 一些的

▶I can't think clearly. I think I need some fresh air.
我無法清楚地思考，我想我需要一些新鮮的空氣。

somebody
◀Track 1964

[`sʌm‚badɪ]

=someone
pron. 某人

▶Somebody told me that you are a medical expert in leukemia.
有人告訴我你是白血病的醫學專家。

somebody's
◀Track 1965

[`sʌm‚badɪz]

abbr. 某人的；某人是

（**somebody is** 的縮寫）

▶Somebody's knocking on the door.
有人正在敲門。

someone [`sʌm‚wʌn]
◀Track 1966

=somebody
pron. 某人；有人

▶I heard someone crying in the room last night.
我昨晚聽到房間有人在哭。

something [`sʌmθɪŋ]
◀Track 1967

pron. 某事；某件事

▶Something is wrong with the TV. The screen is all blank.
電視壞掉了，螢幕是空白的。

sometimes
◀Track 1968

[`sʌm‚taɪmz]

adv. 有時候

▶Sometimes I wonder why people do drugs.
有時候我很納悶為什麼有人要吸毒。

somewhere
◀Track 1969

[`sʌm‚hwɛr]

adv. 某處；某個地方

▶The incident happened somewhere in the 17th century.
這個事件發生在十七世紀某個時候。

son [sʌn]
◀Track 1970

n. 兒子

▶My son has lived in Berlin for ten years.
我的兒子已經住在柏林十年了。

song [sɔŋ]
◀Track 1971

n. 歌曲；曲子

▶The children sang the songs they learned in the music class.
孩子們在唱音樂課學到的歌曲。

soon [sun]
◀Track 1972

adv. 馬上；立刻

▶I didn't finish the project soon enough as I expected.
我的計畫沒有我預料的那樣快完成。

sore [sor]
◀Track 1973

adj. 疼痛的

▶He had a sore throat and a headache.
他的喉嚨和頭都在痛。

n.（身體或精神的）痛處；瘡；潰瘍

▶It is cruel to reopen people's old sores.
重提別人舊時的傷心事是很殘酷的。

初級

sorry [`sɑrɪ]
<audio>Track 1974</audio>

adj. 抱歉的；難過的

▶I'm sorry to hear that you were betrayed by your friend.
聽到你被朋友背叛，我感到很難過。

sort [sɔrt]
<audio>Track 1975</audio>

n. 種類；類型

▶What sort of shoes are you looking for?
你要找什麼樣的鞋子呢？

v. 將……分類；區分

▶He used his laptop to sort vocabulary alphabetically.
他用筆電將單字以字母順序分類。

soul [sol]
<audio>Track 1976</audio>

n. 靈魂；心靈

▶Her music can touch your soul.
她的音樂能觸到你的靈魂。

補充片語 rest in peace
安息

相關片語 body and soul
全心全意地

▶He put his heart and soul into his work.
他全心全意地工作。

soup [sup]
<audio>Track 1977</audio>

n. 湯

▶Mom cooked chicken soup and dumplings for supper.
媽媽煮雞湯和水餃當晚餐。

sour [`saʊr]
<audio>Track 1978</audio>

adj. 酸的；酸臭的

▶The vinegar tastes sour.
這個醋嚐起來酸酸的。

source [sors]
<audio>Track 1979</audio>

n. 源頭；根源；來源

▶The intelligence came from a reliable source.
這個情報來自一位可靠的人士。

south [saʊθ]
<audio>Track 1980</audio>

n. 南；南方

▶The Philippines is to the south of Taiwan.
菲律賓在台灣的南面。

adv. 朝南；往南；向南

▶They traveled south towards the Yellowstone Park.
他們朝南部的黃石公園而去。

adj. 南方的；南部的

▶ASEAN is short for the Association of Southeast Asian Nations.
「ASEAN」是東南亞國家協會的簡稱。

southern [`sʌðən]
<audio>Track 1981</audio>

adj. 在南方的；來自南方的；有南部特點的

▶He lives in southern England.
他住在英格蘭南部。

soy sauce [`sɔɪ-sɔs]
<audio>Track 1982</audio>

ph. 醬油

▶Mom made a scallion sauce and added some soy sauce in it. It was super tasty.
媽媽做的青蔥醬有加入一些醬油，超級好吃的。

soybean [`sɔɪbin]
<audio>Track 1983</audio>

n. 大豆

▶I drink a glass of soybean milk everyday.
我每天都喝一杯豆漿。

補充片語 soybean milk 豆漿

space [spes]
◀ Track 1984

n. 空間；場所；空地；宇宙、太空

▶The operating system takes up a lot of space.
這個作業系統佔太多空間了。

補充片語 take up
佔（地方）

spaghetti [spə`gɛtɪ]
◀ Track 1985

n. 義大利麵

▶They had spaghetti and meatballs for supper tonight.
他們今晚晚餐吃義大利麵和肉丸。

speak [spik]
◀ Track 1986

v. 說；說話

▶My sister can speak German and Dutch.
我的姊姊會說德語和荷語。

speaker [`spikɚ]
◀ Track 1987

n. 說話者；說某種語言的人；演說家；擴音機

▶Prof. Nye will be the speaker of this lecture.
奈伊教授將是這堂課的講者。

special [`spɛʃəl]
◀ Track 1988

adj. 特別的

▶I have an evening gown for special occasions.
我有一件專門在特殊場合穿的晚禮服。

n. 特別的東西；特刊；特餐

▶Friday's special is a $70 cheeseburger and tots.
星期五特餐是一個七十元的起士漢堡和薯球。

speech [spitʃ]
◀ Track 1989

n. 演說；說話；致辭

▶He made an opening speech for the seminar.
他在研討會發表開幕詞。

補充片語 make a speech
發表演說；致辭

speed [spid]
◀ Track 1990

n. 速度

▶The high speed rail traveled at a speed of 120 miles per hour.
這列高速鐵路時速120公里。

v. 迅速前進；加速

▶The police car sped after a stolen vehicle.
警車加速追趕一輛被偷的汽車。

spell [spɛl]
◀ Track 1991

v. 用字母拼；拼寫

▶He can't spell my name.
他不會拼我的名字。

spelling [`spɛlɪŋ]
◀ Track 1992

n. 拼字；拼寫；拼法

▶My spelling has improved since I studied hard everyday.
自從我今天開始用功，拼寫就進步了。

spend [spɛnd]
◀ Track 1993

v. 花費（時間、金錢、精力）；度過

初級

▶She spent twenty dollars on the pencil.
她花了二十元買下那枝簽筆。

spider [`spaɪdɚ]
◀Track 1994
n. 蜘蛛

▶I saw a spider spinning its web.
我看到一隻蜘蛛在織網。

spinach [`spɪnɪtʃ]
◀Track 1995
n. 菠菜

▶Spinach salad is my mother's favorite.
我媽媽最喜歡菠菜沙拉。

spirit [`spɪrɪt]
◀Track 1996
n. 精神；心靈；本意

▶The class showed a very strong team spirit.
這班學生有很強的團隊精神。

相關片語 **in good spirits**
興高采烈的

▶She's been in good spirits and everything seems to be moving in the right direction.
她近來精神奕奕，一切看來都很平順。

spoon [spun]
◀Track 1997
n. 湯匙；一匙

▶The little girl was born with a silver spoon.
這個小女孩是含著銀湯匙出生的。

sport [sport]
◀Track 1998
n. 運動

▶What kind of sport do you like?
你最喜歡的運動是哪一項？

spot [spɑt]
◀Track 1999
n. 斑點；污點；場所；職位

▶A-Li Mountain is one of the most beautiful scenic spots in Taiwan.
阿里山是台灣最美的景點之一。

v. 玷污；弄髒；認出、發現

▶Her sneakers were spotted with mud.
她的步鞋沾有泥漬。

spread [sprɛd]
◀Track 2000
v. 使伸展；張開；塗、敷；散佈

▶She spread some peanut butter on the bread.
她在麵包上抹上一些花生醬。

n. 伸展；擴張；蔓延

▶The spread of the prairies was a wonder to behold.
這片草原的浩瀚是奇景。

square [skwɛr]
◀Track 2001
n. 正方形；方型廣場

▶The food fair will be held in town square.
食品博覽會將在城市廣場舉行。

adj. 正方形的；正直的；平方的；令人滿意的

▶He has a square jaw and beautiful blue eyes.
他有一個方下巴和美麗的藍眼。

squirrel [`skwɝəl]
◀Track 2002
n. 松鼠

▶I saw a grey squirrel in the garden.
我在庭院看到一隻灰色的松鼠。

stage [stedʒ]
◀Track 2003
n. 舞台

▶My daughter is dancing ballet on the stage.
我女兒正在舞台上跳芭蕾舞。

stairs [stɛrz] ◀Track 2004
n. 樓梯

▶He fell down a flight of stairs and was immediately sent to a hospital.
他從一段樓梯摔下來，並馬上被送到醫院。

stamp [stæmp] ◀Track 2005
n. 郵票

▶I bought a set of commemorative stamps.
我買了一套紀念郵票。

v. 蓋印

▶She stamped her name on all of the documents.
她在所有的文件上都蓋上自己的名字。。

stand [stænd] ◀Track 2006
v. 站；站立

▶I'll stand by you.
我會支持你

n. 站立；立場；攤子

▶She has always taken a firm stand on this issue.
她在這個議題上一直立場堅定。

standard [`stændəd] ◀Track 2007
n. 標準；水準；規格

▶The manager asked everyone in the office to come up to his standard.
經理要求辦公室所有同仁要達到他的標準。

補充片語 come up to sb.'s standard
達到某人的標準

adj. 標準的

▶White is the standard color for this brand of cell phone.
白色是這個牌子手機的標準色。

star [stɑr] ◀Track 2008
n. 星星；明星

▶My three-year-old daughter can sing Twinkle, Twinkle, Little Star.
我三歲的女兒會唱《一閃一閃小星星》。

v. 當明星；主演

▶Julia Roberts starred in the film Ben Is Back.
茱莉亞‧羅勃茲主演《班恩回家》這部電影。

start [stɑrt] ◀Track 2009
v. 開始

▶The new semester will start in September.
新學期將在九月開始。

n. 開始；開端

▶She opposed the project from the start.
她一開始就反對這個計畫。

state [stet] ◀Track 2010
n. 狀態；狀況；國家；州

▶The prime minister is in a state of poor health.
總理的健康狀況不是非常好。

v. 陳述；聲明；說明

▶The presidential candidate stated that he would make America great again.
總統競選人表示，他將讓美國再度強大。

statement [`stetmənt] ◀Track 2011
n. 陳述；說明；正式聲明

初級

▶The press secretary made an official statement that the accusation against the president was simply fake news.
發言人發表正式聲明表示，總統所遭受的指控只是假新聞。

station [ˈsteʃən]
🔊 Track 2012

n. 車站；站、局、所

▶I used to listen to this radio station everyday.
我以前每天都聽這個廣播電台。

stationery
🔊 Track 2013

[ˈsteʃənˌɛrɪ]

n. 文具

▶The company supplies office stationery at cheaper prices.
這家公司供應的辦公室文具價格比較便宜。

stay [ste]
🔊 Track 2014

v. 停留；暫住；保持；止住

▶I stayed with a friend while I was in Seattle.
我在西雅圖時住在一位朋友家裡。

n. 停留；逗留

▶We wish you a pleasant stay in Taiwan.
我們祝您在台灣停留的時間愉快。

steak [stek]
🔊 Track 2015

n. 牛排；肉排；魚排

▶Monday's special is steak.
星期一的特餐是牛排。

steal [stil]
🔊 Track 2016

v. 偷；偷竊

▶Someone stole my wallet.
有人偷走我的皮包。

steam [stim]
🔊 Track 2017

n. 蒸汽；水蒸汽；精力；氣力

▶The bath was so hot that the room was full of steam.
澡堂太熱以致於房間都瀰漫著水蒸汽。

v. 蒸煮；蒸發；用蒸汽開動

▶She is health-conscious. She steams vegetables and knows how to cook them so they still have a crunch.
她很有健康意識，她清蒸蔬菜並知道怎麼煮能保有蔬菜的爽脆感。

相關片語 **run out of steam**
耗盡力氣；筋疲力盡

▶We ran out of steam after the basketball game.
我們籃球比賽之後，都筋疲力盡了。

steel [stil]
🔊 Track 2018

n. 鋼；鋼鐵

▶The lunch box is made of stainless steel.
這個便當盒是用不鏽鋼做成的。

step [stɛp]
🔊 Track 2019

n. 腳步；一步的距離；步驟

▶The library is only a short step away from my apartment.
圖書館離我的公寓不遠。

v. 踏、跨步；踏（進）；踩

▶He stepped into the kitchen and looked for something to eat.
他走進廚房找東西吃。

stick [stɪk]
🔊 Track 2020

n. 枝條；棍棒；手杖；棒狀物

▶He threw a stick for his dog to run and pick up.
他丟了一支棍棒讓小狗跑去撿起來。

v. 釘住；黏貼；伸出

▶She stuck a poster on the board with pins.
她用大頭針把海報釘在公告欄上。

相關片語 **stick together**
團結一致

▶As a family, we need to stick together.
我們是一家人，應該團結一致。

still [stɪl]

🔊 Track 2021

adv. 仍然；還是

▶We are still waiting for his reply.
我們還在等候他的回覆。

adj. 靜止的

▶Time stood still the first time I saw him.
我第一次見到他時，時間好像暫時停止了。

stingy [`stɪndʒɪ]

🔊 Track 2022

adj. 吝嗇的；小氣的

▶Mrs. Kelly is mean and extremely stingy.
凱莉太太為人刻薄，極度吝嗇。

stomach [`stʌmək]
=tummy

🔊 Track 2023

n. 胃；肚子；胃口

▶The kid has a delicate stomach.
這個小孩的腸胃不好。

相關片語 **turn one's stomach**
使某人反胃或噁心

▶The film about abortion turned my stomach.
墮胎的影片令我反胃。

stomachache

🔊 Track 2024

[`stʌmək͵ek] **n.** 胃痛

▶He got a stomachache and had no appetite.
他胃痛沒食慾。

stone [ston]

🔊 Track 2025

n. 石頭

▶Some demonstrators threw stones at the police.
有些示威者向警方丟擲石頭。

stop [stɑp]

🔊 Track 2026

v. 停；阻止

▶The heavy rain stopped at about 6:00 P.M.
大雨大概是在晚上六點停了。

n. （車）站

▶Which stop should I get off?
我應該要在哪一站下車？

補充片語 **get off**
下（車）

store [stor]

🔊 Track 2027

n. 店；商店

▶I bought a bottle of soy bean sauce in a grocery store.
我在一家雜貨店買了一瓶醬油。

v. 儲存；存放

▶Mom stored lemons and garlics in a cool dry place.
媽媽把檸檬存放在涼爽乾燥的地方。

storm [stɔrm]

🔊 Track 2028

n. 暴風雨

▶The storm wreaked havoc on many highways and cities.
這場暴風雨對許多高速公路和城市造成重大災害。

初級

stormy [`stɔrmɪ]
Track 2029

adj. 暴風雨的

▶It was a stormy day. There were heavy showers of sleet and rain.
那天是暴風雨天，天空下起了很大的凍雨。

story [`storɪ]
Track 2030

n. 故事

▶I like stories with happy endings.
我喜歡有快樂結局的故事。

stove [stov]
Track 2031

n. 火爐；爐灶

▶She has never cooked on a gas stove before.
她從沒用過瓦斯爐子上煮東西。

straight [stret]
Track 2032

adv. 直地；直接地；正直坦率地

▶I went straight home.
我直接回家。

adj. 筆直的；平直的；正直坦率的

▶He is a straight shooter.
他講話都坦白。

strange [strendʒ]
Track 2033

adj. 奇怪的；奇妙的；陌生的；生疏的

▶Did you hear a strange noise?
你有聽到奇怪的噪音嗎？

stranger [`strendʒɚ]
Track 2034

n. 陌生人

▶Mom warned Johnny not to talk to strangers.
媽媽警告強尼不要和陌生人講話。

straw [strɔ]
Track 2035

n. 吸管

▶Plastic straws are not environmentally-friendly.
塑膠吸管很不環保。

strawberry [`strɔbɛrɪ]
Track 2036

n. 草莓

▶Strawberries are in season now.
現在是草莓當令的時節。

stream [strim]
Track 2037

n. 溪；溪流

▶We crossed the stream and entered a cave.
我們越過小溪，進入一個山洞。

street [strit]
Track 2038

n. 街道；馬路

▶The British prime minister lives at 10 on Downing Street.
英國首相住在唐寧街十號。

stress [strɛs]
Track 2039

v. 強調；著重

▶Our teacher stressed the importance of being honest, especially in today's culture of fake news.
我們老師很強調誠實的重要性，尤其是我們現在處於假消息充斥的文化。

n. 壓力

▶Eric has been under a lot of stress.
艾利克最近壓力很大。

stretch [strɛtʃ]
Track 2040

v. 伸直；伸展；延伸

▶The baby bird stretched its wings and learned how to fly.
幼鳥伸展翅膀學飛。

相關片語 **stretch one's legs**
去散步

▶Nina decided to stretch her legs and enjoy some fresh air.
妮娜決定去外面散散步，享受一下新鮮的空氣。

strict [strɪkt]
adj. 嚴格的；嚴厲的
◀€ Track 2041

▶Our teacher is very strict and doesn't allow late submission.
我們老師很嚴格，不准我們遲交作業。

strike [straɪk]
v 打；擊
◀€ Track 2042

▶The earthquake struck the island and caused serious damage.
地震襲擊這座島嶼，造成嚴重的災害。

n. 打擊；攻擊；空襲；罷工

▶The workers of the airline have been on strike for two weeks.
航空公司的員工已經罷工二個星期了。

string [strɪŋ]
n. 細繩；線；一串
◀€ Track 2043

▶She used a piece of string to tie the parcel up.
她用一條繩子把包裹綑起來。

strong [strɔŋ]
adj. 強壯的；強健的；堅強的；濃烈的
◀€ Track 2044

▶She is very strong and decisive.
她的個性很堅強果斷。

struggle [`strʌg!]
n. 奮鬥；鬥爭；難事
◀€ Track 2045

▶It was an uphill struggle for him to reach his goal, especially after the bankruptcy of his father's business.
他要達成目標會非常困難，尤其是在他的父親公司破產之後。

v 奮鬥；掙扎；艱難地行徑；對抗

▶Many women struggle to keep a balance between work and family.
許多女性在工作和家庭之間努力取得平衡。

student [`stjudnt]
n. 學生
◀€ Track 2046

▶Sarah is a bright student.
莎拉是個聰明的學生。

study [`stʌdɪ]
n. 學習；研究；課題
◀€ Track 2047

▶He left in 1999 to further his studies in Germany.
他於一九九九年赴德國深造。

v 學習；研究；用功

▶I studied data analytics at college.
我大學時攻讀資料分析。

stupid [`stjupɪd]
adj. 笨的；愚蠢的
◀€ Track 2048

▶It is very stupid to believe that your online friend is the defense secretary of the Pentagon and that he is going to marry you.
相信你的網友是美國國防部長而且他會娶你是很愚蠢的。

style [staɪl]
n. 風格；文體；流行款式；式樣
◀€ Track 2049

初級

▶It's not her style to flatter people.
逢迎拍馬不是她的作風。

補充片語 not one's style
非某人所好；非某人風格

subject [`sʌbdʒɪkt] 🔊 Track 2050
n. 主題；題材；科目
▶Music is my favorite subject.
音樂是我最喜歡的科目。

adj. 易受……的；以……為條件的
▶The man is very subject to rheumatism.
這名男士常受風濕之苦。

subtract [səb`trækt] 🔊 Track 2051
v. 減；減去
▶Subtract ten from forty and you have thirty.
四十減十得到三十。

subway [`sʌb͵we]
=underground
=tube （英式英語）
=MRT=metro
🔊 Track 2052
n. 地下鐵
▶She took the subway to work.
她搭地鐵上班。

succeed [sək`sid] 🔊 Track 2053
v. 成功；取得成功
▶You will succeed if you don't give up halfway.
如果你不半途就放棄就會成功。

補充片語 give up halfway
半途而廢

success [sək`sɛs] 🔊 Track 2054
n. 成功
▶He achieved great success in his work.
他在工作方面表現卓越。

successful
[sək`sɛsfəl]
🔊 Track 2055
adj. 成功的
▶David Foster is a successful music producer.
大衛·福斯特是成功的音樂製作人。

such [sʌtʃ] 🔊 Track 2056
adv. 如此地
▶He is such a good student that every teacher likes him.
他是極好的學生，每個老師都喜歡他。

sudden [`sʌdn] 🔊 Track 2057
adj. 突然的
▶The mountain climbers were trapped by a sudden snowstorm.
登山客被突如其來的暴風雪困住。

suddenly [`sʌdnlɪ] 🔊 Track 2058
adv. 忽然
▶She suddenly noticed that a man was stalking her.
她忽然注意到有個男人在跟蹤她。

sugar [`ʃʊgɚ] 🔊 Track 2059
n. 糖
▶Mom put too much sugar in the apple pie.
媽媽在蘋果派裡加太多糖了。

suggest [sə`dʒɛst]
Track 2060

v. 建議

▶ My professor suggested that I apply for Northwestern University.
我的教授建議我申請西北大學。

suit [sut]
Track 2061

n. （一套）西裝；套；組

▶ My son bought a black suit for the prom.
我兒子為了參加畢業舞會買了一套黑色西裝。

v. 適合；與……相配；使適合

▶ The schedule of the meeting suited us both.
會議行程對我們兩人都很合適。

summer [`sʌmə]
Track 2062

n. 夏天

▶ They are going to Vancouver this summer.
他們今年夏天要去溫哥華。

sun [sʌn]
Track 2063

n. 太陽；日

▶ The sun is always setting and always rising.
太陽總是每天起落

Sunday [`sʌnde] =Sun.
Track 2064

n. 星期天

▶ We will have a flea market this coming Sunday.
我們星期天要舉辦跳蚤市場。

sunny [`sʌnɪ]
Track 2065

adj. 晴天的

▶ The apartment has a sunny balcony, spacious living room, and three large bedrooms.
這間公寓有日照充足的陽台、寬敞的客廳和三間大臥室。

super [`supə]
Track 2066

adj. 特級的；特佳的；極度的

▶ The movie is about a super hero who saves the world.
這部電影是關於一位拯救世界的超級英雄。

adv. 非常；極度

▶ The rock star is super cool.
這名搖滾明星超級酷的。

supermarket
Track 2067

[`supə͵markɪt]

n. 超級市場

▶ She bought a dozen of eggs and some apples in the supermarket.
她在超級市場買了一打雞蛋和一些蘋果。

supper [`sʌpə] =dinner
Track 2068

n. 晚餐

▶ We went to the Thai restaurant for supper.
我們去泰式餐廳吃晚餐。

supply [sə`plaɪ]
Track 2069

n. 供應；供給；生活用品；補給品

▶ Demands exceeds supply.
需求超過供給。

v. 供應；提供

▶ Taipower supplies electricity through well-established network.
台電公司透過完整的網絡提供用電。

初級

support [sə`port] 🔊 Track 2070
n. 支持

▶We look forward to your support.
我們期望獲得你的支持。

v. 支持；資助；撫養

▶My parents support my college education.
我的父母資助我唸大學。

sure [ʃʊr] 🔊 Track 2071
adj. 確信的；一定的

▶Are you absolutely sure?
你真的很確定嗎？

adv. 的確；當然

▶I will attend your wedding for sure.
我當然會參加你的婚禮。

surf [sɝf] 🔊 Track 2072
n. 拍岸浪花

▶The roar of the surf is hypnotic.
浪濤聲有催眠的感覺。

v. 衝浪；在網路上或電視上搜索資料或快速地看

▶He surfed the Internet for information about the disease.
他在網路搜尋有關這個疾病的資訊。

surface [`sɝfɪs] 🔊 Track 2073
n. 表面；外表

▶The wall has a rough surface.
牆壁表面很粗糙。

surprise [sə`praɪz] 🔊 Track 2074
n. 驚喜；驚訝

▶We threw a surprise party for Jim.
我們幫吉姆辦了一個驚喜派對。

v. 使驚喜；使驚訝

▶The news surprised everyone on campus.
這條消息讓校園所有的人都很意外。

surprised [sə`praɪzd] 🔊 Track 2075
adj. 感到驚喜的；感到驚訝的

▶She was surprised when she heard the good news.
她聽到好消息，感到很驚喜。

survive [sə`vaɪv] 🔊 Track 2076
v. 活下來；倖存

▶She survived a horrible car wreck.
她從一次可怕的車禍中倖存下來。

swallow [`swɑlo] 🔊 Track 2077
n. 吞；嚥

▶His throat was too hurt to endure any swallow of food.
他的喉嚨很痛，難以吞嚥食物。

v. 吞嚥；吞下；忍受

▶A third loss in four days was a bitter pill to swallow.
四天比賽有三天是敗局，這是令人難以忍受的殘酷事實。

swan [swɑn] 🔊 Track 2078
n. 天鵝

▶Experts said that bread is comfort food for swans.
專家說麵包對天鵝來說是暖心的食物。

sweater [`swɛtə] 🔊 Track 2079
n. 毛衣

▶She wore a sweater and a skirt.
她穿一件毛衣和裙子。

sweep [swip]
◀ Track 2080

v. 掃

▶The students sweep the classroom everyday.
學生每天掃教室。

sweet [swit]
◀ Track 2081

adj. 甜的

▶I had a sweet dream last night.
我昨晚作了一個香甜的美夢。

n. 糖果

▶She is very health-conscious and doesn't eat sweets.
她很有健康意識，不吃糖果。

swim [swɪm]
◀ Track 2082

v. 游泳

▶He can swim really fast.
他游泳的速度真的很快。

swimsuit [`swɪmsut]
◀ Track 2083

n. 泳衣

▶She put her swimsuit on and went to the pool.
她穿上泳衣並到泳池裡。

swing [swɪŋ]
◀ Track 2084

v. 搖擺；擺動

▶Monkeys were swinging from trees to trees.
猴子在樹木之間盪來盪去。

n. 搖擺；擺動；鞦韆

▶The panda is playing on the tire swing.
貓熊在玩輪胎鞦韆。

symbol [`sɪmb!]
◀ Track 2085

n. 象徵；標誌；記號

▶Four-leaf clover is a symbol of good luck.
四片葉子的苜蓿是幸運的象徵。

system [`sɪstəm]
◀ Track 2086

n. 系統；制度

▶We need to reform our current education system.
我們需要改革目前的教育制度。

初級

▶ Tt

　　以下表格是全民英檢官方公告初級「聽、說、讀、寫」所須具備的能力，本書例句皆依此範疇特別設計，只要掃描右方QR code，就能搭配相對應的音軌，實現「眼耳並用」方式，刺激左腦的語言學習功能；同時也可使用本書附贈的紅膠片，將其置於單字上，一面記憶一面自我挑戰，達到雙倍的學習成果！

聽	▶ 能聽懂與日常生活相關的淺易談話，包含價格、時間及地點等。
說	能朗讀簡易文章、簡單地自我介紹，對熟悉的話題能以簡易英語對答，如問候、購物、問路等。
讀	可看懂與日常生活相關的淺易英文，並能閱讀路標、交通號誌、招牌、簡單菜單、時刻表及賀卡等。
寫	能寫簡單的句子及段落，如寫明信片、便條、賀卡及填表格等。對一般日常生活相關事物，能以簡短的文字敘述或説明。

table [`teb!]
◀ Track 2087
n. 桌子；餐桌
▶ Could you help me set the table?
你可以幫我擺餐桌嗎？

Taichung [`taɪ`tʃʊŋ]
◀ Track 2088
n. 台中
▶ He is an English teacher from Taichung City.
他是來自台中市的英文老師。

tail [tel]
◀ Track 2089
n. 尾巴；尾部；尾狀物
▶ My dog is chasing his tail.
我的狗在追著牠的尾巴跑。

Tainan [`taɪ`nan]
◀ Track 2090
n. 台南
▶ Tainan is an ancient city.
台南是一座古城。

Taiwan [`taɪ`wɑn]
◀ Track 2091
n. 台灣
▶ Taiwan's health care system is one of the best in the world.
台灣的健保體系是全球最好的之一。

Taiwanese
[ˏtaɪwə`niz]
◀ Track 2092
adj. 台灣的；台灣人的
▶ Stinky tofu is one of my favorite Taiwanese food.
臭豆腐是我最喜歡的台灣美食之一。

n. 台灣人；台灣話

▶His father is Taiwanese and his mother is Canadian.
他的爸爸是台灣人，媽媽是加拿大人。

---

take [tek]
◀⨏ Track 2093

v. 拿；取；帶去；接受；承擔；花費；占用

▶Dad took us to Disneyland last week.
爸爸上週帶我們去迪士尼玩。

---

tale [tel]
◀⨏ Track 2094

n. 故事；傳說

▶Cinderella is a fairy tale written by Brothers Grimm.
灰姑娘是格林兄弟所寫的童話故事。

補充片語 fairy tale
童話故事

相關片語 tell tales about sb.
道某人長短

▶She's been telling tales about me, hasn't she?
她一直在說我的是非，不是嗎？

---

talent [ˈtælənt]
◀⨏ Track 2095

n. 天賦；能力

▶She has a talent for singing.
她有歌唱的天賦。

---

talk [tɔk]
◀⨏ Track 2096

v. 說話

▶She talks to her boyfriend on Skype every evening.
她每天晚上都用聊天軟體Skype跟男友聊天。

n. 談話；交談

▶His talk was all about space explorations.
他所說的全是關於太空探險的事。

相關片語 talk big
說大話

▶My brother always talks big to impress people.
我哥哥總是吹噓自己來吸引別人對他的好感。

---

talkative [ˈtɔkətɪv]
◀⨏ Track 2097

adj. 喜歡說話的；多嘴的；健談的

▶She is talkative and nosy.
她愛說話又好管閒事。

---

tall [tɔl]
◀⨏ Track 2098

adj. 高的

▶The model is tall and slim.
這名模特兒又高又苗條。

相關片語 tall tale
荒誕不經的故事

▶Loch Ness Monster was probably just a tall tale.
尼斯湖水怪很可能只是一個荒誕不經的故事。

---

tangerine [ˈtændʒəˌrin]
◀⨏ Track 2099

n. 橘子

▶The tangerine is an excellent source of vitamin C.
橘子是很好的維他命C來源。

初級

tank [tæŋk]
◀≣Track 2100

n.（貯水、油、氣的）箱、櫃、槽

▶There is a water tank on the top of the roof.
屋頂上有一個水塔。

相關片語 **fish tank**
水族箱；魚缸

▶It is important to clean the fish tank on a regular basis.
定期清洗魚缸是很重要的。

tape [tep]
◀≣Track 2101

n.（錄音或錄影）磁帶；膠布；膠帶

▶She used some tape to wrap a present.
她用了一些膠帶包裝禮物。

v. 用膠布貼牢；將……錄音；將……錄影

▶They taped their trip in Germany.
他們把在德國的旅途錄影下來。

target [`tɑrgɪt]
◀≣Track 2102

n.（欲達到的）目標；
（攻擊、批評、嘲笑的）對象

▶The kid became a target of laughter due to his obesity.
這孩子因為肥胖而成為別人嘲弄的對象。

v. 以……為目標；以……為對象

▶The animation is targeted at teenagers and children.
這部動畫片是以青少年及孩童為目標對象。

task [tæsk]
◀≣Track 2103

n. 任務；差事；作業

▶Learning physics is a difficult task for some students.
學習物理對有些學生來說並非易事。

taste [test]
◀≣Track 2104

n. 味覺；味道；滋味；一口

▶I like the taste of chocolate.
我喜歡巧克力的味道。

v. 嚐；嚐到；嚐起來；吃起來

▶The watermelon tastes so sweet.
西瓜好甜哦。

tasty [`testɪ]
◀≣Track 2105

adj. 美味的；可口的

▶The fried chicken was tasty and juicy.
炸雞美味又多汁。

taxi [`tæksɪ]
◀≣Track 2106

=taxicab=cab

n. 計程車

▶She flagged down a taxi.
她攔了一輛計乘車。

tea [ti]
◀≣Track 2107

n. 茶

▶My grandfather likes oolong tea.
我祖父喜歡烏龍茶。

teach [titʃ]
◀≣Track 2108

v. 教學；教導

▶He taught social science in the elementary school.
他在小學教社會科學。

teacher [`titʃɚ]
◀≣Track 2109

n. 老師

▶Prof. Allison is a good teacher.
艾利森教授是位好老師。

Teacher's Day
◄€Track 2110

[`titʃɚz-de]

n. 教師節

▶I am going to give a card to my English teacher on Teacher's Day.
我在教師節要送給英文老師一張卡片。

team [tim]
◄€Track 2111

n. 隊；隊伍

▶Michael is the captain of the school basketball team.
麥可是學校籃球隊隊長。

teapot [`ti͵pɑt]
◄€Track 2112

n. 茶壺

▶This teapot is elegant and worth the buy.
這個茶壺很典雅，值得買下來。

tear [tɛr]
◄€Track 2113

n. 眼淚

▶He shed tears when he heard his mother's favorite song being played in the ceremony.
他聽到媽媽最喜歡的音樂在典禮播放，不禁掉下眼淚。

> **補充片語** shed tears
> 掉淚

v. 撕開；拔掉；扯破

▶The boy torn a hole in his trousers.
男孩的褲子扯破了一個洞。

teen [tin]
◄€Track 2114

n. 青少年；十幾歲

▶When Diana met Prince Charles, she was in her teen.
黛安娜遇到查爾斯時，她還是個青少女。

adj. 青少年的；十幾歲的；十幾的

▶The teen actor was bullied online.
這名青少年演員被網路霸凌。

teenager
◄€Track 2115

[`tin͵edʒɚ]

n. 青少年

▶She lived a very carefree life when she was a teenager.
她在青少女時期過著無憂無慮的生活。

telephone
◄€Track 2116

[`tɛlə͵fon]

=phone

n. 電話

▶The doctor talked to his patient on the telephone.
醫師在和病人講電話。

v. 打電話給；打電話告知

▶He telephoned his parents to ask if he could stay with them for a week.
他打電話問父母是否可以在他們家待一個星期。

television
◄€Track 2117

[`tɛlə͵vɪʒən]

=TV

n. 電視；電視機

▶There was nothing interesting on the television last night.
昨晚的電視沒什麼好看的。

tell [tɛl]
◄€Track 2118

v. 告訴；講述；吩咐

▶She told me not to wait for her.
她吩咐我不要等她。

初級

temperature

◀€ Track 2119

[`tɛmprətʃɚ]

n. 溫度；氣溫；體溫

▶The nurse took my temperature and blood pressure.
護士幫我量體溫和血壓。

補充片語 take sb.'s temperature
幫某人量體溫

temple [`tɛmp!]

◀€ Track 2120

n. 廟宇；寺廟；神殿；教堂；禮拜堂

▶She visited the Buddhist temple with her mother each year around her birthday.
她每年大約生日時都會跟媽媽到佛寺參拜。

ten [tɛn]

◀€ Track 2121

pron. 十個

▶She bought twenty croissants, and I ate ten of them.
她買了二十個牛角麵包，我吃了十個。

n. 十；十歲

▶Three plus seven equals ten.
三加七等於十。

adj. 十的；十個的

▶We invited ten guests to our party.
我們邀請十位賓客參加我們的派對。

相關片語 nine times out of ten
十之八九；幾乎總是

▶Nine times out of ten my sore throat is caused by allergies.
我的喉痛幾乎都是過敏造成的。

tennis [`tɛnɪs]

◀€ Track 2122

n. 網球

▶Michael Chen is my tennis coach.
張德培是我的網球教練。

tent [tɛnt]

◀€ Track 2123

n. 帳篷

▶They had to move in the middle of the night because they pitched a tent too close to the ocean.
他們在半夜必須離開，因為他們把帳篷搭在太靠海的地方。

補充片語 pitch a tent
升起；搭造

term [tɝm]

◀€ Track 2124

n. 學期；任期；期限；條款；關係

▶She is on good terms with her sister-in-law.
她跟我小姑的關係和睦。

補充片語 on good terms with sb.
與某人和睦相處

terrible [`tɛrəb!]

◀€ Track 2125

adj. 可怕的；嚇人的；令人不快的；極糟糕的

▶The food in that restaurant is terrible.
那家餐廳的食物很糟糕。

terrific [tə`rɪfɪk]

◀€ Track 2126

adj. 可怕的；嚇人的；非常好的

▶They made a terrific sand castle.
他們造了一座很棒的沙堡。

test [tɛst]

◀€ Track 2127

n. 試驗；測驗；小考

▶I had a bone density test today.
我今天做了骨質密度的測試。

v. 測試；檢驗

▶They tested his blood for HIV.
他們驗了他的血，看看是否有愛滋病病毒。

相關片語 **stand the test**
經得起考驗

▶Shakespeare's literary works have stood the test of time.
莎士比亞的文學作品是經得起考驗的。

textbook [ˋtɛkstˏbʊk] ◀Track 2128

n. 課本；教科書

▶He bought a used textbook for only $100.
他只花一百元就買到了二手教科書。

than [ðæn] ◀Track 2129

conj. 比；比較；與其；除了……之外

▶She swims much faster than I.
她游泳的速度比我快多了。

prep. 比起……；超過

▶He has lived in the United States for more than five years.
他住在美國超過五年了。

thank [θæŋk] ◀Track 2130

v. 感謝

▶We thank you for your opinion.
我們感謝你提供意見。

n. 感謝；謝意

▶She expressed her thanks to Gary for his timely help.
她對於蓋瑞及時的協助向他表達感激。

Thanksgiving ◀Track 2131
[ˏθæŋksˋɡɪvɪŋ]
=Thanksgiving Day

n. 感恩節

▶We'll have Thanksgiving dinner together.
我們會一起吃感恩節晚餐。

that [ðæt] ◀Track 2132

conj. 因為；由於；為了；引導名詞子句

▶She told me that she will move to Japan next month.
她告訴我她下個月要搬家到日本。

pron. 那個；那人

▶That's not the movie I am talking about.
那部電影不是我現在說的這部。

adj. 那個

▶Who's that girl?
那個女孩是誰？

adv. 那樣

▶He is not that into you.
他沒那麼喜歡你。

that's [ðæts] ◀Track 2133

abbr. 那是（**that is**的縮寫）

▶That's a serious problem.
那是很嚴重的問題。

the [ðə] ◀Track 2134

art. 這（些）；那（些）

▶The boy standing over there is my student.
站在那裡的男孩是我的學生。

theater [ˋθɪətɚ] ◀Track 2135
=theatre （英式英語）

n. 劇場；電影院

▶He went to the theater with Mary.
他和瑪莉去看電影。

初級

補充片語 go to the theater
去（電影院）看電影

their [ðɛr]
🔊 Track 2136

det. 他們的

▶ That's their business, not ours.
那是他們的事，與我們無關。

them [ðɛm]
🔊 Track 2137

pron. 他們

▶ Who are they? Do you know them?
他們是誰？你認識他們嗎？

themselves
🔊 Track 2138

[ðəm`sɛlvz]

pron. 他們自己

▶ They finished the task by themselves.
他們靠自己完成這個工作。

then [ðɛn]
🔊 Track 2139

adv. 那時；然後

▶ She was a waitress in that restaurant then.
她當時在那家餐廳當女服務生。

adj. 當時的

▶ The rule was laid down by the then CEO of the company.
這個規則是當時執行長訂下的。

there [ðɛr]
🔊 Track 2140

adv. 在那裡；到那裡

▶ My family lives there.
我的家人住在那裡。

n. 那個地方；那裡

▶ It's about a ten-minute drive from there.
從那裡開車過去要約五分鐘。

therefore [`ðɛr͵for]
🔊 Track 2141

adv. 因此

▶ She had a fever, and therefore she took a day-off.
她發燒了，因此請假一天。

there's [ðɛrz]
🔊 Track 2142

abbr. 那裡有（**there is** 的縮寫）

▶ Where there's a will, there's a way.
有志者事竟成。

these [ðiz]
🔊 Track 2143

pron. 這些人；這些東西

▶ These are my students.
這些人是我的學生。

adj. 這些的

▶ These shoes are too expensive.
這些鞋子太貴了。

they [ðe]
🔊 Track 2144

pron. 他們

▶ They are baseball players.
他們是棒球選手。

they'd [ðed]
🔊 Track 2145

abbr. 他們會、他們已（**they would**、**they had**的縮寫）

▶ They'd arrived at the airport.
他們已經到機場了。

they'll [ðel]
abbr. 他們會（**they will**的縮寫）

▶They'll go to the movie theater tonight.
他們今晚要去看電影。

Track 2146

they're [ðer]
abbr. 他們是（**they are**的縮寫）

▶They're my roommates.
他們是我的室友。

Track 2147

they've [ðev]
abbr. 他們已（**they have** 的縮寫）

▶They've fixed the problem.
他們已經把問題解決了。

Track 2148

thick [θɪk]
adj. 厚的；粗的；濃的

▶They were lost in the thick forest.
他們在茂密的森林中迷路了。

相關片語 a thick head
　　　頭腦遲鈍的

▶The pain is there, and I still have a thick head.
疼痛感還在，我的頭腦仍然很遲鈍。

Track 2149

thief [θif]
n. 小偷

▶The thief was caught by the police last night.
小偷昨晚就被警察抓到了。

相關片語 as thick as thieves
　　　（人與人）感情非常要好

▶She and her twin sister are as thick as thieves.
她和雙胞胎妹妹感情非常要好。

Track 2150

thin [θɪn]
adj. 瘦的；薄的；稀少的

▶She looks very thin and depressed.
她看起來很瘦、很消沉。

Track 2151

thing [θɪŋ]
n. 事情；東西

▶He doesn't eat sweet things.
他不吃甜食。

Track 2152

think [θɪŋk]
v. 想；認為；想起；打算

▶I think we should invite him.
我認為我們應該邀請他。

Track 2153

third [θɝd]
adj. 第三的；三分之一

▶This is my third time visiting Washington D.C.
這是我第三次訪問華盛頓特區。

adv. 第三

▶She arrived third.
她第三個到。

Track 2154

thirsty ['θɝstɪ]
adj. 渴的；口渴的；渴望的

▶He was thirsty for power.
他渴望權力。

Track 2155

thirteen ['θɝtin]
pron. 十三個

▶She has twenty pair of shoes, and I dislike thirteen them.
她有二十雙鞋子，而我不喜歡其中十三雙。

Track 2156

初級

n. 十三；十三個；十三歲

▶My son is turning thirteen tomorrow.
我兒子明天就十三歲了。

adj. 十三的；十三個的

▶The boy has thirteen toy cars.
男童有十三輛玩具車。

thirty [ˋθɝtɪ]　◀ Track 2157

pron. 三十個

▶He had twenty paintings in the exhibition, and I have thirty.
他在展覽展出二十幅畫作，而我展出三十幅。

n. 三十

▶She is thirty.
她三十歲了。

adj. 三十的

▶He has been in the building trade for thirty years.
他在建築業工作三十年了。

this [ðɪs]　◀ Track 2158

pron. 這個

▶Is this the book you recommended?
這本是你之前推薦的書嗎？

adj. 這個

▶This laptop is mine.
這個筆電是我的。

adv. 這麼；像這樣地

▶My cat is about this big.
我的貓大概有這麼大隻。

those [ðoz]　◀ Track 2159

pron. 那些

▶Those are her children.
那些是她的小孩。

adj. 那些的

▶Those children are having a good time.
那些孩子玩得正開心。

though [ðo]　◀ Track 2160

conj. 雖然；儘管

▶Though he came from a humble family, he never gave up.
他雖然出身貧寒，但從不放棄。

adv. 然而；還是

▶The mission seemed impossible. He completed it, though.
這看似是不可能的任務，然而他完成它了。

thought [θɔt]　◀ Track 2161

n. 思維；想法；考慮

▶I'll give serious thought to this proposal.
我會認真考慮這個提案。

thousand　◀ Track 2162

[ˋθaʊznd]

pron. 千個

▶The battle took away thousands of lives.
這場戰爭奪走成千上萬人的生命。

n. 一千；一千個

▶Tens of thousands of visitors went to the zoo to see the polar bear cub.
上萬名遊客到動物園去看小北極熊。

adj. 一千的；成千的；無數的

▶I've warned you a thousand times not to trust him.
我警告過你無數次不要相信他。

three [θri]

◀ Track 2163

pron. 三個

▶All three of his children are medical professionals.
他的三個孩子都是醫學專家。

n. 三；三個

▶One plus two equals three.
一加二等於三。

adj. 三的；三個的

▶I have three cats.
我有三隻貓。

throat [θrot]

◀ Track 2164

n. 喉嚨

▶There was a fish bone stuck in his throat.
他的喉嚨卡了一根魚刺。

相關片語 **lie in one's throat**
　　　　撒大謊

▶She was lying in her throat when she told you how poor she was.
她告訴你她有多窮，這真是天大的謊言。

through [θru]

◀ Track 2165

prep. 穿過；通過

▶The river runs through the city.
這條河穿過了這座城市。

adv. 穿過；通過；從頭到尾

▶She read through the script and decided to take the role.
她把整個劇本看完，決定接演這個角色。

throughout

◀ Track 2166

[θru`aʊt]

prep. 遍佈；從頭到尾；貫穿

▶Chinese New Year is celebrated throughout the Chinese community.
華人世界都在慶祝農曆新年。

throw [θro]

◀ Track 2167

v. 丟

▶They threw stones at the stray dog.
他們拿石頭丟那隻流浪犬。

thumb [θʌm]

◀ Track 2168

n. 拇指

▶He hit his thumb with the hammer by accident.
他不小心用鐵錘敲到自己的姆指。

thunder [`θʌndɚ]

◀ Track 2169

n. 雷聲；雷

▶He was woken up by the loud peal of thunder.
他被一陣大雷聲吵醒。

v. 打雷；發出雷般聲響；大聲斥責

▶It started to thunder and pour rain in the afternoon.
下午天空開始打雷並下起雨。

相關片語 **thunder shower**
　　　　雷陣雨

▶There was a thunder shower this morning.
早上有一場雷陣雨。

Thursday [`θɝzde] =Thurs./Thur.

◀ Track 2170

n. 星期四

▶We have music class on Thursday.
我們星期四有音樂課。

初級

thus [ðʌs]
◀**Track 2171**

adv. 因此

▶He likes eating bread. Thus, he takes a bakery course.
他愛吃麵包，所以去上烘焙課。

ticket [`tɪkɪt]
◀**Track 2172**

n. 票

▶May I book a ticket to Kyoto?
我可以訂一張到京都的機票嗎？

tidy [`taɪdɪ]
◀**Track 2173**

adj. 整齊的；井然有序的

▶Her house is neat and tidy.
她的房子很整潔乾淨。

v. 收拾；使整齊

▶The office cleaner tidied up the pantry room.
辦公室清潔工把茶水間打掃乾淨了。

tie [taɪ]
◀**Track 2174**

n. 領帶；聯繫；束縛

▶We have stable trade ties with the United States.
我們和美國有穩定的貿易關係。

v. 繫；綁；打結；結為夫妻

▶His allergy is tied to flour.
他的過敏症與麵粉有關係。

tiger [`taɪgɚ]
◀**Track 2175**

n. 虎

▶Bengal tigers are rare species.
孟加拉老虎是稀有物種。

till [tɪl]
◀**Track 2176**

=until

prep. 直到……才

▶I didn't know the news till now.
我直到現在才知道這個新聞。

conj. 直到……為止

▶He will not give up till he realizes his dream.
直到他實現夢想以前，他不會放棄的。

time [taɪm]
◀**Track 2177**

n. 時間

▶You really need to take some time to relax.
你實在應該撥出一些時間放鬆一下。

v. 為……計時；預定……的時間

▶The runner was timed at 10.02 second.
這名跑者的成績被測定為十點零二秒。

tiny [`taɪnɪ]
◀**Track 2178**

adj. 極小的；微小的

▶The fish is very tiny.
這種魚很小隻。

tip [tɪp]
◀**Track 2179**

n. 小費

▶We gave our tour guide a tip.
我們付小費給導遊。

v. 給……小費

▶He tipped the waitress $100.
他給女服務生一百元的小費。

tired [taɪrd]
◀**Track 2180**

adj. 疲累的；厭倦的

▶I am tired of her lies.
我對她的謊言好厭煩。

title [`taɪt!] ◀⌇Track 2181
n. 標題;書名;頭銜;名稱

▶The title of the article is As We May Think.
這篇文章的名稱是《如吾人所思》。

to [tu] ◀⌇Track 2182
prep. 向;往;到

▶We are going to Prague for our honeymoon.
我們要去布拉格渡蜜月。

inf. 不定詞

▶To teach is to learn.
教學相長。

toast [tost] ◀⌇Track 2183
n. 吐司;烤麵包片

▶She spread strawberry jam on her toast.
她在吐司麵包上塗上草莓醬。

v. 烤（麵包）;烘（手或腳）

▶She toasted some hamburger buns in the oven.
她在烤箱烤些漢堡麵包。

today [tə`de] ◀⌇Track 2184
adv. 今天

▶He is going to an audition today.
他今天要試鏡。

n. 今天

▶Today is my daughter's birthday.
今天是我女兒的生日。

toe [to] ◀⌇Track 2185
n. 腳趾;足尖

▶She was dancing on her toes.
她踮起腳趾跳舞。

相關片語 **from head to toe**
全身;從頭到腳

▶He was dressed in navy blue from head to toe.
他全身穿著海軍藍的衣服。

tofu [`tofu] ◀⌇Track 2186
=bean curd
n. 豆腐

▶Stinky tofu is one of the most famous dishes in Taiwan.
臭豆腐是台灣最知名的料理之一。

together [tə`gɛðɚ] ◀⌇Track 2187
adv. 一起;合起來

▶My friend and I went to Beijing together.
我和朋友一起去北京。

toilet [`tɔɪlɪt] ◀⌇Track 2188
n. 馬桶;廁所、洗手間

▶He flushed the toil after using it.
他上完廁所後沖馬桶。

相關片語 **toilet paper**
廁紙;衛生紙

▶We bought a lot of toilet paper from the shopping mall.
我們在購物中心買了很多衛生紙。

tomato [tə`meto] ◀⌇Track 2189
n. 番茄

▶She put some tomatoes in the salad.
她放了一些番茄在沙拉裡。

初級

tomorrow
🔊 Track 2190

[tə`mɔro]

adv. 明天

▶We will have a field trip tomorrow.
我們明天要校外教學。

n. 明天

▶Tomorrow will be Wednesday.
明天是星期三。

tone [ton]
🔊 Track 2191

n. 音調；腔調；語氣；色調

▶She spoke in a tone of demand.
她用命令的口氣說話。

tongue [tʌŋ]
🔊 Track 2192

n. 舌頭；說話方式；語言

▶French is my mother tongue.
法文是我的母語。

相關片語 **on everyone's tongue**
被眾人議論

▶Her sudden marriage was on everyone's tongue.
她的閃婚讓大家議論紛紛。

tonight [tə`naɪt]
🔊 Track 2193

adv. 今晚

▶We will go to the movie tonight.
我們今晚要去看電影。

n. 今晚

▶Tonight is hot.
今晚很熱。

too [tu]
🔊 Track 2194

adv. 太；也

▶You are never too old to learn.
活到老，學到老。

tool [tul]
🔊 Track 2195

n. 工具；方法；手段

▶A screwdriver is a simple tool.
螺絲起子是一種簡單的工具。

tooth [tuθ]
🔊 Track 2196

n. 牙齒

▶He had a tooth decay.
他有一顆蛀牙。

相關片語 **have a sweet tooth**
愛吃甜食

▶I have a sweet tooth for cocoa.
我愛吃可可。

toothache [`tuθˌek]
🔊 Track 2197

n. 牙痛

▶She had a toothache yesterday.
她昨天牙痛。

toothbrush
🔊 Track 2198

[`tuθˌbrʌʃ]

n. 牙刷

▶He used an electric toothbrush for cleaner teeth.
他用電動牙刷，把牙齒刷得更乾淨。

top [tɑp]
🔊 Track 2199

n. 頂端；頂部；上方；頂點

▶The temple is on the top of the hill.
佛寺位於山頂上。

adj. 頂上的；最高的；居首位的

▶The restaurant is on the top floor of the building.
這間餐廳在建築物的頂樓。

v. 給……加蓋；達到……的頂部；高於

▶The mountain is topped with snow in winter.
這山頂每年冬天都會積雪。

topic [ˋtɑpɪk] ◀€Track 2200
n. 題目;話題;標題

▶They talked about different topics in the meeting.
他們在會議中談論不同的話題。

total [ˋtot!] ◀€Track 2201
adj. 總記的;全體的

▶Her project ended in total failure.
她的計畫徹底失敗。

n. 總數

▶The budget reached a total of 1 million dollars.
預算總計一百萬元。

v. 合計為;總計

▶The utility bill totals to $500.
水電費總計五百元。

touch [tʌtʃ] ◀€Track 2202
v. 摸;觸碰

▶I was deeply touched by the movie.
我被這部電影深深感動。

n. 觸覺;觸感;接觸;聯繫

▶I still keep in touch with my elementary school teacher.
我仍跟我的小學老師保持聯絡。

補充片語 stay/keep in touch
保持聯繫

tour [tʊr] ◀€Track 2203
n. 旅行;旅遊;巡迴演出

▶The band is on tour in England.
這個樂團在英格蘭巡迴演出。

v. 旅行;在……旅遊

▶He spent his holidays touring Poland.
他去波蘭旅遊度假。

相關片語 group tour
團體旅遊

▶I prefer group tours to DIY tours.
相較於自由行,我更喜歡團體旅遊。

補充片語 DIY tour
自由行;自助旅行

toward [təˋwɔrd] ◀€Track 2204
=towards
prep. 朝;向

▶We drove toward the countryside.
我們朝著鄉間開去。

towel [ˋtaʊəl] ◀€Track 2205
n. 毛巾

▶She used a towel to dry her hands.
她用一條毛巾擦乾雙手。

tower [ˋtaʊɚ] ◀€Track 2206
n. 塔;高樓

▶The Twin Towers used to be an important landmark in New York.
雙子星塔曾是紐約著名的地標。

town [taʊn] ◀€Track 2207
n. 城鎮

▶She came from a small town.
她來自一個小城。

初級

out of town
出遠門

▶My dad is out of town this week.
我爸爸這禮拜出門到外地去。

toy [tɔɪ] ◀Track 2208
n. 玩具

▶This teddy bear is her favorite toy.
這隻泰迪熊是她最愛的玩具。

trace [tres] ◀Track 2209
v. 追蹤

▶The detective tried to trace the criminal.
警探試著追蹤罪犯。

n. 蹤跡

▶She always spoke with a trace of cynicism.
她說話總帶著一絲憤世嫉俗。

track [træk] ◀Track 2210
n. 行蹤；軌道；小徑

▶They followed her tracks in the snow to a cabin.
他們沿著她在雪地上留下的足跡走到一間小木屋。

v. 跟蹤；追蹤

▶The police tracked down the suspects and arrested an armed man.
警方循線追蹤嫌犯並逮捕了一名武裝人士。

補充片語 **track down**
經追蹤或搜索而發現

trade [tred] ◀Track 2211
n. 交易；貿易

▶There is a trade war between China and the United States.
中美正在打貿易戰。

v. 進行交易；交換；做買賣

▶Can I trade my bananas with your apples?
我可以用香蕉和你換蘋果嗎？

tradition [trə`dɪʃən] ◀Track 2212
n. 傳統；慣例

▶This tradition dates back to one thousand years ago.
這個傳統的由來可以追溯到一千年前。

traditional ◀Track 2213
[trə`dɪʃən!]
adj. 傳統的；慣例的

▶He is very traditional and conservative.
他很傳統保守。

traffic [`træfɪk] ◀Track 2214
n. 交通

▶The traffic was very busy on the highway.
高速公路交通很繁忙。

相關片語 **traffic jam**
交通堵塞

▶I was late for work because of the traffic jam.
我今天因為交通堵塞而上班遲到。

train [tren] ◀Track 2215
n. 火車

▶He went to London by train.
他坐火車到倫敦。

v. 訓練；培養；接受訓練；鍛鍊

▶She is training for the Olympics.
她正在為奧林匹克接受訓練。

transit [`trænsɪt] ◀Track 2216

n. 運輸；公共交通運輸系統

▶The cars were damaged in transit.
這些汽車在運輸過程中損壞了。

trap [træp] ◀Track 2217

v. 設陷阱捕捉；使落入圈套；堵塞

▶A deer was trapped.
一隻鹿落入陷阱。

n. 陷阱；圈套

▶He set traps to catch bears.
他設了陷阱要抓熊。

trash [træʃ] ◀Track 2218

n. 垃圾；廢物；無用的人

▶Please put your trash in the garbage can.
請把垃圾投入垃圾筒裡。

> 相關片語 **trash can**
> 垃圾桶

▶She handed him a trash can so he can vomited into it.
她遞了一個垃圾桶給他，好讓他可以朝裡面嘔吐。

travel [`træv!] ◀Track 2219

v. 旅行；移動

▶They are traveling around the world.
他們正在世界各國旅行。

n. 旅行；遊歷；旅遊業；移動

▶They had a ten-day's travel in Germany.
他們在德國旅遊十天。

treasure [`trɛʒɚ] ◀Track 2220

n. 金銀財寶；貴重物品

▶She locked her treasures in a safe.
她把貴重物品鎖在保險箱裡。

v. 珍惜；珍視

▶I treasure my friendship with him.
我珍惜和他的友誼。

treat [trit] ◀Track 2221

v. 對待；處理；治療；款待、請客

▶She treated me like her own daughter.
她待我如同自己的女兒。

n. 請客

▶Today is my treat.
今天我請客。

treatment [`tritmənt] ◀Track 2222

n. 對待；處理；治療；療法

▶The new treatment is more effective than the current one.
新療法比目前的療法更有效。

tree [tri] ◀Track 2223

n. 樹

▶There's a lemon tree in the garden.
庭院有一顆檸檬樹。

trial [`traɪəl] ◀Track 2224

n. 試用；試驗；棘手的事；審問、審判

▶The man will testify at the trial today.
男人將在審判中作證。

triangle [`traɪˌæŋg!] ◀Track 2225

n. 三角形

▶She drew a triangle with three equal sides and three equal angles.
她畫了一個正三角形。

初級

trick [trɪk]
🔊 Track 2226

n. 詭計；花招；竅門；手法；戲法；特技

▶Magic tricks are simply illusions.
魔術的戲法只不過是利用人們的錯覺。

v. 哄騙；戲弄

▶They tricked him into trafficking drugs.
他們騙他走私毒品。

相關片語 **any trick in the book**
各種招數或計謀

▶He tried any trick in the book but still couldn't stop her.
他用盡千方百計卻仍無法阻止她。

trip [trɪp]
🔊 Track 2227

n. 旅行；行程

▶She is on a business trip.
她出差中。

trouble [`trʌb!]
🔊 Track 2228

n. 麻煩；困境；費事；騷亂

▶He got himself into trouble.
他陷入麻煩了。

v. 麻煩；使憂慮；使疼痛；費心

▶He didn't even trouble to look at the gift.
他甚至不屑看一下禮物。

相關片語 **ask for trouble**
自討苦吃；自找麻煩

▶Making friend with her is asking for trouble.
跟她做朋友是自找麻煩。

trousers [`traʊzɚz]
🔊 Track 2229
=pants （美式英文）

n. 褲子

▶He bought a new pair of trousers.
他買了一件新褲子。

truck [trʌk]
🔊 Track 2230

n. 卡車

▶The chickens were loaded onto trucks.
這些雞被卡車裝載。

true [tru]
🔊 Track 2231

adj. 真的

▶The movie is based on a true story.
這部電影是根據真實故事改編而成的。

trumpet [`trʌmpɪt]
🔊 Track 2232

n. 喇叭；小號

▶He can play the trumpet.
他會吹小號。

trust [trʌst]
🔊 Track 2233

n. 信任；信賴

▶She has no trust in her family.
她不信任家人。

v. 相信；信賴；依靠

▶Why do you trust him?
你為什麼信任他？

truth [truθ]
🔊 Track 2234

n. 真相；實情

▶I need to know the truth.
我需要知道真相。

相關片語 **home truth**
關於自己的不愉快事實；不中聽的真話

▶He told her a home truth as kindly as he could.
他盡可能地婉轉告訴她不中聽的真話。

try [traɪ]　🔊 Track 2235

v. 嘗試；試圖；努力

▶She tried to lose weight by exercising regularly.
她嘗試規律運動以減重。

n. 嘗試；努力

▶Maybe you should give it one more try.
也許你應該再試試看。

T-shirt [`ti,ʃɝt]
=tee-shirt　🔊 Track 2236

n. T恤；短袖圓領汗衫

▶She wore a pink T-shirt and a denim skirt.
她穿著粉紅T恤和藍色牛仔裙。

tub [tʌb]　🔊 Track 2237

n. 盆；桶；浴缸；（放冰淇淋的）杯

▶She grows tomatoes in tubs on the roof.
她在屋頂用木盆種番茄。

tube [tjub]　🔊 Track 2238

n. 管；筒；（英）地下鐵

▶He went to London by tube.
他搭地鐵到倫敦。

Tuesday [`tjuzde]
=Tues./Tue.　🔊 Track 2239

n. 星期二

▶Tomorrow is Tuesday.

明天是星期二。

tummy [`tʌmɪ]　🔊 Track 2240
=stomach

n. 胃；肚子；啤酒肚

▶I had a tummy ache.
我肚子痛。

tunnel [`tʌn!]　🔊 Track 2241

n. 隧道；地道

▶The workers are digging a tunnel.
工人正在挖隧道。

相關片語 light at the end of the tunnel 苦盡甘來

▶After years of hard work, I can finally see the light at the end of the tunnel.
辛勤耕耘了多年，我終於能苦盡甘來了。

turkey [`tɝkɪ]　🔊 Track 2242

n. 火雞；火雞肉

▶She roasted a turkey for Thanksgiving dinner.
她烤了一隻火雞當感恩節晚餐。

turn [tɝn]　🔊 Track 2243

v. 轉；翻轉；轉向；轉身；變化

▶Please turn to the next page.
請翻開下一頁。

n. 轉向；依次輪流的機會

▶Students took turns to make presentations.
學生輪流做報告。

補充片語 take turns
輪流

初級

turtle [ˋtɝtḷ] ◀€Track 2244
n. 海龜；龜肉

▶A few sea turtles laid eggs on the shores of North Cyprus.
北塞浦路斯海岸有幾隻海龜下蛋了。

補充片語 lay eggs
下蛋

TV [ti-vi] ◀€Track 2245
n. 電視

▶Turn on the TV. I want to watch the Cartoon Network.
把電視打開，我想看卡通頻道。

補充片語 turn on
打開

twelve [twɛlv] ◀€Track 2246
pron. 十二個

▶Twelve of the participants asked questions in the seminar.
研討會與會者有十二個提問。

n. 十二

▶Twenty minus eight equals twelve.
二十減八等於十二。

adj. 十二的

▶She has twelve students in her class.
她的班上有十二個學生。

twenty [ˋtwɛntɪ] ◀€Track 2247
pron. 二十個

▶We need a meeting room to accommodate twenty of those students.
我們需要一間能容納那二十個學生的會議室。

n. 二十

▶Four times five is twenty.
四乘以五等於二十。

adj. 二十的

▶He bought twenty pounds of rice.
他買了二十磅重的米。

twice [twaɪs] ◀€Track 2248
adv. 兩次

▶He has been to Paris twice.
他去過巴黎兩次。

two [tu] ◀€Track 2249
pron. 兩個

▶The cupcakes are yummy. Can I have two of them more?
這些杯子蛋糕好好吃，我可以再多吃兩個嗎？

n. 二；兩歲；兩點

▶My son will be at the age of two next month.
我兒子下個月滿兩歲。

adj. 二的；兩個的

▶He has two sisters.
他有兩個姊姊。

type [taɪp] ◀€Track 2250
v. 打字；用打字機打

▶How many words can you type a minute?
你每分鐘能打幾個字？

n. 類型；型式；樣式

▶What type of parent are you?
你是什麼樣類型的父母？

相關片語 blood type
血型

▶His blood type is O.
他的血型是○。

typhoon [taɪˋfun]

🔊 Track 2251

n. 颱風

▶Typhoon Morakot is one of the deadliest typhoons to impact Taiwan in the past 50 years.
莫拉克颱風是台灣過去五十年來最致命的颱風之一。

初級

Uu

　　以下表格是全民英檢官方公告初級「聽、說、讀、寫」所須具備的能力，本書例句皆依此範疇特別設計，只要掃描右方QR code，就能搭配相對應的音軌，實現「眼耳並用」方式，刺激左腦的語言學習功能；同時也可使用本書附贈的紅膠片，將其置於單字上，一面記憶一面自我挑戰，達到雙倍的學習成果！

聽	▶	能聽懂與日常生活相關的淺易談話，包含價格、時間及地點等。
說	▶	能朗讀簡易文章、簡單地自我介紹，對熟悉的話題能以簡易英語對答，如問候、購物、問路等。
讀	▶	可看懂與日常生活相關的淺易英文，並能閱讀路標、交通號誌、招牌、簡單菜單、時刻表及賀卡等。
寫	▶	能寫簡單的句子及段落，如寫明信片、便條、賀卡及填表格等。對一般日常生活相關事物，能以簡短的文字敘述或說明。

ugly [`ʌglɪ]　　◀ Track 2252

adj. 醜的；難看的；可怕的

▶ The ugly duckling turned out to be a beautiful swan.
醜小鴨居然變成美麗的天鵝。

umbrella [ʌm`brɛlə]　　◀ Track 2253

n. 雨傘

▶ I left my umbrella on the train.
我把傘落在火車上了。

相關片語 beach umbrella
（海灘）遮陽傘

▶ He sat under a beach umbrella.
他坐在一把遮陽傘下。

uncle [`ʌŋk!]　　◀ Track 2254

n. 叔叔；舅舅；伯伯；姑丈；姨父等對年長男子的稱呼

▶ My uncle is an engineer.
我的叔叔是一位工程師。

相關片語 cry uncle
求饒；認輸

▶ She kept nagging her husband until he cried uncle.
她一直對先生喋喋不休，直到他求饒。

under [`ʌndɚ]　　◀ Track 2255

prep. 在……下

▶ They were sitting under the tree.
他們在樹下坐著。

adv. 在下方；在下面

▶ She was a bad swimmer, so she often went under and swallowed a lot of water.
她不善長游泳，所以經常沉到水下，喝了一些水。

underline

Track 2256

[ˌʌndəˈlaɪn]

v. 在下面劃線

▶ She underlined the topic sentences with a highlighter.
她用螢光筆在主題句下面劃線。

underpass

Track 2257

[ˈʌndəˌpæs]

n. 地下道

▶ The underpass offered fast and convenient access to the city center.
這個地下道提供一個快速、方便到達市中心的通道。

understand

Track 2258

[ˌʌndəˈstænd]

v. 理解；明白

▶ I understand why you don't trust her.
我明白你為什麼不信任她。

underwear

Track 2259

[ˈʌndəˌwɛr]

n. 內衣

▶ He removed his underwear for medical examination.
他為了做健康檢查而脫掉內衣。

unhappy [ʌnˈhæpɪ]

Track 2260

adj. 不高興的；不幸的；對……不滿意的

▶ My husband was unhappy when I needed to work overtime again.
我又必須加班時，先生很不高興。

uniform [ˈjunəˌfɔrm]

Track 2261

n. 制服

▶ Students in this private school are required to wear uniform.
這所私立學校的學生被要求要穿校服。

adj. 相同的；一致的

▶ These fleece jackets have a uniform size.
這些刷毛外套尺寸相同。

unique [juˈnik]

Track 2262

adj. 獨一無二的；唯一的

▶ Her painting style is unique.
她的畫風很獨特。

unit [ˈjunɪt]

Track 2263

n. 單位；單元；一組；一個；一套

▶ The acronym CPU stands for the central processing unit of a computer.
CPU是「電腦的中央處理器」的縮寫。

universe [ˈjunəˌvɝs]

Track 2264

n. 宇宙；全人類；全世界

▶ There are galaxies in the universe that are incredibly far away.
宇宙有許多非常遙遠的銀河。

university

Track 2265

[ˌjunəˈvɝsətɪ]

n. 大學

▶ She is studying at the University of Pennsylvania.
她在賓州大學就讀。

until [ənˈtɪl]

Track 2266

conj. 直到……時；在……之前

▶ He waited until his tea cooled down just enough that he could sip happily.
他等到茶涼到可以喝了才開心地喝了起來。

初級

prep. 直到……時，直到；在……之前

▶He didn't go home until ten o'clock last night.
他昨晚直到十點才回家。

相關片語 **until further notice**
在另行通知之前

▶All the flights to Amsterdam were cancelled until further notice.
在另行通知之前，所有到阿姆斯特丹的班機都取消了。

---

up [ʌp]
◀Track 2267

adv. 向上；增加；上揚

▶She hung the painting up.
她把圖畫掛起來。

prep. 向……上；在……上

▶They walked up the trail in the mountain.
他們在山裡沿著路徑走上去。

adj. 向上的；上行的；起床的

▶Time's up!
時間到!

相關片語 **up and down**
來回地；上下地；到處地

▶The boy's smiley ball is bobbing up and down in the pool.
男孩的笑臉球在水池裡時上時下的浮動。

---

upon [əˈpɑn]
◀Track 2268

prep. 在……之上；在……之後立 即……

▶Upon hearing the good news, she jumped up and down in joy.
她一聽到好消息，就開心地跳上跳下。

---

upper [ˈʌpɚ]
◀Track 2269

adj. 較高的；上層的；上游的

▶This area is where the upper class live.
這個地區是上流階級的人住的。

n. 鞋幫；上舖；安非他命

▶The shoes have suede uppers.
這雙鞋的鞋幫是絨面革的。

---

upstairs [ˈʌpˈstɛrz]
◀Track 2270

adv. 在樓上；往樓上

▶He lived upstairs.
他住在樓上。

adj. 樓上的

▶Many people watched the royal couple from their upstairs windows.
許多民眾從他們的樓上窗戶往下看這對皇室夫妻。

n. 樓上

▶They rent out the upstairs to an American family.
他們把樓上出租給一戶美國家庭。

---

us [ʌs]
◀Track 2271

pron. 我們

▶Our teacher is very strict with us.
我們的老師對我們很嚴格。

USA [ju-ɛs-e]
◀Track 2272

n. 美利堅合眾國；美國

▶Miss USA won the Miss Universe pageant.
美國小姐贏得環球小姐選美后冠。

---

use [juz]
◀Track 2273

v. 使用；利用

▶The superstar used his fame to raise funds for people with AIDS.
這名巨星利用他的名氣幫助愛滋病患募款。

n. 使用；利用

▶He didn't have much money to buy books, so he made good use of the school library.
他沒有很多錢買書，所以他善用學校的圖書館。

補充片語 **make use of sth.**
利用某事

---

used [juzd]
Track 2274

adj. 舊了的；用舊了的

▶She bought a used iPhone.
她買了一支二手的蘋果手機。

v. 曾經

▶I used to work at a cram school.
我曾經在補習班工作。

補充片語 **cram school**
補習班

---

useful [ˋjusfəl]
Track 2275

adj. 有用的；有幫助的；有助益的

▶This guidebook is very useful.
這本旅遊指南很實用。

---

user [ˋjuzɚ]
Track 2276

n. 使用者；用戶

▶The new app has a friendly user interface.
這款新的應用程式擁有對使用者友善介面。

---

usual [ˋjuʒʊəl]
Track 2277

adj. 平常的；慣常的

▶She went to the office later than usual.
她比平時晚進辦公室。

相關片語 **as usual**
像平常一樣

▶She stood quietly as usual.
她像平常一樣安靜地站著。

---

usually [ˋjuʒʊəlɪ]
Track 2278

adv. 慣常地；通常地

▶He usually goes to bed at nine o'clock.
他通常九點上床睡覺。

初級

Vv

　　以下表格是全民英檢官方公告初級「聽、說、讀、寫」所須具備的能力，本書例句皆依此範疇特別設計，只要掃描右方QR code，就能搭配相對應的音軌，實現「眼耳並用」方式，刺激左腦的語言學習功能；同時也可使用本書附贈的紅膠片，將其置於單字上，一面記憶一面自我挑戰，達到雙倍的學習成果！

聽	▶	能聽懂與日常生活相關的淺易談話，包含價格、時間及地點等。
說	▶	能朗讀簡易文章、簡單地自我介紹，對熟悉的話題能以簡易英語對答，如問候、購物、問路等。
讀	▶	可看懂與日常生活相關的淺易英文，並能閱讀路標、交通號誌、招牌、簡單菜單、時刻表及賀卡等。
寫	▶	能寫簡單的句子及段落，如寫明信片、便條、賀卡及填表格等。對一般日常生活相關事物，能以簡短的文字敘述或說明。

vacation [veˋkeʃən]　◀€ Track 2279

n. 假期；休假

▶She went to South Korea on vacation.
她去南韓度假。

相關片語 **winter vacation**
寒假

▶They will spend their winter vacation in Austria.
他們寒假要去奧地利。

Valentine's Day　◀€ Track 2280
[ˋvæləntaɪnz-de]

n. 情人節

▶I overheard some young people talking about how much they hate Valentine's Day.
我無意中聽到有些年輕人討論他們有多麼討厭情人節。

valley [ˋvælɪ]　◀€ Track 2281

n. 山谷；溪谷

▶We visited the Yangtze valley when we were in China.
我們在中國時，有去參觀長江流域。

value [ˋvælju]　◀€ Track 2282

n. 價值；重要性；價值觀

▶Her values seem ancient.
她的價值觀似乎很老舊。

v. 估價；重視；珍視

▶We value your suggestions.
我們很重視你的建議。

VCR [vi-si-ɑr]　◀€ Track 2283
=video cassette recorder

n. 卡式錄放影機

▶I don't know how to use the VCR.
我不知道怎麼用這台卡式錄放影機。

vegetable
Track 2284

[`vɛdʒətəb!]

n. 蔬菜;青菜

▶I like vegetables and fruit.
我喜歡吃蔬果。

adj. 蔬菜的;植物的

▶She prefers a vegetable diet to a meaty one.
相較葷食,她更喜歡素食。

vendor [`vɛndɚ]
Track 2285

n. 攤販;小販;叫賣者

▶I bought a bubble tea from the vendor.
我從攤販買了一杯珍珠奶茶。

相關片語 street vendor
地攤;路邊攤

▶He is a street vendor. He just has a knack for cooking.
他經營一個路邊攤,他就是有烹飪的天份。

補充片語 have a knack for
對……有天份

very [`vɛrɪ]
Track 2286

adv. 非常

▶He was very upset.
他非常生氣。

adj. 正是;恰好是

▶That was the very first time I heard Michael Jackson's song.
那正是我第一次聽到麥可・傑克森的歌曲。

vest [vɛst]
Track 2287

n. 背心;汗衫;內衣

▶The police wore bulletproof vests while investigating the crime scenes.
警方身穿防彈背心調查刑案現場。

相關片語 life vest
救生衣

▶When Titanic sank, there were not enough life vests on the ship.
鐵達尼號沉沒時,船上沒有足夠的救生衣。

victory [`vɪktərɪ]
Track 2288

n. 勝利

▶The president-elect celebrated victory on Wednesday night alongside his wife and children.
總統當選人在週三晚上在妻兒的陪伴下慶祝勝選。

video [`vɪdɪ‚o]
Track 2289

n. 錄影節目;電視

▶You can upload videos of your own to YouTube.
你可以上傳自己的影片到YouTube。

v. 錄像;錄製

▶They hired me to video their own wedding.
他們僱用我幫他們錄製婚禮。

相關片語 video game
電動遊戲;電玩遊戲

▶Their teenage son spent too much time playing video game.
他們處於青春期的兒子花太多時間打電玩了。

view [vju]
Track 2290

n. 景色;看法

▶The view from the hotel was absolutely breathtaking.
從這間旅館望出去的景色真是令人歎為觀止。

初級

v. 觀看；看待；將……視為

▶He is viewed as a potential 2020 White House contender.
他被視為是角逐二〇二〇白宮總統大位頗具潛力的候選人。

village [ˋvɪlɪdʒ]
🔊 Track 2291

n. 村；村落；村莊；村民

▶He lived in a remote village.
他住在一個偏僻的村莊裡。

相關片語 **holiday village**
度假村

▶We went to a holiday village in Italy and we were pleasantly surprised.
我們去義大利的一個度假村，那裡讓我們很驚喜。

vinegar [ˋvɪnɪgɚ]
🔊 Track 2292

n. 醋

▶Homemade apple cider vinegar is better and cheaper than those sold in the supermarket.
自製蘋果醋比起超市賣的風味更好且更便宜。

violin [ˌvaɪəˋlɪn]
🔊 Track 2293

n. 小提琴

▶He practiced the violin after school.
他下課後練習拉小提琴。

visit [ˋvɪzɪt]
🔊 Track 2294

v. 參觀；拜訪

▶We visited a nursing home yesterday.
我們昨天參觀一間安養院。

n. 參觀；拜訪

▶She met her ex-boyfriend during her visit to Salt Lake City.
她在鹽湖城參訪期間遇見了前男友。

相關片語 **pay sb. a visit**
拜訪某人

▶He paid a visit to his uncle.
他拜訪了他的叔叔。

visitor [ˋvɪzɪtɚ]
🔊 Track 2295

n. 訪客；遊客

▶The Vatican attracts more than five million visitors every year.
梵蒂岡每年吸引超過五百萬名遊客前往旅遊。

相關片語 **visitors' book**
訪客登記簿

▶After lunch, they signed our visitors' book before departing.
他們用完午餐後，在離去前於我們的訪客名冊上簽名。

vocabulary
🔊 Track 2296

[vəˋkæbjəˌlɛrɪ]

n. 字彙；詞彙

▶He has a wide vocabulary.
他的詞彙量很大。

voice [vɔɪs]
🔊 Track 2297

n. 聲音

▶I could tell from his voice that he wasn't quite sure.
我可以從他的聲音聽出來他不是很確定。

volleyball [ˋvɑlɪˌbɔl]
🔊 Track 2298

n. 排球；排球運動

▶He coached volleyball for two seasons.
他擔任了兩季的排球教練。

相關片語 **beach volleyball**
沙灘排球

▶The children were playing beach volleyball.

孩子在玩沙灘排球。

volume [`vɑljəm]
◀ミ Track 2299

n. 冊；卷；音量

▶This masterpiece is in fifteen volumes.

這本鉅作有十五卷。

vote [vot]
◀ミ Track 2300

n. 選舉；投票；選票

▶They called a meeting to hold a vote on the issue.

他們召集了一次會議對這個議題進行表決。

v. 投票；表決；投票決定

▶You are still too young to vote in the election.

你的年齡還太小，不能在選舉中投票。

voter [`votɚ]
◀ミ Track 2301

n. 選舉人；投票人

▶Cigarette tax increases are popular with voters.

提高烟品税很受選民的歡迎。

初級

Ww

以下表格是全民英檢官方公告初級「聽、說、讀、寫」所須具備的能力，本書例句皆依此範疇特別設計，只要掃描右方QR code，就能搭配相對應的音軌，實現「眼耳並用」方式，刺激左腦的語言學習功能；同時也可使用本書附贈的紅膠片，將其置於單字上，一面記憶一面自我挑戰，達到雙倍的學習成果！

聽 ▶	能聽懂與日常生活相關的淺易談話，包含價格、時間及地點等。
說 ▶	能朗讀簡易文章、簡單地自我介紹，對熟悉的話題能以簡易英語對答，如問候、購物、問路等。
讀 ▶	可看懂與日常生活相關的淺易英文，並能閱讀路標、交通號誌、招牌、簡單菜單、時刻表及賀卡等。
寫 ▶	能寫簡單的句子及段落，如寫明信片、便條、賀卡及填表格等。對一般日常生活相關事物，能以簡短的文字敘述或說明。

waist [west]　◀ Track 2302
n. 腰；腰部
▶ The skirt is a bit tight around my waist.
這件裙子我穿著腰有點緊。

wait [wet]　◀ Track 2303
v. 等；等候；等待
▶ He's been waiting for you for two hours.
他等你兩個小時了。

waiter [`wetɚ]　◀ Track 2304
n. 侍者；服務生
▶ He was a waiter before he became an actor.
他成為演員前曾是服務生。

waitress [`wetrɪs]　◀ Track 2305
n. 女侍者；女服務生

▶ The waitress met a famous movie star and married him.
女服務生遇到知名的影星並嫁給他。

wake [wek]　◀ Track 2306
v. 醒來；覺醒；喚醒；弄醒
▶ He woke up with a stomachache.
他醒來時覺得胃痛。

walk [wɔk]　◀ Track 2307
v. 走；散步；陪……走
▶ C'mon. Let's walk home.
快點，我們走路回家吧。

n. 走；步行；散步
▶ I had a walk in the park last night.
我昨晚在公園散步。

Walkman [`wɔkmən]　◀ Track 2308
n. 隨身聽

▶She listened to her Walkman while she was running on the treadmill.
她在慢跑機運動時，一邊聽著隨身聽。

wall [wɔl]　◀ Track 2309

n. 牆；牆壁

▶The tapestry on the wall is magnificent.
牆上的絨繡很壯麗。

相關片語 **up the wall**
發狂；氣死

▶My dog is difficult to control. He's driving me up the wall.
我的狗很難控制，快把我氣死了。

wallet [`wɑlɪt]　◀ Track 2310

n. 皮夾；錢包

▶The man took out a credit card from his wallet.
男人從皮夾中拿出一張信用卡。

want [wɑnt]　◀ Track 2311

v. 想要

▶Do you want to go to the movie?
你想看電影嗎？

war [wɔr]　◀ Track 2312

n. 戰爭；競賽；對抗

▶He died in World War II.
他在第二次世界大戰喪生。

warm [wɔrm]　◀ Track 2313

adj. 溫暖的；暖和的

▶Winter is getting warmer and warmer due to climate change.
由於氣候變遷，冬天變得越來越暖和。

v. 使溫暖；使暖和

▶We turned on the heater to warm up the room.
我們打開暖爐讓房間暖和起來。

warming [`wɔrmɪŋ]　◀ Track 2314

adj. 讓人感到暖和的

▶Have a warming bowl of chicken soup.
喝碗熱乎乎的雞湯吧。

wash [wɑʃ]　◀ Track 2315

v. 洗；沖洗

▶He is washing his sports car.
他在洗他的跑車。

wasn't [`wɑznt]　◀ Track 2316

abbr. （過去式）不是、
還沒（**was not**的縮寫）

▶It wasn't the movie that I mentioned to you.
這不是我之前跟你提到的電影。

waste [west]　◀ Track 2317

n. 浪費

▶The movie was a waste of money.
看這部電影是浪費錢。

v. 浪費

▶Don't waist your time waiting for him. He's not worth it.
別浪費時間等他了，他不值得。

watch [wɑtʃ]　◀ Track 2318

n. 手錶；看守；監視；警戒

▶She bought an eco-drive watch for her son.
她買了一支光動能手錶給兒子。

初級

v. 看

▶The children are watching TV.
孩子們正在看電視。

相關片語 **watch out**
注意；小心

▶Watch out! Don't go near the thorn patch.
小心！不要走進荊棘裡。

water [`wotɚ] ◀ Track 2319

n. 水

▶She paused during her speech to drink some water.
她在演講中停頓了一下並喝口水。

v. 澆水；給水

▶She is watering the plants she grows on the balcony.
她正在幫陽台上種的植物澆水。

waterfall [`wotɚ͵fɔl] ◀ Track 2320

n. 瀑布

▶The waterfall is about 15 feet high.
這個瀑布大約十五英呎高。

watemelon ◀ Track 2321
[`wotɚ͵mɛlən]

n. 西瓜

▶The watermelon is so sweet. May I have one more piece?
這顆西瓜真好吃，我可以再要一片嗎？

wave [wev] ◀ Track 2322

n. 波浪；浪潮；揮手；捲髮

▶I gave him a friendly wave.
我友善地向他揮了揮手。

v. 對……揮手；揮動；使形成波浪

▶The princess waved gently to the crowd.
王妃溫和地向群眾揮手。

相關片語 **wave sb. goodbye**
揮手道別

▶We waved goodbye to our host family.
我們向寄宿家庭揮手道別。

way [we] ◀ Track 2323

n. 道路；路途

▶He's on his way to the train station.
他正在去火車站的路上。

補充片語 **on one's way to**
在往……的途中

we [wi] ◀ Track 2324

pron. 我們

▶We are English majors.
我們是主修英文的學生。

weak [wik] ◀ Track 2325

adj. 虛弱的；柔弱的；衰弱的

▶The old man is too weak to carry the luggage.
這名老人太虛弱而提不動行李。

相關片語 **weak in the head**
愚蠢的

▶He must have been weak in the head to have remitted so much money to his online friend.
他匯這麼多錢給網友，真是太愚蠢了。

weapon [`wɛpən] ◀ Track 2326

n. 武器；兇器

▶The robbers had weapons.
搶犯持有武器。

wear [wɛr]
◀✕ Track 2327

v. 穿；戴

▶The bride wore a beautiful wedding gown.
新娘穿著一件美麗的婚紗。

n. 穿；配戴；服裝

▶The T-shirt is for everyday wear.
這件汗衫供日常穿著。

weather [`wɛðɚ]
◀✕ Track 2328

n. 天氣

▶Today's weather is lovely.
今天的天氣很怡人。

相關片語 **under the weather**
身體不舒服

▶He was under the weather yesterday.
他昨天身體有點不舒服。

wed [wɛd]
◀✕ Track 2329

v. 嫁；娶；與……結婚

▶He wedded his high school sweetheart.
他娶了高中的女友。

we'd [wid]
◀✕ Track 2330

abbr. 我們已、我們會（ **we had**、**we would**的縮寫）

▶Don't you know that we'd arrived yesterday?
你不知道我們昨天已經到了嗎？

wedding [`wɛdɪŋ]
◀✕ Track 2331

n. 婚禮

▶The royal wedding was televised around the world.
這場皇室婚禮透過電視轉播到全世界。

Wednesday [`wɛnzde]
◀✕ Track 2332

=Wed., Weds.

n. 星期三

▶We will have a teacher-parent day on Wednesday.
我們星期三會有親師會。

week [wik]
◀✕ Track 2333

n. 星期；週

▶There are seven days in a week.
一週有七天。

weekday [`wik͵de]
◀✕ Track 2334

n. 平日；工作日

▶The studio is open on weekdays.
這個工作室平日是開放的。

weekend [`wik`ɛnd]
◀✕ Track 2335

n. 週末

▶Do you have any plan for the weekend?
你週末有計畫嗎？

相關片語 **long weekend**
週休連假

▶The exhibit will be open to the public this long weekend.
展覽將在這次週休連假展出。

weekly [`wiklɪ]
◀✕ Track 2336

adj. 每週的；一週一次的；週刊

▶The weekly magazine is published on Tuesday.
這份週刊每週二出版。

adv. 每週地；每週一次

▶She goes to church weekly.
她每週上教堂一次。

初級

n. 週刊；週報

▶Business Weekly is one of the most influential Chinese business magazines.
《商業週刊》是最具影響力的中文商業雜誌之一。

weigh [we]
◀ Track 2337

v. 秤重；有……重量；考慮；權衡

▶How much do you weigh?
你的體重是多少？

weight [wet]
◀ Track 2338

n. 體重

▶She exercises regularly to lose weight.
她為了減重而規律運動。

welcome [`wɛlkəm]
◀ Track 2339

v. 歡迎

▶The president welcomed the visiting delegation in the White House.
總統在白宮歡迎來訪代表團。

adj. 受歡迎的；被允許的；可隨意使用 的

▶You are welcome to stay with us when you are in New York.
你到紐約時，歡迎你來我們家住。

n. 歡迎；款待

▶The puppy received a tearful welcome when he was reunited with his family.
小狗和主人的家庭團圓時，受到喜極而泣的歡迎。

well [wɛl]
◀ Track 2340

adv. 很好地；成功地；適當地

▶Did you sleep well last night?
你昨晚睡得好嗎？

adj. 安好的；健全的；令人滿意的

▶He's not well. He has a stomachache.
他不舒服，有胃痛

we'll [wil]
◀ Track 2341

abbr. 我們會（we will的縮寫）

▶We'll go to the concert tonight.
我們今晚要去聽演唱會。

we're [wɪr]
◀ Track 2342

abbr. 我們是（we are的縮寫）

▶We're classmates.
我們是同班同學。

weren't [wɜnt]
◀ Track 2343

abbr. （過去式）不是（were not的縮寫）

▶We weren't pleased with the outcome.
我們對結果並不滿意。

west [wɛst]
◀ Track 2344

n. 西邊；西方

▶He was born in Turkey but spent most of his life in the West.
他在土耳其出生但大部分時間都住在西方國家。

adv. 向西；往西；自西

▶He drove west along the riverbank.
他沿著河岸向西駛去。

adj. 西部的；向西的；由西邊來的

▶We started our trip in the west coast of the USA.
我們在美國西岸展開旅行。

western [`wɛstɚn]
◀ Track 2345

adj. 西部的；朝西的；西方的；歐美的

▶He likes western movies.
他喜歡看歐美的電影。

n. 西方人；歐美國家的人；西部片

▶Brokeback Mountain is a western.
《斷背山》是一部美國西部片。

wet [wɛt]
◀ Track 2346

adj. 濕的

▶He was wet from head to toe.
他全身都是濕的。

v. 弄濕

▶The baby wetted the bed.
嬰兒尿床了。

> **補充片語** wet the bed
> 尿床

we've [wiv]
◀ Track 2347

abbr. 我們已（we have的縮寫）

▶We've been engaged.
我們已經訂婚了。

whale [hwel]
◀ Track 2348

n. 鯨魚

▶Whales are the world's largest mammals.
鯨魚是世界上最大的哺乳動物。

what [hwɑt]
◀ Track 2349

pron. 什麼

▶What do you think?
你認為如何？

adj. 什麼；何等

▶What a sweetheart she is.
她真是個人兒。

whatever [hwɑt`ɛvɚ]
◀ Track 2350

pron. 無論什麼

▶I'll be there for you whatever happens.
無論發生什麼事，我都會陪著你。

adj. 無論什麼的；不管什麼樣的

▶She eats whatever her mother cooks.
她媽媽不管煮什麼她都吃。

what's [hwɑts]
◀ Track 2351

abbr. 是什麼（what is的縮寫）

▶What's the title of the movie?
電影名稱是什麼？

wheel [hwil]
◀ Track 2352

n. 輪子；車輪；方向盤

▶The chair is on wheels to move around easily.
這把椅子有輪子，可以移動自如。

> **相關片語** take the wheel
> 開車

▶He took the wheel during the storm.
他在暴風雪中開車。

when [hwɛn]
◀ Track 2353

conj. 在……的時候

▶I wonder when she became sad.
我想知道她何時變得如此悲傷？

adv. 何時

▶When will you come back?
你什麼時候回來？

pron. 何時

▶Since when did you care?
你什麼時候開始關心了？

whenever
◀ Track 2354

[hwɛn`ɛvɚ]

adv. 無論何時；究竟何時

▶She avoided him whenever possible.
她盡可能躲開他。

初級

conj. 每當；無論何時

▶He travels whenever he can.
他只要有空就去旅行。

when's [hwɛnz]　◀Track 2355
abbr. 是什麼時候（**when is**的縮寫）

▶When's Thanksgiving?
感恩節是什麼時候？

where [hwɛr]　◀Track 2356
adv. 哪裡

▶Where do you come from?
你從哪裡來的？

conj. 在……的地方

▶This is where we live.
這是我們居住的地方。

where's [hwɛrz]　◀Track 2357
abbr. 在哪裡（**where is**的縮寫）

▶Where's Susan? Has anyone seen her?
蘇珊在哪裡？有人看到她了嗎？

wherever [hwɛr`ɛvɚ]　◀Track 2358
adv. 無論在何地；究竟在何處

▶Wherever did you find the book?
你究竟是在哪裡找到這本書的？

conj. 無論在哪裡；無論到哪裡；無論在什麼情況下

▶I'll go wherever you like.
你愛去哪兒我就去哪兒。

whether [`hwɛðɚ]　◀Track 2359
conj. 是否

▶I'll ask whether he likes the movie or not.
我會問他是否喜歡這部電影。

which [hwɪtʃ]　◀Track 2360
adj. 哪一個；哪一些

▶Which is your homeroom teacher?
哪一位是你的級任導師？

conj. 哪一個；哪一些

▶How do I choose which job offer is the right one for me?
我如何選擇哪一份工作適合我？

pron. 哪一個；哪一些

▶Which of these books do you like?
你喜歡這些書中的哪幾本？

while [hwaɪl]　◀Track 2361
conj. 當……的時候；然而

▶She likes romantic movies while her husband likes action ones.
她喜歡浪漫電影，然而她先生喜歡動作片。

n. 一會兒；一段時間

▶He has been around for a while.
他在這兒已有一陣子了。

相關片語 once in a while
偶爾

▶We go to that fancy restaurant once in a while.
我們偶爾會去那家昂貴的餐廳用餐。

whisper [`hwɪspɚ]　◀Track 2362
n. 耳語；私語；傳聞、流言

▶Did you hear whispers outside the room?
你聽見有人在房間外竊竊私語嗎？

v. 低語；私下說；低聲說

▶People are whispering that she's having an affair with her boss.
人們私下說她和老闆傳有緋聞。

white [hwaɪt]
🔊 Track 2363

adj. 白的；白色的

▶She has a white Maltese.
她有一隻白色的瑪爾濟斯 。

n. 白色

▶It is traditional for a bride to wear white.
傳統上新娘要穿白色禮服。

相關片語 **white lie**
善意的謊言；無惡意的謊言

▶Is it OK to tell a white lie?
說善意的謊言是適當的嗎？

who [hu]
🔊 Track 2364

pron. 誰；什麼人（關係代名詞）……的人

▶The boy who is standing there is my son.
站在那裡的男孩是我的兒子。

▶Who is he?
他是誰？

who'd [hud]
🔊 Track 2365

abbr. 誰會、誰已（**who would**、**who had**的縮寫）

▶He wondered who'd given him the chocolate.
他很納悶是誰給了他巧克力。

whoever [hʊˋɛvɚ]
🔊 Track 2366

pron. 無論誰；到底是誰

▶She knew the documents would be very helpful to whoever needed them.
她知道這些文件對需要的人會很有幫助。

whole [hol]
🔊 Track 2367

adj. 全部的；整個的；所有的

▶She spent the whole afternoon chatting with her friends.
她整個下午都在和朋友閒聊。

n. 全部；全體

▶The company on the whole was struggling to find a solid footing at the end of 2016.
整體說來，這間公司在二〇一六年底仍在辛苦地經營佈局。

補充片語 **on the whole**
整體說來；大體上

whom [hum]
🔊 Track 2368

pron. 誰；任何人

▶To whom do you want to cooperate with?
你想和誰合作？

▶He wants his children to be proud of whom they are.
他要他的孩子們以自身為榮。

who's [huz]
🔊 Track 2369

abbr. 是誰（**who is**的縮寫）

▶Who's that little girl?
那個小女孩是誰？

whose [huz]
🔊 Track 2370

pron. 誰的

▶Whose teddy bear is it?
這是誰的泰迪熊？

▶Do you know whose money it is?
你知道這是誰的錢嗎？

why [hwaɪ]
🔊 Track 2371

adv. 為什麼

▶Why is she so happy?
她為什麼這麼開心？

初級

conj. ……的原因；為何

▶Can you tell me why you dislike her?
你可以告訴我你為什麼不喜歡她嗎？

---

wide [waɪd]
《 Track 2372

adj. 寬的；寬鬆的；廣泛的

▶She has a wide knowledge of Russian history.
她具有廣博的俄羅斯歷史知識。

---

widen [`waɪdn]
《 Track 2373

v. 放寬；加大；擴大

▶They are widening the roads in the city.
他們正在拓寬城市的道路。

---

width [wɪdθ]
《 Track 2374

n. 寬度

▶How do you measure the width of a human hair?
你如何測量人類頭髮的寬度？

---

wife [waɪf]
《 Track 2375

n. 妻子；太太；夫人

▶My wife is Korean. 我的太太是韓國人。

---

wild [waɪld]
《 Track 2376

adj. 野生的；未被馴養的；粗野的；瘋狂的；猛烈的

▶We saw wild horses and antelope.
我們看到野生的馬和羚羊。

n. 荒野；未被開發之地

▶Some captive-bred pandas were released into the wild.
有些圈養的貓熊被野放到荒野之中。

---

will [wɪl]
《 Track 2377

aux. 將；會

▶I will call you back as soon as possible.
我會盡快回電話給你。

補充片語 as soon as possible
盡快

---

willing [`wɪlɪŋ]
《 Track 2378

adj. 願意的

▶He was willing to help.
他願意幫忙。

---

win [wɪn]
《 Track 2379

v. 贏；獲勝

▶They won the baseball game.
他們贏得籃球比賽。

n. 獲勝；成功

▶German team has had five wins and one loss so far.
德國隊目前五勝一負。

---

wind [wɪnd]
《 Track 2380

n. 風

▶The strong wind had downed some trees.
強風把一些樹吹倒了。

---

window [`wɪndo]
《 Track 2381

n. 窗戶

▶She leaned out of a window to see who was calling her.
她探出窗外看是誰在叫她。

---

windy [`wɪndɪ]
《 Track 2382

adj. 颳風的；多風的

▶It was a cold and windy day.
那天既冷風又大。

wine [waɪn] ◀╡Track 2383

n. 酒；葡萄酒；水果酒

▶I had a glass of grape wine.
我喝了一杯葡萄酒。

相關片語 **wine bag**
酒鬼

▶His father was a wine bag.
他的父親是個酒鬼。

wing [wɪŋ] ◀╡Track 2384

n. 翅膀

▶The eagle was spreading its wings.
老鷹展開了翅膀。

相關片語 **under sb.'s wing**
在某人的保護下

▶She took her little sister under her wing.
她很保護她年幼的妹妹。

winner [ˋwɪnɚ] ◀╡Track 2385

n. 贏家；獲勝者；優勝者

▶Who is the winner of Britain's Got Talent 2018?
誰是二〇一八年《英國達人秀》的冠軍？

winter [ˋwɪntɚ] ◀╡Track 2386

n. 冬天

▶It's not cold this winter.
今年的冬天並不冷。

相關片語 **winter vacation**
寒假

▶They went to Thailand last winter vacation.
他們去年寒假去泰國。

wire [waɪr] ◀╡Track 2387

n. 金屬線；電纜；電話線

▶Someone cut the phone wires.
有人切斷了電話線。

wise [waɪz] ◀╡Track 2388

adj. 有智慧的；明智的

▶Thomas More said that the wise man learns from the experience of others.
托馬斯‧莫爾說過聰明人會吸取他人的經驗教訓。

wish [wɪʃ] ◀╡Track 2389

v. 希望；但願

▶I wish I could colonize Mars.
但願我能去火星殖民。

n. 願望；心願；祝福

▶I gave you all my wishes.
我給你我全部的祝福。

with [wɪð] ◀╡Track 2390

prep. 和……一起

▶He lives with his parents.
他和雙親住在一起。

within [wɪˋðɪn] ◀╡Track 2391

prep. 在……範圍內；不超過；在……內部

▶We managed to travel in France within our budget.
我們設法在預算內到法國旅遊。

adv. 在裡面；在內部

▶He looks calm, but he's dying within.
他看起來很鎮定，但內心枯竭失落。

without [wɪˋðaʊt] ◀╡Track 2392

prep. 沒有

初級

▶She looks cute even without make-up.
她即使不上妝也很可愛。

wok [wɑk] ◀€Track 2393
n. 鑊；中式炒菜鍋

▶She stir-fried vegetables in a wok.
她用鍋子炒菜。

wolf [wʊlf] ◀€Track 2394
n. 狼

▶Pay no attention. He's crying wolf again.
別理他，他又再喊狼來了。

補充片語 cry wolf
喊狼來了；發假情報

woman [`wʊmən] ◀€Track 2395
n. 女人；婦女

▶It's quite sad that some women have abortions simply because they want baby boys.
令人難過的是，有些女人墮胎純粹是因為她們想生兒子。

wonder [`wʌndɚ] ◀€Track 2396
v. 納悶；想知道

▶I wonder what happened to her.
我很納悶她發生了什麼事。

n. 驚奇；驚歎；奇觀、奇事

▶It is a wonder that she escaped the crash with minimal injuries.
她經歷車禍只受到極小的傷，真是奇蹟。

wonderful ◀€Track 2397
[`wʌndɚfəl]
adj. 美好的；神奇的；極好的

▶They had a wonderful time in Rome last week.
他們上週在羅馬玩得很愉快。

won't [wont] ◀€Track 2398
abbr. 不會（**will not**的縮寫）

▶Don't worry. I won't spill a bean.
別擔心，我不會洩密的。

wood [wʊd] ◀€Track 2399
n. 木頭、木材；森林、樹林

▶We chopped wood to build a fire.
我們砍木頭用來生火。

相關片語 out of the woods
擺脫麻煩、脫離險境

▶The man is still in coma. He is not out of the woods yet.
男子仍陷入昏迷，人尚未脫離險境。

wooden [`wʊdn] ◀€Track 2400
adj. 木製的；僵硬的

▶She has a beautiful wooden wardrobe in her room.
她的房間有一個很漂亮的木製衣櫥。

wool [wʊl] ◀€Track 2401
n. 羊毛；毛線；毛織品

▶The coat is made of wool.
這件外套是羊毛製的。

相關片語 lose one's wool
發怒；發火

▶He lost his wool when you gave him the brush-off.
你對他不理不睬，讓他發火了。

word [wɝd] ◀€Track 2402
n. 字；一句話；言辭；談話

▶May I have a quick word with you?
我可以簡短地跟你説幾句話嗎？

work [wɝk]　🔊Track 2403

n. 工作；事；職務

▶I go to work on foot.
我走路上班。

v. 工作；幹活；（機器）運轉

▶He works in a biopharmaceutical company.
他在生技醫藥廠工作。

worker [ˋwɝkɚ]　🔊Track 2404

n. 工人；勞工；勞動者；工作者

▶Some foreign workers face discrimination in the workplace.
有些外籍勞工在職場受到歧視。

補充片語 **foreign worker**
外籍勞工

world [wɝld]　🔊Track 2405

n. 世界

▶The movie star is popular around the world.
這名影星在世界各地都很受歡迎。

adj. 世界的

▶I enjoy watching World Cup and I'm cheering for Germany.
我喜歡看世界盃足球賽，而且我為德國隊加油。

worm [wɝm]　🔊Track 2406

n. 蟲；蠕蟲；蛀蟲

▶There are worms in the cabbage.
包心菜裡有幾隻蟲。

相關片語 **a can of worms**
複雜的問題

▶You're opening a can of worms on a topic that is highly controversial.
你開啟了一個高度爭議難解的話題。

worry [ˋwɝɪ]　🔊Track 2407

v. 擔心；擔憂

▶Don't worry, be happy.
別擔心，快樂些。

n. 擔心；憂慮；令人擔憂的事

▶Her daughter's illness was a great worry to her.
她女兒的病情是她非常擔心的事。

worse [wɝs]　🔊Track 2408

adj. 更差的；更壞的；更糟糕的；
（並）更重的

▶Nothing is worse than inaction.
沒有比無為更糟的事了。

adv. 更糟；更壞；更惡化

▶The situation of the country is getting worse.
這個國家的情況正在惡化中。

n. 更糟的狀況

▶If you don't take action, there will be worse to come.
你若不採取行動，會發生更糟的狀況。

worst [wɝst]　🔊Track 2409

adj. 最差的；最壞的

▶It was the worst moment of her life.
這是她生命中的最低潮。

adv. 最壞地；最惡劣地；最不利地

▶Of the three candidates, he performed the worst.
三名候選人之中，他表現得最差。

初級

n. 最壞的狀況

▶Let's hope for the best and prepare for the worst.
讓我們一起做周全的準備，同時做最壞的打算。

worth [wɝθ]　◀⋮Track 2410

adj. 有⋯⋯的價值；值⋯⋯

▶The bangle is worth $200.
這支手鐲價值兩百元。

n. 價值；值一定金額的數量

▶The estimated worth of her wealth is about 20 million dollars.
她的財富估計價值兩千萬元。

would [wʊd]　◀⋮Track 2411

aux. 會；將；要；願意

▶Would you be my prom date?
你願意當我畢業舞會的舞伴嗎？

wouldn't [`wʊdnt]　◀⋮Track 2412

abbr. （過去式）不會（**would not**的縮寫）

▶I wouldn't trust her if I were you.
我如果是你，就不會信任她。

wound [wund]　◀⋮Track 2413

n. 傷口；創傷

▶The wound on his arm needed 30 stitches.
他手臂的傷口需要縫三十針。

v. 使受傷；傷害

▶Many passengers were badly wounded after an express train derailed and flipped over.
特快火車出軌翻覆後，許多乘客受到重傷。

wrist [rɪst]　◀⋮Track 2414

n. 腕；腕部；腕關節

▶He sprained his wrist playing hockey.
他打曲棍球時扭傷手腕。

相關片語 **wrist watch**
手錶；腕表

▶This wrist watch is an elegant everyday accessory.
這款腕表是每天都可配戴的優雅配件。

write [raɪt]　◀⋮Track 2415

v. 寫

▶I wrote an e-mail to my friend.
我寫了一封電郵給朋友。

writer [`raɪtɚ]　◀⋮Track 2416

n. 作家；作者；撰稿人

▶She is the column writer for the magazine.
她是雜誌的專欄作家。

wrong [rɔŋ]　◀⋮Track 2417

adj. 錯誤的；不對的；出毛病的

▶What's wrong with you?
你到底怎麼了？

adv. 錯誤地；不正當地

▶You guessed wrong.
你猜錯了。

n. 錯誤

▶She has no sense of right and wrong.
她沒有什麼是非感。

相關片語 **get sb. wrong**
誤解某人

▶Don't get me wrong. I'd love to go to the movie with you, but I've been too busy lately.
別誤會了，我想跟你去看電影，只是我最近實在太忙了。

▶ Xx

以下表格是全民英檢官方公告初級「聽、說、讀、寫」所須具備的能力，本書例句皆依此範疇特別設計，只要掃描右方QR code，就能搭配相對應的音軌，實現「眼耳並用」方式，刺激左腦的語言學習功能；同時也可使用本書附贈的紅膠片，將其置於單字上，一面記憶一面自我挑戰，達到雙倍的學習成果！

聽 ▶	能聽懂與日常生活相關的淺易談話，包含價格、時間及地點等。
說 ▶	能朗讀簡易文章、簡單地自我介紹，對熟悉的話題能以簡易英語對答，如問候、購物、問路等。
讀 ▶	可看懂與日常生活相關的淺易英文，並能閱讀路標、交通號誌、招牌、簡單菜單、時刻表及賀卡等。
寫 ▶	能寫簡單的句子及段落，如寫明信片、便條、賀卡及填表格等。對一般日常生活相關事物，能以簡短的文字敘述或說明。

初級

xerox [ˋzɪraks]   ◀℈Track 2418

n. 靜電複印機；影印機

▶The printing quality of this xerox is excellent.
這台影印機的影印品質非常好。

v. 靜電複印；影印

▶Could you xerox this report and send me a copy of it？
你可以複印這份報告並送一份複本給我嗎？

▶ Yy

　　以下表格是全民英檢官方公告初級「聽、説、讀、寫」所須具備的能力，本書例句皆依此範疇特別設計，只要掃描右方QR code，就能搭配相對應的音軌，實現「眼耳並用」方式，刺激左腦的語言學習功能；同時也可使用本書附贈的紅膠片，將其置於單字上，一面記憶一面自我挑戰，達到雙倍的學習成果！

聽	▶	能聽懂與日常生活相關的淺易談話，包含價格、時間及地點等。
説	▶	能朗讀簡易文章、簡單地自我介紹，對熟悉的話題能以簡易英語對答，如問候、購物、問路等。
讀	▶	可看懂與日常生活相關的淺易英文，並能閱讀路標、交通號誌、招牌、簡單菜單、時刻表及賀卡等。
寫	▶	能寫簡單的句子及段落，如寫明信片、便條、賀卡及填表格等。對一般日常生活相關事物，能以簡短的文字敘述或説明。

yam [jæm]
◀ Track 2419

n. 山芋；番薯

▶My aunt makes the best steamed yam cake in the family.
我嬸嬸做的芋頭糕是全家族中最好吃的。

補充片語 steamed yam cake
芋頭糕

yard [jɑrd]
◀ Track 2420

n. 院子；庭院

▶She grew some vegetables in her yard.
她在庭院種了一些蔬菜。

相關片語 yard sale
庭院舊貨拍賣

▶I bought this painting from a yard sale.
我在庭院舊貨特賣會買到這幅畫。

yeah [jɛə]
◀ Track 2421

interj. 對啊！好啊！

▶"Do you like the new fragrance?" "Yeah, it's fantastic!"
「你喜歡新款的香水嗎？」「對啊，棒極了!」

year [jɪr]
◀ Track 2422

n. 年

▶We wish you a happy new year.
我們祝你新年快樂。

yearly [ˈjɪrlɪ]
◀ Track 2423

adv. 每年；一年一度

▶The GDP per capita data is updated yearly.
國內生產總值的數據每年更新一次。

yellow [ˋjɛlo]　　◀≣ Track 2424

adj. 黃的；黃色的

▶You look good in the yellow shirt.
你穿黃色的襯衫很好看。

n. 黃；黃色；黃色的衣服

▶My favorite color is yellow.
我最喜歡的顏色是黃色。

yes [jɛs]
=yeah　　◀≣ Track 2425

interj. 好極了；真的

▶We won the championship. Yes!
我們贏得冠軍。太好了！

adv. 是；是的

▶"Would you marry me?" "Yes, I would."
「你願意嫁給我嗎？」「是的，我願意。」

> **相關片語** **yes man**
> 唯命是從的人；應聲蟲

▶When will he stop being a yes-man?
他什麼時候才會停止做個濫好人？

yesterday [ˋjɛstɚde]　◀≣ Track 2426

n. 昨天

▶Yesterday was windy.
昨天風很大。

adv. 昨天

▶She went to Australia yesterday.
她昨天去澳洲。

yet [jɛt]　　◀≣ Track 2427

adv. （用於否定句）還沒；已經；

▶I haven't finished my homework yet.
我還沒寫完功課。

conj. 然而；卻

▶He is young, yet he sings like Andrea Bocelli.
他很年輕，然而他唱起歌來像安德烈‧波伽利一樣好。

you [ju]　　◀≣ Track 2428

pron. 你

▶Are you free this weekend?
你週末有空嗎？

you'd [jud]　　◀≣ Track 2429

abbr. 你會、你已（**you had**、**you would**的縮寫）

▶I thought you'd changed your mind.
我以為你已經改變主意了。

you'll [jul]　　◀≣ Track 2430

abbr. 你會（**you will**的縮寫）

▶I hope you'll realize your dreams.
我希望你能實現你的夢想。

young [jʌŋ]　　◀≣ Track 2431

adj. 年輕的；年幼的

▶Many companies prefer to hire young people.
許多公司寧可僱用年輕人。

n. 年輕人們；青年們

▶Couch surfing is popular with the young.
沙發旅行很受年輕人的歡迎。

> **補充片語** **be popular with**
> 受……的歡迎

> **相關片語** **old and young**
> 無論老少；人人

初級

▶Bridging the gap between old and young is never easy.
要消弭老年人和年輕人的代溝從來就不是容易的事。

your [jʊɚ] ◀ Track 2432

pron. 你的；你們的

▶We appreciate your support.
我們感謝你的支持。

you're [jʊɚ] ◀ Track 2433

abbr. 你是（**you are**的縮寫）

▶You're only young once.
青春只一度。

yours [jʊrz] ◀ Track 2434

pron. 你的（事物）；你們的（事物）

▶This is my towel, and that's yours.
這是我的毛巾，你的是那條。

yourself [jʊɚˋsɛlf] ◀ Track 2435

pron. 你自己；你們自己

▶Did you travel by yourself?
你獨自旅行嗎？

youth [juθ] ◀ Track 2436

n. 青春時代；青年；年輕；青春

▶She spent her youth in Singapore.
她青少女時期在新加坡度過。

相關片語 **youth park**
青年公園

▶The youth park is about 20 minutes' drive from here.
青年公園裡離這裡大約要開車二十分鐘。

you've [juv] ◀ Track 2437

abbr. 你已（**you have**的縮寫）

▶You've been watching TV for hours.
你已經看了好幾個小時的電視了。

yucky [ˋjʌkɪ] ◀ Track 2438

adj. 討人厭的；難以下嚥的；難聞的

▶The food in that eatery is yucky.
那家小吃店的食物很難吃。

yummy [ˋjʌmɪ] ◀ Track 2439

adj. 好吃的；美味的

▶The pumpkin pie is yummy.
南瓜派真好吃。

▶ Zz

以下表格是全民英檢官方公告初級「聽、說、讀、寫」所須具備的能力，本書例句皆依此範疇特別設計，只要掃描右方QR code，就能搭配相對應的音軌，實現「眼耳並用」方式，刺激左腦的語言學習功能；同時也可使用本書附贈的紅膠片，將其置於單字上，一面記憶一面自我挑戰，達到雙倍的學習成果！

聽 ▶	能聽懂與日常生活相關的淺易談話，包含價格、時間及地點等。
說 ▶	能朗讀簡易文章、簡單地自我介紹，對熟悉的話題能以簡易英語對答，如問候、購物、問路等。
讀 ▶	可看懂與日常生活相關的淺易英文，並能閱讀路標、交通號誌、招牌、簡單菜單、時刻表及賀卡等。
寫 ▶	能寫簡單的句子及段落，如寫明信片、便條、賀卡及填表格等。對一般日常生活相關事物，能以簡短的文字敘述或說明。

初級

zebra [`zibrə]　◀ Track 2440

n. 斑馬

▶ No zebra is striped like another.
沒有任何一隻斑馬的斑紋是一樣的。

zero [`zɪro]　◀ Track 2441

n. 零；零號；零度；無；烏有

▶ There are two zeros in 2001.
在2001中有兩個零。

adj. 零的；全無的

▶ She has zero experience in foreign policy.
她對外交政策全無經驗。

相關片語 **zero hour**
開始行動的關鍵時刻

▶ It's zero hour to act on climate change.
該是我們行動扭轉氣候變遷的時候了。

zoo [zu]　◀ Track 2442

n. 動物園

▶ The children had a great time in the zoo.
孩子們在動物園玩得很開心。

NOTE

英語學習 系列 007

GEPT全民英檢初級單字100%攻略：
左腦式聽力學習╳紅膠片高效練習

單字全命中！完整收錄英檢官方指定＆名師特選高分單字

作　　　者	張慈庭英語教學團隊
顧　　　問	曾文旭
總 編 輯	王毓芳
編 輯 統 籌	耿文國、黃璽宇
主　　　編	吳靜宜
執 行 主 編	潘妍潔
執 行 編 輯	吳芸蓁、吳欣蓉、范筱翎
美 術 編 輯	王桂芳、張嘉容
封 面 設 計	盧穎作
法 律 顧 問	北辰著作權事務所　蕭雄淋律師、幸秋妙律師

初　　　版	2019年02月
初版三刷	2023年09月
出　　　版	捷徑文化出版事業有限公司——資料夾文化
電　　　話	（02）2752-5618
傳　　　真	（02）2752-5619

定　　　價	新台幣400元／港幣133元
產品內容	1書+1紅膠片+1mp3 QR code

總 經 銷	知遠文化事業有限公司
地　　　址	222新北市深坑區北深路3段155巷25號5樓
電　　　話	（02）2664-8800
傳　　　真	（02）2664-8801

港澳地區總經銷	和平圖書有限公司
地　　　址	香港柴灣嘉業街12號百樂門大廈17樓
電　　　話	（852）2804-6687
傳　　　真	（852）2804-6409

▲本書圖片由 Shutterstock、123RF提供。

捷徑Book站

國家圖書館出版品預行編目資料

GEPT全民英檢初級單字100%攻略：左腦式聽
力學習╳紅膠片高效練習／張慈庭英語教學團
隊著. -- 初版. -- 臺北市：資料夾文化, 2019.02
　　面；　公分（英語學習：007）
ISBN 978-957-8904-59-0（平裝）
1. 英語　2. 詞彙
805.1892　　　　　　　　　　　107019524